THE RANCH

Also by Danielle Steel

SILENT HONOUR
MALICE
FIVE DAYS IN PARIS
LIGHTNING
WINGS
ACCIDENT
THE GIFT
VANISHED
MIXED BLESSINGS
JEWELS
NO GREATER LOVE
HEARTBEAT
MESSAGE FROM NAM
DADDY
STAR
ZOYA
KALEIDOSCOPE
FINE THINGS
WANDERLUST
SECRETS
FAMILY ALBUM
FULL CIRCLE
CHANGES
THURSTON HOUSE
CROSSINGS
ONCE IN A LIFETIME
A PERFECT STRANGER
REMEMBRANCE
PALOMINO
LOVE: POEMS
THE RING
LOVING
TO LOVE AGAIN
SUMMER'S END
SEASON OF PASSION
THE PROMISE
NOW AND FOREVER
GOLDEN MOMENTS*

*Published outside the UK under the title *Passions Promise*.

DANIELLE STEEL

THE RANCH

BCA

LONDON NEW YORK SYDNEY TORONTO

This edition published 1997
by BCA
by arrangement with Bantam Press,
a division of Transworld Publishers Ltd

CN 2900

All of the characters in this book
are fictitious, and any resemblance
to actual persons, living or dead,
is purely coincidental.

Printed and bound in Great Britain by
Clays Ltd, St Ives plc.

To Victoria and Nancy,
special, precious friends,
sisters of my heart,
who make me laugh,
hold my hand when I cry,
and are always, always, always
there for me.

With all my love,
d.s.

THE RANCH

CHAPTER 1

In any other supermarket, the woman walking down the aisle, pushing a cart between canned goods and gourmet spices, would have looked strangely out of place. She had impeccably groomed shoulder-length brown hair, beautiful skin, huge brown eyes, a trim figure, perfectly done nails, and she was wearing a navy linen suit that looked as though she had bought it in Paris. She wore high-heeled navy blue shoes, a navy Chanel bag, and everything about her was perfection. She could have easily pretended she'd never seen a supermarket before, but she looked surprisingly at home here. In fact, she often stopped at Gristede's at Madison and Seventy-seventh on the way home. Most of the shopping was done by their housekeeper, but in a funny old-fashioned way, Mary Stuart Walker liked doing the shopping herself. She liked cooking for Bill at night when he came home, and they had never had a cook, even when the children were younger. Despite the impeccable way she looked, she liked taking care of her family, and attending to every minute detail herself.

Their apartment was at Seventy-eighth and Fifth, with a splendid view of Central Park. They had lived there for fifteen of the nearly twenty-two years of their marriage. Mary Stuart kept an impressive home. The children teased her sometimes about how "perfect" everything always was, how everything had to look and be just right, and it was easy to believe that about her. Just looking at her, it was easy to see that she was somewhat compulsive about it. Even at six o'clock, on a hot June evening in New York, after six hours of meetings, Mary Stuart had just put on fresh lipstick, and she didn't have a hair out of place.

She selected two small steaks, two baking potatoes, some fresh asparagus, some fruit, and some yogurt, remembering too easily the days when her shopping cart had been filled with treats for the children. She always pretended to disapprove, but couldn't resist buying the things they saw on TV and said they wanted. It was a small thing in life, spoiling them a little bit, indulging them bubble-gum flavored cereal was so important to them, she never could see the point of refusing to buy it for them and forcing them to eat a healthy one they'd hate.

Like most people in their world in New York, she and Bill expected a great deal from their children, a high standard for everything, near perfect grades, impressive athletic ability, complete integrity, high morals. And as it turned out, Alyssa and Todd were good-looking, bright and shining in every way, outstanding in and out of school, and basically very decent people. Bill had teased them ever since they were young, and told them that he expected them to be the perfect kids, he and their mother were counting on it in fact. By the time they were ten and twelve, Alyssa and Todd groaned whenever they heard the words. But there was more than a little truth to the speech, and they knew it. What their father really meant was that they had to do their absolute best in and out of school, perform at the top of their ability, and even if they didn't always succeed they had to try hard. It was a lot to expect of anyone, but Bill Walker had always set high standards, and they met them. As rigid as their mother seemed to be sometimes, it was their father who was the real perfectionist, who expected it all from them, and from their mother. It was Bill who really put the pressure on all of them, not just his children, but his wife as well.

Mary Stuart had been the perfect wife to him for nearly twenty-two years, providing him with the perfect home, the perfect children, looking beautiful, doing what was expected of her, entertaining for him, and keeping a home that not only landed them on the pages of *Architectural Digest,* but was a happy place to come home to. There was nothing showy or ostentatious about their way of life, it was all beautifully done, meticulously handled. You couldn't see the seams in anything Mary Stuart did. She made it all look effortless, although most people realized it couldn't be as easy as she made it seem. But that was her gift to him. Making it all seem easy. For years, she had organized charity events which raised hundreds of thousands of dollars for important charities, sat on museum boards, and worked ceaselessly assisting the cause of injured, diseased, or seriously underprivileged children. And now, at forty-four, with the children more or less grown, in addition to the charity events she still organized, and the committees she sat on for the past three years she'd been doing volunteer work with physically and emotionally handicapped children in a hospital in Harlem.

She sat on the board of the Metropolitan Museum of Art, and Lincoln Center, and helped to organize assorted fundraising events each year, because everyone wanted her to help them. She kept extraordinarily busy, particularly now, with no children to come home to, and Bill constantly working late at the office. He was one of the senior partners in an international law firm on Wall Street. He handled all of their most important cases relating to Germany and England. He was a trial lawyer primarily, and the things Mary Stuart did socially had always done a great deal to enhance his reputation. She entertained beautifully for him, and always had, although this year had been very quiet. He had spent much of the year traveling abroad, particularly for the past several months, preparing a massive trial in London, which had kept him away from home. And Mary Stuart had been busier than ever with her volunteer work.

Alyssa was spending her junior year at the Sorbonne. So Mary Stuart had more time to herself this year. It had given her a chance to catch up on a lot of things. She took on some additional charity work, did a lot of reading, and volunteered at the hospital on weekends. Or sometimes, on Sundays, she just indulged herself, and stayed in bed with a book, or devoured all of the *New York Times.* She had a full and busy life, and to look at her, no one would ever have suspected there was anything lacking. She looked at least five or six years younger than she was, although she had gotten thinner than usual that year, which should have been aging, but somehow it wasn't, and it actually made her seem even more youthful. There was a gentleness about her which people loved, and children responded to, particularly the ones she worked with. There was a genuine kindness which came from the soul that transcended social distinctions, and made one unaware of the world she came from. One was simply aware of something very touching about her, something almost wistful, it seemed, as one watched her, as though she understood great sorrow and had endured great sadness, and yet there was no sign of gloom about her. Her life seemed so completely perfect. Her children had always been the smartest, the most accomplished, the most beautiful. Her husband was enormously successful, both financially and in terms of the prestige he earned in winning highly visible, landmark international cases. He was highly respected in business, as well as in their social world.

Mary Stuart had everything most people wanted, and yet as one looked at her, one sensed that edge of sadness, it was a kind of compassion one felt more than saw, a loneliness perhaps, which seemed odder. How could anyone with Mary Stuart's looks and style, accomplishments and family, be lonely?

When one sensed that about her, divining her with the heart rather than the eyes, it seemed strange and unlikely, and made one question one's own intuitions about her. There was no reason to suspect that Mary Stuart Walker was lonely or sad, and yet if one looked hard enough at her, one knew she was. Behind the elegant facade, there was something tragic about her.

"How ya doin' today, Mrs. Walker?" The man at the check-out grinned at her. He liked her. She was beautiful, and she was always polite to him. She asked about his family, his wife, his mother for years before she died. She used to come in with the kids, but now they were gone, so she came in alone and always chatted with him. It would have been hard not to like her.

"I'm fine, Charlie, thank you." She smiled at him, and looked even younger. She looked scarcely different than she had as a girl, and when she came into the store in blue jeans on the weekends, sometimes she looked just like her daughter. "Hot today, isn't it?" she said, but she didn't look it. She never did. In winter, she looked well-dressed despite the brutal cold and the layers everyone wore, the boots against the snow and slush, the hats and the scarves and the earmuffs. And in summer, when everyone else looked frazzled in the deadly heat, she looked calm and cool and unruffled. She was just one of those people. She looked as though nothing ever went wrong, she never lost control, and certainly never lost her temper. He had seen her laugh with her kids too. The daughter was a real beauty. The son was a good kid . . . they all were. Charlie thought her husband was a little stiff, but who's to say what makes some people happy? They were a nice family. He assumed the husband was in town again. She had bought two baking potatoes and two filet mignons.

"They say it's going to be even hotter tomorrow," he said as he bagged her things and saw her glance at the *Enquirer* and then frown in disapproval. Tanya Thomas, the singing megastar, was on the cover. The headline said TANYA HEADED FOR

ANOTHER DIVORCE. AFFAIR WITH TRAINER BREAKS UP MARRIAGE. There were terrible photographs of her, an inset of the muscle-bound trainer in a T-shirt, and another of her current husband fleeing from the press, hiding his face as he disappeared into a nightclub. Charlie glanced at the headlines and shrugged. "That's Hollywood, they all sleep around out there. It's a wonder they even bother to get married." He had been married to the same woman for thirty-nine years, and for him the vagaries of Hollywood were like tales from another planet.

"Don't believe everything you read," Mary Stuart said somewhat sternly, and he looked at her and smiled. Her gentle brown eyes looked troubled.

"You're too nice about everyone, Mrs. Walker. They're not the same kind of people we are, believe me." He knew, he had seen some movie people come in regularly over the years, with different men and women all the time, they were a pretty jazzy crowd. They were a totally different kind of human being from Mary Stuart Walker. He was sure she didn't even understand what he was saying.

"Don't believe what you read in the tabloids, Charlie," she said again, sounding unusually firm, and with that she picked up her groceries with a smile, and told him she'd see him tomorrow.

It was a short walk to the building where she lived, and even after six o'clock it was still stifling. She thought Bill would be home, as usual, at around seven o'clock, and she would have dinner for him at seven-thirty or eight, depending on how he was feeling. She planned to put the potatoes in the oven when she got home, and then she'd have time to shower and change. Despite the cool way she looked, she was tired and hot after a long day of meetings. The museum was planning an enormous fund-raising drive in the fall, they were hoping to give a huge ball in September, and they wanted her to be the chairman. But so far she had managed to decline, and was hoping only to advise them. She wasn't in the mood to put together a ball, and lately she much preferred her hands-on work, like what she did at the hospital with handicapped children, or more recently with abused kids in Harlem.

The doorman greeted her as she came in, took the groceries from her, and handed them to the elevator man, and after thanking him, she rode upstairs to their floor-through apartment in silence. The building was solid and old, and very handsome. It was one of her favorites on Fifth Avenue, and the view as she opened her front door was spectacular, particularly in winter, when Central Park was blanketed with snow, and the skyline across the park stood etched in sharp contrast. It was lovely in summer too, everything was lush and green, and from their vantage point on the fourteenth floor, everything looked so pretty and peaceful. You could hear no noise from below, see none of the dirt, sense none of the danger. It was all pretty and green, and the final late bloom of spring had exploded at last after the seemingly endless, long, bleak winter.

Mary Stuart thanked the elevator man for helping her, locked the door after he left, and walked the length of the apartment to the large, clean white kitchen. She liked open, functional, simple rooms like this one to work in, and aside from three framed French prints, the kitchen was completely pristine, with white walls, white floor, and long expanses of white granite counters. The room had been in *Architectural Digest* five years before, with a photograph of Mary Stuart sitting on a kitchen stool in white jeans and a white angora sweater. And despite the excellent meals Mary Stuart actually prepared, it was hard to believe anyone really cooked there.

Their housekeeper was daily now, and there was no sound at all as Mary Stuart put the groceries away, turned the oven on, and stood looking for a long moment out the window at the park. She could see the playground a block away, in the park, and remembered the countless hours she had spent there, freezing in winter when her children were small, pushing them on the swings, watching them on the seesaw or just playing with their friends. It seemed a thousand years ago . . . too long . . . how did it all fly by so quickly? It seemed like only yesterday when the children were at home, when they had dinner together every night, with everyone talking at once about their activities, their plans, their problems. Even one of Alyssa and Todd's arguments would have been a relief now, and so much more comforting than the silence. It would be a relief when Alyssa came home in the fall, for her senior year at Yale after a year in Paris. At least once she was back, she'd come home occasionally for weekends.

Mary Stuart left the kitchen and walked to the small den, where she often did her paperwork. They kept the answering machine there, and she flipped it on and heard Alyssa's voice instantly. It made her smile just to hear her.

"Hi, Mom . . . sorry I missed you. I just wanted to say hi, and see how you are. It's ten o'clock here, and I'm going out for a drink with friends. I'll be out late, so don't call me. I'll call you this weekend sometime. I'll see you in a few weeks . . . bye . . ." And then, almost as an afterthought, ". . . Oh . . . I love you . . ." There was a click then, when she hung up. The machine recorded the time, and Mary Stuart glanced at her watch, sorry to have missed her. It had been four o'clock in New York when Alyssa had called her, two and a half hours before. Mary Stuart was looking forward to meeting her in Paris in three weeks, and driving to the south of France, and then into Italy for a vacation. Mary Stuart planned to be there for two weeks, but Alyssa only wanted to come home a few days before school began in September. She wanted to stay in Europe as long as she could, and was already saying that, after graduation, she wanted to go back to live in Paris. Mary Stuart didn't even want to think about that now. The last year, without her, had been far too lonely.

"Mary Stuart . . ." The next voice was her husband's. "I won't be home for dinner tonight. I'll be in meetings until seven o'clock, and I just found out I have to have dinner with clients. I'll see you at ten or eleven. Sorry." There was a click and he was gone, the information imparted, clients more than likely waiting for him while he called, and besides, Bill hated machines. He said that he was constitutionally unable to relate to them, and he would never have left her a personal message on the recording. She teased him about it at times. She used to tease him about a lot of things, but not so many lately. It had been a hard year for them. So much had changed . . . so many startling revelations and disappointments . . . so much heartbreak. And yet, outwardly, they all seemed so normal. Mary Stuart wondered how that was possible sometimes. How your heart could break, shattered beyond repair, and yet you went on, making coffee, buying sheets, turning down beds, and attending meetings. You got up, you showered, you dressed, you went to bed, but inside a part of you had died. In years past, she had wondered how other people lived through it. It had morbidly fascinated her at times. But now she knew. You went on living. You just did. Your heart kept beating and refused to let you die. You kept walking, talking, breathing, but inside everything was hurting.

"Hi," the next message said, "this is Tony Jones, and your VCR is repaired. You can pick it up any time you want. Thanks, bye." Two messages about board meetings that had been changed. A question about the museum ball, and the committee being formed for it, and a call from the head of volunteers at a shelter in Harlem. She jotted down a few notes, and remembered that she had to turn off the oven. Bill wasn't coming home. Again. He did that a lot now. He worked too hard. That was how he survived. And in her own way, so did she, with her endless merry-go-round of meetings and committees.

She turned off the oven, and decided to make herself eggs instead, but not yet, and then walked into her bedroom. The walls were a pale buttery yellow, with a white glazed trim, the carpet an antique needlepoint she'd bought in England. There were antique prints and watercolors on the walls, a handsome marble fireplace, and on the mantel silver-framed photographs of her children. There were comfortable overstuffed chairs on either side of it, and she and Bill liked to sit by the fire and read at night, or on weekends. They spent most of their weekends in the city now, and had for the past year. They had sold the house in Connecticut the summer before. With the children gone, and Bill traveling constantly, they never went there.

"My life seems to be on a shrink cycle these days," Mary Stuart had said jokingly to a friend, "with the kids gone, and Bill away, we seem to be paring everything down. Even our apartment is beginning to seem too big for us." But she would never have had the heart to sell it. The children had grown up there.

As she walked into the bedroom, and set down her handbag, her eyes went unwittingly toward the mantel. It was still reassuring to see them there, the children when they were four and five and ten and fifteen . . . the dog they had had when they were small, a big friendly chocolate Lab named Mousse. As always, she found herself drawn to them, and stood staring at their pictures. It was so easy to look at them, to just stand there and remember. It was like being drawn into another time, and she so often wished she could go back to that earlier time, when all their problems had been simple. Todd's blond, cheery little face looked out at her from when he was a little boy and she could hear him calling her name again . . . or see him chasing the dog . . . or falling into the swimming pool when he was three and she dived in after him with all her clothes on. She had saved him then. She had always been there for him, and for Alyssa. There was a photograph of all of them three Christmases before, laughing, their arms around each other, horsing around while an exasperated photographer had begged them to be serious for a moment so he could take their picture.

Todd had insisted on singing outrageous songs to them, while Alyssa laughed hysterically, and even she and Bill couldn't stop laughing. It had felt good to be so silly. It always felt good to be with them. It made the sound of Alyssa's voice on the machine that night even more poignant. And then, as she always did, Mary Stuart turned away from the photographs, the little faces that both caressed and tormented her, that tore at her heart and soothed it. There was a catch in her throat as she went to her bathroom and washed her face, and then looked sternly at herself in the mirror.

"Stop that!" She nodded in answer. She knew better than to let herself do that. Self-indulgence was a luxury she could no longer afford. All she could do now was move forward. But she had moved to an unfamiliar land with a landscape she didn't like. It was bleak and unpopulated, and at times unbearably lonely. At times, she felt as though she had come there by herself, except that she knew Bill was there too, lost in the desert somewhere, in his own private hell. She had been searching for him there for over a year, but as yet she hadn't found him.

She thought about making herself dinner then, but decided she wasn't hungry, and after taking off her suit, and changing into a pink T-shirt and jeans, she went back to the den, sat down at the desk, and looked over some papers. It was still light outside at seven o'clock, and she decided to call Bill and tell him she'd gotten his message on the machine. They had very little to say to each other these days, except about his work, or her meetings, but she called him anyway. It was better than letting go completely. No matter how lost they had been for the past year, Mary Stuart was not ready to let go yet. And she knew she probably never would be. Giving up wasn't something that fit into her scheme of things, it wasn't something she believed in. They owed each other more than that after all these years. When times got rough, you did not abandon the ship. In Mary Stuart's life, you went down with it if you had to.

She dialed his number and heard it ring, and then finally a secretary answered. No, Mr. Walker wasn't available. He was still in meetings. She would tell him Mrs. Walker had called him.

"Thank you," Mary Stuart said softly, and hung up, swiveling slowly in the chair to look out at the park again. If she let herself, she would see couples strolling there in the warm June air at sunset, but she didn't want to. She had nothing to say to them now, nothing to learn from them. All they brought her now was pain, and the memories of what she and Bill once shared. Perhaps they would again. *Perhaps* . . . she let herself think the word, but not the inevitable conclusion if they didn't. That was unthinkable, and prodding herself again, she went back to her papers. She worked for another hour, as the sun went down, making committee lists, and suggestions for the group she'd met with that afternoon, and when she glanced outside again, it was almost dark, and the velvet night seemed to engulf her. It was so quiet in the apartment, so empty in a way that it almost made her want to call out, or reach for someone. But there was no one there. She closed her eyes and lay her head back against the chair, and then as though Providence had been listening to her, and still gave a damn, although she doubted that, the phone rang.

"Hello?" She sounded surprised and very young, she had been pulled back a long way from her own thoughts, and in the twilit room, with her hair a little ruffled, she looked incredibly pretty as she answered.

"Mary Stuart?" The voice was a soft drawl, and it made her smile at once just to hear her. It was a voice she had known for twenty-six years now. She hadn't heard from her for months, but somehow she was always there when she needed her, as though she knew. They shared the powerful bond of ancient friendship. "Is that you? You sounded like Alyssa for a minute." The voice on the other end was feminine, deeply sensual, and still had faint whispers of Texas in it.

"No, it's me. She's still in Paris." Mary Stuart sighed as she felt a strong hand reach out and pull her back to shore. It was amazing how she was always there at odd moments. She often did that. They were there for each other, and always had been. And as she thought about it, Mary Stuart remembered what she had seen at Gristede's. "Are you okay? I was reading about you this afternoon." Mary Stuart frowned, thinking about the headline.

"Pretty, isn't it? It's particularly nice, since my current trainer is a woman. I fired the guy on the cover of the *Enquirer* last year. He called today, threatening to sue me, because his wife is furious about the piece. He's got a lot to learn about the tabloids." Tanya herself had learned it all the hard way. "And to answer your question, yeah, I'm okay. Sort of." She had a soft purr that drove most men crazy, and Mary Stuart smiled when she heard her. It was like a breath of fresh air in a stifling room. She had felt that way about her the first day she met her. They had gone to college together twenty-six years before, in Berkeley. Those had been crazy days, and they'd all been so young. There were four of them then. Mary Stuart, Tanya, Eleanor, and Zoe. They were suite mates in the dorm for the first two years, and then they'd rented a house on Euclid.

They'd been inseparable for four years; they had been like sisters. Ellie had died in their senior year, and after that things changed. After graduation they all grew up and moved on to their lives. Tanya had married right away, two days after graduation. She married her childhood sweetheart from her hometown in East Texas. They were married in the chapel, and it had lasted all of two years. Within a year of graduation, her meteoric career had taken off and blown her life to bits, and her marriage along with it. Bobby Joe managed to hang on for another year, but it was too much for him. He was way out of his element, and he knew it. It had been frightening enough for him to have a wife who was educated and talented, but a superstar was more than he could deal with. He tried, he wanted to be fair, but what he really wanted was for her to give it all up and stay in Texas with him. He didn't want to leave home, didn't want to give up his daddy's business, they were contractors and they were doing well, and he knew what he could handle and what he couldn't. And to his credit, tabloids, agents, concerts, shrieking fans, and multimillion dollar contracts were not what he wanted, and they were Tanya's whole life. She loved Bobby Joe, but she wasn't about to give up a career that was everything she'd ever dreamed of. They got separated on their second anniversary, and were divorced by Christmas. It took him a long time to get over her, but he had since remarried and had six kids, and Tanya had seen him once or twice over the years. She said he was fat and bald and as nice as ever. She always said it a little wistfully, and Mary Stuart knew that Tanya was always aware of the price she had paid, the dues that life had collected from her in exchange for her wild success, her fantastic career. Twenty years after she'd begun, she was still the number one female singer in the country.

She and Mary Stuart had stayed good friends. Mary Stuart had married the summer after graduation too. But Zoe had gone on to medical school. She had always been the rebel in their midst, the one who burned for all the most revolutionary causes. The others used to tease her that she had come to Berkeley ten years too late, but it was she who always rallied them, who demanded that everything be fair and right, she who fought for the underdog in every situation. . . . It was she who had found Ellie when she died, who had cried so desperately, and had had the guts to call Ellie's aunt and uncle. It had been a terrible time for all of them. Ellie had been closest to Mary Stuart, and she had been a wonderful, gentle girl, full of idealistic ideas and dreams. Her parents had been killed in an accident junior year, and her three roommates had become family to her. Mary Stuart wondered at times if she would ever have been able to cope with the pressures of the outside world. She was so delicate as to be almost unreal, and unlike the others, with their life's goals and their plans, she had been completely unrealistic, a total dreamer. She died three weeks before graduation. Tanya almost delayed her wedding over it, but they all agreed Ellie would have wanted it to go on and Tanya said that Bobby Joe would have killed her if she'd postponed it. Mary Stuart had been Tanya's maid of honor, and Zoe was her only bridesmaid.

Tanya would have been in Mary Stuart's wedding too, except that she was giving her first concert in Japan at the time. And Zoe hadn't been able to leave school. Mary Stuart was married at her parents' home in Greenwich.

The second time Tanya got married, Mary Stuart had seen it on the news. Tanya was twenty-nine, married her manager, and had a quiet ceremony in Las Vegas, followed by tabloids, helicopters, TV cameras, and every member of the press that could be deployed within a thousand miles of Vegas.

Mary Stuart had never liked Tanya's new husband. Tanya said she wanted kids this time, they were going to buy a house in Santa Barbara, or Pasadena, and have a "real life." She had the right idea, but this time her husband didn't. He had two things on his mind, Tanya's career, and her money. And he did everything he could to push the one in order to obtain the other. Professionally, Tanya always said, he did a lot of good things for her. He made changes she could never have made on her own, set up concerts around the world for her, got her record contracts that broke all records, and pushed her from superstar to legend. After that, she could ask for just about anything she wanted. In the five years they were married, she had three platinum records, and five gold ones, and won every Grammy and musical award she could lay her hands on. And in spite of the small fortune he took from her in the end, her future was assured, her mom was living in a five-million-dollar house in Houston, and she had bought her sister and brother-in-law an estate near Armstrong.

She herself had one of the prettiest houses in Bel Air, and a ten-million-dollar beach house in Malibu she never went to. Her husband had wanted her to buy it. She had money and fame, but no kids. And after the divorce, she thought she needed a change, and started acting. She made two movies the first year, and won an Academy Award the second. At thirty-five, Tanya Thomas had anything and everything that most people thought she might have dreamed of. What she had never had was the life she would have shared with Bobby Joe, affection, love, and support, someone to be with her, and care about her, and children. And it was another six years before she married her third husband, Tony Goldman. He was a real estate developer in the Los Angeles area, and had gone out with half a dozen starlets. There was no doubt that he was impressed with Tanya's career, but even Mary Stuart, always fiercely defensive on her friend's behalf, had to admit that he was a decent guy and obviously cared deeply about her. What worried Tanya's friends, and they were numerous by then, was whether or not Tony could keep his head in the heat of Tanya's life, or would it all be too much for him, and he'd go crazy. From all Mary Stuart had heard in the past three years, she had the impression that things had gone well, and she knew better than anyone, after being close to Tanya for the twenty years of her career, that what she read in the tabloids meant nothing.

The big draw Tony had had for her, Mary Stuart knew, was that Tony was divorced and had three children. They had been nine, eleven, and fourteen the day of the wedding, and Tanya loved them dearly. The oldest and youngest were boys and were crazy about her, and the little girl was completely bowled over by her and couldn't believe that Tanya Thomas was marrying her father. She bragged about it to everyone, and even started trying to look and dress like Tanya, which on an eleven-year-old was less than appropriate, and Tanya used to take her shopping and buy her things constantly to tone it down, but still make her feel pretty. She was great with the kids, and kept talking about having a baby. But having married Tony at forty-one, she was hesitant about getting pregnant. She was afraid she was too old, and Tony was not keen on having more children, so Tanya never pushed it. She had enough on her plate without negotiating with Tony about having a baby. She had two concert tours back-to-back in the first two years of their marriage, the tabloids were going crazy with her, and she had been battling a couple of lawsuits. It was hardly an atmosphere conducive to sanity, let alone conception. It was easier to just take on Tony's kids, and she had, wholeheartedly. He even said that she was a better mother to them than his first wife. But Mary Stuart had noticed that in spite of Tony's easy, friendly ways, Tanya always seemed to be handling everything herself, managers, lawyers, concert tours, death threats, facing all the agonies and worries alone, while Tony closed his own business deals, or went to Palm Springs to play golf with his buddies. He seemed less involved in her life than Mary Stuart had hoped he would be. She knew better than anyone how rough Tanya's life was, how lonely, how hard she worked, how brutal the demands of the fans, how painful the betrayals. Oddly enough, Tanya rarely complained, and Mary Stuart always admired her for it. But it annoyed her when she saw Tony waving to the cameras as they went to the Oscars or the Grammys. He always seemed to be around for the good times, and none of this hard stuff. Mary Stuart thought of that now, as Tanya mentioned the trainer's wife who had called threatening her, over the headlines in the tabloids. Tanya had learned better than anyone over the years that there was nothing anyone could do to fight the tabloids. "Actually, Tony wasn't too thrilled either," Tanya said very quietly. The tone of her voice concerned Mary Stuart. She sounded tired and lonely. She had been fighting all the same battles for a long time, and they were very wearing. "Every time the tabloids claim I'm having an affair, he goes crazy. He says I'm embarrassing him with his friends, and he doesn't like it. I can see his point." She sighed, but there was nothing she could do about it. There was no way to stop them. And the press loved to torment her, with her splendid blond mane, her huge blue eyes, and her spectacular figure. It was hard for any of them to believe that she was just a regular woman, and would have rather drunk Dr Pepper than champagne. But that bit of news wouldn't have sold their papers.

Tanya had always worn her hair blond, and constant, careful cosmetic repair kept her looking sinfully young. She was claiming to be thirty-six now, and had successfully shed the additional eight years that she and Mary Stuart had in common. But no one would have suspected from looking at her that she was lying. "I don't exactly love it myself when they claim I'm having an affair, but the people they talk about are usually so ridiculous, it doesn't bother me most of the time . . . except for Tony." And the kids. It was embarrassing for all of them, but there was nothing she could do to stop it. "I think they just run off a list of possibles on a computer somewhere, and throw you together with anyone they feel like."

Tanya shrugged, and put her feet up on the coffee table in front of her, as she narrowed her eyes and thought of Mary Stuart. She hadn't talked to her in months. They were the two closest of the old group. Tanya knew that Mary Stuart no longer talked to Zoe, and hadn't for years, and even she had all but lost track of Zoe. She called her every year or two, and they still exchanged Christmas cards, but Zoe's life seemed so separate from theirs. She was an internist in San Francisco. She had never married, never had kids. She was completely devoted to her work, and gave every spare moment of her time to free clinics. It was the kind of work she had always believed in. Tanya hadn't even seen her in the last five years, since the last concert she'd done in San Francisco.

"What about you?" Tanya suddenly asked Mary Stuart pointedly. "How are you doing?" There was an edge to her voice, a pointed end she used to probe into her old friend's soul, but Mary Stuart saw her coming and silently dodged her.

"I'm fine. Doing all the same things, committee work, board meetings, volunteer work in Harlem. I just spent the whole day at the Metropolitan talking about a big fund-raising event they're planning for September." Her voice was even and controlled and cool, but Tanya knew her far better than that, and Mary Stuart knew it. She could fool a lot of people, even Bill at times, but never Tanya.

"That's not what I meant." There was a long silence while neither woman was sure what to say, and Tanya waited for what Mary Stuart would answer. "How are you, Mary Stuart? Really?"

Mary Stuart sighed, and looked out the window. It was dark now. And she was alone in the silent apartment. She had been alone for all intents and purposes for over a year. "I'm okay." Her voice trembled, but only slightly. It was better than when Tanya had seen her a year before, on a disastrous rainy day when Mary Stuart wished that her own life had ended. "I'm getting used to it." But so much had changed. So much more than she had expected.

"And Bill?"

"He's fine too, I guess. I never see him."

"That doesn't sound so fine to me." There was another long pause, but they were used to it, Tanya was thinking. "What about Alyssa?"

"She's fine, I think. She loves Paris. I'm meeting her there in a few weeks. We're going to spend a month running around Europe. Bill has a big case in England, and he's going to be over there for the summer, so I thought I'd go over and see her." She sounded happier as she spoke of it, and Tanya smiled. Alyssa Walker was one of Tanya's favorite people.

"Will you be in England with him?" Tanya asked in her soft drawl, and Mary Stuart hesitated and then answered quickly.

"No, I'll be here. He's really too busy to pay any attention to me during a case like that, and I have so much to do here." *So much to do here.* She knew all the right things to say, all the cover-ups, the language of despair. . . . We'll have to get together sometime . . . no, things are fine . . . everything is just terrific . . . Bill is so incredibly busy with work right now . . . he's on a trip . . . I have a meeting . . . have to see my board . . . have to go downtown . . . uptown . . . to Europe to see my daughter . . . The politics of hiding, the correct thing to say in order to buy solitude and silence, and a place to grieve in peace away from prying eyes and pity. A way of pushing people away without saying how bad it really was.

"You're not okay, Mary Stuart." Tanya went after her with the single-mindedness she was known for. She would leave no stone unturned until she found the truth, the answer, the culprit. It was that determination for the pursuit of truth that she and Zoe had had in common. But Tanya had always been far subtler about it, and far kinder when she discovered whatever it was she wanted. "Why won't you tell me the truth, Stu?"

"I am telling you the truth, Tan," Mary Stuart insisted . . . Stu . . . Tan . . . Tannie . . . the names of so long ago . . . the promises . . . the hope . . . the beginning. It always felt so much like the end now, when everything winds down and you begin to lose it all, instead of find it. Mary Stuart hated that about her life now. "We're fine, honest."

"You're lying, but I'm not sure I blame you. You're entitled." That was the difference between Zoe and Tanya. Zoe would never have let her lie, let her hide. She would have felt an obligation to expose her, to shine a bright light on her pain, thinking she could heal it. At least Tanya understood that she couldn't. She had her own worries now. The tabloids weren't right about the affair, but they weren't far off the mark that she and Tony were having problems. Despite the fact that he had thought it was fun for a while, he was no longer enjoying the spotlight placed on them by the press, or the lies, the threats, the stalkers, the lawsuits, the people constantly trying to take advantage of her, and either embarrass or use her, whatever it cost them. It was utterly exhausting, and impossible to have any kind of decent private life. How could you even find the real woman amidst all the nonsense? Lately, Tony had complained about it constantly, and she sympathized with him, but other than retire, which she didn't want to do, and he didn't expect it of her, there was really nothing she could do to change it. All they could do was get away from time to time, and that helped, but a trip to Hawaii, or even Africa, or the south of France, did nothing to solve the problems. It provided a brief, pleasurable escape, but no real solution. As insane as it sounded even to him, despite her phenomenal success, her vast fame, and millions of adoring fans, in fact the very life she led made her a victim. And little by little,

Tony had come to hate it. For the moment, all she could do was promise him to keep as low a profile as she could. She hadn't even gone to Texas to see her mother the week before, as planned, because she was afraid that if she left town, she'd fuel the rumors. Lately, he said constantly that it was all getting to be too hard on him, and on his kids, and just the way he said it, made Tanya feel panicked. Particularly since she knew there was nothing she could do to change the situation. Their torments all came from outside sources.

"I'm coming to New York next week, that's why I called," Tanya explained. "I figured in your busy life I'd better make a date with you, or you'd be having dinner with the governor and hitting him up for money for one of your causes." Over the years, Tanya had been incredibly generous with the groups Mary Stuart cared about most, and twice she had donated her time and given a performance, but not in a while. Lately, she was just too busy. She never seemed to have a moment for herself now. And her current agent and manager were tougher than the ones she'd had before, who had cut her a little slack, but the new ones were pushing her to do more concerts. There were fortunes to be made, from albums made from the concerts, licensing deals for dolls and perfume and cutting new CD's and tapes and Tanya was hotter than she ever had been. They wanted her to capitalize on it, but at the moment she was leaning more toward making another movie. "I'm doing a TV show in New York," she told Mary Stuart, "but actually I'm talking to some agent about writing a book. I got a call from a publisher, and I don't think I'm interested, but I'll listen to them. What's left to say about me?" There had already been four unauthorized biographies about her, all of them cruel, and mostly inaccurate, but she was generally good-natured about them. After the first one, which had come as a terrible blow, she had called Mary Stuart in the middle of the night in hysterics. They had been there for each other a lot over the years, and by now they both felt certain that they always would be. It was the kind of friendship you don't reproduce in later life. It begins, it grows, you nurture it from sapling to oak tree. Later on, the roots don't form the same way. Theirs had taken hold long since, and were there, buried in solid ground, for the duration.

"When are you coming in? I'll meet you at the airport," Mary Stuart offered.

"I'll pick you up on the way into town, and we can go to the hotel and talk. I'll be in on Tuesday." Tanya was flying in on the recording company's plane, as she always did. It was just like hopping in a car for her, and the casual way she flew around always amused Mary Stuart. "I'll call you from the plane."

"I'll be here," Mary Stuart said, feeling suddenly like a kid. There was something about the way Tanya swept her up and took her under her wing that made her feel young again, instead of a thousand years old. She grinned at the thought of seeing her again, it had been ages since the last time, she couldn't even remember when, although Tanya could, distinctly.

"See you, kiddo," Tanya said, smiling at her end. And then, sounding more serious, and as gentle as Mary Stuart always remembered, "I love you."

"I know." She nodded as tears sprang to her eyes. It was kindness which Mary Stuart could no longer tolerate. The loneliness was so much easier to deal with. "I love you too," she said, choking on her own words, and then, ". . . I'm sorry. . . ." She closed her eyes, fighting back the waves of her own emotions.

"Don't be, baby . . . it's okay . . . I know . . . I know." But the truth was she didn't. No one knew. No one could possibly understand what she felt now. Not even her husband.

"I'll see you next week," Mary Stuart said, sounding composed again, but Tanya wasn't fooled. There was a flood of agony held behind the dam that Mary Stuart had built to keep her grief in check, and Tanya couldn't help wondering how long she could stand it.

"See you Tuesday. Just wear jeans. We'll go have a hamburger, or order room service or something. See ya . . ." And then she was gone, and Mary Stuart was thinking of her, and the days in Berkeley, before they had all moved on to their lives, before life had gotten so full, and so hard, and they had all had their dues to pay. It had all been so easy then . . . at first. Until Ellie had died, just before graduation. That had been their entry into the real world, and as she thought of it, she glanced at a photograph on her night table, of the four of them in freshman year. They looked like children to her now, even younger than her own daughter. She saw Tanya with her long blond mane, looking sexy and sensational, and Zoe with long red pigtails, so earnest and intense, and Ellie so ethereal with a little halo of blond curls, and Mary Stuart herself, all eyes and legs and long dark hair, looking straight into the camera. It seemed a hundred years ago, and it was. She thought about them for a long time, and eventually she fell asleep on her bed, in her jeans and her pink T-shirt. And when Bill came in at eleven o'clock, he found her there. He stood looking at her for a long time, and then turned off the light. He never spoke to her and never touched her, and she slept in her jeans all night. And when she woke the next morning, he had already gone back to the office. He had simply passed through her life once again, like the stranger he was now.

CHAPTER 2

When Tanya Thomas woke up in her Bel Air bedroom the next day, Tony was already in the shower. They shared a single bedroom, and two huge, separate dressing rooms, each with their own separate bathroom. The bedroom was large and airy, decorated in French antiques, with enormous pink silk curtains, and miles of pink floral fabrics. Her dressing room and bath were pink marble, and the fabrics were pale pink silk there too. And Tony's bathroom was done entirely in black marble and granite. Black towels, black silk drapes, it was the consummate male bathroom.

She had bought the house years before, and had it all redone to suit Tony when they got married. Although he was extremely successful too, she knew he loved showing off her success. In spite of all the headaches associated with it, he loved letting people know that he was married to Tanya Thomas. The Hollywood scene had always appealed to him, and after years on the fringe, being catapulted into the very heart of it had always seemed like an extraordinary bonus. He loved going to Hollywood parties, and chatting with the stars, and he liked going to the Academy Awards and the Golden Globes, and especially Barbara Davis's gala events, far more than Tanya did. After eighteen hours of work, she was happier staying home at night, sinking into a warm tub, and listening to someone else's music.

She put a pink satin robe over her lace nightgown while he was still getting dressed, and she went downstairs to make him something for breakfast. There were other people in the house who could have done as much for him, but Tanya liked doing it, and she knew it meant a lot to Tony. She cooked for his kids whenever she could too, and she was a good cook. She cooked a good steak, and had introduced them all to grits, and took a lot of teasing for it, but they loved them. She liked making pasta for him too. There were a lot of things she liked doing for Tony. She liked making love to him, and being alone with him, and going on trips with him, and discovering new places, but there was never enough time, there were always rehearsals, and recording sessions, movies, and concerts, benefits, and countless hours spent poring over documents and contracts with her attorneys. Tanya was more than a singer or an actress now, she was an empire, an industry unto itself, and she had learned a lot about the business, the hard way.

She poured orange juice while she waited for him, and broke eggs into a frying pan as the butter began to sizzle. And as she dropped the toast into the toaster, and started the coffee for him, she opened the morning paper. Her heart sank as she read the second lead item. It was about a former employee suing her, allegedly for sexual harassment. It was the first she had heard of it, and as she read the article, she recognized the name of a bodyguard they'd had for two weeks the year before, and had fired for stealing. He had given a lengthy interview, claiming that she had tried to seduce him, and when he refused her, she fired him without reason or explanation. Tanya knew as she read the piece, with a sickening feeling, that like all the other lawsuits in which she'd been involved, in the end they'd wind up paying him off just to settle it, and unload him. There never seemed to be any way to defend herself anymore, to prove to anyone that she was innocent, that it was all lies, and that it was a form of blackmail. She knew that her husband knew that too, and he was always the first one to tell her to settle, no matter how outrageous the claim, or the attack. It was just simpler that way. But she also knew that Tony would be livid when he saw the paper. She folded it carefully and put it away, and a moment later, he walked into the kitchen wearing his golf clothes.

"Aren't you going to work today?" she asked conversationally, trying to look relaxed as she sliced an avocado, and put the finishing touches on his breakfast.

"Where have you been for the last three years?" He looked startled by her question. "I always play golf on Fridays." He was a good-looking man with dark hair, and a powerful build, in his late forties. He played a lot of tennis and golf, and worked out in a gym he had built at the opposite end of the house, with his personal trainer, not the one who had recently appeared in the tabloids. "Where's the paper?" he asked as he sat down and looked around. He read the *Los Angeles Times* and the *Wall Street Journal* every morning. He was an outstanding businessman, and had made a fortune in real estate development in the years when it really counted. But his money was of no interest to Tanya. It was his kindness which had originally appealed to her, his decency, his kids, and his family values. As far as she was concerned, he was just a regular guy going to work every day, and playing ball with his sons on the weekend. And she particularly liked the fact that he wasn't in "the business." What she hadn't figured on originally was that he liked all of the Hollywood trappings a lot more than she did. He liked all of it, but he didn't like paying his dues for the lifestyle. He liked the glitter but not the price you had to pay to be there. And Tanya knew you couldn't have one without the other. In fact, Tony complained constantly about the aggravations they had to endure, and the infuriating stories in the tabloids.

"You can't have it both ways," she had explained to him early on. "You can't have the glory without the pain," she'd said softly, and offered to retire the first time after they were married that the tabloids made ugly accusations about her, and talked about all her old boyfriends. But he insisted that he didn't want her to retire. He thought she would be bored. She had suggested they give it all up and have a baby. But he liked what she did, and so did she, so she kept doing it, and they kept rallying from the attacks, and the death threats, and the lawsuits. She still refused to have a bodyguard full-time, and only hired one when she went to an event wearing a lot of borrowed jewelry.

"So where's the paper?" he asked again, digging into his eggs, and glancing up at her, and he saw immediately in Tanya's eyes that something had happened. "What's up?"

"Nothing," she said vaguely, pouring herself a cup of coffee.

"Come on, Tanya," he said, looking annoyed. "It's written all over your face. You won't win the Oscar for this one." She smiled ruefully at him and shrugged. He'd find out anyway. She just hadn't wanted it to be over breakfast. Without saying another word, she handed the paper to him, and watched as she saw him read the story. She could see the muscles work in his jaw and neck, but he didn't say a word until he finished it, and put down the paper. And then he looked up at her with a grim expression. "That's going to cost you. I hear sexual harassment suits are really paying big now." He said it unemotionally, but it was easy to see that he was very angry. "What did you say to him?" His eyes bore into hers as he asked her, and Tanya looked at her husband in amazement.

"What did I *say* to him? Are you crazy? Do you think I said anything to him? I told him where the studio was and what time I had to be at rehearsal. That's what I said to him. How can you even ask me?" There were tears in her eyes as she looked at him, and Tony seemed uncomfortable as he took a sip of coffee.

"I just wondered if you said anything he could build this on, that's all. I mean, hell, the guy certainly tells quite a story."

"So does everyone," she said sadly, her eyes never leaving Tony's. "It's no different than anything else. It's just plain greed and envy. He saw money, and he wants it. He figures he can embarrass me into paying him to shut up." She'd been through it before, not just with discrimination suits, but with unlawful terminations, real estate claims, accident claims from previous employees. Everyone hoped that by suing her they would get a piece of the action. It was old news in Hollywood, and other places these days, but it still wasn't pretty when it happened. And although he understood the reasons for it, Tony had never gotten used to it, and he didn't like it. He said it was hard on his kids and his family, it made him an object of ridicule and even gave his ex-wife something to complain about. He just didn't need it. Tanya knew only too well how Tony reacted to these stories. First he pretended they didn't bother him, then he got increasingly more disagreeable as the plot unfolded, and eventually he put as much pressure on her as the lawyers did to just get out of it, and settle. But through it all he acted like the injured party. And eventually, after he had made her pay for it for a while, he decided to forgive her. It was becoming an old familiar story, and she didn't enjoy it.

"Are you going to pay him off?" Tony asked, looking anxious.

"I haven't even talked to my lawyer yet," she said, looking annoyed. "I just read it in the paper this morning, like you did."

"If you'd handled it right a year ago, when you fired him, this would never have happened," he said, putting a jacket on and looking at her from the doorway.

"That's not true, and you know it. We've been through this before. It just goes with the territory, no matter what you do." She had always been so careful, and so circumspect, but no one ever gave her credit for it. She had never been promiscuous, behaved badly, used drugs, treated her employees badly, or got drunk in public. But no matter what you did, or didn't do, in her kind of life, people made outrageous claims, and in most cases, the public believed them. And sometimes so did Tony.

"I'm not sure I know what you do anymore," he said, looking angry. He hated the embarrassment he said she caused him. And then he turned on his heel and left. And a minute later she heard his car speeding down the driveway.

She dialed her attorney, Bennett Pearson, almost as soon as Tony had left, and her attorney apologized. They had received the papers late the day before, and hadn't had time to call her and warn her.

"It sure made a nice surprise this way, over breakfast," she said, sounding very Texas. "Next time, it might be nice to have a little warning. You know, Tony is not exactly crazy about these things." Last week the trainer in the *Enquirer,* now the bodyguard. On top of being a target for lawsuits and blackmail of varying degrees, she was also a sex symbol, and the papers loved honing in on anything they could about her. There were tears in her eyes when she hung up from the lawyers. The bodyguard was insisting that she had propositioned him, embarrassed him, and that he had suffered emotional distress over it. And he had some quack psychiatrist who was willing to testify for him. According to her attorneys, the claim wasn't particularly unusual, but Tanya remembered that the guy was a real sleaze and would probably really stick it to her. In earlier days, she would probably have sat and cried over it. But after over twenty years, it was all too familiar, and she knew why it happened. She was successful and powerful, and had managed to stay on top of her career with hard work and an incredible amount of determination, and people were willing to line up ten deep to try and take it from her. In Hollywood, like anywhere else, there were armies of frustrated people who were only too happy to take what they could from anyone else. It was an unusual work ethic certainly, but it was by no means unheard of.

She had asked her attorney what he wanted her to do about the case, and he told her to just forget it. He would handle everything, and he was sure that after the initial public blast, the gentleman in question was going to be anxious to settle. He was sure that that had been his intent anyway, and warned her that settlements in harassment suits these days were easily up in the millions.

"Great. What would you like me to do? Why don't I just give him the house in Malibu? Ask him how he feels about the sun, or maybe he'd rather have the house in Bel Air, but it's a little smaller." It was impossible not to be cynical, harder still not to be angry, or to feel abused, or betrayed, by people who were willing to hurt you or use you, although they never even knew you. In some ways, the attacks on her were so obvious and so impersonal that they had the same quality as a drive-by shooting.

It was nine o'clock by then, and her secretary had arrived, a high-strung girl named Jean who had worked for the president of a record company previously, and had worked for Tanya for more than a year. She was efficient and trustworthy, but Tanya didn't like the fact that the girl always seemed to increase the feeling of urgency around her, rather than diminish it for her. And she did just exactly that that morning. Within the first hour she was there, there were three calls from New York, two from entertainment magazines, wanting interviews, and one from the show she was going to be on. The lawyer called her back two more times, and her agent called to press her into a decision about her next concert tour. She hadn't committed herself yet, and they had to know immediately because it would be impossible to include Japan otherwise, and the agent she used in Britain called wanting to know about a contract. They got word of another tabloid story coming out, and they called about a technical problem as well in her current record. She was doing a benefit the next night, had to get to the recording studio by noon, and had rehearsals that night for the benefit. And her film agent called, wanting to talk to her about another movie.

"God, what is today? A full moon, or is everyone in this town just going crazy?" Tanya brushed the long blond hair out of her eyes with one hand, while Jean handed her a cup of coffee, and reminded her that she had to give an answer about the tour before four-thirty. "I don't have to do anything, goddammit, and if they don't include Japan, then too bad. I'm not going to be pressured into making a decision before I'm ready." She was scowling when she said it, which was uncharacteristic of her. Tanya had always had an easygoing disposition, but there was enough pressure on her to make a volcano erupt, and she was only human, and could only take so much.

"What about the interview with *View*?" Jean asked relentlessly. "They really need an answer from you this morning."

"Why didn't they call my PR people?" Tanya asked, feeling increasingly stressed with every passing moment. "They're not supposed to be calling me directly. And why aren't you telling them that?"

"I tried, but they didn't want to hear it. You know how it is, Tanya, the minute they get your number, everyone wants to talk to you directly."

"Yeah, and so do I." It was Tony. He was back from playing golf, and he was standing in the doorway of her office, looking anything but happy. "Can I talk to you for a minute, Tan?"

"Sure," she said, looking up at him, feeling suddenly nervous. She had to be at the studio in half an hour, but she didn't want to put him off. He didn't look as though he'd be willing to wait another minute. Whatever was bothering him seemed urgent.

Jean left them alone, and Tanya waited for him to sit down. He looked as though he had something major to say to her, and she wasn't sure she was ready to hear it. "Is something wrong?" she asked in an anxious whisper.

"Not really," he sighed, and looked away from her out the window. "No more than usual. And I don't want you to get me wrong." He turned and looked at her, but she could see in his eyes how angry he still was, how betrayed he felt, not just by her, or the story the bodyguard had told, but by the fact that their life required that kind of abuse, and there was never any way to escape the torture. As celebrities, they had no right to privacy, or even honesty, and every invented tale about her, every story made up by anyone, enjoyed the protection of the First Amendment. "I'm not angry about the thing in the paper today," he lied to himself more than to her, but he liked to believe he was fair to her, even when he wasn't, "it's not much worse than anything else they've said about us. I have a lot of respect for you, Tan. I don't know how you take all the shit you do," and they both knew there was plenty of it. The previous Christmas, they'd had to have bodyguards for all his kids, because there'd been a very serious death threat on all of them, particularly Tanya, and his ex-wife had a fit over it. "I think you're an amazing woman." But she didn't like the way he looked at her when he said it. It was all in his eyes and she had seen it coming for a year. He was sick of it, and he could still walk away from it. The difference was, she couldn't. Even if she decided to retire that afternoon, it would go on for a long, long time, maybe forever, and she knew it.

"What are you saying to me?" She tried not to sound cynical, but it was hard not to. She'd been there before, in various ways, with different people. She told herself she was ready for it, but in her heart of hearts, she knew she wasn't. You never were, you always hoped that this time it would be different, that he would be strong enough, that he would really care, that it would be worth it to him to stick by her and help her. It was all she'd ever wanted, maybe even more than children, just a solid, real relationship with a man who would stick around when the shit hit the fan, because it would. She had told Tony that at the beginning. And he'd been good about it, for nearly three years now, but lately he was getting testy. Too much so.

"Are you telling me I'm too good for you, that I deserve better than you have to give? One of those noble little speeches that makes me feel that I'm rising to greatness while you run out the door?" She looked him in the eye, and spoke clearly. There was no point hiding from what was coming. And she knew it was now.

"That's a lousy thing to say. I've never run out on you." He looked hurt and she felt sorry. Maybe she was premature in her accusations.

"No, but you're thinking about it, aren't you?" Tanya asked softly.

He sat looking at her for a long time, neither confirming nor denying what she had asked him. "I don't even know what I'm saying to you. I'm just telling you I'm getting tired. This is a hard life you live, harder than anyone ever knows until they get here."

"I warned you of that," she said, feeling like a climber on Everest halfway through the climb, as her companions began to fail her. "I told you what it was like. It's a tough life here, Tony. There are wonderful things about it, and I love my work, but I hate what all the other stuff does to me . . . and to you . . . and to us . . . and the kids . . . I know how hard it is. But the bitch of it is, I can't do anything to stop it, and you know that."

"I know, I know . . . and I have no right to complain." He looked at her with eyes filled with embarrassment and agony, but she knew as she looked at him that, for Tony, it was over. You could just see it. He'd had his fling with Hollywood, and for him, the romance had faded. "I know how hard it is on you, and I don't mean to make it any worse. I know how hard you work, and what a perfectionist you are . . . but that's part of it too. There's no time in your life for me anywhere, all it is is concerts and rehearsals and recordings. You're doing great things, Tan, and meanwhile I'm sitting here reading about us in the tabloids."

"And believing it?" she asked him bluntly. Maybe that was

it. Maybe he thought it was true. The bodyguard who was suing her had been a real son of a bitch, but he was very attractive.

"No, I'm not believing it," he sighed, "but I'm not enjoying it either. The guys I played golf with this morning made a big deal about it. Actually, some of them thought it was pretty funny, to have a wife who gets sued for sexual harassment, most of them claim their wives never want to sleep with them." He looked embarrassed by what he was saying, but Tanya got the deeper meaning. His friends had been harassing him, and Tony was tired of being humiliated. It was a reasonable complaint, but she was tired of it too. The problem was that he could get a ticket to freedom anytime, and she couldn't. The tabloids, and the potential "suers," were gunning for her, not her husband. "I don't know what I'm saying to you," Tony said unhappily, "it's not much fun like this, is it?"

"No, it's not," she said sadly, too decimated by the look in his eyes to even argue with him about it. Somehow, the bad guys always won in the end. The tabloids and the lawsuits and the threats and the pressure of all of it proved to be too much for any relationship with any normal human being. "Are you telling me you want out?" she asked miserably. He was not the love of her life, but she was comfortable with him, she trusted him, she loved him and his kids. If it had been up to her, she would never have ended their marriage.

"I'm not sure," he admitted to her. He had been thinking about it for a while, but he hadn't come to any definite conclusions. "I'm not sure how many more rounds of this I can take, to be honest with you. And I don't want to be unfair to you. It's really starting to get to me, and I thought you should know that."

"I appreciate your honesty," she said, looking at him, already feeling betrayed that he wasn't there for her, that the "embarrassment" of being married to her, and what it entailed, was making him want to leave her. "I wish I could make it better."

"I wish it didn't bother me. I never thought it would. It all seems much more human scale until you step into it, and then it's very Alice-in-Wonderland. It's all very unreal as you begin to fall and fall and fall . . ." he said, and listening to him reminded her again that she loved him. He was a bright man, and despite their differences, they still had a lot in common.

"That's an interesting way to put it," she said, smiling wistfully at him, knowing in her heart of hearts that for him anyway, it was probably already over. "What about the kids?" she asked, looking suddenly distraught. "If you leave, will you still let me see them?" There were tears in her eyes as she asked him. It had all been so bloodless so far and so reasonable. The first of many talks to begin the unraveling of their marriage. But he reached out and touched her hand when he saw the devastated look in her eyes. He felt terrible at what he was seeing. And he hated himself for doing this to her, but he had known for a while that he couldn't take it much longer. And the story in the morning paper had really gotten to him.

"I still love you, Tan," he said in a whisper, and she hated him for looking so handsome as he said it. He still appealed to her a great deal, he was sexy, handsome, and smart, even if he wasn't there for her a lot of the time but she'd always been willing to forgive him. "I just wanted to tell you what I was feeling. And even if things don't work out for us, I would never stop you from seeing the kids. They love you," he said, looking kindly at her in a way that tore her heart out. He was saying good-bye without saying the words, but she knew it wouldn't be long now. It was over for him, if not for her.

"And I love them." She began to cry softly, and he went to sit next to her and put an arm around her shoulders.

"They love you too, and so do I, Tan, in my own crazy way," he said, but she didn't believe him. If he really loved her, he wouldn't want to leave her.

"What about Wyoming? Will they still come? Will you?"

she asked, feeling desperate and suddenly very frightened. She was losing him, and probably them too. Why would they want to see her if their father left her? Had she established enough of a relationship in the past three years for them to want to do that? And when she looked up, Tony was looking at her strangely.

"I think they ought to go with you. I think it would be a great experience for them," he said, looking uncomfortable, and she understood immediately what he was saying.

"But you won't come. Is that it?"

"I don't think so. I think it would be a good time for us to take a break. I think I'm going to go to Europe."

"When did that come up? Today on the golf course?" What was happening here? How long had he been planning this defection? She suddenly wondered as she listened. And as her eyes bored into his, he looked a little sheepish.

"I've been thinking about this for a while, Tan. It didn't just happen this morning over breakfast. I think that was kind of the catalyst. But it was the *Enquirer* last week. The *Star* the week before. It's been lawsuits and crises and death threats and tabloids ever since we got married."

"I thought you were getting used to it," she said, sounding startled.

"I don't see how anyone can. You're not used to it either." He had worried at times about the incredible stress it all caused her, he knew that even people as young as she was sometimes keeled over and died from too much stress. Sometimes he seriously wondered how she didn't. "Anyway, Tanya, I'm sorry."

"So what do we do now?" She wanted to know if she was supposed to go upstairs and pack his bags for him, or make wild passionate love to him and talk him out of it. What was the protocol, and what did he expect? And even more important than that, what was it she wanted? She didn't even know herself. She was still too hurt and too startled by what he was saying.

"I'm not sure what we do," he said honestly. "I want to think about it for a while. But I wanted to warn you of the direction I'm going."

"Kind of like a hurricane, or a flood, sort of a natural disaster," she said, trying to smile, but tears kept springing to her eyes, and then Jean knocked on the door and stuck her head in.

"You're an hour late at the studio. The producer called, and he wanted to remind you the meter's running. The musicians want to know if they can take an early lunch and come back in an hour. And your agent called to remind you, he needs an answer from you today by four-thirty. Bennett Pearson called too. He needs you to call him as soon as you're finished."

"Okay, okay." Tanya put up a hand to stop her. "Tell the musicians to take lunch now. I'll be there in half an hour. Tell Tom to wait and we'll go over the arrangements." And how in hell was she supposed to sing, and decide about Japan, a new film, another tour, and whether or not to pay a settlement to the blackmailer who had told his story in the morning paper? As Jean left the room again, she looked up at her husband. "I guess you're right. None of this is much fun, is it?"

"Sometimes it's lots of fun," he said, "but most of the time it isn't. There's too high a price to pay for it," he said honestly as he stood up. He felt like hell, but secretly he was relieved, as far as he was concerned, her life was an absolute nightmare. "Go do your recording, Tan. I'm sorry I made you late. We'll talk another time. There's nothing to resolve now. I'm sorry I took so much time." No problem. An hour. Three years. It was great fun. Hell, who can blame you for wanting to bail out now? She watched him leave the room, torn between sorrow and hatred.

"Everything all right?" Jean was back in with a stack of messages for her, and a reminder that she had to leave for the studio in the next five minutes.

"Okay, okay, I'm going, and yes, I'm fine." Fine. Everything was always fine, even when it wasn't. And she couldn't help wondering how long it would take the press to find out, if Tony left her. It shouldn't have been a consideration, but it was. The prospect of another round of stories on her seemed exhausting.

She washed her face before she left, and tried not to cry. She put on dark glasses, and Jean drove the car. She returned some of her calls from the car, and told her agent she'd do the concert tour, including Japan. She would be on the road the following year for nearly four months, but she could fly home from time to time, and she knew how important the concert tour was. She went straight into the studio when they arrived, and stayed until six o'clock, and then she went on to the rehearsal for the benefit, and didn't get home again until eleven o'clock that evening. And when she did, she found a note from Tony on the kitchen table. He had gone to Palm Springs for the weekend. She stood for a long moment, holding the note in her hand, wondering where their life had gone, and how long it would take him now to end it. The handwriting was on the wall, and it didn't take a clairvoyant to guess that he was on his way out. She thought about stopping him, about calling him in Palm Springs, and telling him how much she loved him, how sorry she was for all the pain she'd caused. But when she picked up the phone, she just stood there. Why wasn't he there for her? Why couldn't he take the same abuse that was being heaped on her? Why was he so willing to run? The only conclusion she could come to as she thought about it was that it was entirely possible Tony Goldman had never really loved her. And if that was truly the case, she would very probably never know it. She set down the phone, and with tears in her eyes, she walked quietly toward the silence of their bedroom.

CHAPTER 3

When Tanya flew to New York, she took the record company's plane, and in order to be alone, she decided not to take her secretary with her. She really didn't need Jean for one TV show, and a meeting with a literary agent. Besides, she wanted some time to think about Tony. After his weekend in Palm Springs, he had come home dutifully on Sunday night. They'd had dinner with the kids, and nothing more was said about his unhappiness, or the stories in the tabloids. She didn't have the courage or the energy to broach either subject with him. And he was careful not to say anything more to her. He didn't even mention it when *People* magazine picked up the story of the lawsuit. He knew he had said enough, and he had already gone to the office when she left for the airport to go to New York on Tuesday.

The plane was waiting for her, and it was almost like having a commercial airliner all to herself. There was a company executive heading for New York onboard. He obviously knew who she was, but other than a curt hello, he said nothing more to her. And she made notes, and telephone calls, and worked on some music. Halfway to New York her lawyer called to tell her the ex-bodyguard wanted a million dollars to drop his lawsuit.

"Tell him I'll see him in court," Tanya said coolly.

"Tanya, I don't think that's smart," Bennett Pearson said calmly.

"I'm not going to pay people to blackmail me. He can't prove anything, he has no case. It's a complete fabrication."

"It's his word against yours. You're a big star, and according to him, you went after him, you traumatized him, you fired him, you ruined his life because he wouldn't have sex with you . . ."

"It's all right, Bennett. You don't have to go through all of it. I know what he's claiming."

"People could feel sorry for him. Juries are unpredictable these days. You have to think about that. What if they award him ten million dollars for his pain and suffering? How would you feel then?"

"Like I wanted to kill him."

"Think about it. I think you should buy your way out. And a million is a nice clean number."

"Do you know how hard I have to work for that? They don't just give that stuff away, you know."

"You're going on tour next year. Take it out of that, and chalk it up to bad luck, like a fire in the house not covered by your insurance."

"That's sick. This is nothing more than a holdup."

"That's right, and it's been done before. To you, and to a lot of others."

"It makes me sick to pay people like that."

"Just give it some thought. You have enough other things on your plate without adding a lawsuit to it. The last thing you need is to give a deposition that will end up in the tabloids. It would be a matter of public record, and so would the proceedings."

"All right, all right."

"Call me from New York." Why was it all so unpleasant? No wonder Tony wanted out. She wished she could walk out of her life too sometimes, but it was all inescapably attached to her, like warts, or cancer.

The flight to New York took only five hours, and she called Mary Stuart just before they landed. She said she'd be there in half an hour to pick her up, and Mary Stuart sounded excited to see her. Tanya called her again half an hour later from the car, and when she got there, her old friend was waiting downstairs, in jeans and a little cotton sweater. The two women hugged each other close, and Tanya took a long look at her friend in the dark car. Mary Stuart looked thinner and far more serious than she had a year before. The last year had obviously taken a tremendous toll on her. Tanya knew with Alyssa in Paris, it was even harder. But Alyssa had needed to be away from them, and Mary Stuart knew it, so she didn't complain about it.

"God, you never change," Mary Stuart said, admiring her, amazed at how beautiful Tanya still looked, even at their age. It was as though the hands of time never touched her. "How do you do that?"

"Professional secrets, my dear," she laughed, looking sexy and mysterious, and then they both laughed. But in spite of whatever surgery she'd had, she also had great skin, beautiful hair, and a fantastic figure. And she had a youthful look about her that had never left her. Mary Stuart looked well too, but she looked closer to their age than Tanya ever had. But keeping her looks wasn't Mary Stuart's business. "You're looking pretty good too, kid, in spite of everything," Tanya dared to say it. It was hard to believe it had been a year, the worst in Mary Stuart's life, and probably Bill's, although he would never admit it.

"I think you've made a pact with the devil," Mary Stuart complained. "It's not fair to the rest of us. What do you admit to now? Thirty-one? Twenty-five? Nineteen? They're going to think I'm your mother."

"Oh, shut up. You look ten years younger than you are and you know it."

"I wish." But Mary Stuart knew just how hard the past year had been on her. In spite of what Tanya said, she could see it in the mirror.

They went to J.G. Melon's, as they had for years, and commented on the faces they still saw, or no longer did, and Tanya told her she was going on tour that winter.

"What does Tony think about that?" Mary Stuart looked at her over her hamburger, and there was a brief lull in the conversation, and then Tanya glanced up at her, and her expression spoke volumes.

"I haven't told him. I haven't actually seen much of him in the past few days. We . . . uh . . . I think I have a little problem." Mary Stuart frowned in concern and listened. "He . . . uh . . . went to Palm Springs for a few days, and he thinks maybe we need a break this summer. He says he's going to Europe, while I take the kids to Wyoming."

"Is he going on a religious pilgrimage, or is there something you're not saying?"

"No." Tanya put her hamburger down, and looked at her old friend soberly. "I think there's something he's not saying yet, but he will. He just doesn't know it yet. He thinks he's still trying to make the decision. But I know the signs. He's already made it."

"What makes you think he has?" Mary Stuart felt sorry for her, but she was not surprised either. Tanya's lifestyle inevitably caused a lot of casualties, and both of them knew that. But as she talked about it, Tanya looked disappointed and unhappy.

"I think he has, because I'm not as young as the doctor makes me look." Mary Stuart smiled at her comment. "I've seen a lot of fatalities. He's already gone, he just doesn't know it. He can't take this pressure anymore, apparently, the lawsuits, the tabloids, the attacks, the slurs, the embarrassment, the humiliation. I can't say I blame him."

"Aren't you forgetting something? What about the good stuff?" Mary Stuart asked gently.

"I guess it kind of gets lost in the shuffle. You forget about that. I forget about it too, so I guess I can't really blame him. The only time I really like what I do is when I'm singing . . . when I'm recording, or in concert and I'm singing my guts out. I don't even care about the applause . . . it's just the music . . . and he doesn't get that, I do.

"He gets all the shit. I get the glory. I suspect he's sick of it. There was a story in the paper this week by some ex-employee we hired last year, the guy claims I came on to him, and then fired him when he wouldn't screw me. You know, your usual nice, homespun little story. It made the front page and embarrassed Tony with all his friends. I think it was kind of the last straw for him."

"What about you? Where does that leave you?" Mary Stuart looked genuinely worried. They had worried about each other for years, even if they didn't talk all the time, or see each other constantly, or even live in the same city. But they both knew that they were always there for each other. "You're telling me that it's getting too hot for him, so he's leaving?"

"He hasn't said that yet, but he's going to. Right now, he wants 'time off' so he can go to Europe. Which leaves me taking his kids to a ranch in Wyoming, but that's okay too. I really love them."

"I know you do. But I'm not exactly impressed by their father's chivalry and devotion."

"So what else is new?" Tanya smiled ruefully, and squeezed Mary Stuart's hands. "What about you? How's Bill doing these days? Has it been as hard on him as it has on you?" It was written all over her face how much she'd been through.

"I suppose so." She shrugged. "We don't talk about it much. There's nothing to say. You can't undo what happened." Or the things they had said to each other about it.

Tanya dared to ask her something then that she had wondered for the past year, and she suspected was the root of the problem. "Does he blame you?" It was barely more than a whisper, but even in the crowded restaurant Mary Stuart heard her.

"Probably," she sighed. "I suppose we both blame ourselves for not seeing what was happening. But I know in the beginning he felt that I should have seen it coming. I should have been able to foresee disaster before it struck us. Bill bestows magical qualities on me, when it suits him. In any case, I suppose I blame myself too. It doesn't change anything. The delusion is that you can turn the clock back, and stop it from happening, if you assign the blame to the right person. But it doesn't work that way. It doesn't matter. It's over." Tears filled her eyes and she looked away, and Tanya was instantly sorry she had brought up the subject.

"I'm sorry . . . I shouldn't have said anything . . ." What was the point now? Tanya was silently berating herself for being so stupid, as Mary Stuart dabbed at her eyes, and looked reassuringly at Tanya.

"It's all right, Tan. It doesn't matter. It hurts all the time anyway. Like a severed limb, it never stops, sometimes it's sharper than others, sometimes it's really unbearable, sometimes you can live with it, but it never stops aching. You didn't make it hurt. It's with me every moment."

"You can't live like that forever," Tanya said, looking devastated for her. It was clearly the worst thing that had happened to any of them, and there was nothing she could do about it.

"Apparently you can live like that forever," Mary Stuart answered her desperately. "People do it all the time, they live with constant pain of all kinds, arthritis, rheumatism, indigestion, cancer, and then there's this, the destruction of the heart, the death of hope, the loss of everything you ever cared about, it's a challenge to the soul," she said, looking agonized, but so strong that Tanya almost couldn't bear it.

"Why don't you come to Wyoming with me and the kids?"

she suddenly blurted out. It was the only thing she could think of to help her.

Mary Stuart smiled at her. "I'm going to Europe to see Alyssa, otherwise I'd love to. I love to ride." And then she frowned, confused by an old memory, and grateful to get off an unbearably painful subject. "I didn't think you did though."

"I don't." Tanya laughed. "I hate it. But this is supposed to be a fabulous place, and I thought it would be good for the kids." She looked awkward for a moment then. "I thought Tony would like it too, but he's not coming. But the kids are twelve, fourteen, and seventeen now, and they all love to ride. I thought it would be perfect for them."

"I'm sure it will be. Are you going to ride too?" Mary Stuart asked her.

"Depends how cute the wranglers are," Tanya said, sounding very Texas and they both laughed. "I think I'm the only girl in Texas who always hated horses." But Mary Stuart remembered she rode well, she just didn't like it.

"Maybe Tony will change his mind and go with you."

"I doubt it," Tanya said quietly. "It sounds like he's made his mind up. Maybe the time away will do him good." But Tanya didn't really think it would make a difference, and Mary Stuart was silently of the same opinion. Things definitely seemed to be on their way downhill between Tanya and her husband.

They chatted on for a little while, about Alyssa, and Tanya's next movie, and the concert tour she had signed on for the following winter. Mary Stuart could only imagine how rigorous it would be, and she admired Tanya for doing it. And then they talked about the show she was going to be on the next morning. It was the number one daytime talk show in the country.

"I had to come to New York for that meeting anyway, so I thought I might as well do it. I hope to hell they don't want to talk about the lawsuit. My agent already told them I didn't want to, for whatever that's worth." And then she remembered an invitation she wanted to extend to Mary Stuart. "I have a friend who opened in a play here last week. They said it's pretty good, and she got great reviews. They're going to run it through the summer and see how it does, and if they do okay, they're going to run it through next winter. I'll get you tickets if you want. But she's giving a party tomorrow night, and I said I'd go. If you want to come, I'd love to take you. Would Bill enjoy something like that? He's welcome too, I just didn't know if it was his cup of tea, or if he'd be too busy." Or if he was currently speaking to Mary Stuart.

"You sweetheart." Mary Stuart smiled at her, Tanya always brought so much sunshine and excitement into her life. It reminded her of over twenty years before. It was always Tanya who rallied everyone, got them all going on some crazy project she had, or made everyone have fun, sometimes in spite of themselves. But she couldn't see Bill being willing to do that. They hadn't gone out in months, except for business purposes, and he was working late every night now, getting ready for London. He was leaving in two weeks for the rest of the summer, but she hoped that at the end of her trip, with Alyssa, they would spend a weekend at Claridge's in London, visiting him. But he had already told her he would be too busy to have them stay any longer. And after that, Mary Stuart was flying back to the States. He said he'd let her know how the trial was going, and if she could come over again to visit. In some ways, it didn't sound too much different to her from what Tony had said to Tanya. And perhaps it wasn't. They both seemed to be losing the men in their lives, and had no way to stop them from going.

"I'm not sure Bill would be able to join us. He's working late every night before he leaves for London for the trial. But I'll ask him."

"Would you want to come without him? She's a nice girl," and then Tanya looked embarrassed. She was acting as though she was an unknown actress. "I should probably tell you it's

Felicia Davenport, so you don't faint when you meet her. I've known her for years, and she's really terrific."

"You disgusting name-dropper." Mary Stuart was laughing at her, she was one of the biggest stars in Hollywood, and she was taking her first stab at Broadway. Mary Stuart had just read about it in the *New York Times* on Sunday. "It's a good thing you told me before I met her. I would have died, you're right. You dummy." They were both laughing as they left the restaurant, and Tanya told her she could let her know about the party in the morning. It was at Felicia's rented town house in the East Sixties.

Tanya dropped Mary Stuart off at her apartment then, and she promised to watch Tanya on the show the next morning, and she hugged her tightly as she left her. "Thanks for tonight, Tan. It's so good to see you." She hadn't even realized how brittle and lonely she was until she saw her friend. She and Bill had barely spoken to each other all year, and she felt like a plant that hadn't been watered. But seeing Tanya had been like standing in a rainstorm getting revitalized again. And she was smiling when she walked into the building with a spring in her step, and nodded at the doorman.

"Good evening, Mrs. Walker," he said, and tipped his hat to her, as he always did. The elevator man told her Bill had come in just a few minutes before her. And when she let herself in, she found him in the den, putting away some papers. She was in good spirits, and she smiled at him, as he turned to face her. And he looked startled to see her expression, as though they had both forgotten what it was like to have a good time, to be with friends, to talk to each other.

"Where were you?" He looked surprised. She looked like an entirely different person, and he couldn't imagine where she'd been at that hour, in blue jeans.

"Tanya Thomas is in town, we just had dinner. It was great to see her." She felt like a drunk in church, as she grinned at him, and seemed to have suddenly forgotten the solemnity of the last year, the silence that had sprung up like a wall between them. She felt suddenly too loud, too jovial, and surprisingly awkward with her husband. "I'm sorry to come home so late . . . I left you a note . . ." She faltered, feeling herself shrink as she looked at him. His eyes were so cold, his face so expressionless. The handsome, chiseled features that she had loved for so long had turned to stone in the past year, along with everything else about him. He had taken so much distance from her that she couldn't even see him anymore, much less find him. All she could hear was an echo of what had been.

"I didn't see the note." It was a statement more than an accusation. And as she looked at him, she often found herself wishing he weren't still so handsome. He was fifty-four years old, and he was well over six feet tall, with an athletic physique, and a long lean body. He had piercing blue eyes, which had looked like ice for a year now.

"I'm sorry, Bill," she said quietly. She felt as though she had spent a lifetime apologizing to him for something she should never have been blamed for. But she knew he would never forgive her. "I left the note in the kitchen."

"I ate at the office."

"How's it going?" she asked, as he put the rest of his papers in his briefcase.

"Very well, thanks," he said, as though talking to a secretary or a stranger. "We're almost ready. It's going to be a very interesting trial," he said, and then turned off the light in the den, as though to dismiss her. He was carrying his briefcase to their bedroom. It was something he would never have done a year before, and it was a small thing, but it no longer mattered. "I think we're actually going to leave for London a little early." He had said nothing to her until now. He had just made his plans, and that was it, as though he no longer had to consult her. She wanted to know what "early" meant in this case, but she didn't dare ask him. It would probably just annoy him.

If he was leaving early, maybe she would too, although she

still didn't have the final details. They had reservations in hotels in Paris, St.-Jean-Cap-Ferrat, San Remo, Florence, and Rome, and they were going to be staying at Claridge's with Bill in London. It was going to be a terrific trip, and after their months apart, Mary Stuart was really looking forward to traveling with her daughter. She had just turned twenty in April. Her birthday was a week before her brother's. And both days had been important to Mary Stuart.

And as Bill put down his briefcase and headed for their bathroom to put his pajamas on, Mary Stuart remembered Tanya's invitation, and she told him about it. "I think it's a cocktail party or something. It's being given by Felicia Davenport. Apparently, she's a friend of Tanya's." And at the look on his face, she felt like a fourteen-year-old asking her father to go to the senior prom. He looked appalled that she had even dared to ask him. "I think you might enjoy it. Her new play has gotten rave reviews, and Tanya says she's a nice woman."

"I'm sure that's true, but I have to work late again tomorrow night. This is an enormous case we're preparing, Mary Stuart. I thought you understood that." It was a reproach even more than a refusal, and his tone suddenly annoyed her.

"I do, but you have to admit, it's an unusual invitation. I think we should go." She wanted to do it. She was tired of sitting home and grieving. Seeing Tanya had reminded her there was a whole world out there—even with her own problems, and worries about Tony, her lawsuits, and the tabloids, she wasn't sitting at home, crying in the corner. It had reminded Mary Stuart that there were other options.

"It's out of the question for me," he said firmly, "but you're welcome to go if you want to." He closed the door to the bathroom and when he came out, his wife was waiting for him with a purposeful look.

"I will," she said, with a stubborn look in her eyes, as though she expected him to fight her.

"Will what?" He looked completely confused by what she

was saying. And if he didn't know her better, he would have thought she'd been drinking. She was behaving very strangely. "What are you talking about?" he said, looking annoyed, and unaware of the fact that she seemed more relaxed than usual and actually looked very pretty.

"I will go to the party," she said, looking determined.

"Fine. And I will *not,* as long as you understand that. It'll be fun for you to meet people like that. Tanya certainly seems to have interesting friends, but that's hardly surprising." He seemed to forget about it then, and went to bed with a stack of magazines he needed to glance through for legal and business purposes. There were several articles about some of his clients. And Mary Stuart disappeared into the bathroom, and emerged ten minutes later in a white cotton nightgown. She could have worn chain mail or a hair shirt and he wouldn't have noticed, and she lay in bed quietly while he read, thinking about her conversation with Tanya, and the things she had said about Tony. She wondered if Tanya was right, and if he really would be leaving soon, or if he would stick around and work it out. It seemed so unfair of him not to stand by Tanya, but she seemed resigned to his defection, and almost to expect it. Mary Stuart couldn't help wondering if Tanya should take a less accepting role, and at least try to stop him. It was so easy to look at someone else's life and decide what they should do. She had been completely unable to do it in her own life. In the past year, she had been completely helpless to reverse the tides, or to reach Bill at any time. He was totally beyond her reach, behind a wall of ice that grew thicker and thicker by the moment. She felt as though she hadn't really seen him in months, and she had begun to lose hope of ever reaching him again. She had no idea what they would do about their future. And he was certainly not open to discussion about that either. She had the feeling that if she had even mentioned it to him, he would have acted as though she were crazy. As he had tonight, when she came home with a lighter step, and a smile on her face. He had looked at her as though she came from another planet. It was obvious that laughter was no longer to be tolerated, and any kind of closeness between them was a thing of the distant past. And she only really noticed how bad it had become when she saw them through other people's eyes. Alyssa had looked horrified when she came home at Christmas, and couldn't wait to go back to Paris. And yet, as awful as it was for all of them, Mary Stuart had no idea how to stop it. And Bill didn't want to.

He turned out the light when he finished reading, and said nothing at all to Mary Stuart. She was lying on her side, with her eyes closed, pretending to be asleep, wondering if he would ever become human again, if he would ever reach out to her, if anyone would ever care about her, or touch her, or tell her they loved her, or if that was all in the past now. At forty-four, in more ways than one, her life was not only shrinking, it was over.

CHAPTER 4

Mary Stuart diligently stayed home to watch Tanya on television the next day, and wanted to leap out of her seat and smash the screen when the interviewer segued from a question about Tanya's childhood in a small town in Texas right to one about the recent rumor linking her to a trainer, and then a snide reference to the lawsuit she'd just been slapped with for sexually harassing an employee. But in spite of Mary Stuart's fury, Tanya handled it gracefully and seemingly with ease and a friendly smile, as she brushed it off as blackmail, and typical fare for the tabloids. But when she came off the set, her arms were glued to her sides, and she felt as though she'd spilled a glass of water under each armpit, not to mention the beginnings of a massive headache.

"So much for daytime TV," she said to the publicity woman who had accompanied her to the set, and escorted her to her next stop, the appointment with the literary agent about doing a book about her life. But in the end the meeting held little appeal for her. All they wanted was sensationalism, not substance. She was sick of all of them by the time she called Jean that afternoon, and found out that she was once again all over the L.A. papers, and there was something in the tabloids about her husband spending a weekend in Palm Springs with an unidentified starlet.

"Was that harlot?" she asked pointedly, and Jean laughed. It was not a pretty story. Jean read the L.A. piece about the lawsuit to her, and Tanya had to fight back tears as she listened. The ex-bodyguard was claiming that she had taunted him repeatedly by strolling around the house naked when they were alone, which would have made her laugh, if she hadn't been so distressed by the story. "I wish I could remember the last time I was alone in that house," Tanya said, feeling depressed. She could just imagine Tony's reaction. But she declined Jean's offer to read the tabloid story about him to her. She went out and bought it herself after she hung up, and it was a beauty. There was a photograph of him trying to hide from a photographer, and a picture of a young actress Tanya knew, who couldn't have been a day over twenty. But it was also impossible to tell if the photograph had been computerized, and the paper just made it look as though they were together. These days you could never be sure about pictures. But she didn't like it anyway, and although at first she resisted, she eventually called him at the office. She caught him just as he was leaving.

"I gather my name's been up in lights again today," she said, trying to inject a little humor into a dismal situation.

"You could say that. Your friend Leo seems to have a lot to say about you. Have you read it?" he said, sounding really furious and barely able to conceal it from her.

"Jean read it to me. It's all bullshit though. I hope you know that." She sounded very calm, and very much in control, and very Southern.

"I'm not sure what I know anymore, Tan."

"What they wrote about me is no worse than the tabloid

story on you and the girl you supposedly took to Palm Springs. They even printed a picture of you," she said, trying to tease him. "And that's not true either. So what's the big deal here?"

There was a long pause, and then he spoke very slowly. "As a matter of fact, it is true. I was going to tell you about it, but I didn't get a chance before you left." She felt as though he had hit her with a club. He had cheated on her, it was in the tabloids and he was admitting it to her. For a long moment, she was silent. She didn't know what to say.

"That's quite a story. What do you expect me to say now?"

"You have a right to be real pissed off, Tan. I wouldn't blame you at all. I think someone tipped them off. I have no idea how they turned up at the hotel. I figured it would hit the papers."

"You're a little too old to be that naive, you know that? You've been around Hollywood long enough to know how it works. Who do you think called them? She did. This is a big coup for her, walking off with Tanya Thomas's husband. Big time, Tony. How could she pass up an opportunity like that?" It was a nasty thing to say, but it was probably true, and he knew it. It hadn't even occurred to him when it happened. And at his end of the phone, there was a long, long silence. "You're a celebrity now, Mr. Goldman. How do you like it?"

"There's not much I can say, Tan."

"No, there isn't. You could have at least been discreet, or taken someone who wouldn't sell out your ass and mine to the tabloids."

"I don't want to play this game with you, Tanya," he said, sounding embarrassed and angry. "I'm moving out tomorrow." There was another long silence, while she nodded and fought back tears.

"Yeah, I figured that," she said hoarsely.

"I can't live like this anymore, being a constant target for the tabloids."

"I don't like it either," she said sadly. "The only difference is you have a choice, I don't."

"I'm sorry for you then," but he didn't sound it. He had turned mean suddenly. He'd gotten caught with his pants down, and he didn't like it. He didn't like playing second fiddle to her, he didn't like being sold out and betrayed and made a fool of. He didn't like any of it, and he couldn't wait to get out of her house and her life, and the spotlight he had been forced into while he was married to her. At first he had wanted it, but when they'd turned the heat up too high, he found he didn't like it.

"I'm sorry, Tan . . . I didn't want to do it over the phone. I was going to tell you tomorrow when you got home." She nodded, as the tears rolled down her cheeks, and he inquired if she was still there, and she finally answered.

"Yeah, I'm here," more or less, what was left of her. It was all so damn hard, and so unbearably lonely. She had been through so much for so long, been so used and so exploited and treated so unkindly. She had been robbed blind by the manager she'd married, and now Tony didn't have the balls to stick it out after three years, and he was running off to Palm Springs to fuck starlets. Just what did he think the tabloids would do with that? How could he have been so careless and so stupid?

"I'm sorry," he said weakly, but by then it didn't matter.

"I know . . . never mind . . . I'll see you when I get back," she said, anxious to get away from him. He had hurt her enough. She didn't have anything else to say. And then she had another thought. "What about Wyoming?"

"Take the kids. It'll be good for them," he said grandly, relieved to be off the hook himself. He was anxious to be off to Europe, and he was taking the same starlet with him.

"Thanks . . ." And then, "Tony . . . I'm sorry too . . ." She started to sob then, and a moment later she hung up the phone. She was still crying when it rang again. She almost didn't answer it, she was sure it was Tony, calling back to see if she was all right. But it wasn't. It was Mary Stuart, and she could hear instantly how upset Tanya was. And through tears,

Tanya managed to explain that Tony had just left her. She told her about the two articles, and that Tony had been cheating on her in Palm Springs. It was all tangled and nearly unintelligible, but Mary Stuart managed to figure out what was happening, and insisted she come over. They had plenty of time before the party, if they even went after all. All Tanya wanted to do was go home, but they weren't sending the plane for her until the next morning.

"I want you to come up here for a cup of tea, or a Kleenex, or a glass of water . . . come on, you. If you don't come, I'll come and get you," Mary Stuart insisted, and Tanya was reluctant but touched by the offer.

"I'm okay." But she sounded anything but convincing while she cried harder.

"No, you're not okay, you liar." And then, the ultimate threat. "If you don't come, I'll call the tabloids," Mary Stuart said firmly, and Tanya laughed.

"You're disgusting," Tanya said, laughing through her tears. "I don't see you for a year, and what do I do, I end up getting divorced in the two days I do finally see you."

"At least I can be here for you. Now come on over, before I call the *Enquirer* and the *Globe* and the *Star,* and any others I can find. Do you want me to come and get you, Tan?" she asked gently, but Tanya blew her nose again at the other end.

"No, I'm okay. All right . . . I'll come over. I'll be there in five minutes." And she was, with uncombed hair, and red eyes and a red nose. But in spite of it all, she still looked gorgeous, as Mary Stuart told her, as she put her arms around her and held her like a child crying in her arms. She had had a lot of practice with Todd and Alyssa, and she was a good mother. She had done a lot of comforting and consoling in twenty-two years. But sadly, not enough for Todd. If she had, things might have been different.

"I can't believe this . . . it's all fallen apart in about five minutes," Tanya said about her marriage. Except they both knew that it had actually taken a lot longer. Tony had been steaming for a long time, about all the things that irked him in her life, he just hadn't said so. And she realized now that he had been unhappy for a lot longer than she thought. Looking back, she could see all the signals, but she had missed them as they happened.

Mary Stuart made her a cup of tea, despite the heat outside, and Tanya sat down in the immaculate white kitchen and drank it.

"What do you do in this place anyway?" Tanya asked, as she looked around her. "Order out?"

"No, I cook here," Mary Stuart said primly, but with a smile at her friend. Tanya looked battered and bruised, but a little bit better for the comfort. "I just like things clean and organized."

"No," Tanya corrected her. "You like things perfect, and you know it. But it can't always be perfect, sometimes everything is a mess and that's just the way it is, and you can't change that. Maybe you need to accept that. I keep getting the feeling that you're beating yourself up for what happened." It was true, and Tanya wanted more than anything to release her friend from the torment she could still see in her eyes.

"Wouldn't you beat yourself up?" Mary Stuart asked softly. "How could I not blame myself? Bill blames me . . . I know it . . . he can't even look at me anymore. We live here like strangers. We're not even enemies anymore . . . at first we were, there's not even that now."

"Is he coming tonight?" Tanya asked her, feeling sad for both of them. The hands life had dealt them had not been easy. At least not lately.

But Mary Stuart shook her head in answer. "He said he has to work late at the office."

"He's hiding." Like most people, she was wise about everyone's life but her own, but Tanya was also smarter than most people. She just picked lousy husbands.

"I know he is," Mary Stuart said as they wandered to her bedroom. "But I can't find him. I've looked everywhere, and I don't know where he is anymore. It's like *Invasion of the Body Snatchers.* There's a man living here, and he looks like Bill, but I know he isn't. But I have no idea where they've put the real one."

"Keep looking," Tanya said, and surprised Mary Stuart with her earnestness. "It's not over till it's over." Somehow Tanya felt they had something worth saving. They'd been married for nearly twenty-two years. That was a long time to walk out on. On the other hand, people did it, and if Mary Stuart never found him again, it was wrong of her to waste her life with him forever, and Tanya knew that. She just hated to see her give up so soon, after everything that had happened to them. And it was so unfair that he should blame Mary Stuart.

"Is that true for you too?" Mary Stuart asked her, as they walked back down the hall toward the living room, past a bunch of closed doors that Tanya suspected were other bedrooms. "It's not over till it's over?"

"I think in my case, it's different," Tanya said with a sigh. "Maybe it never was, or never should have been. But I think it's been over for a while, and I didn't want to see it. I never realized how unhappy he was with all the garbage I can't control. But if that's going to make him crazy, then I can't do anything about it." She still loved him, but she was also smart enough to know when she was defeated. And in some ways, it had never been completely right between them since the beginning and she knew that too, although she would have hated to admit it.

They settled in the living room and talked for a while, and then Tanya got up and said she had to go to the powder room, and Mary Stuart told her where to go. There was a tiny guest bathroom down the hall, on the left, and Tanya walked swiftly toward it. She opened the door, turned on the light, and then gasped. She had opened the wrong door, and she was standing in Todd's bedroom, staring at the trophies and the pictures and the memorabilia all around her. Everything in the room was perfectly in place, and it was as if he was in school, and would be home from Princeton any minute. And as she stood looking at all of it, Tanya didn't hear Mary Stuart come up behind her, or see the look of devastation in her eyes as she looked around her.

"I never come in here anymore," she said in a whisper that made Tanya jump, and she turned to see the ravaged look in her friend's eyes and instinctively put her arms around her. Tanya didn't think she should have left the room that way. It was like a shrine to him, and just knowing it was there, so close to her every day, had to be incredibly painful. There was a wonderful photograph of him on the desk, with two friends from school. Tanya had forgotten how exactly he looked like his mother when he smiled, but now she remembered, and it made her cry to see it.

"Oh, Mary Stuart," she said as tears filled her eyes too, "I'm so sorry . . . I opened the wrong door, and I just kind of fell in here . . . ."

The boy's mother smiled through her tears and pulled away, standing next to Tanya and staring at the same picture. "He was so wonderful, Tanny . . . he was such a terrific kid . . . he always did the right thing . . . he was always the star, the boy everyone wanted to be, the kid everyone fell in love with. . . ." There were tears slowly rolling down her cheeks and Tanya stood staring at the picture, it was as though she expected him to speak, or appear in the room, but they both knew he wouldn't.

"I know. I remember him perfectly . . . he looked so much like you," Tanya said in a soft voice.

"I still can't believe it happened," Mary Stuart said, looking at Tanny, and then sitting on the bed. She hadn't done that since Christmas. She had come in here alone, late on Christmas Eve, and lay on his bed, clutching his pillow, and cried for hours. As usual, she hadn't dared tell Bill she'd been in there. He had told her once before that he thought the room should be kept locked, but when she asked him what he thought she should do with Todd's things, he had told her to do whatever she wanted. And she hadn't had the heart to take any of it apart. She just couldn't bring herself to do it.

"Shouldn't you put his things away?" Tanya asked her sadly. She could only imagine how difficult it would be, but she wondered if it would be healthier for them. Or maybe they should think about selling the apartment. But she didn't dare say that.

"I just couldn't," Mary Stuart answered her. "I just can't put his things away," she said, and tears rolled down her cheeks all over again, thinking of the child who had once lived there. "I miss him so terribly . . . we all do. Bill doesn't say anything, but I know he must too. It's killing him . . . it's killing all of us . . ." She knew how it hurt Alyssa too. She had seen her go into his room once. And she didn't think it was a complete mystery why she wanted to stay in Paris. Who could blame her for that? Coming home was pretty depressing, and for the moment, there was no relief in sight. Neither she nor Bill seemed to have recovered.

"It wasn't your fault," Tanya suddenly said firmly, taking her friend by both arms, and looking into her eyes with a sense of purpose. It was as though she was meant to be here. "You have to believe that. You couldn't have stopped him once he made his mind up."

"How could I not see what was happening to him? How could I love him so much and miss it completely?" Mary Stuart knew she would never forgive herself for what she hadn't seen and what had happened.

"He didn't want you to see it. He was a grown man, he had a right to keep his own secrets. He didn't want you to know, or he would have told you. You're not expected to know everything, to see into someone's mind. You couldn't have known, Mary Stuart, you *have* to believe that." What Tanya couldn't believe was that Bill had tortured her for the past year and hadn't released her from her own guilt. Instead, he had confirmed it to her, both by his actions and by his silence.

"I'll always think it was my fault," Mary Stuart said sadly, but Tanya would not let her go. She was determined to free her from the hooks that held her. It was the ultimate act of friendship, and a matter of Mary Stuart's survival.

"You're not that important," she said quietly. "As much as he loved you, you weren't that important to him. He had his own life, his own friends, his own dreams, his own disappointments, his own tragedies. You couldn't have made him do it if you wanted to, and you couldn't have made him not do it, no matter how much you wanted to. Not unless he had come to you, and begged you to stop him. And he would never have done that, he was too private a person, just like you are." Tanya was very serious as she looked her in the eye, determined to help her friend now.

"But I would never do anything like that," Mary Stuart said, still staring at her son's picture, as though she could still ask him why it had happened. But they all knew why now. It was so pathetically simple. The girl he had loved for four years had died in a car accident, on an icy New Jersey road four months before, and he had quietly sunk into an ever deeper depression. No one had realized how depressed he was, or the full extent of his despair after she died. They had thought he was coming out of it at Easter. But in retrospect, Mary Stuart had realized that he only seemed happier at Easter because he had probably decided to do it when he went back after the vacation. He had been so close to his mother then. They had gone for a long walk in the park, and talked philosophically and laughed, he had even talked in vague terms about his future. He told her he knew now he would always be happy. And then he did it, the night he went back. He committed suicide two weeks before his twentieth birthday, in his room in Princeton. The boy in the next room had found him. He had come in to borrow something and he had found Todd in bed, asleep, and something about the way he lay there aroused suspicion. He had checked him immediately and administered CPR, until the police and the fire department came. But they said later that Todd had been dead for several hours when the boy found him. He had left a note to each of them, telling them that he felt so peaceful and so calm, and so happy at last. He said it was cowardly of him, he knew, and he regretted any pain he would cause them, but he simply couldn't live without Natalie anymore. He said he had truly tried. And he hoped that once they forgave him, they would be relieved to know that he and Natalie would be together forever in Heaven. Although his parents had said they were too young, he had wanted to marry her, after graduation, the following summer. And in a sense, Todd said in his note, they were married now.

And through it all, once they heard the news, and long afterward, Bill had blamed Mary Stuart. He said that she had filled his head with foolishness and romantic notions, she had allowed him to become too seriously involved with Natalie for the past four years, and if she hadn't forced religion on him, he would never have had such absurd notions of the hereafter or of God. According to Bill, Mary Stuart had, in fact, set the stage for disaster. And he laid Todd's suicide entirely on the conscience of his mother. At the time, what he said to her had almost killed her. But more than anything he could have said to her was the agony of her loss of her older child, her only son . . . her firstborn . . . the child who had always been her sunshine, and brought her so much joy and pride.

And as Tanya listened to her, she wanted to go to Bill Walker and shake him. His accusations were the most insane she had ever heard, and she sensed easily that he was trying to ease his own pain, and feelings of failure, by blaming it all on Mary Stuart. It was so cruel, it was almost beyond bearing. And it was easy to see what had happened to Mary Stuart as a result. She was nearly dead inside.

"The poor kid." Mary Stuart was sobbing quietly as they sat in his old room, still trying to understand why he had done it, a whole year after he had. "He was so in love with her, when he got the call after Natalie's accident, I thought it would kill him." And in the end, it had. It had killed all of them. There was nothing left of Mary Stuart now, or Bill, or their marriage.

They had all died with Todd, the important parts of them anyway, their hearts and their souls, and their dreams, had all died with the boy they had so loved and had lost so unfairly.

"Have you ever gotten angry at him for all this?" Tanya asked, and Mary Stuart looked startled.

"With Todd? How could I?"

"Because he hurt all of you. Because he took something from you. Because he chickened out when he should have had the guts to live through it, and he should have told you how much pain he was in."

"I should have known." Mary Stuart turned it on herself again, but Tanya wouldn't let her do that.

"You can't know everything. You're not a mind reader, you're just a human being. And you were a wonderful mother to him. He shouldn't have done this to you." Mary Stuart had never even allowed herself to think those things, and it frightened her to hear them. "It wasn't fair of him, and you know it. And it's not fair of Bill to blame you. Maybe it's time for you to get good and mad at both of them. They've put an awful lot on your back, Mary Stuart."

For a long moment, she didn't say a word as she looked at Tanya. "I've felt it was my fault since the night he died."

"I know you have. But that was kind of convenient for everyone, wasn't it? Maybe even now, Todd needs to take responsibility for what he did. Maybe you need to give that back to him, and tell Bill what you think. You can't just silently accept all the guilt and all the burden of what happened. Todd goes down in history as a hero, and not a poor, sick, foolish kid who did an incredibly stupid thing we'll all regret forever. But whatever it was, for whatever reason, maybe that was his destiny. And it is what happened. It can't be changed now. You can't take it back, or make it your decision, or your fault. It was all his doing. And Bill has no right to blame you, that's how he absolved himself. It was all *your* fault, so he could be free to be angry and miserable and rotten. Mary Stuart, you're not the responsible party here, you're the scapegoat."

"I know," she said softly. "I figured that out a while back, but it doesn't change anything. Bill will never admit it. As far as he's concerned, it's all my fault."

"Then maybe you should leave him. Or are you going to let him punish you for the rest of your life? Are you going to stay on your knees for the next forty or fifty years, whispering 'mea culpa'? That's a long time to feel guilty. You're way too young for that." Listening to her was like having someone pull the drapes back in a dark room and let in huge splashes of sunshine. She had been sitting in a dark corner for a year, lost in the gloom, and grieving. And it was odd sitting in this room while they talked about it. It was almost as though Todd was with them. And listening to Tanya speak to her suddenly made it all seem very different. She wanted to be angry at Bill, wanted to shout at him, and to shake him. How could he be so stupid? How could he have destroyed their marriage?

"I don't know what to think anymore, Tan. It's been so confusing. And poor Alyssa, it must have been a nightmare coming home for Christmas last year. We were all such a mess, she couldn't wait to go back to Paris." In the end, she had left four days early. And that had made her mother feel even more guilty.

"You've got years to make it up to her. What you have to do is think of yourself, and what you need. You can't keep letting Bill do this to you. You have to find your peace over what happened. You have to have a long talk with yourself, and with your son, and see what you come up with. And then you have to talk to Bill. He's gotten out of this pretty easy so far."

"I don't think he has," Mary Stuart said wisely. "I think it's so painful for him that he's hidden behind a wall of ice until he was completely numb. I think he's terrified to come out now."

"If he doesn't, he'll destroy you and your marriage." If he hadn't already. Tanya wasn't sure how much her friend could salvage, but at least she was thinking about it. And Tanya was glad she had ventured into Todd's room and been in it with her.

"Thank you, Tanny," Mary Stuart said, standing up again, and Tanya put an arm around her shoulders. Mary Stuart pulled open the curtains then, and the room filled with light, as she looked around her. "He was a great kid. I still can't believe he's gone."

"In some ways, he isn't," Tanya said softly, "we'll all remember him forever." There were tears in their eyes as they left the room, arm in arm, and walked slowly back to the kitchen. Tanya had another cup of tea and then went back to her hotel to dress for the party. And after she left, Mary Stuart took another look into Todd's room, closed the curtains, and then quietly closed the door, and went back to her own room. Maybe Tanya was right. Maybe it wasn't all her fault. Maybe it was Todd's fault and no one else's. But she still couldn't bring herself to be angry at him. It was so much easier to be angry at his father. Just as it was easier for Bill to blame Mary Stuart, and not himself, for not anticipating what had happened.

And she was still sitting and thinking about it when Alyssa called and they chatted for a little while, and she told her about Tanya's visit, but not about their conversation in her brother's bedroom. She told her Tanya had invited her to a party given by Felicia Davenport, but she was thinking of not going. She was feeling emotionally drained by their conversation. But Alyssa was outraged at the thought of her losing out on an opportunity like that.

"Are you crazy? You'll never get another chance like that, Mom. Go. Get dressed. I'm hanging up now so you can get ready. Wear the black chiffon Valentino."

"The one you wear all the time?" she teased, but it had been wonderful talking to her. She had always been close to her daughter, but after Todd's death they had grown even closer. And in many ways Alyssa had been there for her mother. She wanted to apologize for being so depressing for such a long time, but she didn't want to bring up painful subjects. Instead, she hung up, and forced herself to bathe and dress and put on the Valentino. It was a pretty dress, and she looked subdued and elegant as she put on high heels, and brushed her hair till it shone. And she had very carefully put on makeup. She put on diamond earrings that Bill had given her years before, and as she looked in the mirror, she smiled. She looked all right, she decided, maybe even slightly better than that, but it felt odd to be going out without her husband.

Tanya called and made arrangements to pick Mary Stuart up. She was waiting downstairs when the limousine came, and Mary Stuart slipped inside and looked impressed when she saw Tanya. She was wearing a loose, nearly see-through pink chiffon blouse, over black satin pants that showed off her trainer's hard work and her spectacular figure. She had on high-heeled black satin pumps, and her blond hair stood out like a huge mane. She looked incredibly beautiful and very sexy, but her assessment of Mary Stuart was satisfactory too.

"You look so elegant," she said admiringly, there was a quality about Mary Stuart that she had always envied. Everything about her was so completely perfect, down to the very last detail, the last hair, the last nail. She had sensational legs, and great hair, and tonight, for the first time in a year, her big, warm, brown eyes looked a little less haunted. "You look great."

"You're sure I won't disgrace you?" Tanya asked shyly.

"Hardly. You'll have to be kicking the men away all night." She grinned, and then raised an eyebrow. "Unless of course you don't want to." But Mary Stuart shook her head at that. She wasn't looking for anyone else. Not yet, at any rate. And more than likely never. But she didn't like feeling that part of her life was entirely over, and for the past year it certainly had been, and in spite of her talk with Tanya in Todd's room that afternoon, for the moment, there was certainly no light at the end of the tunnel. But it just felt good to be dressed up again, and going out, and meeting new people. And the party, when they got there, was better than they'd expected.

Felicia Davenport was wonderful and warm and hospitable to both of them, and she and Mary Stuart spent a long time talking about New York and theater and even children. Mary Stuart loved her. She was a fascinating woman, and obviously a great friend to Tanya. Tanya spent most of the evening surrounded by men, and Mary Stuart had her fair share of admirers as well. She let everyone know she was married, and her wedding ring was plainly visible, but she had several very interesting conversations, and the whole evening was good for her ego. She felt great when they finally left, and Tanya offered to take her out for hamburgers again, but she really thought she should get home. She didn't want to push her new independence, and set Bill off.

Tanya dropped her off at home, and Mary Stuart invited her up, but she said she wanted to get back to the hotel and make some calls and relax, since Mary Stuart didn't want to go out to dinner.

"Thank you for a great time . . . for a lot of things . . ." Mary Stuart smiled at her gratefully. "As usual, you saved my life. It's funny how you always do that."

"I don't do anything except turn up once a year like a bad penny."

"You take care of yourself now, you hear," Mary Stuart scolded her, and they both laughed and then hugged, and Mary Stuart stood on the sidewalk and waved until the limousine disappeared, and as she turned and walked inside, she felt like Cinderella. Tanya's visits always transformed her life while she was there, and they always reminded her of what good friends they had been, still were, and probably always would be. It was a good thing to remember. And she felt better than she had in months, maybe over a year. Tanya's timing couldn't have been better. And even though she was having problems herself, she had still managed to give so much to Mary Stuart.

"Mr. Walker just went upstairs," the elevator man announced when she walked in, and a moment later she was in the apartment, and she saw him walk into their bedroom. He heard her come in, but he didn't turn around and look at her. It was like a slap in the face as she saw him walk away from her and refuse to see her.

"Hello, Bill," she said as she walked into the room shortly after him, and only then did he acknowledge her, as he glanced over his shoulder. He was holding his briefcase.

"I didn't see you come in," he said, but she knew he had heard her. He hadn't wanted to see her. He was the master of denial and rejection. "How was the party?"

"Very interesting. I met a lot of very intelligent people, it was kind of refreshing. Felicia Davenport was wonderful, and I liked most of her friends. I had a good time," she said, without apology for once. She suddenly didn't feel that she needed to crawl to him, to beg his forgiveness for her unforgivable failure. It was an odd thing to think, but it was as though that afternoon, Tanya had freed her. "It's too bad you couldn't make it."

"I left the office twenty minutes ago, while you were playing," he said unkindly, but he smiled as he said it. "We're leaving for London in three days." It was almost two weeks earlier than he'd planned.

"That's a lot earlier than you said, not just a few days," she chided him, but she felt punished again, and abandoned. There was no real reason why she couldn't stay in London with him. But he had long since made it clear to her that that was out of the question. He didn't want her there while he was working. It was yet another way he kept his distance from her, to punish her for her transgressions.

"I'll see you when you come over with Alyssa," he said, as though reading what was in her head. But two days in three months was hardly sufficient to sustain a marriage, particularly when there was no real reason for her not to be there, except that he didn't want her, which was the only reason that would keep her away from London. After her trip with Alyssa she would spend the rest of the summer in New York alone. And for a crazy moment, she thought of flying to California for a few days to visit Tanya. She had nothing else to do, and most of her boards and charities would be on hiatus for the summer. It was a thought, at least, although she knew full well she'd probably never do it.

A moment later, Bill disappeared into the bathroom and came out in his pajamas. He didn't even seem to notice her, or the dress she wore, or how pretty she looked. It was as though she had stopped being a woman for him the moment their son died.

She went into the bathroom after that, and slowly took the Valentino dress off, and with it went the illusion of her being either attractive or independent. She came out in her dressing gown, and Bill had his back to her again, and she saw that he was reading some papers. And before she could stop herself, it was as though a force deep inside her made her confront him. She spoke very clearly and very quietly in the room, and even she was surprised by her own words, but not as startled as he was.

"I'm not going to do this forever, Bill." She stood there for a moment after she said it, and slowly he turned and looked at her, holding his glasses in his hand with a look of amazement.

"What exactly does that mean?" He was the trial attorney at his most daunting, but she refused to be intimidated by him this time. The things Tanya had said had given her courage.

"It means exactly what I just said. I am not going to live like this forever. I can't do it. You never speak to me. You act as though I don't exist. You ignore me, you shun me, you reject me, and now you're going to London for three months, or two at least, and you expect me to be satisfied with a two-day visit. This isn't a marriage anymore. It is slavery, and people must have been a lot nicer to their slaves than you are."

It was the most outrageous thing she had ever said to him, certainly in the past year, and he did not look pleased with what he was hearing. "Do you think I'm going over for pleasure? You seem to have forgotten I'll be working." His tone was glacial.

"You seem to have forgotten we're married." He knew exactly what she meant, and she did not need to explain it further.

"This has been a very difficult year. For both of us." They had recently passed the anniversary of Todd's death, and that had only seemed to make it harder.

"I feel as though we died with him," Mary Stuart said sadly as she looked at her husband, but she was relieved that they were at least speaking. "And our marriage with us."

"That's not necessarily true. I think we both need time," he said, but she could see that he wasn't being honest, neither with her nor himself. He thought it was all going to fix itself one day, and Mary Stuart could have told him it wasn't. It was going to take a lot more now than just waiting.

"It's been a year, Bill," she reminded him, wondering how far he would be willing to be pushed. She suspected not much farther.

"I'm aware of that," he said, and then there was silence. "I'm aware of many things. I did not know, however, that you were planning on issuing ultimatums." He was not pleased by any means with her opening statement.

"It wasn't intended as that. It was information. Even if I wanted to do this indefinitely, I don't think I could."

"You can do anything you want to."

"Then maybe I don't want to. I don't want to be treated like a piece of furniture for the rest of my life. This isn't a marriage, it's a nightmare." It was the first time she had told him. And this time he said nothing, he simply turned his back on her again, put his glasses back on, and concentrated on his reading. "I can't believe you're going to ignore me again after what I just said to you."

He spoke to her with his back to her, and it was hard to remember, watching him, that there had been warmth or love or laughter between them. It was harder still to believe that she had been deeply in love with him, and he was the father of their children. "I have nothing more to say to you," he said, as he read on. "I've heard your statement, and I have no further comment." He was being unbelievable, and she couldn't help wondering if he was so frightened and in so much pain that he was simply frozen. But whatever it was, and however it had come, she had finally faced the fact that she couldn't stand it for much longer.

She went to bed, and he turned off the light, and he never turned back to her again, or said another word to her, and she lay in bed that night in the dark for a long time thinking of Tanya and the people she had met at Felicia's party. Even at forty-four, there was a life out there for her, and people who were willing to talk to her, and show a little interest. It was as though Tanya had opened a window for her, and she had dared to look outside for the first time in ages. It was all very intriguing, and she had no idea what to do now. And after hearing what she had said to him that night, neither did her husband. They were trapped on opposite sides of what had become the Grand Canyon, and had once been their marriage.

CHAPTER 5

For the next three days, Bill and Mary Stuart's paths rarely seemed to cross. He worked until nearly midnight every night, and it was beginning to feel as though he lived at the office. But Mary Stuart was used to it now. She had been more or less alone all year, and this really wasn't any different. The only change in the past week was that she no longer had to cook dinner. She was getting thinner as a result, and in the past Bill would have worried about her, but as things were now, he didn't even notice.

And on the day before he was scheduled to leave, Mary Stuart called him at the office, to see if he wanted her to pack for London. She assumed he would, as he had never packed for himself before, but he said he was coming home that afternoon to do it.

"Are you sure?" She was surprised, it was as though she didn't know him anymore. Nothing he did, or wanted from her, was the same as it once had been. But their son had died, and as far as he was concerned, it was her fault, or at least that was her reading of the situation. And as far as she was concerned, they were no longer the same people. "I don't mind packing for you." It seemed the least she could do, and it would keep her busy. She was still trying to absorb the fact that her husband was leaving for two or three months. It had only just that day really hit her. With the exception of her trip with Alyssa, she was going to be alone for the entire summer. And in some ways, it scared her. It underlined the distance between them that he didn't want her staying with him in London. He claimed it would be too boring for her, and it would distract him. But in years past, there would never have been a moment's doubt about her going. "I don't mind packing for you," she said again on the phone, but he insisted that he needed to pick his clothes himself, as he wanted to be very careful about what he wore in court in London.

"I'll be home at four," he explained, sounding pressed. Leaving his office for several months was complicated, and there were a million details to think of. He was taking one of his assistants with him, and had she been younger and more attractive than she was, Mary Stuart would have come to the obvious conclusion. As it was, she was a heavyset, intelligent, but very unattractive woman in her early sixties.

"Do you want dinner at home, or would you rather go out tonight?" Mary Stuart asked, feeling depressed, but trying to make it sound festive. It was as though there was no pretense between them anymore, not even the illusion of closeness, and it somehow seemed more acute now that he was leaving.

"I'll just grab something out of the fridge," he said absently, "don't go to any trouble." They had both come to hate their awkward, silent dinners, and she had been relieved when he preferred staying at the office, and working late. And as a result, they had both gotten thinner.

"I'll get something cold at William Poll or Fraser Morris," she said, and went out to do some errands. She had to buy a book she knew he wanted for the plane, and pick up all of his dry cleaning. And as she hurried east toward Lexington she was suddenly glad that she was leaving in a few weeks. Despite the chasm between them now, it was going to be incredibly lonely without him.

She picked up some dinner at William Poll, got the book and some magazines, some candy and gum, and she had all of his clean shirts hanging in his dressing room for him when he got home from the office at four-thirty. And he went straight to his packing, without saying a word to her. He was busy taking suitcases out of storage bins high above his closet. And she didn't see him again until seven o'clock when he appeared in the kitchen. He was still wearing his starched white shirt from work, but he had taken his tie off, and his hair was a little ruffled. It made him look young suddenly, and the painful part of it was that he looked so much like Todd now, but she tried valiantly to ignore it.

"All packed? I would have been happy to do it for you," she said softly, setting out dinner on the table. It had been another hot day, and it was nice having cold meats to put out, and not having to cook dinner.

"I didn't want to give you a lot of trouble," he said, sitting down on a high stool at the white granite kitchen counter. "I don't give you much happiness anymore, it doesn't seem fair to give you the work and the grief, and not much else. At least I can stay out of your hair and make things easy." It was the first time he had even acknowledged their situation, and she stared at him in amazement. When she had even tried to say something to him a few days before, she had met a wall, and he had completely ignored her. She wondered now if he had actually heard her.

"I don't expect you to stay out of my hair," she said, as she sat down across from him, and her eyes looked like pools of dark chocolate. He had always loved looking at her, loved her looks, and her style, and the expressiveness of her eyes, but the pain he had seen there for the last year had been too much to bear, and it was easier to avoid her. "Marriage isn't about keeping your distance. It's about sharing." And they had. They had shared joy for nearly twenty-one years, and endless grief for the last year. The trouble was that they hadn't really shared it. They had each grieved silently in their separate corners.

"We haven't shared much of anything lately, have we?" he said sadly. "I guess I've been too busy at the office." But it wasn't that, and they both knew it. She said nothing as she watched him, and he reached out slowly and touched her hand. It was the first gesture of its kind in months, and there were tears in her eyes as she felt his fingers.

"I've missed you," she said in a whisper, but all he did was nod. He had felt it too, but he couldn't bring himself to say it to her.

"I'm going to miss you while you're away," she said quietly. It was the first time in their marriage they would be apart for that long. But he had been so adamant about her not going with him. "It's such a long time."

"It'll go quickly. You'll come over next month with Alyssa, and I hope to be home by the end of August."

"We'll be together two days in two months," she said, looking at him in despair, and slowly pulling her hand away from his. "That's not exactly the stuff of which marriages are usually made, at least not good ones. I could stay at the hotel and fend for myself during the day." They had enough friends in London to keep her busy night and day for months, and he knew that. And it felt awkward suddenly to be begging him to let her be there.

"It will be just too distracting," he said unhappily, they had been over it before and he had been definite about it with her. He did not want her coming to London, other than for a brief weekend with their daughter.

"I've never distracted you before," she said, feeling like the supplicant again, and hating both herself and him for it. "Anyway . . . it's a long time . . . that's all. I think we both know that." His eyes suddenly bore into hers, and there was a question in his eyes as he watched her.

"What do you mean by that?" For the first time, he actually

looked worried. He was an attractive man, and she was sure that there would be plenty of women running after him in London. But she couldn't imagine that he was worrying about her. She had always been the perfect wife, but he had also never left her for an entire summer, after a year like this one.

"I mean that two months is a long time, especially after the year we've just had. You're leaving for two months, maybe more . . . I'm not exactly sure what I'm supposed to think about it, Bill." She looked worried as she watched him, and then he startled her even further.

"Neither am I. I just thought . . . maybe . . . we could use some time apart, to get a grip on things again, to figure out what we do now, and how we put back all the pieces." She was amazed to hear him say it. She hadn't even been sure he would have been willing to acknowledge how totally they'd come apart in the last year, let alone the fact that they needed to put the pieces back together.

"I don't see how being apart for two months is going to bring us any closer," she said matter-of-factly.

"It might help clear our minds. I don't know . . . I just know that I needed to be away from you, to think about something else for a change, to lose myself in work." She was startled when he looked up at her, and she saw tears in his eyes. She hadn't seen him cry since the day they'd picked Todd's body up at Princeton. Even at the funeral, he had looked stern, and she had never seen him cry since. He had been hiding behind his wall for all this time, and this was the first time he'd ventured out from behind it. Maybe he was upset about leaving too. At least that was something. "I wanted to be alone to work over there, Mary Stuart. It's just that . . ." His lips trembled as his eyes filled with tears, and she reached for his hand again and held it gently. "Every time I look at you . . . I think of him . . . it's as though we're all irreversibly bound to each other. I needed to get away from it, to stop thinking about him, and what we should have done or known or said, or how things could have been different. It's almost driven me out of my mind. I thought London might be a good way to change that. I thought leaving you behind might be good for both of us. You must feel the same way about me whenever you see me.''

She smiled through her own tears then, touched but dismayed by what he was saying. "You look so much like him. When you came into the kitchen a little while ago, you startled me for a moment.''

He nodded. He understood perfectly. They were both haunted. He was sick of the apartment, the occasional mail that still came for Todd, the room he knew was there but never stepped into. Even Alyssa looked like Todd at times, and he had had his mother's eyes and smile. It was all so unbearably painful.

''We can't run away from each other to escape the memory of our son,'' Mary Stuart said sadly. ''Then it's a double loss for us, we not only lose him, we lose each other.'' In fact, they already had, and they both knew it.

''Will you be all right while I'm gone?'' he asked, feeling guilty for the first time. He had told himself it was so sensible leaving her. He was going to London to work, after all. But in fact, he had been relieved at the opportunity to escape her, and now it seemed awkward and stupid, yet he didn't want to change it and take her with him.

''I'll be fine,'' she said with more nobility than truth. What choice did she have now? To tell him she'd sit home and cry every day? That it was more than she could take? It wasn't. She was almost used to it. In fact, Bill had abandoned her when Todd died, emotionally anyway, and now he was just taking his body with him. She had been alone for a year, in truth two more months wouldn't make much difference.

''You can call me whenever you have a problem. Maybe you should stay in Europe with Alyssa for a while.'' She felt like an aging aunt being foisted off on relatives or sent on cruises. But she knew she would be better off at home, than languishing alone in hotels around Europe.

"Alyssa is going to Italy with friends, she has her own plans." And so did he. They all did. Even Tanya had her trip to Wyoming with Tony's children. Everyone had something to do, except for her. All she had was a short trip with Alyssa, and he expected her to spend the rest of the summer waiting. It was extraordinarily presumptuous of him, but given what their life had become, it no longer surprised her.

They picked at the food she'd bought without much appetite, talked about some things she needed to know, about their maintenance, an insurance premium that he was waiting for, and what mail he wanted her to send him. He was expecting her to pay the bills and take care of most of it. He would have precious little spare time while he worked on the case in London. And after they'd talked for a while, he went back to their bedroom, and packed the rest of his papers. He was in the bathroom taking a shower, when she came in, and when he walked into the bedroom, he was wearing a robe and his hair was damp. He smelled of soap and aftershave, and for a moment, seeing him that way gave her a jolt. He seemed to be relaxing with her a little bit now that he was leaving. She wondered if it was because he was sorry to go and it made him feel closer to her suddenly, or if on the contrary he was so relieved it made him careless.

And when they went to bed that night, he didn't move close to her, but somehow, even at a distance, he seemed less rigid. There were things she would have liked to say to him, about how she felt, and what she still wanted from him, but she sensed that despite the slight warming of the cold war, he was not yet ready for her to bear her soul, or tell him how she was feeling about their marriage. She was feeling bereft these days, incredibly sad, and oddly cheated. She had been cheated out of a son, and Todd in turn had been robbed, or robbed himself, of his future. But it was as though when the spirits took him away, they took his parents with them. It would have been nice to be able to say that to Bill openly, but knowing that she would barely see him for the next two months, she didn't think it was the time, or that he was ready. And as she lay on the other side of the bed, thinking about him, Bill fell asleep without saying another word, or putting an arm around her. He had said all he was able to say for now, earlier in the kitchen.

And when he got up the next day, he was in a hurry to get organized. He called the office, closed his bags, showered and shaved, and scarcely had time to glance at the paper over breakfast. She had made eggs and cereal for him, and the whole wheat toast he ate every day, and then gone to get dressed herself, and she appeared in a black linen pantsuit and a black-and-white striped T-shirt. As usual, she looked like a magazine ad when he saw her.

"Do you have a meeting today?" he asked, glancing over the paper.

"No," she said quietly. There was a pain in the pit of her stomach.

"You're awfully dressed just to sit around at home. Are you going out to lunch?" She couldn't help wondering why he cared, he was leaving for two months anyway. What difference did it make what she did now?

"I didn't want to take you to the airport in blue jeans," she said, and with that, he raised an eyebrow.

"I wasn't expecting you to take me. I have a limo coming at ten-thirty. I'm giving Mrs. Anderson a ride. They're picking her up first, and actually Bob Miller is coming too. We were going to do some work in the car on the way to the airport." They couldn't bear to lose a single moment. The human robots. Or was it just an excuse to get away from her sooner?

"I don't have to go if you'd rather not," she said quietly, and he picked up the paper again and went back to reading.

"I don't think it makes much sense. It'll be simpler to say good-bye here." And less embarrassing. God forbid someone would ever think he loved her. Or did he? The faint humanity he had shown in the same room only the night before seemed to have disappeared, the wall was up again, and he was hiding not only behind it, but also behind the paper. "I'm sure you have better things to do today. The airport is a mess this time of year, it'll take you hours to get back into the city." He smiled at her then, but there was no warmth in it. It was the kind of smile you'd bestow on a stranger. She nodded, and said nothing, and when he got up, she put their dishes in the sink, and tried to keep herself from crying. It was so strange watching him leave, going through all the procedures and plans, and almost before she had come to terms with it, he had rung for the elevator and his bags were on the landing. He was wearing a light gray suit and he looked unbearably handsome. And it had been tacitly decided by then, she was not going to the airport. She stood in the doorway watching him as the elevator man took his bags, and then took a discreet step back so he couldn't see them.

"I'll call you," Bill said, looking like a kid again, and she had to fight back tears as she watched him. She wanted to tell him that she couldn't believe he was leaving, without a single loving gesture to her.

"Take care of yourself," she said awkwardly.

"I'll miss you," he said, and then bent to kiss her cheek, and without meaning to, she put her arms around him.

"I'm sorry . . . about everything . . ." About Todd, about the past year, about the fact that he felt he needed a two-month break from her while he worked in Europe. About the fact that their marriage was in shards around their feet. There was so much to be sorry for, it was hard to remember all of it, but he knew what she was saying.

"It's all right. It'll be all right, Stu . . ." He hadn't called her that all year. But would it? She no longer believed that. And they would be apart for two months now. She knew instinctively that they would only get farther apart from it, not closer. He was so foolish to think this was what they needed. If anything, it would make the gap unbridgeable in future.

He took a step back from her then, without kissing her, and looked down at her with immeasurable sadness. "I'll see you in a few weeks.'' All she could do was nod as the tears began to course down her cheeks and the elevator operator waited.

''I love you,'' she whispered as he turned away, and then he turned as he heard her. But he only looked at her, and nodded, and then the elevator door closed silently behind him. He hadn't answered.

When Mary Stuart walked back into the apartment, the force of her loneliness took her breath away. She couldn't believe how awful it had felt to see him go, and know that he wouldn't be home for months, that she wouldn't even see him except for a few days with her daughter. At least she had that, but even so, it felt like the end of their marriage. No matter what he said, the fact that he needed time away from her, and that he was no longer able to respond to her in any way, told its own story.

She sat on the couch and cried for a while, feeling sorry for herself, and then she walked slowly into the kitchen. She put the dishes in the dishwasher, and put the rest of his breakfast away, and when the phone rang she almost didn't answer. She thought it might be Bill calling from the car, telling her he had forgotten something, or maybe even that he loved her. But when she answered, it was her daughter.

''Hi, sweetheart.'' Mary Stuart tried to sound brighter than she felt. She didn't want to tell Alyssa how unhappy she was that her father had left. They had had enough unhappiness without Mary Stuart complaining about her marriage, particularly to her daughter. ''How's Paris?''

''Beautiful and hot and romantic,'' she said. It was a new word in her vocabulary, and Mary Stuart smiled, wondering if there was a new man in her life. Maybe even a young Frenchman.

''Am I allowed to ask why?'' she said cautiously, still smiling.

''Oh, it just is. Paris is so wonderful. I love it here. I never want to leave.'' But she was going to have to in a few weeks.

They were giving up her apartment when Mary Stuart came to Paris.

"I can't blame you for that," she said, glancing at Central Park from her kitchen window. It was pretty and green too, but it was also filthy and full of muggers and bums, and it was definitely not Paris. "I can't wait to see you," she said, trying not to think of Bill leaving an hour before. By then, he would have been at the airport. But she doubted that he'd call her. There was nothing to say, and she had made him too uncomfortable with her display of emotions. She had gotten the message very clearly.

But at Alyssa's end there was a strange silence. Her mother hadn't even noticed.

"Have you gotten organized a little bit?" Mary Stuart had asked her to get some maps together for their driving trips. That part of the trip was Alyssa's assignment. The rest had been taken care of by Bill's office. "Did you get the maps of the Maritime Alps? I heard about a great little hotel just outside Florence." But still there was no sound from her daughter. "Alyssa? Are you all right? Is something wrong?" Was there a problem? Was she in love? Was she crying? But when she spoke again, Mary Stuart could hear that she wasn't. She just sounded very awkward.

"Mom . . . I have a problem . . ."

Oh, my God. "Are you pregnant?" She was nearly twenty years old and it would have been a calamity Mary Stuart would have preferred not to face, but if she had to, she would go through it with her.

But Alyssa was outraged at the suggestion. "Mom, for God's sake! Of course not!"

"Well, excuse me. How should I know? So what's the problem?"

Alyssa took a deep breath and launched into a long, complicated tale that sounded like one of the stories she had told in third grade that went on forever and had no ending. What it boiled down to finally was that a group of her friends were going to the Netherlands and they wanted her to go with them. It was a rare opportunity, and they would travel into Switzerland and Germany, staying with friends, or at youth hostels, and then Italy, where she had planned to meet them later. But the whole earlier part of the trip had just been organized, and as far as Alyssa was concerned, it was the opportunity of a lifetime.

"That sounds great. But I still don't understand the problem."

Alyssa sighed. Her mother was so dense at times, but at least not always, like her father. "They're leaving this week. They're going to be traveling for two months, before we meet in Capri. I could give up the apartment now, and go with them except . . ." Her voice trailed off as Mary Stuart understood. She no longer wanted to travel around Europe with her mother. It was understandable certainly, but it was also a huge disappointment for Mary Stuart. It was all she had in her life at the moment. And she had hoped for a healing trip, alone with her only daughter, her only child now.

"I see," Mary Stuart said quietly. "You don't want to go with me." And then she cringed at her own words. She hadn't meant it the way it sounded.

"That's not it at all, Mom. And I'll still go with you if you really want to. It's just . . . I thought . . . this is such a great opportunity . . . but whatever you want . . ." She was trying to be diplomatic about it, but she was dying to go with her friends, and Mary Stuart knew it would be so much more fun for her. It didn't seem fair to stop her.

"It sounds wonderful," her mother said generously. "I think you should do it."

"Are you serious? Do you mean it? Really?" She sounded like a little kid, jumping up and down in her Paris apartment. "Oh, Mom, you're the best. I knew you'd understand . . . but I was afraid you'd think . . . I . . ." And then Mary Stuart suddenly understood even more, but it didn't really shock her.

"Is there a gentleman included in this plan?" She could hear it in her daughter's voice, and it made her smile, although it also made her feel nostalgic.

"Well . . . maybe . . . but that's not why I want to go with them. Honestly, it's just such a great trip."

"And you're a great kid, and I love you. You owe me a trip in the fall. We'll go away somewhere together for a few days before you go back to Yale. Is that a deal?"

"I promise." But Mary Stuart knew it wouldn't be the same, she would be anxious about her friends and starting school, and coming home again. She would be easily distracted. The trip through France and Italy would have been wonderful for her, but the trip through the Netherlands with her friends would be a lot more fun for her daughter. And Mary Stuart had never hesitated to sacrifice herself for her children.

"How soon do you leave?"

"In two days, but I can get everything done." They talked about how she would ship things home, and payments that had to be made. And Mary Stuart needed to wire her money. She told her to buy traveler's checks with it, and how much to get, and they talked for a long time about the details of Alyssa's travels. And then her mother asked her if she was still planning to go to London.

"I don't think so. We weren't going to go to England at all, and when I talked to Daddy the other night, he said he was going to be really busy." He was avoiding all of them, not just his wife, but his daughter. It was of little comfort to Mary Stuart to hear it.

When they hung up, Mary Stuart sat looking out the window for a long time, at mothers and children hurrying toward the playground, and the children running there while the mothers sat on benches and chatted. She could remember those days now, as though they had happened only the day before. She had spent every afternoon in the park with her children. Some of her friends had gone to work, but she had always felt it was more important for her to be at home, and she was lucky that she had always been able to do it. And now they were gone, one grown and on her own and traveling around Europe with friends, the other to a distant place in eternity where she hoped she would one day see him again. Believing that was all she had left to hold on to.

"Take care of them," she wanted to whisper to the mothers she could see far below. "Hold on to them while you can." It was all so short, and then it was over. Like her marriage. That was over now too. She knew it for sure, had for months, and had refused to see it. But when she thought of the way he had gone, the things he had left unsaid, and the way he had walked away from her when she told him she loved him, there was no longer any doubt in her mind. And she didn't even have the comfort of thinking it was another woman. It was no one, it was him, it was her, it was time, it was the fact that tragedy had struck them, and they hadn't survived it. It was Life. But whatever had done it, she knew that her marriage had died. All she had to do now was adjust to it. She had two months to try freedom on for size, and see how she liked it.

She went out for a walk that afternoon, and thought about all of it, about Alyssa traveling with her friends, and Bill being in London for two months, and she realized something she had always known and somewhat feared, that in the end you're alone, just as she was now, without them. It was up to her to pick up the pieces, to go on, to make peace with what Todd had done, and learn to move past it. Tanya had been right when she was in town, she couldn't hide from it forever. Maybe it wasn't her fault after all, but even if it was, she couldn't continue to wear his death like a shroud until it killed her.

She went back to the apartment, and as she walked in, and set her handbag down, she knew what she needed to do. She had known it for a long time, and she had never had the courage to do it. She would have preferred not to do it alone, but it was time. It almost felt as though he were waiting for her, as though he would have approved and wanted her to do it. She opened the door to his room, and stood there for a long time, and then she opened the drapes and the blinds and let in the sunlight. She sat down at his desk, and began opening drawers, and at first she felt like an intruder going through all of Todd's papers. There were letters and old exams, and assorted memorabilia from his childhood, and an old note from Princeton about his eating club initiation. One by one, she went through his drawers, and then, fighting back tears, she went out to the kitchen. There was a stack of boxes there and she brought them back to Todd's room, and as soon as she began packing them, she started crying. But it was almost a relief to give in to tears. She spent hours in his room that night, and the phone never rang. Bill never called. He was supposed to land at 2:00 A.M. London time and would be at Claridge's by 3:30. He had no idea what she was doing, and he had told her long since to do whatever she wanted.

It took her hours to pack his room, and when she was through there was nothing left. She had packed all his clothes into boxes, and kept only a few special things, like his old Boy Scout uniform that she found put away on a shelf, his favorite leather jacket, a sweater she had once made him. The rest was to be given away, and the papers and books she was going to put in their storage vault in the basement. She had left all his trophies lined up on a shelf. She wanted to find a home for them, and she had taken all the photographs from his room, and spread them around the apartment. It was as though he had suddenly shared something with them, as though he had left them a gift, yet another memory. She put an especially nice photograph of all of them in her own room, and another of him in Alyssa's bedroom. It was two o'clock in the morning before she was through, and it was all done by then. It was dark outside, as she stood alone in the stark white kitchen. She could almost feel him next to her, she could still see his face, his eyes, hear his voice so clearly. Sometimes she thought she was forgetting, but she knew she never would. Todd was so much more than the sum of his things to her. None of that mattered anymore, it was all gone, and what really mattered would be with her forever.

She took the dark green bedspreads off the beds, and put them in the closet to send to the cleaners, and she made a mental note to change the drapes. She had never noticed how badly they had faded. It was sad looking at his old room, it seemed so empty and so bereft, with boxes stacked everywhere all around her. It was as though he was moving somewhere. But he was already long gone. She was a year late putting away his things. She was a year late saying good-bye to him, but in the important ways she had. He would never be forgotten, and things would never be the same again. It seemed only a matter of time before she would be packing the rest of the apartment.

She looked around for a last time, and gently closed his door again. The next day, she was going to have the Goodwill pick up the things to give away, and the service manager take the rest of the boxes down to the basement. And as she walked slowly back to her room, she thought of everything that had happened in the past year, how far they had come, and how alone they all were. Alyssa was in Europe with her friends, Todd was gone, and Bill was in London for the summer. And now she was here, putting away memories, and letting go of her older child, her first baby. She looked long and hard at a photograph of him as she stood in her bedroom. His eyes were so big and bright and clear, and he had been laughing when she took the picture. She could still hear the sound of his laughter. "Oh, come on, Mom . . . hurry up . . ." He was in a wet bathing suit in Cape Cod, and he'd been freezing. He was pretending to strangle his sister, it was all in good fun, and he had run halfway down the beach afterward with the top of her bikini, with Alyssa running after him, clutching a towel and screaming. It seemed a thousand years ago, when there was still more to her life than just memories, and an empty apartment.

Mary Stuart didn't get to bed till several hours later, and

when she did, she lay dreaming of all of them, Alyssa was saying something and shaking her head, and Todd was thanking her for packing his things for him. And when she looked up, she could see Bill in the distance, walking away from her, and as she called after him, he never turned around and looked at her, he just kept walking.

CHAPTER 6

When Tanya got back to Los Angeles, she hadn't been sure what she would find. Tony had said he was moving out, but there was always the off chance that he hadn't. But as soon as she got home, she checked his closets and saw that they were empty. Jean was at the house, waiting for her, anxious to give her the latest report, and show her the latest horror from the tabloids. She was in the front pages again, and as usual the stories about the bodyguard who was suing her were appalling. Someone had told them that Tony had rented his own apartment, but it was only temporary, they explained, and there were more photographs of him with the starlet he had gone out with. This time he had been having dinner with her.

"It's all right . . . it's all right . . ." Tanya said to Jean, looking tired. "I know. I've seen it." She had picked up a copy at the airport. "I think I'll go to Santa Barbara for a couple of days." She needed to get away from there, from the photographers and the prying eyes and the empty closets. She didn't even have time to mourn for him, all she could think about was how to protect herself from the media.

"You can't go," Jean said matter-of-factly, handing her four sheets of schedules. "You're doing a benefit tomorrow night, and you have rehearsal for two days after that. And you have to meet with Bennett about the lawsuit over the weekend."

"Tell him I can't," Tanya said unhappily. "I need a couple of days off." She would never have welched on a benefit or skipped rehearsals. But she was not about to spend her weekend with Bennett Pearson, preparing for depositions.

"I think that's pretty firm. They're already scheduling you for depositions in the Leo Turner case, and Bennett said he got a call from Tony's lawyer this morning."

"That was fast," Tanya said, dropping into a large, comfortable, pink satin chair in her bedroom. "He sure didn't waste much time." It was as though three years had vanished into thin air overnight, and now they had to get down to business. Sometimes she wondered if that was all everything was. It was all about money, greed, and business. The agents, the lawyers, the people selling stories about her, those who wanted to be paid off so they wouldn't sue, the endless number of people who thought she owed them for her success, because she'd been fortunate and they'd been less so.

"I need a day to myself," she said to her secretary quietly, and no one in her world had any idea how much she meant it. She just couldn't do it anymore, couldn't go on, couldn't keep plugging and smiling and singing and working, for all of them. Sometimes she felt as though she worked only to pay them. There was no life left anymore. It was just work and payments.

"He thinks he can buy Leo off for five hundred grand," Jean said, pressing on, and she still had an armful of appointments and clippings, but Tanya was looking grim, and the secretary hadn't noticed.

"Fuck Leo. And you can tell Bennett I said so."

Jean nodded and went on, while Tanya wished she would drop through the floor, but Jean was not only thorough, she was relentless. "We got a call from the *L.A. Times* today. They want to know the details of the divorce, if Tony wants alimony or a settlement or both, and if you're going to give it to him."

"Was that from his lawyer or the paper?" Tanya looked confused and upset. There was certainly no such thing as privacy in her life, or decency, or anything even remotely human.

"It was the paper, and Tony called. He wants to talk to you about the children."

"What about them?" She lay her head back against the chair and closed her eyes, as Jean sat down across from her and went on. She never missed a beat. And she still had to tell Tanya about all her new appointments. An attorney, an accountant, a decorator who thought she should redo the house, an architect who was going to help her alter the kitchen at the beach house. Everyone had to be paid and met with and listened to, and if they somehow decided she had fallen short of their expectations of her, they would sue her. It was just the way things were, and Tanya knew it. And it didn't matter that Tanya's lawyer made them all sign confidentiality agreements, assuring her that they would not sell information to the tabloids. "Why does Tony want to talk to me about the kids?" she asked Jean again, who went back in her notes and checked. She worked a ten- or twelve-hour day sometimes. It was not an easy job, but she was well paid, and most of the time Tanya was nice to work for. And Jean liked the glory of it, going to concerts with her, being seen with her, wearing her old clothes, and living an odd kind of half-life in her shadow. She had wanted to sing too, but she didn't have the voice, the luck, or the talent. Tanya did, and she was happy just to stand beside it.

"I'm not sure," Jean answered her about the kids. "He didn't say. But he asked you to call him."

She had another half hour of business to listen to, and Jean pointed out that the housekeeper had left dinner for her in the kitchen. Tanya poured herself a glass of wine instead, went over some notes, took a file of contracts from Jean. They had been dropped off by her lawyers and were all from the promoters of the concert tour. And when Jean finally left at nine o'clock, Tanya picked up the phone and called Tony.

"Hi," she said, sounding utterly exhausted. It had been a long day from her start in New York early that morning, and there was so much waiting for her here. Sometimes she wondered if she'd survive it. "Jean said you wanted me to call."

"Yes, I did," he said, sounding uncomfortable and distant. "How was New York?"

"Nice, more or less. I saw Mary Stuart Walker, it was worth it just for that, and Felicia Davenport. They screwed me on the morning show I did, and hit me full face with all the garbage from the tabloids." She'd been through it before, nothing surprised her anymore, but she still never liked it. "And seeing the literary guy was a waste of time." But she realized as she listened to herself that she was getting sidetracked. He wasn't interested in her life anymore. "That's beside the point, isn't it, right now? Or is that all that's left, just business?"

"That's all there ever was, wasn't it? What else was there, Tanya? Your work, your concerts, your career, your benefits, your rehearsals, your music."

"Is that how you see it now? I think you've left out a few things. The things we did together . . . the trips we took . . . the kids . . ." There had been more in their life than just her career and her music. It wasn't fair of him now to say that, just to absolve himself for leaving her, but she was beyond arguing with him. It wasn't just her work and the pressures that got to him, she knew she had lost him because he was so humiliated over the tabloids. You had to have a thick skin to love someone with a show business career, and apparently he didn't. "What have you told the kids, by the way?" She was worried about that. She had wanted to call them from New York, but she didn't want to talk to them before Tony told them.

"Their mother took care of it for me," he said, sounding angry. "She showed them everything they ran in the tabloids."

"I'm sorry," Tanya said with genuine humility. It was so hurtful for all of them, especially the children.

"Yeah, me too," he said without sincerity. He sounded more relieved than unhappy. And then, suddenly, he sounded awkward. "In fact, Nancy wanted me to talk to you. With everything they're writing about us, she doesn't think . . . she thought the kids . . . she doesn't want to expose them to your lifestyle at the moment." He spat out the words like bad oysters.

"My lifestyle?" Tanya was totally baffled by his comment. "What lifestyle? What's changed since last week?" And then she understood. Nancy had read all the stories, and all of Leo's claims about her harassing him sexually and walking around naked. "Tony, your kids have nearly lived with us for the past three years. Has any harm ever come to them? Have I done anything wrong? What does she think I'm going to do now? What could possibly be different?"

"I'm not there anymore. She doesn't see why they should stay with you if I'm gone. They can visit you, if I'm along," he said, nearly choking on the words, even he was embarrassed by what Nancy had told him. "But she doesn't want them to stay there."

"Are we talking about visitation?" Were they already there? Was she already negotiating her divorce? And where were their lawyers?

"Eventually we will be," he explained, and they'd be talking about other things too, like the house in Malibu she'd bought with her own funds after she married Tony, but he was extremely fond of. He was the only one who used it. She never had time to. "Right now, she's talking about Wyoming."

There was a long silence on Tanya's end as the light began to dawn. Nancy was not willing to let Tanya take her stepchildren to Wyoming. "Can this be negotiated?" she asked, sounding bitterly disappointed. It was going to be such fun, and she had looked forward to it for months. Now everything had gone wrong. Tony had left her, and the kids were being kept home by their mother. "It's a great place, Tony. Everyone says it's fabulous and the kids would love it." He hadn't even wanted to go at first. None of them had. And she had a huge, luxurious three-bedroom cabin reserved for two weeks. "What am I supposed to do with my reservations?"

"Cancel them. Will they give you a refund?"

"No. But that's not the point. I wanted to do something special and different with the children."

"I can't help it, Tan," Tony said, sounding uncomfortable again. The whole thing was embarrassing. He knew how she'd been looking forward to it, and he really felt awkward, particularly since he had just left her. "Nancy says no, Tan. I did my best to convince her. Take a couple of friends. What about your old friend in New York? Mary Stuart."

"Thanks for the suggestions." But she was worried about something else now, something much more important. "I want to know what's happening here. Am I going to be allowed to see them again?" She wanted to hear it from him. They had no right to do this to her. And her eyes filled with tears as she asked him.

"Who?" He tried to sound vague, but he knew what she was asking. And it wasn't up to him, it was up to their mother.

"You know who I mean, dammit, don't play with me. The kids. Am I going to be allowed to see them?"

"Sure, I . . . I'm sure Nancy . . ." But she could tell that he was hedging.

"The truth. What deal did you make with her? Am I going to be able to see them?" She said it as though she were speaking to a foreigner, or someone from another planet. But he had very clearly understood the question, he just didn't know how to answer, without making her crazy.

"You'll have to work it out with your lawyer," he said vaguely, hoping to avoid a confrontation.

"What the hell does that mean?" She was shouting at him, and rapidly losing control. She was suddenly overwhelmed by a feeling of panic. Why was everyone always so able to take everything away from her? The money she worked so hard to earn, her reputation, now even her children. "Are you going to let me see them or not?" She was screaming and he was cringing.

"It's not up to me, Tan. If it were, you could see them anytime. It's up to their mother."

"My ass it's up to her. That bitch doesn't give a damn about them and you know it. That's why you left her." That and a few other things, like a drinking problem, a penchant for gambling, and the fact that she had slept with every man he knew. More than once, he had had to go looking for her and the kids in Vegas. But in spite of that, his children were terrific, and Tanya knew she had been good for them. She wanted to remain a part of their lives now, and Nancy had no right to stop her.

"Just work it out with your lawyer." They talked for a few more minutes and hung up, and she paced around the house that night like a lion looking for his dinner. She couldn't believe what was happening to her. He had left her, taken his life, his kids, cheated on her in Palm Springs, made a fool of her in the press, and now his ex-wife wouldn't let her see the children. But when her lawyer called her back later that night, he was not encouraging when she explained it.

"There is something called stepparents' rights," Bennett explained patiently to her, and she began to hate the sound of his voice as he went through it. It was always the same. They explained what normal people's rights were, and what celebrities' rights were, and why they were different. And with extenuating circumstances, you could count on being screwed completely. "But you have to understand, Tanya," he went on, "you have not exactly been painted like the Virgin Mary in the press of late, with the kind of accusations Leo is making. The guy has told some pretty ugly stories, and I guess Tony's ex-wife doesn't want the kids exposed to that sort of behavior. I think if you got on the stand, and her attorney questioned you, no matter how innocent you are, by the time he got through, no one would let you take those kids to high tea in St. Paul's Cathedral, let alone stay at your house, or go to Wyoming for a vacation.'' There were tears in her eyes as he said it. He had no idea how he had hurt her. ''I'm sorry, Tanya. That's just the way it is. I think you have to let it go for now. At least until the dust settles around this lawsuit.''

''But what about the next one?'' she said, blowing her nose. She knew the scenario much too well now.

''What next time?'' She had succeeded in confusing Bennett for a minute. ''Did you pick up another case? Were you just served?'' He hadn't heard anything about it.

''No, but I'm sure I will be. It's only been a week since the last one. Give me a few days.''

''Don't be so cynical,'' he said, but she was right, and he knew it. In her position, she was nothing more or less than a constant target. No wonder Tony had left her. At the moment, she hated her life as much as he did. ''Anyway, let's talk about Leo,'' Bennett went on, ignoring her current frustration over Tony's children. There was nothing he could do about it, and he didn't want to argue in court, inevitably in front of cameras, about whether or not Tanya was in the habit of walking naked around the house in front of bodyguards, or sleeping with her trainer. He was sure she did neither, but whatever she had done in her life would come out with a vengeance. And she was, after all, a grown woman.

''I don't want to talk about Leo,'' she said bluntly. She was unhappy, and exhausted.

''He's willing to come down to four hundred and ninety if we jump on it now. And frankly, I think you should take it.'' He said it matter-of-factly, and she almost jumped off the couch and hung up on him as she listened.

''Four hundred and ninety thousand dollars?'' She screamed at him and he didn't bat an eye. ''Are you *nuts*? The guy made the whole story up, and we're going to pay him half a million bucks for it? Why doesn't he just get a part in a feature?''

''Because no one's ever heard of him and he'd have to work in four or five movies to get that. That could take him a couple of years, if he's lucky. Hitting you up for it is a lot quicker.''

''That's disgusting.'' But it was true, that was the worst part. ''I can't believe this.''

''If we wait, he could double it again. May I call his lawyer tonight and say we agree? I want to make it contingent on confidentiality, of course. His attorney says he's already talking to one of the networks about a TV movie.''

''Oh, my God,'' she groaned, and closed her eyes again. What kind of nightmare did she live in? No wonder Tony had left. Who could blame him? Tanya would have liked to leave too, but this was the only way she knew to make a living. ''This is so sick, isn't it? What kind of business is this? How did I ever get into it, and why have I stayed here?''

''Would you like to see your tax returns for last year? That might offer some small comfort,'' he said fliply but she shook her head sadly. It was all too much. Way, way too much. It was more slime and sleaze than she had ever dreamed she'd have to live with.

''You know what, Bennett,'' she answered him. ''It's not consolation enough for this kind of shit. This is my life these people are playing with. This is *me* they're telling lies about. I've become a thing, a cash register, an object.'' Anyone who wanted an extra dime, a cool half mil, and was willing to either lie, cheat, or blackmail her, could have anything they wanted. For the first time, listening to her words, Bennett was silent. And he hated to press her, but he knew he had to.

''What do I say to Leo's lawyer, Tan? Give me a break here.''

There was a long, unhappy pause, and then finally she nodded. She knew when she was beaten. ''All right,'' she said hoarsely, depressed by all of it. ''Tell him we'll pay him . . . the bastard . . .'' And then, trying to push the horror from her mind, and the fact that she had just paid a man half a million dollars to tell vicious lies about her to the press, she asked Bennett another question. "What about Wyoming? Can you do something about that?"

"Like what? Buy it for you?" He was trying to tease her out of her gloom, but he knew he was not succeeding, and he didn't blame her. It was a difficult business being a celebrity, in spite of what people thought. From the outside, it looked great, from the inside, it was filled with heartbreak. And it was impossible not to take it personally. They were human, they all did.

"Can you get her to agree to let me take the kids with me? I'll cut it down to a week if that makes a difference," although she had the reservations for two weeks.

"I'll try if you want, but I think it's pretty hopeless. And I think it's a fair bet that it'll hit the papers that you were turned down, which doesn't exactly make you look like a very moral person. And since we're pressing Leo on the confidentiality issue here, I'd rather not have all this crap dragged back into the papers."

"Great. Thanks," she said, trying to sound unaffected by all of it, but it was obvious that she was distraught over the entire conversation.

"I'm sorry, Tan," he said somberly.

"Sure, thanks. I'll talk to you tomorrow." She was crying as she said it.

"I'll call you. We have to go over the contracts on the concert tour. I'll call you in the morning."

Her heart sank as she hung up. Her life had turned to shit over the years, and it was only at times like these that she really saw it. For all the adulation, and the thrill they talked about, the applause, the concerts, the awards, the money, this was what it really boiled down to. People making you look like a two-bit tramp, a husband who walked out without looking back, and stepchildren you never saw again. It was a wonder anyone in Hollywood could still hold their head up, or bothered to put one foot after the other.

She sat alone in her house in Bel Air that night, thinking

about it, and wishing she were dead, but too unhappy and too scared to do anything about it. She thought of Ellie for the first time in years, and Mary Stuart's son, Todd. It seemed such an easy way out, and yet it wasn't. It was so totally the wrong thing to do, and yet it required a peculiar mix of cowardice and courage, and she found that she had neither.

She sat in her living room until the sun came up, thinking about all of it, wanting to hate Tony for as much as she could, and she found she couldn't do that either. She couldn't do anything except sit there and cry all night, and there was no one to hear her. And at last, she got up and went to bed. She had no idea what she was going to do about Wyoming, and she didn't even care now. She'd let Jean go and take friends, or her hairdresser, or Tony with a girlfriend. And then she remembered he was going to Europe with his girlfriend. Everyone had friends and children, and a life, and even a decent reputation. And all she had were a bunch of gold and platinum records, hanging on a wall, and a row of awards sitting on a shelf below them. But there was not much more beyond that. She couldn't imagine trusting anyone again, or even having a man willing to put up with all the garbage. It was laughable. She had made it all the way to the top, in order to find that there was nothing there that anybody wanted. She lay down on her bed, still thinking of it, and the children she would probably never see again, or not for more than a few minutes. It was as though she and Tony and his kids and their life had vanished into thin air, none of it had ever existed. Gone. In a puff of smoke . . . in a giant blaze . . . a whole life up in flames . . . with tabloids used as kindling.

CHAPTER 7

When Tanya woke up later that day, she felt as though she had been beaten. She had hardly slept at all, and something about the settlement, the news about the kids, the fact of coming home and seeing that Tony had taken all his things, left her feeling bullied and broken. She got out of bed, and felt as though she had a hangover as she grimaced and looked in the mirror. She hadn't even had a drink the day before, but she felt rotten, and she had a dismal headache.

"God, I'm going to need another trip to the plastic surgeon after all this," she said to her reflection once she walked into the bathroom. She ran a hot bath, and slipped slowly into it, and she felt a little better. She had a benefit to do that night, and it was a cause she really cared about, and she wanted to deliver for them. She had a short rehearsal that afternoon, and by noon she had to be on the merry-go-round again, chasing all her myriad obligations.

She walked into the kitchen in her dressing gown, made

herself a cup of coffee, and reached for the morning paper. For once, she hadn't made the front page, and neither had her soon-to-be ex-husband, or any of her employees, past or present. That at least was something. She turned each page gingerly, as though waiting to find a tarantula between the pages. But the only thing that caught her eye was a story about a doctor in San Francisco called Zoe Phillips. Tanya read it avidly, and when she finished it she was smiling. Zoe was one of her old college roommates. She sounded as though she was doing remarkably, not surprisingly. She had started the most important AIDS clinic in the city, and apparently ran it with an absolute genius for obtaining funds, and turning loaves into fishes. She was feeding homeless people with AIDS, housing them, treating them, and also large segments of the more affluent AIDS-infected population. The article made her sound like the Mother Teresa of San Francisco. And Tanya was so touched after what she read, that she reached for her telephone book, looked up the number, and called her. She hadn't talked to her in two years, but they always exchanged cards at Christmas. Tanya knew she was the only one still in touch with her. Mary Stuart had lost contact with her years before. They had never patched up the rift between them that occurred when Ellie died, and Mary Stuart didn't even like to hear about her. But Tanya was fond of both of them, and when a nurse answered the phone, she asked for Dr. Phillips.

At first, the nurse said the doctor was administering a treatment, and she asked if she could take a message.

"Sure," Tanya said agreeably, without hesitation.

"May I ask who's calling?"

"Tanya Thomas."

There was a long pause. Normally, the nurse would have thought it was a coincidence, but the doctor had an odd knack for getting in touch with famous people to participate in benefits for them, or just outright donate money.

"*The* Tanya Thomas?" She felt stupid asking.

"I guess so," Tanya laughed. "I went to college with Dr.

Phillips,'' she explained. It was interesting that Zoe never bragged about it. Her only interest in Tanya was their history together.

The nurse listening to her was clearly impressed that Tanya and the doctor were friends, and she said she was going to see if Dr. Phillips had finished her procedure. There was another wait, and a moment later, Tanya heard a familiar voice on the line. She had a soft smoky voice, and a seriousness which she conveyed even over the telephone lines, but she dealt with a serious subject.

''Tan?'' she asked, with a small, slow voice. ''Is that you? My nurses almost went crazy.''

''It's me. You sound like Dr. Salk from what I'm reading in the paper. You've been pretty busy, and you forgot to send me a Christmas card last year.'' It always felt like being kids again when she talked to her. It brought back old times, just as it did when Tanya saw Mary Stuart.

''I didn't send any. I was too busy. I had a baby.'' She said it with the same gentle smile, and Tanya could just see her as she listened.

''You did what? Are you married?'' But she doubted it. Zoe had never wanted to get married. She was satisfied with her career and long-term monogamous relationships, but she was more interested in issues and changing the course of medical history than in getting married, and she always had been. ''What are you telling me? Have you joined the rest of the bourgeois population? What happened?''

''Don't get too worked up. I adopted. And no, I'm not married. I haven't changed that much. I've just been really busy.''

''How old is the baby?'' It was so sweet just thinking about it, and in some ways, so unlike Zoe. She had never struck Tanya as terribly maternal. And judging from the age she knew so well, Zoe had done it when she was forty-three. She must have decided to give motherhood a try before it was too late, but it was interesting that she hadn't decided to get pregnant.

"She's nearly two now. She just kind of happened into my life. Her mother was a patient, and fortunately, she did not have AIDS, but she was homeless. She didn't want to keep Jade, so I did. She's half Korean. And it's been perfect. I would never have been able to take the time out of my practice to get pregnant." And she had never been involved with anyone she wanted that permanent a tie to. Not in recent years at least. Her heart was in her work, and she would have done anything in life for her patients.

"When am I going to see her?" Tanya asked wistfully, thinking about her old friend and the little Korean girl she had adopted. Jade. She loved the name. And it was so like Zoe.

"I'll send you a picture," Zoe said apologetically, as she signaled to a nurse waiting for her in the doorway. She pointed to her watch and held up five fingers to her. She wanted five more minutes to talk to Tanya. But there were over forty patients waiting for her in the waiting room, some of them too ill to be there. It was a familiar story to Zoe. But she could take at least five minutes out for old times' sake.

"How about doing better than a snapshot? How about coming to Wyoming?" Tanya had just decided to ask her on the spur of the moment. What if Zoe came, and Jade, and Mary Stuart . . . but she knew that was silly. Mary Stuart was going to Europe with her daughter. "It's just a thought. I've rented a cabin at a fancy dude ranch for two weeks in July and I have no one to go with." She sounded tired and forlorn, and Zoe knew her well enough to sense that things weren't going well, and if it were true, she was sorry to hear it.

"What about your husband?"

"That proves what I always suspected about you. You don't buy groceries, and you don't read tabloids." Zoe had been much too thin all her life, and was the envy of every woman who knew her, but she laughed at Tanya's comment.

"You're right on both counts. I never have time to eat, and I wouldn't read that junk if you paid me."

"That's comforting. Anyway, to answer your question, he's

gone. He moved out this week, as a matter of fact. And now his ex-wife won't let me see his kids, because I'm being sued by a bodyguard who claims that I tried to seduce him. Actually, it's all so sick it's not worth trying to explain to a rational human being. Don't bother to figure it out. I can't, and I live here." But what Zoe heard more than the words was the distress in her friend's voice. She sounded genuinely distraught over the state of her life at the moment.

"It doesn't sound like much fun. Wyoming sounds like a great idea. I wish I could go with you." The nurse was standing in the doorway flailing again, but Zoe didn't want to cut Tanya off. It sounded like she needed someone to talk to. So Zoe signaled for another five minutes, and the nurse disappeared again with a look of desperation.

"Don't you think you could come, Zoe? Maybe just for a weekend?"

"I wish I could. I don't have anyone working with me right now. I'd have to leave a call group covering me, and my patients really hate it. Most of them are so sick they want to know I'm going to be here."

"Don't you ever take time off?" Tanya said in amazement, not that she took much time off either. But what she did was a lot less rigorous than caring for dying patients.

"Not very often," Zoe confessed. "In fact," she said apologetically, "I'd better get back to work now, or they're going to break my office door down and lynch me. I'll call you sometime. Don't let the assholes get you down, Tan. They're all lesser beings, and it's just not worth it."

"I try to remember that most of the time, but they get you anyway. Somehow they always win, in this town anyway, or at least in this business."

"You don't deserve that," Zoe said in her gentle voice, and Tanya smiled broadly for the first time that morning.

"Thanks. Oh, I saw Mary Stuart the other day, by the way."

"How is she?" Zoe sounded tense when she asked, but it was still the same old thing, and Tanya never paid any attention to it. She had continued to give each of them news of the other over the years, and she still had fantasies about getting them back together, like the old days.

"She's all right, more or less. Her son died last year. I don't think any of them have recovered. I think right now everything is still a little shaky."

"Tell her I'm sorry," Zoe said softly, and she was. "What did he die of? An accident?"

"I think so," Tanya said vaguely, she didn't want to tell her it was a suicide. She knew how private and pained Mary Stuart felt about it. "He was at Princeton. He was twenty."

"That's a shame." She dealt with death so constantly, but she had never grown blasé about it. It was a defeat she still hated, and knew she would never accept with grace. Every time she lost a patient, she felt cheated.

"I know, you have to go . . . but think about Wyoming, if you can. It would be fun, wouldn't it?" It was a crazy dream, but it appealed to Tanya, and Zoe smiled at the thought. For her, it wasn't even a dream. She hadn't had a vacation in eleven years now. "Call me sometime." She sounded wistful and lonely, and Zoe wished that she could reach out to her and hold her. It was odd to think that someone with so much could be so vulnerable and unhappy. For those who didn't know her life, they would never have believed the beatings Tanya and people like her had taken, and the price Tanya's fame had cost her.

"I'll send pictures of Jade, I promise!" she said before she hung up, and as soon as she did, three nurses descended on her, complaining about the crowds in the waiting room, but the one who had taken the call looked at her with amazement.

"I couldn't believe that was really her. What's she like?" Everyone always asked, but it was such a dumb question.

"She's one of the nicest women I know, the most decent. She works like a dog, and she's so talented she doesn't even realize it. She deserves a much better shake than she's had in life. Maybe one day she'll get it," Zoe said wisely, as she followed them out of her office, but the nurse who had taken the call couldn't understand what Zoe was saying.

"She's won Grammys, Academy awards, platinum records, they say she makes ten million dollars when she does a concert tour, and a million bucks a concert when she doesn't. What else is there?"

"A whole lot, Annalee, believe me. You and I have more in our lives than she does." It was heartbreaking to think that she had to call a friend from college to find someone to go on vacation with. At least Zoe had her baby.

"I don't get it," the nurse said, shaking her head, as Zoe disappeared into a treatment room. And in Los Angeles, Tanya sat staring at the photograph of Zoe in the paper. And then, just for the hell of it, she decided to call Mary Stuart.

"Hi there, guess who I just talked to five minutes ago?"

"The president," Mary Stuart teased, happy to hear her voice again. Ever since she'd come through New York, she'd missed her.

"No. Zoe. She's running an AIDS clinic in San Francisco. There was a big article about it in this morning's *L.A. Times,* and she adopted a baby. She's almost two, her name is Jade, and she's half Korean."

"That's sweet," Mary Stuart said, trying to feel generous about her old friend, but even after more than twenty years, some of the old wounds still smarted. "I'm happy for her," she said, and meant it. "It's so typical of her, isn't it? Adopting, I mean, and an Asian child. She really turned out to be just who she started out to be. And the AIDS clinic doesn't surprise me either. Is she married?"

"Nope. I guess she's smarter than we are. Has Bill left for London yet?"

"Yesterday." She was suddenly silent then, as she thought about what she'd done the night before, and she knew Tanya would think she had done the right thing, although it had been very painful. "I put Todd's things away last night. I guess it was long overdue, but I just wasn't ready before this."

"No one's keeping score," Tanya said gently. "You do what you have to do to survive around here." And then she told Mary Stuart about Nancy not letting her take the kids to Wyoming. She was bitterly disappointed about it, and Mary Stuart could hear it. She knew how much those children meant to her. In some ways, they had been the best part of her marriage.

"That's rotten," she said with feeling.

"What isn't? I just agreed to pay half a million dollars to that blackmailer who sold his ass and mine to the tabloids."

"God, that's awful. Why so much?"

"Because everyone's scared. My lawyers are terrified of juries. They figure they could never win a jury trial. The other side would make me look like a monster rolling in money. There's no way to portray anything good or wholesome to them. *Celebrity* equals *slut,* or at the very least a person who deserves to cough up large sums of money to those either less fortunate, less honest, or extremely lazy. They ought to put that definition in the dictionary," she said, munching on a piece of toast, and Mary Stuart smiled. Tanya sounded upset, but not as devastated as she could have, considering everything that was happening to her. She could have been in bed with the covers over her head, and she wasn't. Tanya always had a lot of guts. Mary Stuart admired that about her. Whatever life did to her, she picked herself up, and went on her way again, dented, scratched, with broken corners here and there, but she was back on her feet, with a big smile, singing her heart out. "Have you heard from Bill since he left?" Tanya asked, thinking about what Mary Stuart had told her. She still found it remarkable that he didn't want his wife with him in London. And from what Mary Stuart said, she didn't even think he was cheating on her. He just didn't want her with him.

"Not yet. Alyssa called yesterday though. Our trip has been canceled."

"It has?" Tanya sounded stunned. "What happened?"

"She got a better offer. With a boy in tow." Mary Stuart smiled, but her voice sounded disappointed. "You can't beat that at her age."

"Or mine either," Tanya laughed, thinking about it. "So where does that leave you?"

"Pretty much beached, I guess. I'm trying to figure out what to do for the next two months. Bill and I talked about it again before he left, but he's adamant about not wanting me to come over. He thinks it would be 'distracting.' To tell you the truth, I was thinking of coming out to visit you for a few days, if you have time. I can stay at a hotel. New York is just so awful in July and August, and we didn't do anything about a summer house this year because we knew Bill would be gone all summer."

"What about Wyoming?" Tanya's face lit up as she asked her. At least half the dream could come true. Even if Zoe couldn't come, she and Mary Stuart could go to Wyoming for two weeks and play cowgirls. "Would you come with me? I have a cabin on this great ranch. It's supposed to be the height of luxury, Western style, and I can't see myself going alone. I've got the time blocked out, and I was going to give it away to someone else today, my secretary probably, or someone I work with."

Mary Stuart looked pensive, as she sat in her kitchen, thinking about it. "It sounds like fun. I don't have anything else to do. I'm not sure what a great rider I am anymore, although I'm certainly well padded."

"Don't give me that, you're fifteen pounds underweight. But who cares if we never ride? Who'll know? We can stare at the mountains and drink coffee, or champagne, or chase wranglers."

"Oh, great. Here come the tabloids. I'm not going anywhere with you if you're going to trash my reputation." But Mary Stuart was laughing at her. She loved the idea of going to a ranch with Tanya. Before, when Tanya had mentioned it, she hadn't even thought about it, because she was going to Europe to meet Alyssa, and Tanya was going to Wyoming with Tony's children.

"I promise, I'll behave. Just come. I'd love it." Tanya's eyes were shining as she said it. "Will you, Stu?"

Mary Stuart grinned when she heard her old college name. "I'd love it. When do we go?" She had the whole summer before her.

"Right after the Fourth. Go buy yourself some boots. I've still got my old ones."

"I'll go shopping this afternoon. How do I get there?" She had so much to do, arrangements to make, cowboy boots to buy. All of a sudden she felt like a kid again, and the thought of spending two weeks with Tanya thrilled her. It was just what she needed.

"Why don't you come to L.A., and we'll ride my bus to Jackson Hole. We can do it in two days easy. We can sleep, eat, read, watch movies, whatever you want. My driver never even talks to me. You can do anything you want on the way to Wyoming." She had a real rock-star bus, with two huge living rooms, hidden beds, a marble bathroom, and a full kitchen. It was perfect.

"I'll be there."

"I'll pick you up at the airport." Tanya gave her the dates, and Mary Stuart wrote them down carefully. This wasn't what she had expected to do by any means, but suddenly she realized that this was her ticket to freedom.

She sent Bill a fax as soon as she hung up, telling him that Alyssa had canceled their trip, and they would not be coming to London. Instead she and Tanya Thomas would be spending two weeks in Wyoming, and she promised to send him the details when she had them. She said that she hoped everything was going well, and that they were settling in at the hotel. She told him she'd be leaving for Los Angeles the following week, after the Fourth, and she'd fax him from there. She signed it *love,* but this time she didn't say that she missed him.

After she sent the fax to him, she picked up her handbag, and went out to buy cowboy boots at Billy Martin's.

And in California, Tanya was hopping around her kitchen like a kid, thinking about their trip. She and Mary Stuart were going to have a ball. She was in great spirits all day thinking about it, and that night at the benefit she looked spectacular in a black sequined dress that clung to her extraordinary figure, and everyone said her performance had never been better.

"You were hot!" Jean whispered as Tanya came off the stage, spent but pleased. It had been a great night, and the crowd had loved her. "You're the best!" There were curtain calls and encores, and people pressing around her everywhere. There were wild screams from the crowd, and flowers flung at her, and gifts pressed into her hands, and even someone's underwear flying through the air, but she dodged it. They adored her, and as the police whisked her away, she couldn't help thinking about the insanity of her life, the wild dichotomies of which celebrity was made, how passionately she was loved, how desperately she was hated.

CHAPTER 8

The rest of Zoe Phillips's day, after Tanya called, went like all her days, it just flew by as she went diligently from patient to patient. Most of her patients were homosexual men, but in recent years, she was seeing more and more women and heterosexuals, who had contracted the disease either sexually, or with IV drugs, or transfusions. But the cases she hated most, and she had had many of them, were the children. It was like working in an underdeveloped country. She could offer them no cure, and there was so little she could do to help them. Sometimes only a gesture, a touch of the hand, a gift of time, a moment at their bedside before they died. She spent untold hours visiting her patients. She was tireless and had been for years, since the first cases were documented in the early eighties. In the years since, AIDS had become her nemesis, her obsession, and her passion.

By the end of each day, she was drained of all energy and emotion. The only human being she could still think of offering anything to at all was her daughter. She tried to spend as much time as possible with her, she even went home for lunch sometimes, just to be with her. Early on she had brought her to work with her, and kept her in her office in a basket. But once Jade began to walk, it was all over. She was just getting ready to go home to her on the day Tanya called, when Sam Warner, her only relief doctor at the time, dropped by to see how things were going. He was a good doctor and a nice man. Zoe had known him for years professionally, and they had been good friends in medical school, when they'd gone to Stanford. They'd been inseparable for a while, and when they were young, Zoe had always suspected that Sam had a crush on her, but she'd been far too intent on her work to acknowledge it, and he'd never done anything about it. He moved to Chicago for his residency, and they had lost touch for a while, long enough for him to get married, and then divorced. And when he finally moved back to California, they eventually ran into each other again and resumed their old friendship. But it was nothing more than that now. They were buddies, and he loved doing relief work in her practice.

"How's it going here? I haven't heard from you in weeks." He popped his head around her office door as she put away her papers. He had the look of a large, cuddly teddy bear. He was tall and broad and warm, with ever tousled brown hair and big brown eyes, and no matter how hard he tried, he always looked rumpled. But Zoe knew he was brilliant with her patients. He was great with people of all ages and sizes, and he was the only relief doctor she trusted. "Don't you ever take a day off?" he asked, with a look of concern. His specialty was doing locum tenens for an interesting assortment of doctors. That meant he was a full-time "relief doctor," with no practice of his own. This was what he did for a living. And he particularly enjoyed Zoe's practice. She ran a tight ship, and he thought she was a truly great physician, working in a nearly impossible field at the moment.

"I try not to take time off," she said in answer to his question. "My patients don't like it." Although they liked Sam, she felt an obligation not to let them down or desert them. She did rounds at the hospital, and visited them in their homes sometimes, even on Sundays, and Sam knew that.

"You need to take time off," he scolded as he watched her take off her white coat and toss it in the laundry. "It's good for you, and besides," he grinned at her, "I need the money."

"I think I still owe you from last time, Sam. I've got a new bookkeeper and so far she's a disaster." She smiled at him, he was always incredibly patient about payment. She had learned in medical school that he was from a wealthy family in the East and had independent means, but he never said anything about it, and nothing about him suggested ostentation. He drove a battered old car, wore simple clothes, mostly work shirts and jeans, and he wore an ancient pair of boots that he obviously loved and looked as though they'd been worn by ten thousand cowboys.

"Anything new around here?" he asked. He liked keeping up to date on her practice, so he wasn't flying completely blind whenever she asked him to take over. And the only time she did was when she was sick, or had a special event to go to. But she hadn't gone out much lately. She'd been too tired at night, and incredibly busy in the daytime, and she was just as happy to stay home with her baby. And when she went out on a date, which she did occasionally, she wore her beeper and took her own calls, and sometimes, if she had to, she walked out of a play, or left dinner even before she'd touched it. It didn't make her a very exciting date, but it made her one hell of a good doctor.

"Nothing much new." She filled him in as she changed her shoes. "We seem to have a lot of new kids at the moment, young ones." They had contracted AIDS during gestation, from their mothers.

"I'll take a look around after you're gone." She never minded him looking at her files. She had no secrets from Sam. "Kiss Jade for me."

"Thanks." She smiled, and left the office. She took a quick look at her watch, it was one of those rare nights when she had a date, and knew she had to hurry. But it was already too late for that. It was six forty-five, and Richard Franklin was picking her up at seven-thirty. He was a well-known breast surgeon at UC, and they'd met two years before when they'd both been speaking at the same medical convention. And she'd been intrigued by the natural rivalry of their fields, he had been irked at the attention AIDS got in the press, citing the fact that more people died of breast cancer than AIDS, and the research funds should have been directed toward cancer. It had provided a lively argument for them, and a basis for an interesting friendship. And over the past two years, she'd gone out with him several times, especially lately. He was a brilliant man, and she enjoyed his company, and sometimes even more than that, but Richard Franklin was not the kind of man one fell in love with. There had been others in her life who had meant a great deal to her, but no one in a long time. The last man she had really cared about had died of AIDS from a blood transfusion ten years before, and that had been the beginning of her clinic when he left her all his money. There had been one or two special people since, but no one like him, and no one had ever made her want to get married. Certainly not Richard Franklin.

She drove home in her old Volkswagen van. She had bought it when she adopted Jade, and she often used it to help transport patients, and eventually she thought she'd use it for car pools. And she used it now to drive home as quickly as she could. She had bought a lovely old house on Edgewood, close to UC Hospital, near the forest. She went for walks in the woods there with Jade, and the view from her living room was spectacular. She had a clear view of the Golden Gate and the Marin Headlands. And as soon as she opened her front door, Jade let out a scream of excitement. "Mommy!" Zoe swept the little girl into her arms, and held her there, cuddling her, while Jade waved her arms and told her all about a dog and a rabbit and raisins and play group. It wasn't highly intelligible, but Zoe knew exactly what she was saying. "Babbit! Babbit!" she said, clapping her hands excitedly, and Zoe knew immediately that she had seen it at their neighbor's. "Mommy, Babbit!"

"I know. Maybe we'll get one, one of these days." She set the toddler down in the kitchen then, and took a bite of her dinner. It was hamburger and rice, prepared by the Danish au pair, Inge. It wasn't fabulous, but it was wholesome, and Jade was brandishing a handful of raw carrots she had gnawed on, as Zoe hurried upstairs to her bedroom. She wanted to change as quickly as she could, and then come back to spend a few minutes with Jade before she went out with Dick Franklin. This was exactly why she hated going out at night. It gave her absolutely no time with her daughter. But her outings and dates were rare, just as her days off were.

She came downstairs twenty minutes later in a long black velvet skirt and a white lace blouse, she looked like an old family portrait, and her long red hair had been brushed and rebraided. She wore it in a long braided tail down her back, just as she had in college.

"Pitty Mama!" the little girl said, clapping her hands again, and Zoe smiled as she pulled her onto her lap. She was incredibly tired.

"Thank you, Jade. How's my big girl today?" she asked, as the child snuggled close to her, and Zoe smiled as she held her. This was what life was all about, not excitement, not glamour, not even money or success, and certainly none of the things Tanya had talked to her about. The important things in life, as far as Zoe was concerned, were good health and children, and she never lost sight of their importance. She had no chance to, she had daily reminders in her office.

She and Jade played with some big pink Lego blocks for a little while, and then the doorbell rang. It was Richard Franklin. He looked very sleek and cool when he walked in. He was wearing gray slacks and a blazer, but she saw that he was wearing an expensive tie, and as usual, he looked as though he'd just had a haircut. Dr. Franklin always looked impeccable, and as though he was expecting to give a lecture to the hospital's most important donors. He knew his specialty perfectly, and it was impossible not to admire his knowledge, if not his bedside manner. He and Zoe had always been extremely different, but fascinated somehow with each other.

"And how are you tonight, Dr. Franklin?" she asked after the au pair let him in. She was crouched on the floor, still playing blocks with her daughter.

"I'm impressed," he said, managing to look both very handsome and extremely lofty. There had always been something very arrogant about him, and Zoe suspected that was what appealed to her, there was an irresistible desire to tame him. But until the present, in any case, she had controlled it. "Do you do that often?" He indicated the game she was playing with Jade, where she built a large pink house of Lego blocks, and Jade destroyed it.

"As often as I can," she said honestly, knowing full well that it made him uncomfortable. He had confessed to her long since that he felt uneasy around children. He had never had any of his own, and like her, he had never been married. He claimed that the opportunity had never presented itself to him at the right time, but she sensed fairly accurately that he was basically too self-centered. "Would you like to play?" she teased, she couldn't imagine him on his hands and knees on the floor, playing anything. He might mess up his hair, or uncrease his trousers. She knew that most of her contemporaries thought he was a stuffed shirt, and he was in a way, but he was so incredibly smart, and at fifty-five, he was extremely attractive. On the surface he was the kind of man her family would have liked her to marry years before, but her parents were long dead, and it seemed exotic enough to her just to date him.

"Are you ready?" he asked expectantly, not particularly amused to be watching her play with Jade. He had gotten tired of it in less than a minute. And their reservation at Boulevard was at eight, and it was quite a distance from Edgewood, and so popular they didn't like holding tables, even for important doctors.

"Ready, sir," she said, shrugging into a little velvet jacket. Even in June, it was cold at night in San Francisco, and she looked very pretty as she picked Jade up again and kissed her.

"I love you, little mouse," she said, rubbing noses with her, and then giving her a butterfly kiss on the cheek with her eyelashes as the little girl giggled. "I'll see you later." As she said the words, Jade's lower lip began to stick out, and Zoe could see instantly that tears were about to happen. She gave her quickly to the au pair, and waved just as Jade let out a wail, but by then they were out the door, and the au pair turned her around to distract her. In the past year, Zoe had become the master of the fast exit.

"You do that very well," he said admiringly. It was very unusual for him to go out with women with young children. Most of the time he preferred women who were too involved in their careers to marry or have kids, which was exactly what Zoe had been when he met her. And then she had stunned him by adopting a baby. It hadn't been at all what he'd expected of her, and it had somehow altered their relationship, but he still found her agonizingly attractive, and he would have liked to spend a lot more time with her. But she was too busy with her practice most of the time, and now with the child, so he did the best he could, and accepted crumbs from her table. "I haven't seen you in two weeks," he complained as he started his dark green Jaguar.

"I've been busy," she said simply. "I have a lot of very sick patients," she said matter-of-factly. She had lost several of late, and it had been very depressing for her because she always got so close to them, particularly in the end, when it was always so touching, and so pathetic.

"I have very sick patients too," he said, sounding mildly irritated, as he headed toward downtown, and through the Haight just below her.

"Yes, but you have partners."

"True. You ought to think about that some time. I don't see how you manage the way you do. You're going to get sick one of these days, a bad case of hepatitis, or worse yet, get AIDS from one of your patients."

"That's a pleasant thought," she said, looking away from him, out the window.

"It happens," he said seriously, "you should think about what you're doing. There's no point being a hero, or a martyr."

"I have thought about it, and this is where I belong. They need me, Dick."

"So does everyone else. So does your daughter. You need to take more time off." He was the second person who had told her that that night, and she glanced over at him, wondering why he had said it. He wasn't usually that solicitous, or that concerned. He wasn't much of a nurturer, although he was a doctor. "You look tired, Zoe," he said simply, and then he patted her hand with a smile. "A nice dinner out will do you good. You probably never eat either." She couldn't even remember if she'd had breakfast or lunch that day, she had hit the deck running the moment she got to the office. Most of her days were like that.

But when they got to the restaurant, she was inclined to agree with him. It was so pretty and well lit, and the table was so inviting that she was sorry she didn't see him more often. He ordered wine for both of them, and they decided to split the rack of lamb, and they ordered soufflé for dessert. It was certainly a far cry from the leftover hamburgers she ate at home off of Jade's plate, or the cold pizza she found in the fridge at the office.

"This is lovely," she said, looking grateful.

"I've missed you," he said simply, reaching out for her hand. But she wasn't in the mood for romance, and there was something about his arrogance that always kept her from falling for him, although she found him physically attractive. But, tonight, in spite of the candlelight and the wine, she was inclined to keep her distance.

"I've been busy," she said, explaining her two-week absence."

"Too much so. What about a weekend somewhere? I've rented a house at Stinson Beach for July and August. What about coming over for a weekend?"

She smiled at him then. She knew him better than he thought. "With Jade?" she asked, and he hesitated, and then nodded.

"If you prefer, but it might do you good to get away from her too."

"I'd miss her," she said, and then laughed at herself. "I'd probably be an awful guest right now, I'm so tired I'd probably sleep all weekend."

"I might think of ways to wake you," he said, looking alarmingly sensual as he raised his glass to her, and then sipped it.

"I believe you would, Dr. Franklin." She smiled at him again, and the evening sped by with talk of the hospital they both practiced in, the politics that were typical of all major teaching hospitals, and several intriguing rumors. They each talked about their specialties, and he described a new technique he had perfected which was already going into textbooks. He was good at what he did, and not particularly modest, but Zoe didn't mind it. It made for fascinating conversation, and she liked talking medicine with him. Although when she said as much to Sam from time to time, he accused her of being too single-minded, and said he hated going out to dinner with female doctors and discussing liver transplants over pasta. He thought she should expand her horizons, besides which, he couldn't stand Dick Franklin. He thought he was impossible and pompous.

Zoe and Dick both had cappuccino after the soufflé was gone, and it was almost eleven o'clock by then, and Zoe didn't want to admit it to him, but she was exhausted. It was all she could do to stay awake at the table. And she was planning to do rounds at seven o'clock the next morning, which meant she'd be up at five or five-thirty with Jade. She got up with her every morning, and played with her before she went to work. It was her favorite time of day with her baby.

But Dick didn't even seem to notice how tired she was when he took her home and reminded her again about the weekend in Stinson. "Let me know when it works for you," he said, with a warm look at her. "I'm at your disposal."

"I have to line up my relief doc first, and make sure the au pair can stay over on Sunday." Despite teasing him, she would never have inflicted Jade on him for an entire weekend. She would have driven him crazy, even though she was a good baby. But he wanted to listen to classical music, make love in the afternoon, and discuss surgical techniques with an equal, not change diapers, or wipe applesauce off a baby. And Zoe understood that. "I'll see when they're both free, and I'll call you." They were sitting in his car outside her house, he had wanted to take her to his place first, in Pacific Heights, but he could see as they drove across town that she was already yawning, and she apologized for being such bad company, as he drove past his place toward Edgewood.

"The trouble is you're not," he said gently, looking longingly up at her house, but he wasn't sure about tackling the child and the au pair, and he knew Zoe preferred to go to his place. "Every time I see you, I want to spend more time with you, and you're always too busy." He understood that about her life though. He himself had a busy schedule with an enormous number of patients to see, he was considered the preeminent breast surgeon at UC, and he still managed to lecture all over the country.

"Maybe that's what keeps things interesting," Zoe said, smiling at him, as she sat in the comfortable car, watching him. He was incredibly smooth and good-looking, and yet, although she enjoyed his company a great deal, she knew she could never love him. "Maybe if we spent more time together, I'd bore you."

But he laughed at her when she said it. "I don't think that's very likely." She was one of his favorite women, and she tantalized him in some ways, as she did now. She managed to be both vulnerable and unattainable, both powerful and gentle, and the contrasts excited him more than he cared to tell her. "I don't suppose I can talk you into shocking your household tonight, can I?" he asked hopefully, and she shook her head slowly. She never did that. Not with the au pair and the baby around, and she wasn't going to start that, even for Dr. Franklin.

"I'm afraid not, Dick. I'm sorry."

"I'm not surprised," he smiled good-naturedly, "only disappointed. Well, go look at your calendar and pick a date for a weekend. Soon, please."

"Yes, sir." He walked her upstairs, and opened the door for her with her key, and kissed her chastely on the lips. There was no point getting anything started that they couldn't finish, as far as he was concerned. And he was a patient man, he could wait a week or two to see her again, although he would have preferred to make love to her that evening. But he was willing to accept her limitations. She thanked him for dinner, and he left, and the moment he was gone, she hurried to her bedroom, took off her clothes, and slipped into bed without even putting on her nightgown or brushing her teeth. She was too tired to do anything but sleep, and she lay dead to the world until six o'clock the next morning.

Jade was already awake when she went in to check on her, and playing happily with the toys the au pair had left in her crib the night before for exactly that purpose. She was alternately talking to herself and singing softly, but she stood up and squealed when she saw her mother.

"Hi there, monkey face," Zoe said as she picked her up and took her to change her diaper. But she noticed as she did that Jade seemed heavier than usual, and Zoe was still tired after a night's sleep. That was happening more and more lately, and it reminded her to call the lab when she got into the office.

She left the house at six forty-five, and was at UC Hospital to do rounds at seven, and in her office at eight-thirty, and there were already two dozen patients waiting for her. It was one of the busiest days she'd had in months, and she didn't have time to call the lab till lunchtime. And when she did, they didn't have the results for her, and for once she lost her temper.

"We've waited two weeks for this, dammit. It's not fair to keep people waiting that long," she complained. "These are life-and-death situations, we're not talking about a urinalysis here, for chrissake. How soon can I have it?" They apologized for being backlogged and promised her that if she called back at four o'clock she'd have the results, but she didn't get a chance to stop again until five-thirty, and she still had patients waiting for her. But she wanted the results before the close of business, so she called them. They fumbled around for a while, while she fumed, and pushed several messages around her desk, and then they came back on the line and told her.

"Positive," the lab tech said matter-of-factly. It was no big surprise. Her patients tested positive for the AIDS virus all the time. That was why they came to see her.

"Positive?" she said, as though she'd never heard it before. *"Positive?"* She could feel the planet spinning.

"That's what I said," he said easily. "Is it a surprise this time?" The trouble was, it wasn't. It explained how tired she had been, how exhausted, the weight she had lost, the diarrhea she had had from time to time, and the symptoms that had been troubling her for six months, since Christmas. The results were her own this time, and she knew exactly when it had happened. She had stuck herself with a dirty needle by accident, nearly a year before, when she was doing a blood test on a little girl who had died of AIDS two months ago, in April.

She thanked the lab tech for the results, and hung up the

phone ever so quietly, feeling as though the world had just come to an end, just as her patients did when she told them. There had been nothing subtle about it, nothing gentle about what he said. "Positive" . . . positive . . . she had AIDS . . . What would she do with Jade? . . . How was she going to work? Who would take care of her when she got sick? . . . What was she going to do now? And as she contemplated the enormity of it, she was overwhelmed by the intensity of her feelings. She had had denial about it at first, but she had suspected it for weeks, when she had gotten a funny sore on her lip. It had disappeared fairly rapidly, but her suspicions didn't. Her own medical background had finally forced her to face it, and at least get tested. It was exactly what she dealt with, with her patients. But her concerns had been vivid enough to make her avoid Dick Franklin for the last few weeks, although she had always been extremely careful with him. Ever since her lover had died of AIDS ten years before, she had always exercised every precaution, and warned the men in her life about him. She had told Dick, and they had both been unfailingly cautious. She had never exposed him to any risk. But if she were to continue seeing him now, she would tell him, just so he'd know what she had to contend with. But she had no desire to see him, or tell him. She couldn't imagine him taking care of her or even being very sympathetic. He had even warned her of the risks she was taking, with her kind of practice. It had happened to other doctors before, just as it had to her. And he didn't think the dangers were worth it.

He was a scientist, and they were good friends certainly, but he wasn't the kind of person you went to with a problem. He was the kind of man you went out with for a nice evening. But she was sure he'd be appalled, if she told him. And she knew, without even thinking about it, that their dating career had just ended. So had a lot of things, maybe not her medical career for now, but certainly her future. She had an overwhelming urge to burst into tears, but she knew she couldn't, she still had to see patients. But suddenly, she could hardly think straight.

"Anyone home?" Sam Warner popped his head around her door again, and looked startled when he saw her expression. She looked as though someone had just shot her out of a cannon. And they had. A big one. "Are you okay? You look awful," he said bluntly.

"I think I'm coming down with something," she said vaguely, groping for an excuse to explain her complete discomposure. "A cold, a flu . . . something."

"Then you shouldn't be here," he said firmly. "I'm not hustling you for work, but your patients can't afford to catch anything from you, and you know it."

"I'll wear a mask," she said, fumbling in her desk with trembling fingers, and he saw how badly her hands shook when she tried unsuccessfully to tie it. But he didn't say anything. He just looked worried. "I . . . really . . . I'm fine . . . I just . . . I have a headache . . ."

"You're a mess," he said, taking the stethoscope from around her neck and putting it on the table. "Go home. I'll see the rest of your patients, and I won't charge you. It's a gift from me. Some people just don't know when to quit." He wagged a finger at her and almost pushed her out the door, but she didn't refuse him. Suddenly she couldn't think, she couldn't breathe, she couldn't believe what she'd heard. She had AIDS . . . AIDS . . . the killer that all her patients died of . . . her life was over. It wasn't, of course, she could live for years with the proper care, and she knew that. But she had the virus in her blood, waiting there, like a sniper or a time bomb. "Go home," Sam was saying to her, "get into bed, and stay there. I'll come by and check on you later."

"You don't have to, I'm fine. And thank you for finishing up for me." He was a great guy and she was deeply fond of him. He was so incredibly kind and gentle with her dying patients. She wondered if she should tell him what had happened, it made perfect sense to tell him, but she didn't want anyone to know. Not yet. Not until she had to. Not Sam. Not her friends. No one. Not even her nurses. Except Dick Franklin, of course, she knew she'd have to tell him she was infected with the AIDS virus, although she had been scrupulously careful, and knew there had been no risk to him. But purely ethically, she wanted to tell him, although she had no intention of sleeping with him again. But there was no one else she wanted to share her bad news with. As she did with everything else, she kept it to herself. Zoe Phillips did not cry on anyone's shoulder.

But Zoe cried all the way home, in the old Volkswagen van, and when she reached her house, she looked almost as ravaged as she felt. The au pair looked shocked when she walked in, and even Jade stared at her for a moment. "Mommy sad?" she asked, looking worried.

"Mommy loves you," she said, holding her close, thinking that she would have to be very careful not to cut herself, or go anywhere near Jade if she did. She wondered if she should wear a mask and gloves in the house now, and then realized she was being ridiculous and panic was settling in. She was a doctor, she knew better than that. But this was so different. It was her life. It was hard to be rational and objective.

She took Sam's advice and went to bed, and Jade crawled in with her, and Zoe lay there for a long time, holding her little girl. It was as though the child sensed that something was terribly wrong, and she might lose her mother somehow. It wasn't that she "might," it was that she would one day, Zoe reminded herself, the question was when, not if, as it was for anyone with the AIDS virus. But in Zoe's case, because of how she'd contracted it, it would be sooner rather than later, and she panicked again at the realization that she had no one to leave Jade with when she died. She'd have to think it over before too long, and decisions had to be made.

An hour later, Inge came in to tell her that Dr. Franklin was on the phone. Zoe hesitated for a moment, and then shook her head. She asked Inge to tell him that she was out, and when Inge returned, she gave Zoe a number at Stinson Beach. But she didn't want to talk to him on the phone, she had already decided to send him a note. It would be easier to tell him in writing. Her conscience was clear because she had been scrupulously careful, she always was, and she knew she hadn't exposed him to any risk. But she still felt she had to tell him, she only hoped that she could trust him, and that he wouldn't spread the word. The medical community was so small and gossipy, she just didn't want anyone to know yet, although eventually, she supposed, once she got very sick, the news would get around. But if she was lucky that might not be for a very long time. And in the meantime, she didn't want Dick Franklin filling everyone in. She didn't want her colleagues talking and gossiping about her. It wasn't anyone's business that she had AIDS. But despite the fact that she didn't feel close to Dick, she felt she had no choice but to tell him the truth. And in fact, wanting to get it off her chest, she wrote a brief letter to him that afternoon. It said only what it had to, that she had tested positive, and she felt he ought to know, but she reminded him that they had never taken any risks. She also told him that she needed to be on her own for a while, and she felt that it was best now if they both moved on. She let him very gently, and very graciously, off the hook, and reading her note again, she wondered if he'd even call her after he got it. Dick Franklin was interesting and intelligent, but he had never been particularly warm. She couldn't imagine him offering her any comfort, or even calling to see how she was, let alone wanting to know if he could help her with Jade. Dick was strictly a dinner partner, a companion for the theater or the opera, or an adult weekend, he was a person for good times, and not bad. But she had no expectations of him. All she wanted from him was that he not tell everyone at UC. It seemed very little to ask of him.

After she wrote the letter to him, Zoe went back to bed, and cuddled with her daughter again. And after a little while, Inge came to take Jade away and give her dinner, and she looked at her employer worriedly. She had never seen Zoe look so lifeless or so distressed, and Zoe had never felt as devastated as she did now, except perhaps when her friend died. She didn't feel ill, she felt terrified, all she wanted to do was run and hide and put the covers over her head, and cling to someone, but there was no one there to hold on to.

She didn't bother to turn on the lights and it was still light outside, although it was twilight. And she could hear Jade playing in the next room with Inge, as the au pair fed her dinner. And at the comforting sounds, Zoe drifted off to sleep, and she slept until she heard someone speaking to her, and she looked up in surprise to see Sam Warner. He was standing next to her, and feeling her neck for a fever.

"How do you feel?" he asked softly, and she had never been as grateful to him as she was at that moment. She could see why her patients loved him. He had a good heart, and a gentle manner. Sometimes that was more important than being a doctor.

"I'm okay," she said honestly. And she was, for the moment, but she was so scared she almost felt ill, and she was angry at herself for being so pathetic.

"No, you're not," he said bluntly. He sat down on her bed carefully and looked at her, checking her eyes and her color without ever touching her, and he was puzzled. "You're not feverish, but you look like shit." She looked terribly upset more than anything, and then he had a thought, and he decided to ask her. "Could you be pregnant?" She smiled in answer, would that it were that simple, or that happy.

"I'm afraid not," she said sadly, "but it's a sweet thought. I almost wish I were."

"I'd be happy to help out if that would cheer you up." She laughed and he reached out and took her hand. "Zoe, I know this sounds like I'm looking for work, but I'm not." She smiled at him, knowing how busy he was already doing locum tenens for other doctors. There were a lot of doctors who asked him to cover for them, he didn't need her business. "Kiddo, you need a break. I don't know what's bothering you," he was beginning to think it was emotional rather than physical, but it was obvious to him she needed some time off, "but I think you need some time away from work. You can't give four hundred percent of yourself all the time, and not have it take a toll eventually. Why don't you try and get away?" She thought of Dick Franklin's invitation to Stinson the night before, but that was inappropriate now, and besides, she didn't want to. But she also understood what Sam was saying. She needed to do something for herself. And if she was going to have to fight for her life, she was also going to have to try and prolong it. And maybe now that meant taking some time off and building her strength up.

"I'll think about it."

"No, you won't. I know you. You'll be back doing rounds at seven o'clock tomorrow morning. Why don't you at least let me do that for you for a few days, and you can arrive at the office like a civilized person at nine o'clock." The offer was very tempting, and she wasn't sure what to say to him. If nothing else, she would have been grateful for just one night off to sleep and think and get her bearings.

"Would you cover for me tonight and tomorrow morning?" she asked, feeling exhausted again. She wasn't sure if it was due to the disease she was carrying, or if she was just emotionally drained by the confirmation that she had it.

"I'll do anything you want," he said kindly, as Zoe's heart went out to him, and she was tempted to tell him what she had just found out. But she didn't want to tell anyone at this point, not even Sam. Later, she would need him. Eventually, she would have to cut down her practice, maybe he would even come in with her for a while, but it was still too soon to ask him, and it depressed her to have to think about it.

"I really appreciate this," she said softly as he stood up.

"Just shut up and get some sleep. I'll call the service for you. You'll probably feel great when you wake up tomorrow, but I don't want to see you at the hospital. And come to think of it, why don't you come in around ten?"

"You're going to make me lazy, Sam," she said, lying back against her pillows, as he stopped in the doorway.

"I don't think anyone could do that." He smiled across the room at her. There was a lot he would have liked to say to her, about respect and friendship, and the kind of working relationship they shared, but he never seemed to find the opportunities to tell her. He had wanted to ask her out ever since he came back to San Francisco, but she always kept her distance. And he'd seen her out once or twice with the illustrious Dick Franklin. He didn't think it was serious between them, but he also didn't think it was appropriate to ask. Despite the longevity of their friendship, she was extremely private about her life. Yet it was hard for him not to respond to her warmth and compassion. He admired her more than he could ever tell her, and he would have done anything for her.

"Thanks, Sam," she said, and he waved and closed the door behind him. She lay in bed, lost in her own thoughts after that, for a long time. There was so much to think about, her practice, her daughter, her health, their future. It was all racing through her head, and as she closed her eyes again, it all seemed like a blur. And then suddenly, as she lay there, she thought of Tanya. It was exactly the kind of thing she would have recommended for one of her patients, and as she thought about it again, she decided to take her own good advice and call her.

She looked in her address book and dialed the number. She knew it was a private line, somewhere in Tanya's house. For a minute, Zoe thought she wasn't there, and then she answered on the fourth ring. She sounded out of breath and there was music in the background. She was alone at that hour, and she had been outside doing exercises by the pool.

"Hello?" She sounded exactly the way she had in college, it was odd how some things about them had never changed, and others had far too much.

"Tanny?" Zoe's voice was soft and tired and vulnerable as she reached out to her, and for a moment she wanted to melt into her arms and dissolve in tears. But she forced herself to be strong as she spoke to her, and Tanya never suspected how distressed Zoe was, or that she had a problem.

"I didn't think I'd hear from you so soon." Tanya sounded surprised but pleased to hear her. They had talked to each other only the day before, after two long years, and it surprised her to get another call so soon from Zoe. "What's up?"

"Something crazy happened today." Something very crazy, in fact, but she didn't say that. "There's a doctor who does relief for me sometimes. He's kicking me out of my office for a few days. He says he needs the work."

"Are you serious?" Tanya still sounded startled, she still didn't understand why Zoe had called her.

"I am . . . and I was thinking . . . the trip you talked about . . . Wyoming . . . I don't suppose . . . I wouldn't want to intrude or anything . . . are you going with anyone? I just thought . . ." Tanya understood the reason for her call then, and it was the perfect opportunity for them to be together. But she knew that if Zoe knew Mary Stuart was joining them, she probably wouldn't come. There was plenty of time to explain it to them once they got there, and Tanya was sure that if they made it that far, everything would be all right at long last between them.

"No, I'm going alone," she lied. She quickly gave her all the details and suggested she fly directly to Jackson Hole. If Zoe came to L.A. to drive to Wyoming with them, Tanya didn't want to take a chance on Mary Stuart's refusing to get on the bus with them. She was sure that once they were at the ranch, it would be a wonderful reunion. But before they got there, she didn't want to give either of them a chance to back out.

"I can only come for a week though," Zoe said firmly. She was already panicking at the thought of leaving her practice. But it was the kind of thing she was going to have to do now, if she wanted to maintain her health. But in any case, a week was long enough.

"That's fine. Maybe we'll talk you into the second week once you get there," Tanya said happily. She couldn't think of anything nicer than a vacation with her two oldest friends from college.

"You're not bringing a date, are you?" Zoe asked, having heard the first person plural, but when Tanya said she wasn't, she figured the *we* was just a figure of speech. It never even occurred to her that Tanya had invited Mary Stuart.

"What about your baby?" Tanya asked her candidly. She would have made adjustments either way. And Zoe thought about it for a long moment and then shook her head slowly.

"I don't think so, Tan. She's really too little. She won't enjoy it at her age, and it might do me good to really get away for a change." Although in some ways, Zoe hated to do it. She was reluctant to leave the baby and her patients.

"You're all right though, right?" There was something in Zoe's voice that worried Tanya, but it was nothing she could put her finger on, and Zoe kept insisting that there was no problem. But there was something in the way she sounded that Tanya vaguely remembered, something about her voice that was reminiscent of when Zoe was in trouble or distraught over something years before, like Ellie. But it had been so long since they'd seen each other that Tanya didn't dare press her, or accuse her of lying.

"I'm fine," Zoe reassured her. "And I can't wait to see you." She was a good rider, a good friend, and with any luck at all, Tanya thought, by the first night, Zoe and Mary Stuart would have made peace with each other, and they'd all be together again, just like old times.

"See you at the ranch," Tanya said as she signed off. She was so happy that Zoe had called her.

"See you then." Zoe smiled, and rolled over on her side in bed and hung up. It was so unlike her to drop everything and leave her practice, and yet she knew she had to do it. She was going to do everything she could now to prolong her life. It had been precious to her before, but with little Jade to think about, it was even more precious now. And knowing what she'd have to fight eventually, the trip to Wyoming became suddenly very important.

CHAPTER 9

Sam worked with Zoe for several hours the following week, to acquaint himself with her current patients. There were a number of them he knew from covering for her on the odd night, here and there. But when he read all the current files of her most acutely ill patients, he was stunned by how many she handled. She had roughly fifty terminally ill patients, and there were more arriving on her doorstep every day, and sometimes every night.

They were brought in by friends, or relatives, or just simply people who had heard about what she was doing. They were all very sick, some who had AIDS, and others who didn't. She took care of all of them, and Sam was particularly touched by the children. There were so many little ones with AIDS. It made you grateful for every healthy child you'd ever seen. Sam knew why Zoe was particularly appreciative of Jade. She was a truly remarkable baby, and wonderfully healthy.

"I can't believe the number of patients you see every day," Sam commented late one afternoon, "it's inhuman. No wonder you're tired all the time.'' It would have been so easy then to just tell him she had AIDS. But it wasn't his problem, or his business. She had already decided she wasn't going to make it anyone's burden but her own, for as long as she could do it. She was planning to save money for herself to put aside for medical care and treatment, for nursing care if it ever came to that. The only real problem she had was Jade, and what to do with her when she died. It seemed awful to be thinking like that, but Zoe knew she had to. Part of her was still resisting it, but another part had already accepted her fate. It seemed an incredible end to a bright career, and if she let herself, she could dwell on her bad luck and ill fate, but she really didn't want to do that. She just wanted to enjoy whatever time she had. And she knew she might have years, even a decade, it didn't happen often, but it happened to some that way, and she was going to do everything she could to ensure that it happened to her. The trip to Wyoming was part of that, the rest, the scenery, the altitude, the air, along with the comfort of seeing her old friend Tanya.

''What about this one?'' Sam interrupted her reverie to hold out a file to her. It belonged to an extremely sick young man. He had already entered the last stages of AIDS dementia, and Zoe doubted that he would last much longer. He had put up a valiant fight for months, and there wasn't much she could do now, except make him comfortable, and console his lover. She visited him every day. She explained it all to Sam and he shook his head. Hers was the most unorthodox of all the practices he worked for, but it was also the most creative in terms of treatment, and he was deeply moved by her compassion. She seemed to leave no stone unturned in seeking out new antibiotics, medications, ways of treating infection and pain, and even unusual holistic treatments. She did anything she could to beat the disease, right till the bitter end, and to comfort the patient.

''One of these days we'll get lucky,'' she said sadly. But not soon enough for all of them. Or even for herself now.

"I think they got lucky when they found you," he said, looking at her with ever increasing admiration. He had always liked her so much, and he liked her even more now. She was everything a physician should be, and most weren't accessible personally but she was. He wondered if it had anything to do with the lover who had died of AIDS years before. He wondered if she had loved anyone since then, and guessed that she hadn't. Surely not Dick Franklin. Sam would have liked to be closer to her. She had always been very open with him, and very friendly, but he never felt there was any interest on her part in being more than friends and business associates and collaborating physicians.

And particularly lately she felt she couldn't allow herself to be close to anyone. She was very careful to put a safe distance between herself and the rest of the world, even Sam, whom she had known since med school. She didn't want to mislead him or anyone, to lead them on, or provide a come-on. She wanted to make it clear to everyone that she was not available as a woman, only as a doctor. It seemed the only fair way to handle her situation. She had even thought about buying herself a cheap wedding band, and she forced herself not to think of the lonely path she was taking.

But as they worked on the last of the files, Sam glanced at her again and wondered if he could ask her out to dinner. There was still plenty to talk about, and he was in no hurry to go home. "Can I talk you into something to eat while we finish up? I thought we could go out for pasta in the neighborhood or something. Any interest?" he asked, nearly holding his breath and feeling stupid for it. She made him feel like a kid sometimes, and he liked that. He liked everything about her. He always had. And over the years, he had come to admire her more, and like her better.

"That sounds fine," she said with no clue at all that he found her even remotely attractive. She had wanted to take him out anyway, to thank him for giving her the opportunity to leave town and have a real vacation. She felt a little guilty leaving Jade, but he had promised he'd keep an eye on her too, and stop in and see her and the au pair when he left the office.

"You're really a full-service on-call doctor," she teased as she slid into the booth in a little Italian restaurant in the Upper Haight. She had come here for years, and she liked it. It was quiet, and the food was good, and it was the first time she and Sam had sat down and talked to each other over dinner since med school. They laughed about how long it had been. Although their paths had crossed regularly over the past eighteen years, they'd never really had time alone together, they were always working.

They both ordered ravioli, and he offered her wine but she refused, and then they settled down to talk about work again. They were halfway through dinner when he looked at her with his boyish grin, and something warm and friendly in his eyes that made her feel surprisingly easy with him, more than ever.

"Don't you do anything but work?" he asked gently. He admired her, but he felt sorry for her too. She did so much for so many people, and he knew firsthand how draining it was. But there didn't seem to be anyone to do anything for her. And he couldn't imagine her deriving any real comfort from her relationship with Dick Franklin, or anyone like him.

"Not lately," she answered him, "except for Jade." And then he wondered about something.

"Have you ever been married?" He didn't think so, and he realized he'd been right when she shook her head.

"Never." She didn't seem in the least bothered about it. She was comfortable with her life, and happy with her daughter. Her life seemed enormously fulfilling.

But Sam was curious about it. "Why not? If you don't mind my asking."

She smiled. She didn't mind at all. Except for her illness, she had no secrets from him. "I never really wanted to, when I was young. And the only man I probably should have married died over ten years ago. He contracted AIDS from a transfusion. Thanks to him, I started the clinic. He was in research and he was brilliant. He had bypass surgery at forty-two, and eventually it killed him. He didn't live a year after the transfusion. I thought about going into research with him. I'd always been intrigued with unsolved mysteries, and remote diseases. And then AIDS came along, and I got caught up in the physical-care end of it and not the research."

"It would have been a real loss to a lot of people if you'd done something different," he said gently, and he meant it. She was a fantastic physician. He knew about the doctor who'd died too, but he'd heard about him from other people. And he watched her as she told him. She looked sad, but not devastated, and he sensed that she'd recovered, although she'd obviously never found anyone who meant as much to her. "Before AIDS, I was fairly involved in juvenile diabetes. In its own way, that's another scourge like this one, although it gets a lot less attention."

"I've always been interested in it too. And I guess I'm a scavenger of sorts, I love visiting other people's practices, picking up little bits and pieces of information, and solving problems, doing what I can, and then moving on. It probably sounds irresponsible, but I've never wanted my own practice. That just seems like a lot of paperwork and red tape, and issues that have nothing to do with medicine or patients. I like doing hands-on work, I don't want to waste time with contracts and insurance and worrying about property, and all the politics established doctors get involved with. Maybe I just haven't grown up yet. I keep waiting for it to happen, I keep thinking that one of these days I'll want to associate with a group of docs and join their office, but I never do. What I see of most of them turns me off completely, except on a rotating basis, the way I do it with you. This way, I get to do all the good stuff."

She smiled at what he said. It was a little bit like the philosophy of emergency room doctors. They wanted to deal with the patients and not the paper or the overhead or the problems. But in her case she would have missed the long-term relationships she developed. "You remind me a little of the Lone Ranger," she said, smiling, ". . . who was that masked man, Tonto? . . . My patients love you. You do a great job. And I can't really blame you for avoiding all the crap that goes with an ordinary practice. I've really missed not having partners, it's so much more work like this. But I also like not having the headaches, the arguments, the petty jealousies, and all the problems. When Adam died, he made it possible to set up the kind of clinic I wanted, and do it exactly the way I thought it should be. But it's still awfully hard not having adequate help, except on occasion." She smiled at him again, and he found himself wondering again how involved she was with Dick Franklin, but he was afraid to ask her.

"Were you planning to marry Adam before he got sick?" He was curious about her, about them, about the baby she'd adopted and why, and why she seemed so comfortable alone. She was an intriguing woman.

"Not really. I think we might have eventually, but we didn't talk about it. He'd been married, and he had kids. And I was busy building up my practice as an internist. I was in a practice with two other docs then, but I left it when I set up the clinic. I never felt compelled to be married, or even to be with anyone indefinitely. We saw each other a lot, and we were very close, but we didn't live together actually until he was dying. I took three months off work and took care of him. It was very sad," but she looked as though she had made her peace with it. She was serious, but not grieving. It had been a long time since he'd died and a lot had happened in the meantime. She still saw his children from time to time, but she hadn't been close to them, it was only after Jade was born that she actually understood the extraordinary joy of having children. He asked her about that too, and she told him how it had come about. Jade's mother had been nineteen years old, unmarried, and had no desire to keep the baby. And her family had refused to take her in when they discovered that the baby was Asian.

"She's the greatest thing that ever happened to me," Zoe

said simply. And then she turned the tables on him. "What about you?" She knew he'd been married briefly in Chicago. "What happened with your marriage?" They had lost track of each other during their residencies, and by the time he came back to San Francisco, his marriage was behind him and he said very little about it, and it was rare for Sam and Zoe to take a night off, just to talk, like this.

"The marriage lasted for two miserable years, while I was doing my residency," he explained, looking thoughtful. "Poor kid, I never saw her. You know what that's like. She hated it. She said she'd never get involved with another doctor. But she was genetically doomed. Her father was a big thoracic surgeon in Grosse Pointe, her brother is a sports doctor in Chicago, and after me she wound up marrying a plastic surgeon. She has three kids and lives in Milwaukee, and I think she's very happy. I haven't seen her in years. And when I first came back to California, I lived with a woman for several years, but neither of us ever had any interest in getting married. We'd both had bad experiences before, and neither of us was ready. You remind me a little bit of her actually. She's kind of a saint like you. She had a real need to make a difference, and she was always pressuring me about it. In the end, she did what she had to do, and I stayed behind. She's a nurse-practitioner in a leper colony in Botswana." Zoe vaguely remembered hearing about her, but it was before Sam had done locum tenens for her, and Zoe had never met her.

"Wow! That's serious." Zoe looked at him, fascinated by what she was hearing. "And she couldn't talk you into joining her?" Zoe thought it sounded vaguely appealing, but Sam clearly didn't, as he shook his head, with a look of horror.

"Not on your life." He grinned. "No matter how much I loved her. I hate snakes, I hate bugs, I was never in the Boy Scouts, and I think camping trips and sleeping bags are sheer torture. I was definitely not cut out for a life serving mankind in the jungle. I like my nice comfortable bed at night, a good meal, a warm restaurant, a glass of wine, and the wildest vegetation I want to see is in Golden Gate Park on a weekend. Rachel comes over here about once a year, and I'm still crazy about her, but we're just friends now. She lives with the head of the leper colony, and they have a baby. She loves Africa and she says I don't know what I'm missing."

"By not having children, or by living here?" Zoe was laughing, but it was quite a story.

"Both. She says she'll never leave Africa. But you never know. The politics over there get pretty scary. It's definitely not for me. She's a great gal, and she did the right thing. She left five years ago, and I don't know, the time has just flown. I'm forty-six years old and I guess I've just forgotten to get married."

"Me too," she laughed at him, "my parents used to go crazy over it. They both died in the last few years, so there's no one to bug me about it anymore." And now she knew she certainly wouldn't be getting married. But talking about his own life suddenly made Sam feel braver.

"What about Dr. Franklin?" He felt nervous asking her, but he was curious. And she definitely didn't put out vibes that said she was open to invitations. He wanted to know if it was because of Dick Franklin, or if there were other reasons, maybe even someone else he didn't know about. It was hard to believe that a woman like Zoe only cared about her practice and her baby.

"What about Dick?" Zoe asked, looking puzzled. "We're good friends, that's all. He's an interesting man," she said kindly, but Sam was looking into her eyes for deeper meaning.

"You don't give much away, do you?" he said, and she laughed at him.

"What exactly do you want to know, Dr. Warner? How serious is it? It isn't. As a matter of fact, I'm not seeing him anymore. I'm not seeing anyone, and that's the way I intend to keep it." There was something very firm about her voice as she said it that startled him. He couldn't figure out what she was saying. But there was a message there for anyone who chose to listen.

"Are you planning to go into a convent sometime soon?" he teased. "Or are you just going to freelance?" Looking at him, she suddenly had to laugh at herself. This was very new to her, and she realized she could have learned a lot from her patients. How did they manage it? What did they say? She knew that many of them told people they had AIDS before they began relationships, but she didn't want to do that either. She just wanted to keep to herself, and enjoy her life with Jade. It would have been different if there had been someone in her life when it happened, but since there wasn't, as far as she was concerned, the doors were closed now.

"I don't have time for a relationship," she said simply, and he looked startled. The way she said it sounded so final, and seemed so unlike her. She was such a warm person, and it was such a waste to think of a woman like Zoe without a man in her life. It really bothered Sam.

"Are you telling me you've made a conscious decision to that effect, at your age?" He looked horrified by the prospect.

"More or less." She was referring to the decision she'd made, but she didn't want to get into it with him, and they were getting onto dangerous ground, which she didn't want to happen. But he was ready to pursue the subject with her with dogged determination. "I can't give anything to anyone, Sam, I'm too involved in my practice, and with my daughter." It was an excuse, but Sam felt certain that she meant it.

"Zoe, that's bullshit," he said firmly, "you're wrong if you think you can't give anything to anyone. There's more to life than just devoting yourself to your work and your baby." He wondered why she was so determined to stay alone, if she was still mourning her old flame, though he doubted it, since he knew she'd gone out with Dick Franklin. But why wouldn't she get involved with anyone? Why was she hiding? She couldn't be that obsessed with her child and her work, or was she? "You're too young to close the doors on a relationship in your life. Zoe,'' he said firmly, ''you have to rethink this.'' He felt a sense of personal loss as he looked at her and realized that she meant it.

She smiled at him, but she was unmoved by what he had said so far. ''You sound like my father. He used to tell me that overeducated women threaten men, and I was making a big mistake when I went to Stanford. College was okay, but medical school was pushing. He said that if I'd wanted to be in medicine, I should have gone to nursing school and saved him a lot of money.'' She was laughing as she said it, and Sam shook his head. He knew about people like her. His whole family were doctors, including his mother.

''Well, you should have gone to nursing school, if becoming a doctor was going to make you come to a dumb decision like that one. Zoe, that's just plain stupid.'' He wondered if she'd had a bad experience, been raped perhaps, or if Franklin had actually done something to upset her and it was still fresh, or maybe she was involved with someone secretly, maybe someone married. Or maybe she was just telling him, nicely, that she wasn't interested in him, but he hoped that wasn't the case either. Otherwise he just couldn't understand it, but she seemed very firm about it.

She turned the conversation then to other things, which frustrated him even more. He found that they had even more in common than he'd previously thought, people, plans, their shared views about medicine, and passion for all it represented. Worse yet, he realized that he was even more attracted to her than he'd previously suspected. She had a great sense of humor, and a quick mind. She had traveled extensively, and there was something wonderfully honest and genuine about her. She told things the way they were, analyzed situations very astutely, and as she talked about her patients to him, it was obvious how much she loved them. She was the first woman he had met in a long time that he was really crazy about and wanted desperately to go out with. He had been attracted to her for years, but he had always hesitated to do anything about it, and having dinner with her and talking to her about a variety of things had infatuated him with her completely. And she was even more tantalizing because she was so insistent that she had given up on having any relationship and she wouldn't even discuss it with him. He felt sure there was another reason, most likely an affair with someone she was protecting, and the more he thought about it, the more he wondered if it was someone married. But as far as he was concerned, she could have said that. In fact, everything in her life pointed to it, the fact that she had so much time available to spend on her work, that she had no desire to get married, she was obviously involved and didn't want to admit it. And he was very sorry to know that.

And as Zoe watched him as they ate, and afterward as they sat and drank cappuccino, she found that she liked him too. He was exactly what he had always seemed, a real teddy bear of a man, someone intelligent and kind, someone you could really count on. And he was as enamored as she was with her clinic. He thought it had been an incredible thing to do, an enormous undertaking, and he admired her a great deal for it.

"I think of all the practices I've seen, yours is the one I most enjoy, and most respect. I really like the way you handle your patients, particularly the home care."

"That was the hardest part to set up actually, to find the right people that you could trust without monitoring them constantly. I watch them very closely, but they still have a lot of leeway. The patients take a lot of responsibility too, though." Many of her patients' lovers and families cared for them almost without professional assistance, until the very end when they were assisted by hospice groups. Dying of AIDS was not an easy business.

They talked again for a while then of what she wanted him to do while she was gone, and he smiled as he listened to her. He knew it was going to be hard for her to leave them, and he tried to reassure her that her patients would be in good hands with him, and she believed him.

"So tell me about Wyoming," he asked genially over their second cup of cappuccino. But he noticed when it came that Zoe was looking exhausted. He had noticed several times recently how tired she looked, but he didn't think much about it. Her practice was so draining that it wasn't surprising she was pale, and it was only tonight that he also noticed a certain gauntness to her figure. She was obviously in serious need of a vacation, and he was glad for her that she was going. "Who are you going to Wyoming with? You're not going camping, are you?" he asked, wishing for an insane moment that he were going with her.

She laughed at his question. "I don't think so. I'm actually going with an old friend, from college. She's an incredible woman, and I haven't seen her in a while, but she called the other day and invited me. At first, I turned her down, but when I felt so lousy, I decided to do it. But believe me, knowing my friend, it won't be camping. She's even more spoiled than I am." Zoe was not a camping aficionado either, and never had been. Like Sam, she didn't like bugs, snakes, or creepy-crawlies. "She lives in L.A., and I'm sure we're going to the Hollywood ranch of all time, if she could find one."

"Who is she?" he asked casually as the check came, and he opened his wallet. "Is she a physician?"

Zoe smiled before she answered. "Not exactly. She's a singer. We've been friends since school, and she's never changed, not that anyone would believe it. The media give her a bad break, it's really not fair." She looked thoughtful as she said it. "I almost hate telling people who she is, they immediately leap to a million inaccurate conclusions."

"I'm fascinated," he said, looking straight at Zoe as the waitress took the check away with his money. He was so intrigued by her, by the deep green eyes, and everything he saw there. "So who is she?"

"Tanya Thomas," Zoe said quietly. To her, it was just a name, to everyone else it was a lifetime of hype, a million lies, a golden voice, a thousand images they'd seen, she was the legend, and Sam had the usual reaction. His eyes widened, his mouth dropped, and then he laughed at his own reflexes and grinned, feeling sheepish.

"I don't believe it. You know her?"

"She was my best pal in college. We were roommates. I love her more than any other friend I've ever had," she said quietly. "I don't see her enough, but whenever we can get together it's all still there. It's amazing, no matter what happens to either of us, nothing ever changes. She's a remarkable woman."

"Wow! I'm impressed." He couldn't help saying it, and he meant it. "I know that sounds dumb, but it always amazes me that someone knows people like that, that they hang out with them, that they sit around and eat pizza and drink coffee like the rest of us, and wash their hair and wear pajamas. It's pretty hard to think of them as real people."

"She's suffered a lot from that. I gather she's getting divorced again. I think it would be impossible to have a normal life with the kind of pressures she lives with. She married a really nice guy when we got out of college, her high school sweetheart, but within a year, she hit it big, she had a gold record and a career, and I think it just blew her marriage. Poor Bobby Joe didn't know what hit him, and neither did Tanny. She married a real shit after that, her manager, and he ripped her off, predictably, and was pretty abusive to her. I think it was fairly typical for the milieu, but it was miserable for her. And three years ago she married some guy in L.A., I think he's a developer. I thought it was going to work, but now they're breaking up, and he won't let her take his kids to Wyoming, as planned, so she had this cabin at a dude ranch, and she asked me to go with her." She made it all sound so ordinary that it amused him.

"Lucky you!" he said, and meant it. "What fun!"

"Yeah, seeing Tanny will be fun more than anything. Neither of us are that crazy about horses," she laughed. "Actually, all I want to do is sleep for the whole week."

"It might do you good," he said, looking at her with concern, and then he looked at her oddly. "You're all right, Zoe, aren't you? You've been looking tired, and I know you weren't feeling great last week. I think you're really pushing." He said it very gently, and what he said touched her deeply. She was so used to taking care of other people, that when anyone took care of her it surprised her.

"I'm fine. Honestly," she said, but she wondered what he had seen. She wondered suddenly if she looked ill. She was tired, but she didn't look any different to herself when she looked in the mirror. She had no sores, no other signs. There were no indications that she had AIDS, and she knew there might not be for a long time, or there could be a lot of them at any moment. And her greatest risk was from infection. But she knew what she had to do to protect herself, and she was being careful. "You're sweet to ask," she said, and was surprised when he reached across the table and took her hand. She hadn't expected him to do that.

"I care about you. I want to help you, but most of the time you're pretty stubborn." The way he said it made her look into his eyes. They were dark brown, and infinitely gentle.

"Thank you, Sam . . ." Feeling a wave of emotion wash over her, she looked away from him, and then took away her hand a moment later. She knew more than ever that she couldn't let her guard down. No matter how kind and appealing he was, she couldn't let herself do it.

It had been so easy with Dick, when she went out with him. They were just friends, and if they took it a little further than that once in a while, there was no harm done. She had no illusions about how he felt about her. He just wanted a comfortable companion from time to time, someone to go to the theater with him, or the symphony, or the ballet, or an expensive dinner. But he wanted nothing more from her than she wanted to give. In fact, if she'd given him more than that, it would have scared him. Dick knew exactly how far he wanted to go with her, and he was always careful to keep his distance.

And although she would have liked a serious relationship with someone, there hadn't really been anyone who'd appealed to her that way in years, and it was easier to avoid the cheap imitations. And now that her whole life had changed, it was such bad luck to discover that Sam Warner might have once been important to her. She had never realized how deep he was, how kind, how compassionate, how in tune with what she was doing. She had just thought of him as a good doctor, a good friend. And now she found that there was more to him, and to what she felt for him, and she had no right to explore it further. The door to that part of her life was closed forever. What could she possibly give anyone now? A few months? A few years? Even if it were five or ten, it wouldn't be fair to them. And through it all, there was always the remote but potential risk of illness for them. She had lived through all of that with Adam. She couldn't do that to anyone. And she had no intention of doing it to Sam. There was not a chance in the world that she was going to let him come any closer to her. They were colleagues and friends, and nothing more, and she absolutely would not let him come beyond her limits, and he sensed that. It made him sad as they left the restaurant. As much as he liked her, he could sense that she was pulling back from him. He didn't know why, but he didn't like it, and he sensed correctly that there was nothing he could do about it.

He looked at her for a long moment as they sat in his car outside the restaurant. "I had a great time tonight," he said honestly, and she nodded.

"So did I, Sam."

"And I want you to have a good time in Wyoming," he said as he looked into her eyes, and she felt as though she could feel his thoughts and she didn't want to. She didn't want him to open his heart to her, or ask her to open hers, or worse yet have to tell him why she couldn't. As far as she was concerned, no one had the right to know that.

"Thank you for covering for me," she said, and meant it. It was a relief to talk about their work and not their feelings. She sensed easily that she was on dangerous ground with him, and as she looked at him in his tweed jacket and gray turtleneck, she forced herself not to feel any attraction to him, but it wasn't easy.

"You know I'll cover for you anytime," he said, still not starting the car. There was something he wanted to say to her, and he wasn't sure how to do it. "I want to talk to you when you come back," he said, and she didn't dare ask him why. She was suddenly afraid that after all this time he was suddenly going to press her. It wasn't fair that it should happen now. It was just too bad they hadn't discovered their attraction for each other sooner. She had been completely blind to what he felt before, and even to the fact that he was actually very attractive. "I think some of what we said tonight deserves a little more conversation," he said, sounding very definite and a little daunting.

"I'm not sure that's such a good idea," she said quietly, slowly looking up at him. There was a lifetime of sorrows in her eyes, and it took all the strength he had not to put his arms around her, but he knew that for now at least it was not what she wanted. "There are some things best left unsaid, Sam."

"I don't agree with you," he said, his eyes boring into hers, begging her to listen. "You're a brave woman. I've seen you look death in the eye and defy it many times. You can't be cowardly about your own life." It seemed odd to her that he should say that, and for a moment she panicked about what he was thinking. But she knew that he couldn't have discovered her secret. The lab results had had no name and had been numbered.

"I don't think I am cowardly about my own life," she said sadly. "I've made some choices that are right for me, not out of cowardice, but out of wisdom."

"That's bullshit," he said, leaning frighteningly close to her, and she turned away from him and looked out the window.

"Sam, don't . . . I can't." There were tears in her eyes, but he never saw them.

"Just tell me one thing," he asked, staring straight ahead of him. All he wanted to do was take her in his arms and kiss her, but out of respect for her and her crazy ideas, he didn't. "Is there someone else? Tell me honestly. I want to know."

She hesitated for a long time. It was the perfect out. All she had to do was tell him that she was involved with someone else, but she was too honest to do that. She hadn't even bought the wedding band she had planned to. She shook her head as she looked back at him. "No, there isn't, but that doesn't change anything. You have to understand that. I can be your friend, Sam, but I can't give anyone more than that. It's just that simple."

"I don't understand," he said, trying not to look angry or as bereft as he felt. But he was so frustrated by what she was saying. "I'm not asking you to make a commitment to me. I'm just asking you to be open, that's all. If I don't appeal to you, if there's nothing there you'd want to explore further, then I understand, but you keep telling me that the door to that whole part of your life is closed, and I don't understand that. Is it the man who died? Are you still mourning him?" Eleven years later that seemed unreasonable to him, but who was he to decide that? But she shook her head again as he watched her.

"No, it isn't. I made my peace with Adam's death a long time ago. Sam, trust me, let's be friends. Besides," she smiled gently at him and touched his hand, "believe me, I'm hard to get along with."

"You certainly are," he said as he started the car. She had completely tantalized him, and he hadn't expected that. He had been attracted to her for years, but his feelings had always been in check, and had long since settled into an easy friendship. He had never expected to be completely bowled over by her, and then find that the door behind which she hid had been locked and sealed forever. The very thought of it drove him crazy. And as he drove her home, he kept glancing at her, she was so peaceful and beautiful, she seemed almost luminous as she sat there. She was like a young saint, and he knew just looking at her that she had a remarkable spirit. He kept trying to remind himself that you can't always have everything you want in life, but it seemed incredibly unfair when he thought about Zoe. And when they reached her house, he came around and opened the door for her, and she seemed almost waiflike as he helped her out, and her arm in his hand felt like a child's as he held it.

"Try to fatten up a little at the ranch," he said with a look of concern, "you need it."

"Yes, Doctor," she said, looking up at him with tenderness in her eyes. She almost wished that things could have been different. "I had a wonderful time. You'll have to come and have dinner with Jade and me when I get back. I make a great hot dog."

"Maybe I should take the two of you out to dinner." He smiled, wishing he could pull her out from her fortress. He could sense more than anything else about her that she was hiding. He didn't know why, but he could see it in her eyes, and try as he might he couldn't reach her. But he had, more than he knew that night, so much so that she was frightened of him.

"I had a lovely time. Thanks, Sam."

"So did I, Zoe . . . and I'm sorry if I pressed you." He was afraid he might have driven her into hiding even further.

"It's all right. I understand." She understood more than she wanted to, and she was flattered and touched but unmoved by it. Her own resolve was still stronger.

"I'm not sure you do understand. I'm not sure I do," he said sadly. "I've been wanting to do this for a long time. Since medical school actually. Maybe I just waited too long." He looked unhappy as he stood there.

"Don't worry about it, Sam. It's all right," she said, and patted his arm, and he walked her slowly to her door. And as they stood there he wished he could kiss her. He wasn't coming to the clinic the next day, but she knew she would see him again before she took off, and she took comfort in that. If nothing else, they could at least occasionally work together.

"I'll see you in a few days," he said, and kissed the top of her head, and then as she opened the door, he ran swiftly down the steps back to his car, and then he stood there and watched her go in. She turned, and their eyes met for one last time, and then she waved and went inside. And a moment later, she heard his car drive away, and inside the car, he looked dazed by the power of what he was feeling. The evening had been nothing like what he'd expected. But neither was Zoe. And despite all he felt for her, and their old friendship, more than ever, she was a mystery to him.

CHAPTER 10

The day Mary Stuart left New York she stood for a last time in her living room and looked around her apartment. The shades were drawn, the curtains were closed, the air-conditioning was off, and the apartment was slowly warming up. For the past week there had been a tremendous heat wave. She had talked to Alyssa in Holland the night before, she was having a fantastic time traveling with five friends, and Mary Stuart suspected she was having her first really serious romance. She was happy for her, and still more than a little sad to have missed their opportunity to travel around Europe together.

She had spoken to Bill several times too. He was working hard, and he sounded startled when she told him she was going to Wyoming. He couldn't understand why and thought she should go to Martha's Vineyard, or the Hamptons to stay with their friends, as she had on the Fourth. He had never really approved of her friendship with Tanya Thomas. And he didn't see why she wanted to go to a dude ranch. He never thought she had any particular affinity for horses. He said all the things which, years before, would have made her reconsider, but this time did not affect her. She wanted to spend two weeks at the ranch with Tanya. She wanted to be with her friend, to talk to her, and look up at the mountains in the morning. She suddenly realized that she needed to get away and reevaluate her life, and if he didn't understand that, then that was his problem. He was in London for two months and didn't want her with him, and he had no right now to make her feel uncomfortable about what she was doing. He had given up that right when he had told her he didn't want her in London with him. He had given up a lot of things that year, intentionally and otherwise, and she wanted to do some serious thinking about it. She couldn't imagine coming back to their relationship the way it had been, the way it had become. She couldn't live in the airless, loveless, joyless atmosphere he had created. And even though the night before he left she had caught a glimpse of him again, there was no promise that she would find him again at the end of the summer. Or ever again for that matter.

She was beginning to realize that what they had once had was gone, very probably forever. And she doubted if what had been left in its place was worth keeping. She couldn't believe what she was thinking. But she couldn't imagine going back to him, couldn't think about living with him that way again, never speaking, holding, touching. They had lost their dreams, their lives, more than just Todd had died. In many ways, she felt they had. And going to Wyoming was a way of leaving what had been, and trying to figure out what was still possible between them. And for an odd moment, as she looked around, she felt as though she were leaving their old life forever. It would never be the same again. She would never come back to the man who had left her so bereft and so abandoned for the past year. Either she would come back to the man she had once known, or she wasn't coming back at all. And in either case she wanted to think about whether or not to tell Bill to sell the apartment. But nothing was ever going to be the same again, nor had it been for the past year, and she knew it.

The prospect of being on her own again at her age was a frightening one. But the thought of being alone with him, in the tomb he had created for both of them, was an even worse fate. She walked down the long hall, and stopped for a long moment in front of the room that had been Todd's. The curtains were gone, the bedspreads were out being cleaned. It had all been put away, and there was nothing left of him. What she still had was in her heart and her memories. He was free now.

She picked her suitcase up again and walked slowly down the hall, thinking about him . . . and about Bill . . . and Alyssa, how happy they had once been, and how different it all was now. The cruel hand of fate, with a quick flick of the wrist, the dream was over. It had all ended so quickly. It was strange to think about it now. She felt as though she had been treading water in icy seas for a long time, she had almost drowned, but she was beginning to move forward again, still frozen, still numb, injured and bruised, but she was beginning to think she might not drown after all. There was the very faintest chance now that she might make it. And as she stood in the doorway with the keys in her hand, she wanted to say good-bye to someone . . . her husband . . . her child . . . the life they had once shared here. "I love you," she said softly into the empty hall, not sure which of them she meant, Bill or Todd . . . or the life they had shared together. And then, with a last look, she closed the door softly behind her.

The doorman put her in a cab downstairs, and she reached Kennedy Airport just under an hour later. And the flight to Los Angeles was uneventful.

When Tanya left her house, it was in a flurry of activity. She had packed six bags, two boxes full of hats, and nine pairs of cowboy boots in assorted shades of alligator and lizard. Her housekeeper was putting bags of food on the bus, and she had bought a dozen new videos to keep them entertained on the trip across Nevada and Idaho. It was a long, boring ride, she'd been told, and she'd even brought half a dozen new scripts to look at. She was currently being offered parts in several new movies.

It was eleven o'clock and Mary Stuart's plane was coming in at twelve-thirty. But she wanted to make one last stop before they left, for a little more food at Gelsen's. The bus was already fully stocked, but she wanted to pick up just a few final goodies.

The driver was waiting patiently outside as she kissed her dog good-bye, thanked her housekeeper, reminded her about the security, grabbed her hat, her handbag, her address book, and ran up the steps of the bus, with her hair flying loose, looking sensational in a white T-shirt and skin-tight blue jeans, and her oldest pair of bright yellow cowboy boots. She had bought them in Texas on her sixteenth birthday, and they looked it. She had worn them all through college, and everyone who knew her knew how much she loved them.

"Thanks, Tom," she said, waving to the driver as she got on, and he began slowly maneuvering the giant vehicle through her gates, and down her narrow driveway. The bus was huge, and it was divided into two huge rooms. A living room all done in teak and navy blue velvet, with comfortable easy chairs, two couches, and a long table that seated eight, and a series of small groups set for conversation. The back room was done in forest green, and transformed easily from another sitting room into a bedroom. And between the two was a large, functional kitchen, and a white marble bathroom. She had bought the bus years before when she had her first platinum record. It looked very much like a yacht, or a very large private plane, and it had been almost as expensive.

On the way, she and Mary Stuart would sleep in the bedroom, and they would park outside a motel, so they could get a room for Tom. And an elaborate alarm system would keep them safe. In some cases, Tanya took security along, but she felt that this time she wasn't likely to need it. She was looking forward to the trip, and to spending two whole days chatting with Mary Stuart. Driving ten-hour days, they should be able to reach Jackson Hole the following day in time for dinner.

They reached the airport ten minutes before Mary Stuart's plane, and Tanya was waiting at the gate in dark glasses and a black cowboy hat when Mary Stuart came off in jeans and a blazer, carrying a Vuitton tote bag. As usual, she looked immaculate, and as though someone had pressed her jacket on the plane, and her hair looked as though she'd just had a haircut.

"I wish I knew how you did that," Tanya said, smiling at her, and then hugging her tight. "You always look so damn neat and clean."

"It's congenital. My kids hate me for it. Todd always used to try and 'mess me up,' just so I'd look 'normal.' " She looked faintly apologetic, and arm in arm they walked toward the baggage claim, where Tanya's bus driver was waiting to help them. She stood a little to one side with her friend, and within less than a minute heads began turning, she saw a few people whispering, some shy smiles, and five minutes later a cluster of teenagers came over with a pen and some paper.

"May we have your autograph, Miss Thomas?" they asked, giggling and shoving each other. She was used to it, and she always signed when she was asked to. But she also knew that if they didn't move quickly then, she would be surrounded by fans in less than five minutes. She knew from experience that once she was recognized it was only a matter of moments before it became a mob scene. And she smiled over the kids at Mary Stuart, as her old friend watched her. As she signed the last piece of paper, she whispered to her, "We gotta go . . . it'll be crazy in a minute." She said something to Tom, and Mary Stuart gave him her baggage stub and described her bag, she'd only brought one with her, and Tanya hustled her as quickly as she could toward the exit. But there was already a large group of women and young girls heading toward her, and two rough-looking guys grabbed her arm, and one of them shoved a pen in her face.

"Hey, Tanya, how 'bout signing something for me, hey sweetheart, like your bra." The two of them were laughing, thinking they were very amusing, and Tom, the bus driver, had been watching and came right over.

"Thanks, guys, another time . . . see ya . . ." and before Mary Stuart realized what had happened to them, they were out the door and across the pavement, right in front of the women who had been hurrying toward her. They zipped right by just as two women took her picture. But Tom had the key in his hand, and unlocked the bus, shoving Tanya ahead of him, and Mary Stuart just behind her. They were inside and the door was closed in a fraction of a second. But there was already the breathless feeling of having been stampeded. And it reminded Mary Stuart instantly of how difficult Tanya's life was. She had almost forgotten. It happened to her everywhere. The supermarket, the doctor, the movies. She couldn't go anywhere without attracting attention. No matter what she did to hide, they always found her.

"That was awful," Mary Stuart said succinctly, as Tanya took two Cokes out of the fridge in the kitchen and handed her one through the doorway with a smile at her driver.

"You get used to it . . . almost . . . Thanks, Tom. That was very smooth."

"Anytime." He told her he was going back for Mary Stuart's bags, and reminded Tanya to keep the door locked.

"Hell, no, I thought I'd hang out in the doorway and sell tickets." She grinned with her cowboy hat still on. In her hat and her boots, she looked very Texas.

"Be careful," he warned again as he left, and the two women could see a small crowd forming on the sidewalk, taking pictures of the bus, and pointing to it, although they couldn't see into the bus and there was nothing to identify it. It was just a long, sleek, black bus with no markings. But they knew. Word had gotten out. They had seen her. And by the time Tom got back, there were fifty people outside, pushing and shoving and talking. They tried to stop him as he came in, wanting to push their way past him, but he was a powerful guy, and no one was going to get by him. He was on the bus, with Mary Stuart's bags, and the door was locked again before anyone could get near him.

"Jesus, the natives are aggressive today, aren't they?" Tanya said, watching the crowd outside. They still frightened her at times. It was scary to be so pursued, so devoured, so compulsively hunted. And as Mary Stuart watched her face, she was overwhelmed with pity.

"I don't know how you stand it," Mary Stuart said softly, and then they both sat down, as the bus began rolling.

"Neither do I," Tanya said as she put her Coke can down on a white marble table, "but you just do, I guess. It goes with the territory. It's just that no one really explains it to you when you grab that mike for the first time and sing your heart out. At first you think it's all about you and the music. But it isn't. After a while, it has nothing to do with that. You can have that anytime, all by yourself, out in a field, in the bathtub, anywhere you are . . . but it's all about the rest that comes with it. They eat you up, if you let them. They give you everything, their hearts, their minds, their souls, their bodies if you want them, and then they take yours, everything you got, and you never get it back again if you're not careful." She knew whereof she spoke. She had fought long and hard to get where she was, and she had paid a high price for it, and given up parts of herself she knew she would never get back now. She had given trust and caring and love, and worked harder than anyone Mary Stuart had ever known, and in the end, she stood alone at the top of the mountain. It wasn't an easy place to be. Mary Stuart could only guess at it. But Tanya knew it.

"So how's it going? . . . How was the flight? . . . How's Alyssa?" Tanya asked, settling back in one of the big club chairs for the long drive to Winnemucca, Nevada, where they were sleeping.

"Alyssa's fine. She's in Holland, and she's in love. She sounds so happy it almost hurts to hear her. And Bill's fine too," she volunteered, but her face saddened instantly as she said it. "He sounds very busy," and he didn't want her with him, she thought. That said it all as far as she was concerned. She didn't say any more, but it was obvious that she was unhappy.

"How's that going, or should I ask?"

"I'm not sure." She hesitated for a long moment, looking out the window. "I've been doing a lot of thinking." And then she looked into her friend's eyes and remembered the endless confessions in Berkeley, the hours they spent talking about their lives and their dreams, and what they really wanted. All Tanya had wanted was to marry Bobby Joe. Mary Stuart had wanted a job and a great husband, and good children. She had married Bill two months after graduation, and for a while seemed to have everything she wanted. But she wasn't as sure now. "I'm not sure I want to go back after the summer," she said softly, and Tanya looked startled.

"To New York?" She couldn't imagine her living in California. Tanya was her only friend there, and everything about her was so Eastern. It would have been a brave decision, but Mary Stuart shook her head at the question. Her answer shocked Tanya still further.

"No, to Bill. I don't know. Something happened when he left. It's as though he thinks he can do whatever he likes now. He has the option to do what he wants, to go to London for two months alone, even though I could have been there. The firm would even have paid for it, but he didn't want me. And yet I'm expected to be there for him, to run his home, to take his messages, to cook his dinner. But he no longer has to speak to me, or care for me, or take me anywhere. He's silently blaming me for killing Todd, or at least not stopping him from what he did. But Bill no longer acts married to me now. That's my punishment. I'm married, and he's not. Like a sentence in purgatory, and I've been letting him punish me because I felt so guilty. But a funny thing happened when I put Todd's things away, it freed me. I feel sad, I feel loss, I still feel terrible grief sometimes." She had cried for him again the night before she left, and for her marriage as well. She had sensed before she left that she might never come back in quite the same way to their apartment. "But I don't feel as guilty. It wasn't my fault. It was terrible. But it was something Todd did. And no matter how terrible it was, or how foolish, even though I'm his mother, I couldn't have stopped him."

"Do you really believe that?" Tanya asked, looking relieved. It was exactly what she had tried to tell her, but Mary Stuart hadn't been ready to hear it. Or maybe Tanya had started the process for her. She hoped so, as she listened.

"I believe it now," Mary Stuart said quietly. "But I don't think Bill does. I think he's going to go on punishing me forever." And then she looked out the window as they drove out of Los Angeles County, thinking of her husband. "We're not married to each other anymore, Tan. It's all over. I don't think he'd admit it if I asked him. But there's nothing left, and I think he knows it too. If there were, I'd be in London with him."

"Maybe he just can't face you yet," Tanya tried to say fairly, but she suspected Mary Stuart was right. What she had told her in New York had been a nightmare. The silence, the loneliness, the agony of his rejection. And even to Tanya the fact that he didn't want her in London with him told its own story.

"I don't think there's anything to go back to. It took me a long time to face that. I think it was especially hard for me because I used to think we had such a great marriage. More than twenty years isn't bad. And it was so good when it was good," Mary Stuart said sadly. "I always thought we were so close and so happy. It seems amazing that a blow like that could end it all. You would think it would bring us closer."

"I don't think it works like that," Tanya said honestly. "Most marriages don't survive the death of children. People blame each other, or they just wither up inside. I don't know, but I've read a lot about it. I don't think what happened is surprising."

"It's as if all those years before don't count at all. I thought it was like money in the bank, you store it up so that when you really need it you have it, and then when the roof fell in I found out our piggy bank was empty." She smiled wistfully, but she had begun to make her peace with it, oddly enough only in the past few weeks. And she'd had a lot of time to think once he left for London. "I just don't think I could go back to what it was like last year, and I don't think we could ever fix it."

"Would you try if he asked you to?" Tanya was curious. Like Mary Stuart, she had always thought they had a great marriage.

"I'm not sure," Mary Stuart said cautiously. "I just don't know now. What we went through was so painful that I don't want to go back, I just want to go forward." Tanya and she sat silently for a few minutes as they headed into the San Bernardino Mountains, and then Mary Stuart asked her a question. They were both stretched out on the couches by then, and Tanya had taken her hat and boots off. It was a great way to travel. "What's happening with Tony?"

"Not much. He called an attorney. Mine is taking care of it for me. It's all pretty predictable and relatively nasty. He wants the house in Malibu, and I won't give it to him. I bought it and put most of the money into it, and in the end I'll have to give him a bunch of money to keep it. And some other stuff. He took the Rolls, and he wants alimony and a settlement, and he'll probably get it. He says that my lifestyle caused him pain and suffering and he wants to get paid for it." She shrugged, but it made Mary Stuart livid.

"You'd think he'd be embarrassed," Mary Stuart said with a disapproving frown. She had always hated the things people did to Tanya. It was as though they thought it was all right because of who she was. Even Tony had given in to it finally. It was hard for anyone to remember she was a person, and harder still for people to resist just grabbing for what they wanted.

Tanya hated it too, but it was something she had long since understood and made her peace with. It was just what happened when you became that famous.

"Not much embarrasses him, or anyone else for that matter," Tanya said, with her hands behind her head as she lay there. "That's just the way it is. Sometimes I think I'm used to it, and sometimes it makes me crazy. My lawyer keeps telling me that it's just money and not to let it upset me. But it's my money and my life, and I worked like a dog for it. I don't see why some guy, any guy, should just get to come along, sleep with you for a while, and then take half of what you've got. It's a hell of a price to pay for a couple of years in the sack with a guy who cheats anyway. What about my 'pain and suffering'? I guess that's not the issue. We go to court next month, and the media will love it."

"Will they be there?" Mary Stuart looked horrified. How could they do this to her? But they would, and they did, and they had, for nearly twenty years now.

"Of course they'll be there. Courtrooms are open to the press and TV. First Amendment, remember?" She looked cynical, but she knew what went with the trappings of her business.

"That's not First Amendment, that's bullshit, and you know it."

"Tell it to the judge," Tanya said, and crossed her ankles. She looked glorious, but there was no one there to see it. This was a rare bit of privacy for her, and she trusted Tom, the driver. He had driven for her for years, and was the soul of discretion. He had a wife and four kids, and never told anyone who he worked for. Sometimes he just said "Greyhound." He admired her a lot, and would have done just about anything to protect her.

"I don't know how you stand the crap that goes with your life," Mary Stuart said admiringly. "I think I'd go completely berserk after about two days."

"No, you wouldn't. You'd get used to it, just like I did. There are a lot of perks. That's what kind of sucks you in at first, they don't hit you with the rough stuff until later, and then it's too late, you're too far in to get out, and you figure you might as well stay for the whole show. I'm not sure yet myself if it's been worth it. Sometimes I doubt it. And sometimes I love it." She hated the pressure and the press and the ugliness of what was hurled at her. But she still enjoyed what she did, and most of the time, she stayed in it for the music. The rest of the time she didn't know why she did it.

They rode on in silence for a while, and then Tanya went to the kitchen and made popcorn. They made sandwiches late that afternoon, and Tanya took one to Tom, with a cup of coffee. They only stopped once, so he could stretch, and the rest of the time they just pressed on, chatting and reading, and Tanya watched a video she'd gotten from the Academy of a first-run movie, and Mary Stuart slept while she watched it. She was exhausted from all her emotions before she left New York. Ever since Bill had left, she'd been moving toward a decision about their life and now she thought she had made it. As sad as it was, it was a relief in a way. It was time to cut their losses. And Tanya didn't disagree with her. But she was sure Alyssa would be upset when her mother told her. She had no idea how Bill would react. She thought it might be a relief for him too. Maybe it was what he had wanted all year, and hadn't had the guts to tell her. She was going to wait, and tell him when he got back from London in late August, or September. And in the meantime, she was going to make plans for her future. After the two weeks at the ranch, Mary Stuart said she was going to L.A. for a week to visit Tanya, and then she had decided to go to East Hampton for a few weeks to get out of the city. She had lots of friends there. It was going to be an interesting summer.

And Tanya was smiling at her when she woke up from her nap. They had traveled far from southern California by then, and had moved on through Nevada.

"Where are we?" Mary Stuart asked, sitting up and looking around. And even half asleep, she barely looked tousled. Tanya leaned over and messed up her hair for her, just as she had done in college, and they both laughed.

"You look about twelve years old, Stu. I hate you. I spend half my life at the plastic surgeon, and you look like that naturally. You're disgusting." They both looked great and nowhere near their ages. "By the way, I talked to Zoe again last week," she said casually. "She's really doing an incredible thing with her AIDS clinic in San Francisco." They both agreed that it was just like her, and Tanya commented that it was too bad she had never married.

"Somehow, I never thought she would," Mary Stuart said thoughtfully.

"I don't know why not. She had plenty of boyfriends."

"Yeah, but her sense of nurturing was on a grander scale . . . orphans in Cambodia, children starving in Ethiopia, refugees from underdeveloped countries. Her AIDS clinic doesn't surprise me in the least, it's exactly what she should have done. The only thing that does surprise me is the baby she adopted. I never figured she'd have kids either. She's too idealistic. I can imagine her dying for a cause she cares about, but not cleaning up throw up." Tanya couldn't help laughing at the description. She was right on the money. It had always been Mary Stuart and Eleanor who cleaned up the suite. Zoe was always out demonstrating somewhere, and Tanya was either on the phone with Bobby Joe, or rehearsing some music department concert. The domestic arts had never been her strong suit.

"I'd really like to see her," Tanya said cautiously, wondering just how mad Mary Stuart was going to be, and hoping it wouldn't be very. It was going to break her heart if one of them refused to stay at the ranch. If either of them left, Tanya thought it was going to be Mary Stuart and not Zoe. It was Mary Stuart who had been so hurt by what Zoe had told her.

But when Tanya mentioned wanting to see Zoe, Mary Stuart didn't answer. She just looked out the window, remembering what had happened. It had been a tragic time for all of them, just before graduation, a sad way to end it. And they'd never really gotten back together. Mary Stuart had never seen Zoe again, although she thought of her sometimes. And Tanya saw them both at different times. None of them had ever been back to a reunion. Berkeley was just too big to make it appealing.

They drove on for the next few hours, and they both read. Mary Stuart had brought a stack of books with her, and Tanya was poring over magazines, and relieved not to find herself in them. And at nine o'clock, they finally rolled into Winnemucca. It was a brassy little town filled with restaurants and casinos along the main drag, which was actually just a piece of the highway. And Tom pulled the bus into the parking lot of the Red Lion Inn, where he had booked a room. Tanya was happier staying on the bus with Mary Stuart, but she wanted to go into the restaurant for dinner, and play some slot machines. It was really more of a coffee shop than a restaurant, but there were fifty or so slot machines, and some blackjack tables.

She put on her boots and the cowboy hat, and a pair of dark glasses. She had brought along a short black wig, but it was hot, and it itched, and she really didn't want to wear it, unless she had to. And she and Mary Stuart stood in the marble bathroom, washing their faces and putting on lipstick. Mary Stuart was looking relaxed and they both laughed about how silly they felt, going gambling together in Winnemucca.

"Listen, kid, this is serious. One of us could hit a jackpot. Just don't tell Tony," Tanya said and winked. She was still amazed at how quickly he could leave her life, and how totally all feelings between them had been canceled. It was as if he had hardly known her. And he was making her so angry these days, that she didn't even miss him. Now and then, she had a flash of nostalgia for him, remembering something they did, but in a minute, remembering the rest, it was over. It had been a mistake, a marriage that should have been an affair. It hurt, but not as much as she had feared when he left her, and that surprised her. She wondered if she was getting callous, or if it had never been what she pretended. It was very strange watching the whole relationship recede into the mists as though it had never existed. The only thing she missed now were his children.

They got off the bus, with Tom watching them, and Tanya told him they'd be fine. He should go relax, gamble, sleep, do whatever he wanted. And he went inside to check in and have dinner. And with that, Tanya and Mary Stuart hurried inside to change two fifty-dollar bills into quarters, and they put the money in a bucket. They had a great time playing the quarter slot machines, making a dollar back here and there, and staring at the people. There were lots of women with blue hair wearing large polyester tops in assorted floral patterns and pastel colors. Most of them had cigarettes hanging from their lips, and the men were playing blackjack and drinking. There were men playing the slot machines too, but there were more women at the slot machines, while the men preferred the poker and blackjack tables. And as Tanya clapped her hands when ten quarters came back to her, a man playing a nearby machine grinned at her, and a minute later, he sidled over. He had long thin legs and no hips, and his jeans seemed to be sliding south. He had a two-day stubble on his face, and rough hands, and he was wearing a cowboy hat not unlike Tanya's.

"How much did you win?" he asked conversationally, and Mary Stuart glanced nervously at Tanya. She was not anxious to get picked up by a drunk in Winnemucca.

"Couple of bucks," she said, ignoring him and frowning, pretending to be intent on the two machines she was playing.

"People ever tell you, you look just like Tanya Thomas, except you're taller and younger."

"Yeah, thanks," she said, never looking him in the eye. Cher had told her that once, that if you never make eye contact they don't recognize you. Sometimes it worked for her, and other times it didn't. She was hoping it would this time. "People tell me that all the time. I think she's real short though."

"That's what I said. You're taller. She's good though. You like her singing?"

"She's all right," Tanya said, slipping into her old Texas drawl, and Mary Stuart tried to keep from laughing. "The stuff she sings is kind of dumb though." She was really pushing it, and she looked unconcerned as she went on playing.

"Naaw, she's good," he argued with her, "I really like her." Tanya shrugged, and a few minutes later he went over to the blackjack table and sat down, and Mary Stuart leaned over and whispered.

"You've got a lot of balls," she said with a broad grin, and Tanya laughed at her and won a twenty-dollar jackpot. So far, between the two of them, they were just about breaking even. They had agreed on the bus that when they lost the hundred dollars, it was over. They would go on however long it lasted.

"That's the only way to do it," Tanya giggled, and a little while later she heard some woman say, "Look, that's Tanya Thomas," but the man who had talked to her said she just looked like her, and was a lot taller, and the woman who had spotted her agreed immediately, and nothing happened. "And younger," Tanya added under her breath, as Mary Stuart pushed her. They were down about fifty dollars by then. And at ten o'clock they walked into the restaurant for a hamburger, and she saw several people stare at them, but Tanya pretended not to notice. The waitress was particularly intent on watching them, but she wasn't quite sure, and she didn't dare ask, and they actually got to eat a meal in peace, which was rare for Tanya. And then they went back to the slot machines till nearly midnight. In the end, they had forty dollars left and split it between them.

"Wow! We won forty dollars," Mary Stuart said happily, as they locked the door of the bus behind them.

"No, dummy." Tanya laughed at her. "We lost sixty. Remember? We started with a hundred."

"Oh," Mary Stuart said, looking momentarily crestfallen, and then they both laughed like kids as they got undressed and got ready to go to bed on the bus. The two long couches in the green sitting room in the rear turned into beds, and there was a good-size table between them.

"You know, you look just like Tanya Thomas!" Mary Stuart drawled at her as Tanya brushed her mane of blond hair in the bathroom. It was like being roommates again in college, and Tanya stuck her chin out. She'd had a small implant put in years before, and a little liposuction just beneath it, which gave her the neck of a very young woman.

"But taller and younger!" they intoned together, laughing still harder.

"And don't forget the 'younger,' " Tanya reminded her. "I paid a fortune for having all this shit done."

"You're hopeless," Mary Stuart said, laughing as she put on her nightgown. She hadn't had this much fun in years, and for the first time in months, she didn't miss Bill at all. Suddenly, she had her own life, and his rejection of her seemed sad but much less important. "You don't look any different than you used to," she said, looking at Tanya carefully in the mirror. But neither did she, and she had done nothing for it.

"That's the whole point," Tanya explained. "What I'd like to know, though, is how come *you* don't look any different, and you claim you've done nothing. I think you're lying," she teased, but she knew better. Mary Stuart just had great bones, a great face, great genes, and she was a beautiful woman. They both were.

They went to bed chatting like young girls, and they talked until two in the morning with the lights off, and then finally they went to sleep, and didn't wake up until nine the next morning. She had told Tom she'd call him in the hotel when they were ready.

Tanya made coffee in the kitchen, and sweet rolls in the

microwave, while Mary Stuart showered. And then Tanya showered afterward, and they were both dressed in blue jeans and cowboy boots by nine-thirty. Neither of them had bothered to put on makeup.

"You know, I never do this," Tanya confessed, looking in the mirror with amazement. She never went out that way in L.A., she couldn't afford to, but here it didn't matter. And it was a real luxury for her to have the freedom to do that. "I'm always afraid I'll run into a photographer somewhere, or a reporter. But here, what the hell," she said, smiling. She felt better just being there, and so did Mary Stuart. They both felt free of their heavy burdens.

And a few minutes later, they walked back into the casino. Tanya had called Tom and told him they were almost ready to get going. They had closed up their beds, and he was going to finish cleaning up for them, and get gas, while the two women went to spend another twenty dollars on the slot machines. And this time they each doubled their money. Their friend of the night before was gone, and in his place were a dozen more like him, but absolutely no one paid any attention to Tanya. Mary Stuart thought it was amazing.

"Maybe you should go out without makeup more often," she said as they boarded the bus. Tom was waiting for them, and he put on another pot of coffee.

"Thanks, Tom," Tanya said when she saw how nice the bus looked. Mary Stuart had to agree with her, she thought it was the only way to travel. She loved it, and she could see why Tom called it a land yacht.

They drove out of Winnemucca shortly after ten, and continued their trek across Nevada all though the afternoon, and when they got to Idaho, the countryside began to look greener. It had been unbelievably barren in the desert. But Idaho was more inviting. And they rolled on doing just what they had before, reading and sleeping and talking. Tanya checked in with her office and returned some phone calls. But for once, there was no crisis. No one wanted anything from her, and there were no new traumas or lawsuits.

"How boring," she teased Jean on the phone when she told her how quiet it was. But Tanya was grateful for the respite. There was only a message from Zoe confirming her flight time. She was going to arrive at Jackson Hole shortly after they did. And a van from the hotel was picking her up at the airport. Tanya figured they'd arrive at the ranch around five-thirty, just in time to change their clothes and have dinner. But she said nothing to Mary Stuart about the message from Zoe, although she was beginning to wonder if she should warn her. But Mary Stuart had been so relaxed on the trip, Tanya hated to spoil it, so she didn't. And for the last few hours of the trip, they both slept, and when they awoke, they were dazzled by the Tetons. They were the most spectacular mountains either of them had ever seen. Mary Stuart just sat and stared at them, and without even realizing it, Tanya starting humming and then singing.

It was a moment neither of them would forget for a lifetime. And as Tanya sang, Mary Stuart reached a hand out to her, and they sat holding hands, as they drove through Jackson Hole, toward Moose, Wyoming.

CHAPTER 11

"You have to check our stock of AZT constantly," Zoe warned Sam as he handed her bags to the skycap. "You have no idea how quickly we run out. And I try to give away as many free samples as I can. It's expensive," she said, handing the man a tip and her ticket so he could check her baggage. "And you have to kick the lab constantly. If you let them, they'll take forever. Particularly with the kids, that can be a disaster. You want to know as fast as you can what's happening to their white counts." She was frantic as she got her ticket back and he walked her to the gate. She was frowning as she talked to Sam, and tried to remember all the concerns she had wanted to share with him at the last minute.

"This could come as a shock to you," he said gently, as they went through the metal detector, and then past it. "But I went to medical school. I'm board certified, and I have a license. Honest. I swear." He held up a hand, and she laughed nervously.

"I know, Sam. I'm sorry. I can't help it."

"I know you can't. But you have to try and relax, or you're going to have a heart attack right here, and never get to Wyoming. And I hate doing CPR in places like this. It's so obvious, and it makes me look like an ER doc, instead of a humble locum tenens." He was teasing her, and she wanted to relax, but she just couldn't. She felt so guilty, about leaving all of them and Jade, that she was sorry she was going, and if she could have backed out without feeling like a total jerk, she would have. But she had promised Tanya, and she knew she needed the rest. Otherwise, she would have stayed home and gone to work. She had just gone through the same performance at home with Inge, about instructions for Jade, and when the baby had started crying, Sam almost had to drag her down the stairs with her suitcase.

"I can see why you never go anywhere," he said as they sat down to wait for the plane. He thought she looked pale and he wondered if she was sick again, or just stressed and nervous. Probably a little of both. He was glad she was taking a vacation and he loved doing locum tenens in her practice. He liked working for her too. But he was willing to sacrifice her company for the moment, she was obviously in dire need of some time off.

They had never talked about her personal life again. Ever since their first night out, Zoe had kept the conversation entirely to business. But he still hadn't given up. He had promised to cook dinner for her and Jade when she got back from Wyoming, and she had at least accepted. She saw it as an opportunity for continued friendship. Sam didn't.

"You won't forget to check on Quinn Morrison, will you? I promised him you'd come by every afternoon after the office." He was one of her favorite patients, a sweet man in his seventies, who had contracted AIDS after prostate surgery, and he was doing poorly.

"I swear," Sam promised. She had also left him ten thousand instructions at the office. And as he looked at her with a gentle smile, he put an arm around her shoulders. "I'm also going to check up on your daughter, and make sure your au pair isn't beating her, or having sex in your bedroom while Jade watches Big Bird."

"Oh, God, don't say that," Zoe groaned at the prospect. She hadn't even thought of Inge doing a thing like that, and he laughed at her reaction.

"I'm going to put you on Prozac if you don't stop it. Or at least Valium."

"What a nice idea," she said. Actually, she had just started AZT that week, as a precaution. She was a great believer in doing that prophylactically, even before symptoms, and recommended it to all her patients. She had even told Sam that, in case he saw any new patients. "I really shouldn't have gone on this trip," shc said, torturing herself further, and he suggested they go and get a cup of coffee.

"I don't know another human being who deserves it more," he said seriously, as he ordered two cappuccinos. "I'm just sorry you're not going for two weeks instead of one." But they both knew she could never have done it.

"Maybe next year."

"I'm impressed," he teased. "You actually think you might do this again? I figured this was a once-in-a-lifetime deal." It might be, but not for the reasons he was thinking, and she didn't say that.

"We'll see." She looked coy then over her coffee. "Depends how much I like it."

"What's not to like?" He had been to Yellowstone Park once, and absolutely loved it.

"Depends how cute the cowboys are." She was teasing him, and he didn't think he liked it, but he was nonetheless willing to take it from her.

"Oh, great. You tell me you're becoming a nun, and now you're going to Wyoming to chase cowboys. Terrific. See if I cover for you again. Maybe I'll give all your patients placebos."

"Don't you dare!" she laughed.

"I wear cowboy boots too, you know. And I can buy one of

those dumb hats, if that's what gets to you. Funny though, I can't see Dick Franklin playing cowboy," he mused, and she laughed at him. He loved to give her a hard time about the illustrious Dr. Franklin. Sam really didn't like him. He thought he was a pompous, pretentious asshole. They had disagreed about surgical treatment for breast cancer at a medical meeting in L.A., and Franklin had treated Sam like a novice. And although he wasn't a surgeon himself, he certainly had valid opinions. But Dick Franklin didn't think so.

"I'll bring you back a cowboy hat," Zoe promised him, and he grinned. She still hadn't convinced him about the validity of her celibacy, and he had every intention of continuing to annoy her about it.

"Just don't bring home a cowboy."

"I'll call you," she said as the plane pulled in. She was flying to Salt Lake City, and then transferring to a smaller plane to Jackson Hole, Wyoming. She had timed it perfectly to arrive at almost the same time as Tanya.

"Say hello to your friend for me. I'd love to meet her sometime."

"I'll tell her to call you," she teased. Everyone in the world wanted to meet Tanya. She was everyone's dream girl. And then suddenly he looked serious as she picked up her bag and got ready to board the aircraft. "Take care of yourself. You need a break, Miss Z. Use this time for yourself. You've earned it." She nodded, touched by the way he looked at her, but unable to respond to him, and then she saw him narrow his eyes with an unspoken question. "I just thought of something. Do you have a medical bag with you?" he asked, looking worried.

"Yeah. Why? I put one in my suitcase, but I checked it. Do you need it?" She looked around, wondering if he had seen something she hadn't. She was usually careful about volunteering her assistance in public, but if she was needed urgently, she always did it. "Is someone hurt?"

"Yeah. You. After I hit you over the head with my shoe.

You're on vacation, you dope. I thought you'd do something like that. I want you to leave it in your suitcase."

"Well, I wasn't planning to run around the ranch with it. I just thought I should have it in case something happened." And then she looked at him pointedly and asked him a question. "Are you telling me you don't take one when you go somewhere? I'd feel lost without it." She knew damn well he would too. They all did.

"That's different. I do relief work." He looked mildly embarrassed, and she laughed at him, and then he put an arm around her and pulled her closer, but he knew she would never have let him kiss her. "Just be good to yourself. Forget all of us, if you can. If I really need you, I'll call you."

"Promise you'll do that?" She looked genuinely concerned, and he nodded. It was why she liked leaving her practice in his hands, because he listened, he cared, and he did exactly what she wanted. He didn't try to change the world and turn everything upside down while he was on duty. And he was truly a great doctor, and she knew that. She had always thought he was foolish being satisfied with doing locum tenens.

"I promise you I'll call if anything comes up," he reassured her again. "Promise me you'll get some rest and come back with pink cheeks and a little fatter, even if you do spend all your time chasing cowboys. Get a little sunshine too, and lots of sleep."

"Yes, doctor." She smiled at him, and she thanked him again for keeping an eye on her practice, and a moment later she walked slowly down the gangway toward the plane. And he waved for as long as he could see her.

He stood watching the plane until it pulled away, and then he walked slowly out of the airport. And almost before he'd reached the door, his beeper went off, and he went to a phone to answer a call from one of her patients. He was off and running. And she was in the air by then, on her way to Wyoming.

The flight to Salt Lake took just over two hours, and she had a two-hour wait then for the next plane, and they had already had a time change. She thought about calling Jade, but she decided it might upset her to hear her voice so soon and not understand where she was. She decided to wait till she got to the ranch instead, and she sat in the airport and drank coffee and read the paper and sat lost in her own thoughts. She so rarely had time to do that. And she mused over the fact that she had heard from Dick Franklin the day before. Much to her surprise, he called her. He had been stunned, and very moved when he got her note. He didn't ask to see her again, but he said that if she needed anything, she should call. He appreciated her honesty, though he wasn't worried, and he assured her that her secret was safe with him. He asked her how it had happened, and she told him, and he said he wasn't surprised. And she had the feeling, when they hung up, that she wouldn't hear from him again. But in her mind, it was just as well. She had no room for him or any man in her life now.

It was a luxury just sitting there on the airplane, without phones, without beepers, without patients, without anyone needing or wanting her, without having to figure out how she could help them. As much as she liked her work, she knew she would really enjoy the vacation. And she really wanted to shore up her energy and her strength. She knew she would need them. She had every intention of continuing her practice till the bitter end. She had already made that decision. She was going to give her patients everything she had to give, until there was nothing left to give them. And Jade too. But she had to figure out what to do about Jade. She had no family to leave her with, and no friends she thought were responsible enough to take good care of her, or else they were people she liked but weren't good with children. She'd been thinking of talking to Tanya, and she had no idea what she'd think of it. But it was a possibility at least. Zoe knew that eventually she had to do something.

The flight to Jackson Hole left on time, and Zoe landed on

schedule at exactly five-thirty. She had no idea where Tanya was by then, she knew she was arriving by bus that afternoon. She had planned to reach her at the ranch, and the hotel was sending a van for her. Her bags were among the first ones off, the driver was waiting for her, and everything went smoothly.

The young man who drove the van was wearing jeans, boots, and a cowboy hat, and he looked like everyone else in Wyoming. He was long, lanky, and lean, had short blond hair, he said his name was Tim, and he was from Mississippi. He was attending the University of Wyoming in Laramie, and working at the ranch for the summer. He said he loved it because of the horses. And as he drove her there, he told her about it. But Zoe found she could barely listen to him, she was mesmerized by the mountains. They were the most beautiful thing she'd ever seen, and the late afternoon sun shimmered on them in blues and pinks. There was snow at the very top, and they looked like the Swiss Alps to her. She had never seen anything like it.

"They're spectacular, aren't they, ma'am? They kinda take your breath away, don't they?" She agreed with him entirely, and let him rattle on for the half hour it took them to get there. He said he had an uncle who was a doctor too, he was an orthopedist and he'd set Tim's arm once. Did it real good too, because when he rode in the rodeo last year, the arm he'd broken before hadn't bothered him at all, but he'd broken the other one, and his leg too. But he was riding again this year. The story definitely had local color.

"Is there a rodeo here?" she asked with interest.

"Yes, ma'am. Wednesdays and Saturdays. Bull riding, broncos, the young kids ride steers, calf roping. You been to the rodeo before?"

"Not yet," she smiled, but she was sure Tanya would want to see it. She used to talk about the rodeos in Texas. "My friend is from Texas."

"I know." He looked a little embarrassed as soon as she said it. "I know who she is, but we're not supposed to talk about it at the ranch. Mrs. Collins gets real mad if anyone makes celebrities uncomfortable, and we get them from time to time, you know. We've had some real big ones at the ranch since I've been there.'' He looked at her staunchly then, and she imagined that that was why Tanya had chosen this one. ''We don't give anyone no information.''

''I know she'll appreciate it,'' Zoe said kindly.

''They're supposed to be arriving by bus any minute.'' She wasn't sure who he meant by ''they,'' except maybe her bus driver, but Zoe didn't bother to ask him, and five minutes later they pulled off the road, through some gates, and down a long winding road Tim called ''the driveway,'' but it seemed to go on forever. It was another full ten minutes before they reached some foothills, and she saw half a dozen buildings cleverly nestled into the base of them, a big barn, and several huge corrals filled with horses. There were lovely trees everywhere, and the buildings were impeccably maintained, and looming high above them, across the valley, were the ever present Tetons.

Tim took her to check in, and she was told at the desk that Miss Thomas hadn't arrived yet, but she was instantly given a warm welcome. The ranch house itself looked old and was very beautiful. There were antelope heads, and a buffalo on the wall, beautiful skins on the floor, and a spectacular picture window that showed a huge span of mountains. And there was an enormous fireplace that a tall man could have stood up in. It looked like a cozy place to spend a long winter's night, and there were a few guests chatting quietly in the corner. The woman at the desk explained to her that at that hour most of them were in their cabins, changing for dinner. Dinner was at seven.

There was a handful of informational sheets and a brochure for her, and then Tim drove her to the cabin. It was a humble euphemism for what would have been a handsome home for a family of five in the suburbs of any city. There was a big, cozy living room, with a fireplace and a potbellied stove, a small kitchen area, and couches covered in handsome textured fabrics. The feeling in the room was Southwestern, and somewhat Navajo, but it looked like a spread in *Architectural Digest,* where it had recently been featured. And there were three huge bedrooms, each one with a splendid view, and there were trees all around them.

It was really beautiful, and Zoe felt totally spoiled as she set down her tote bag, and Tim put down her suitcase. He asked her which bedroom she preferred, and she wanted to wait for Tanya to make the selection. There was one slightly larger than the other two, but they were all large and comfortable with huge king-size beds, and rough-hewn furniture, and a fireplace in each bedroom. For a minute she wanted to jump up and down on the beds and scream, like a little kid, and she was beaming when Tim left her. For a few minutes she wandered from room to room, and she helped herself to a nectarine from a large bowl of fruit on the coffee table. There was a big tin of freshly baked cookies too, and a box of chocolates. They had also asked Tanya's secretary for all her preferences, and the room was full of them. There were flowers everywhere, soda and especially root beer, Tanya's favorite, in the fridge, there were the cookies she preferred, the correct brand of crackers and yogurt she ate for breakfast, and there was an abundance of towels and her favorite soap in all three bathrooms.

"Wow!" Zoe said out loud as she looked around, and then she sat down on the couch and waited. She watched the news on television, helped herself to a Diet Coke, and ten minutes later she could hear the bus lumbering slowly up the driveway. It was perfect timing. And Zoe stood in the doorway, like the lady of the house, waiting to greet her, as Tanya walked off the bus, and ran toward her as soon as she saw her. The two were locked in a fast embrace, as suddenly Zoe saw over her shoulder that someone else was getting off the bus too. And she looked instantly startled, but not nearly as much so as Mary Stuart. Mary Stuart stood rooted to the spot, and she didn't know whether to get back on the bus, or march down the driveway. Instead she just stood there staring at Tanya. And when the other two took a step back, Mary Stuart was staring at them in fury.

"I can't believe you did this," she said to both of them, but even she would have had to admit that Zoe looked genuinely amazed to see her. It was obvious that she hadn't known either.

"It's not her fault," Tanya said rapidly, as Tom began to take their bags off. "It's mine. Let me explain what happened."

"Don't bother," Mary Stuart said sharply. "I'm leaving." Tom looked surprised and glanced at Tanya with a silent question. But she was too busy dealing with her friend to answer.

"That's not fair, Mary Stuart. Give it a chance, at least. We haven't been together in so long . . . I just thought . . ."

"Well, you shouldn't have. After the year I've just had, I don't understand how you could do this. It was a rotten thing to do, and you know it." She was livid and there were tears in Tanya's eyes as she listened, realizing it had been selfish on her part. She had just wanted both of them to be with her. But she'd been worried about it since she'd done it. It had been over twenty-two years, that was a long time for their old wounds to fester.

"I'm sorry, Mary Stuart," Zoe said quietly. "I shouldn't have come anyway. I have a lot to do in San Francisco, and a small child at home. It makes more sense for me to leave. I shouldn't have come in the first place. I'll catch a flight out after dinner." She spoke very calmly and very gently, but in the past two decades she had spent a lot of time dealing with very sick, very unhappy, often agitated, even demented people, and she was able to speak sensibly even when in the throes of her own emotions.

"You don't have to do that," Mary Stuart said, trying to regain her composure, and suddenly feeling she'd been rude, but she had been so stunned to see her, and the moment had been so awkward. "I'll be perfectly happy to fly back to New York in the morning." But she had to admit, it was a disappointment.

"You're both a couple of jerks," Tanya said, near tears. "I can't believe you can keep this bullshit going for more than twenty years. We're almost forty-five years old, for chrissake. Don't you have anything else to think about than to be pissed off at what happened when we were kids? Christ, I deal with so much shit every day, I can't even remember last week, let alone over twenty-one years ago. Give me a break, guys." She stood watching them, and Mary Stuart and Zoe looked at each other, as Tom took their bags into the cabin. He was planning to stay at a hotel in Jackson Hole, and be on call in case Tanya wanted to go on any excursions. But he wondered now about what they were doing. "Can we at least go inside to discuss this?" Tanya asked, looking hurt and angry, and the three women moved inside, as Tom put the groceries in the kitchen, and then left them.

The three women were standing awkwardly in the living room, and Tanya was wondering what to do now. "Will you at least sit down? You're both making me very nervous," she said, pacing the room, as Zoe looked at her. Unlike the other two, who were the same age, Zoe was almost a full year older, but they all looked terrific. "Look," Tanya said as they sat down, "I probably shouldn't have done it, I apologize. It was a stupid, sophomoric thing to do, but I thought I could get the three of us back together. I've missed you. I don't have any other friends like you. Nobody else in this whole world cares about me, absolutely no one. I don't have a husband, I don't have kids, I don't even have stepkids anymore. All I have is you . . . and what I wanted was what we used to have . . . that's all . . . maybe it was crazy . . . but I wish you would at least try it."

"We both love you," Mary Stuart said calmly, trying to regain her composure. "Or at least I do, and I'm sure Zoe does too, or she wouldn't be here. We didn't just come here for the view and the cowboys,'' Zoe smiled and nodded as she listened, ''but we don't love each other, Tan. That's the problem. I think it would be a very hard two weeks if we all stayed here.'' Zoe nodded again, and Tanya looked even more disappointed. She had expected some kind of reaction when they arrived, but she hadn't expected both of them to insist on leaving. She realized now that her idea had been really stupid. She would have been better off extending the invitation to either Mary Stuart or Zoe, and not undertaking such an ambitious reunion.

''What about just for tonight? We've been driving all day, and we're both tuckered out.'' She spoke of herself and Mary Stuart, and turned to Zoe. ''You've had two flights just to get here, and you look tired . . . you look good,'' she corrected herself, ''but you look bushed. We all are. After all, we're not kids anymore,'' she teased, but neither of them smiled. They were both thinking about what to do now. ''Why can't we just stay here for tonight, and then it's up to you what you want to do. I won't make a fuss, and if you're both pissed and tell me to get lost, and leave, it's my own fault. But then I'm leaving too. I'm not going to stay here alone for two weeks. It would be too depressing.'' It was a beautiful place, and a real shame to waste the vacation.

Zoe was the first to speak up, and she looked at both women when she did it. ''I'll stay tonight. You're right. It's a long trip back, and I'm not even sure there is a flight out tonight. This is not exactly Kennedy Airport.'' She smiled at Tanya, and looked hesitantly at Mary Stuart. ''Would that suit you, Stu?'' She slipped easily into their old nicknames.

''I'm all right with that,'' Mary Stuart said politely. ''I'll go back to New York in the morning.''

''No, you're not,'' Tanya said bluntly, ''you promised you'd spend a week with me in L.A.'' She was starting to look annoyed. She thought Mary Stuart was being unreasonable, but she knew just how deep the old wounds went.

''I'll fly back tomorrow,'' Zoe said matter-of-factly, and

Tanya decided to quit while they were ahead. They were spending the night, it was a start, and maybe a miracle would happen before morning.

"What bedrooms do you all want?" Tanya asked, taking off her hat, and tossing it on a hat rack. The rooms had every possible thing they could have wanted. Coatracks, boot jacks, gloves in case the mornings were chilly. There were rain ponchos in the closet in case there was a storm. Everything was comfortable and luxurious and well thought out. Even Tanya had never seen any place like it. "I love this place," she said with a cautious smile, and this time the other two joined her. In spite of their amazement at being together again, they all had to agree that the ranch was fabulous, and their cabin even better.

"Do they just do this for you, Tan?" Zoe asked, "or does everyone get this kind of treatment?" She doubted everyone did, she had never seen so many thoughtful little touches, including every magazine they could possibly have wanted.

"Supposedly, every cabin is like this," she said, helping herself to a root beer. "They called my secretary the week before we left to ask what I like to eat and drink and read, what kind of soap I like, how many pillows and towels, what videos, if I needed a fax in the room, or additional phone lines. I told them one phone was fine, but I had them put in a fax, and three VCR's, and I guessed at the foods and drinks you like. If there's anything you want, just tell them."

"This place is amazing," Mary Stuart concurred as she went to look at all the bedrooms, and on her way back she almost ran into Zoe.

"How've you been, Stu?" Zoe asked solicitously, and the look in her eyes startled Mary Stuart. There was a lot of sorrow and pain there.

"I've been fine," Mary Stuart said softly, wanting to ask her about her own life for the past twenty years. But she knew about the clinic from Tanya.

"I'm sorry about your son," Zoe said, and instinctively

touched her arm. "Tanya told me . . . it's so unfair . . . I deal with it all the time, and it's never right, but especially at his age. I'm really sorry."

"Thanks, Zoe," she said, her eyes filled with tears as she turned away from her. She didn't want Zoe to see it, but Zoe had sensed it, and she moved away so as not to offend her.

"Have we figured out what bedrooms yet?" Tanya came back into the room and she saw that Mary Stuart had been crying, and she wondered if they'd been fighting, but neither of them looked angry, and then she suspected it was about Todd, and when she raised an eyebrow Zoe nodded.

In the end, they all selected rooms. The slightly larger one had a sunken bathtub and a Jacuzzi, and Zoe and Mary Stuart both insisted that Tanya have it, although she would have given it up to either one of them. And when she agreed to use it, she told them to use the Jacuzzi anytime, but they both pointed out they'd be leaving in the morning. And Tanya almost told them she thought they were both disgustingly stubborn, but she didn't say it. She just went to her own room to change for dinner, and the others did the same a moment later.

Zoe called home from her room, and everything was fine. Jade was eating dinner when she called, and Inge said everything was going smoothly and she put Jade on the phone, and she didn't even cry when she heard her mother. She thought of paging Sam, just to see how things were, but she decided not to. He would be paged by plenty of her patients, so she didn't.

And shortly before seven o'clock they all met in the living room. Tanya was wearing skin-tight black suede pants, and a beaded cowboy shirt, with her blond hair loosely tied in a black ribbon behind her. And she was wearing tall, black suede cowboy boots that she had bought for the occasion. Zoe was wearing jeans, a soft, pale blue sweater and hiking boots, and Mary Stuart was wearing gray slacks, a beige sweater, and Chanel loafers. They were all as they had always been, surprisingly compatible, and yet totally different. There was a kind of mesh between them that, even now, with the rift between two of them, was still more powerful than they were. And Tanya knew that if they'd been honest with each other, they would have admitted that they felt it. She did, she felt drawn to both of them, as though there was an invisible cord around them pulling them closer. When she came back into the living room, Mary Stuart was asking Zoe about her clinic, and she was talking animatedly about it, while Mary Stuart listened in fascination.

"What an enormous undertaking," Mary Stuart said admiringly, but as they left for the dining room, they both fell silent, as though they had each remembered they weren't supposed to be speaking to each other. But once they were at the dinner table, the conversation got under way again. Tanya talked at length about her next concert tour, and the movie she was about to close a deal on, and they were both excited for her. It was obvious that they were both genuinely fond of her and wanted to protect her. They had been put at a table in the corner of the room, and although they all saw heads turn, no one came to ask for autographs, or to speak to them, except eventually the head of the ranch, Charlotte Collins, who stopped at the table to make them feel welcome.

She was a remarkable woman with a wide smile and piercing blue eyes, who seemed to see all, and kept her hand in every pie, and in every room, and on every person. She knew exactly what every one of her employees was doing at the time, and what each guest needed at that precise moment. And somehow, she managed to coordinate the two to the nth degree. Tanya was enormously impressed by the entire operation, as were the others, and they said so.

"Well, we hope you'll enjoy your stay with us. It's very important to us," she said, and looked as though she meant it. And neither Zoe nor Mary Stuart had the courage to ask her about planes or tell her they were leaving in the morning.

"I'll ask at the desk after breakfast," Mary Stuart said, after

Charlotte Collins moved on. There would be plenty of time then, and she could always fly to L.A. and spend a night at the Beverly Wilshire. Or to Denver. And Zoe's route was fairly simple. She would just go home the same way she had come there.

"I don't want to talk about this now," Tanya said sternly. "I want both of you to think about what you're doing. Do you really have so many friends that you can afford to lose someone you've known for half your life?" But what had blown them apart had been pretty brutal and Tanya knew it. She just didn't want it to go on forever. After twenty-one years, they had a right to end it. They all needed each other too badly to let go and walk away forever.

They talked about other things after that, Alyssa for a while, and Jade, but not Todd. And neither Mary Stuart nor Tanya talked about their husbands. They talked about trips and music and friends, books they cared about and Zoe's clinic, and then they started reminiscing about college. The people they had hated most, the funny ones, the ones they'd heard about in recent years, the dorks, the nerds, the drips, the tarts, and the heroes. A number of people they knew in school in the early years had died in Vietnam just before the peace was signed. It had been particularly cruel to lose friends in the final hours, but it had happened. And others had died since then. Several members of their class had died of cancer, and Zoe seemed to know that. She knew it through the medical community or through friends, or maybe because she lived in San Francisco, and a lot of their classmates had never left there. It had been a short, easy jump from Berkeley to the city. And through it all none of them ever mentioned Ellie. They were still talking about other friends as they walked back to the cabin, and it was only when they were back in their living room that Tanya said it. She knew Ellie was on all their minds, and it would be easier if someone just said it. So she did.

"You know, it's amazing, after all these years, I still miss her." There was a long pause, and then Mary Stuart nodded.

"So do I," she admitted in a soft voice. In some ways Ellie

had been the heart and soul of the group. She had always been the gentlest of them all, and yet she had often been the life of the party. She was a funny, zany girl, who would do almost anything for a laugh, including walking into a party with nothing but white paint on. She had done that once, and now and then she wore a lamp shade to chapel. She did crazy, silly things, and she always made them laugh, and then she made them cry. It had broken everyone's heart when she died, particularly Mary Stuart's. They had been best friends and roommates. And they were all sitting there thinking about her, when Zoe broke the silence.

"I wish I'd known then what I know now," she said gently to Mary Stuart, as Tanya watched them. "I had no right to say the things I did to you. I can't believe how young and stupid I was. I've often thought about it. I almost wrote you a letter once, when my first patient committed suicide. It was like God's vengeance for my having been so cruel and so outrageous to you. It was as if he were trying to teach me everything I hadn't learned with Ellie, that it was no one's fault, that we couldn't have stopped her if we tried, oh, we might have for a while. But not in the end, not if that was really what she wanted. I was so damn ignorant when I was young, I kept thinking that one of us should have seen it, that you should have because you were closest to her. I couldn't understand why you didn't know that she'd been taking pills and drinking. She must have been doing it for months, I think, and I guess she'd gotten away with it. But she really didn't want to. Ellie got exactly what she wanted." But as Mary Stuart listened to Zoe's words, she started crying. It was like listening to her talk about Todd, but Zoe didn't know that. And Tanya put a gentle arm around her. "I should have written you the letter, Stu," Zoe said with tears in her own eyes. "I never forgave myself for what I said to you, I guess you didn't either. I don't blame you," she said sadly. It had blown them all apart. Zoe had been vicious with her, she had raged at her for days, and even at the funeral, she had refused to sit beside her. She had blamed

Mary Stuart completely for not being able to stop her, and Mary Stuart had been overwhelmed by the accusations, and she had believed her. It had taken years to overcome her sense of having failed to save her friend's life. It was almost as though she had killed her. And then it had all come back to her with Todd. It was as though the horror had never ended. Only this time it was worse, and now it was Bill blaming her, and not Zoe. "I'm so sorry," Zoe said as she walked across the room and sat beside her. "I've wanted to say that to you all night. Even if we both leave tomorrow morning, especially if we do, I can't live with myself unless I tell you how wrong I was, and how stupid. You were right to hate me for all these years and I'm really sorry." She was crying when she said it. It was important to her now to confess her sins and make peace with the people she had injured. And in Zoe's life, there weren't many.

"Thank you for saying that," Mary Stuart choked on a sob as she hugged her, "but I always thought you were right. How could I not know what she was doing? How could I have been so blind?" They were the same questions she had asked herself about her son's death. Todd's death had, in some ways, been very similar to Ellie's. It was like a recurring nightmare. Only there was no waking. It seemed to go on forever.

"She was very sneaky, and she wanted to die," Zoe said simply. Her practice had taught her a great deal in the past two decades. "You couldn't have stopped her."

"I wish I believed that," Mary Stuart said sadly, confused suddenly if they were talking about her son, or their roommate.

"I know," Zoe persisted, as firm in this position as she had once been in the other. "She didn't want you to know what she was doing. If she had, you could have stopped her, but you couldn't."

"I wish I had," Mary Stuart said, staring at her hands folded in her lap, as the other two watched her. And Tanya was worried. "I wish I had known, about both of them." She raised her eyes to her friends', and they could both see the agony she held here.

"Both of whom?" Zoe was confused now, and Mary Stuart didn't answer, but the others just waited. "Mary Stuart?" She looked at her, and then she understood as Mary Stuart looked at her, and she wished she could have died for her, for both of them. She could only begin to imagine the agony she'd been through. Even more so after the distant memory of Ellie. It must have been like reliving it all again, but it had been so much worse for her. It made Zoe sob to realize what had happened. "Oh my God," she said, as she clutched her old friend and they both cried. "Oh, God . . . Stu . . . I'm so sorry . . ."

"It was so awful," Mary Stuart cried, "it was so terrible . . . and Bill said all the same things you did, and more." She went on sobbing as though her heart would break. But Mary Stuart knew it couldn't, it had broken long before that. "And Bill still blames me," she explained. "He hates me. He's in London now, without me, because he can't bear the sight of me, and I don't blame him. He thinks I killed our son, or let him die, at the very least . . . just as you thought about Ellie."

"I was a fool," Zoe said, still holding Mary Stuart in her arms, but it was small comfort in the face of what had happened. "I was twenty-two years old and an inexperienced moron. Bill should know better."

"He's convinced I could have stopped him."

"Then someone needs to tell him the truth about suicides. Stu, if he really wanted to, wild horses couldn't have stopped him. If he really wanted to, he would never have given you any warning."

"He didn't," she said sadly, blowing her nose in the tissue Tanya handed her, as Zoe sat back and put an arm around Mary Stuart's shoulders.

"You can't blame yourself. You have to try and accept what happened. As awful as it is, you can't change it, you can't stop it. You couldn't have stopped it then. All you can do now is go on, or you'll destroy yourself and everything around you."

"Actually, we've done a fairly good job of that." She blew her nose again and smiled at both her friends through the tears she was still crying. "There's nothing left of our marriage. Absolutely nothing."

"Well, not if he blames you. Somebody needs to talk to him."

"Probably my lawyer," Mary Stuart said, laughing grimly, and the other two smiled at her. She sounded a little more herself, and Tanya held one hand, and Zoe the other. "I've kind of decided to give it up. I'm going to tell him when he comes back from London."

"What's he doing there?" Zoe was curious. She didn't think they lived there.

"He has a big case there for the next two or three months, but he wouldn't let me come with him."

Zoe raised an eyebrow, and looked like her old cynical self as the other two watched her. She had mellowed a lot over the last twenty years, but there was still quite a lot of spice there. "Is he involved with someone else?"

"Actually, I don't think so. We haven't made love in a year, not since the night before Todd died. He's never touched me since. It's like the ultimate silent punishment. I think I so revolt him he can't touch me. But anyway, I really don't think there is someone else. That might be easier to understand than what's happened."

"Not really," Zoe looked clinical more than sympathetic.

"Some people just freeze up after traumas like that. It's pretty typical. I've heard it before. It's not exactly therapeutic, however, for a marriage."

"Not really." Mary Stuart smiled briefly. "Anyway, I think I've finally figured out what I need for myself. He's never going to forgive me anyway, and I might as well get it over with. Living with him is like living with my guilt every day, and I just can't do it."

"You shouldn't," Zoe said quietly. "He either has to deal with it honestly, or you need to get out. I think you're doing the right thing," she said matter-of-factly. "What about your daughter?"

Mary Stuart sighed as she answered. "I think she'll probably blame me for the divorce. I don't think she understands how rotten her father has been to me. She just thinks he's busy. I did too, at first. But he made pretty clear what he was feeling. I can't stay there anymore, just for Alyssa, or even for him. I'm not even a wife to him now. We don't speak, we don't go anywhere, he doesn't want to be with me. And just seeing the way he looks at me is like being beaten."

"Then get out," Zoe said firmly. They hadn't seen each other for twenty years, and it was suddenly as though they had turned the clock back, to the beginning.

"You'll be better off without him if he's making you miserable," Tanya said gently. "I survived it. You will too. We all do."

"We've been married for twenty-two years. It's incredible to watch it all go out the window."

"It sounds like it already did a while ago," Zoe said honestly, and Tanya nodded, and Mary Stuart couldn't disagree with them. Even now that he was gone, he hardly ever called her. And when they spoke, he was in a hurry to get off the phone because it was so awkward. Lately, she had taken to sending him faxes, as she had that night when they arrived, just confirming her location. And even then, he didn't answer.

"You're still young," Tanya said encouragingly, "you could meet someone else, and have a whole new life with them, with someone who wants to be with you." Mary Stuart nodded, wishing she believed them. She couldn't imagine anyone ever wanting to be with her again, after the way Bill viewed her.

"It sounds like it's time to move on," Zoe confirmed, and Mary Stuart didn't disagree with them. She just hated the fact that it had come to this after all these years. She dreaded telling him, and then packing up her things, and telling Alyssa they were getting divorced. It was all so difficult, and she shuddered at the prospect of dating. She almost couldn't bear it. But it was the same boat Tanya was in, except she was Tanya Thomas, and Mary Stuart said that. "Are you kidding? I haven't had a date since Tony left. Everyone is scared to death of me. No one's going to ask me out, except some damn hairdresser who wants to say they were out with me. Like Everest. No onc wants to live there, but the whole world wants to say they climbed it." All three of them laughed at that, and Mary Stuart wasn't sure if she felt better or worse. Just talking about her plans made it all seem so final. And in a way it seemed a betrayal of Bill, who didn't even know what she was thinking. But it was real, and it was what she was feeling, and what she thought she'd do at the end of the summer. At least she had time to think about it now while he was in England.

They sat and talked for a long time. Nothing was resolved, but their friendship was restored, and none of them said anything more about leaving in the morning. Zoe's apology had meant a great deal to Mary Stuart. And Zoe was deeply moved to realize her words had hurt her friend for all these years, worse still since her son had been a suicide, not unlike Ellie. Life was so cruel sometimes. It always boggled her, but it was also so kind at others. And in the morning, when the phone rang at six o'clock, it was Zoe who answered. She was used to coming awake instantly for the phone at night, and the other two were still sleeping.

"Hello?"

"Zoe?" It was Sam, and she instantly thought of Jade and felt a wave of panic . . . appendicitis . . . crib death . . . an earthquake . . .

"Is Jade all right?" They were the first words out of her mouth. It was as though Jade had been born to her, she loved her as much as any natural mother and had all the same instincts.

"She's fine. I'm sorry if I scared you. But I wanted to call you. I thought you'd want to know." He hated calling her with bad news, but he was sure she'd never forgive him if he didn't. "Quinn Morrison died an hour ago. He went peacefully, and his family was with him. I'm sorry you weren't here with him, but I did everything I could. His heart just gave out finally." In a way, it had been a mercy, and she knew it. But she was sad anyway, and she cried when he told her. She cried for most of them, the old, the young, and especially the children. At least Quinn Morrison had been seventy-four years old, he'd had a full life, and AIDS had only ruined the last year of it, not an entire lifetime, and it hadn't cut it much shorter than most people his age with other diseases. But she was sad anyway, she felt a sense of loss, and of having been defeated. It was a familiar feeling to her, she lost so many patients to the dread killer. "Are you all right?" Sam sounded worried.

"I'm fine. I just feel badly not to have been there."

"I knew you would. That's why I called. He said he was glad you went to Wyoming." She smiled at that. It sounded just like him. He'd spent the whole year telling her she should get married and have children.

"Is everyone else all right?"

"Peter Williams had a rough night. I spent an hour at his house before I went to Quinn's. He's got pneumonia again. I'm going to admit him in the morning." He was thirty-one years old, and getting close to the end too. But in his case, it was far more disturbing because he was so young.

"Sounds like you had a busy night."

"The usual," he said, smiling. He loved it. This was what he had gone to school for. "What about you? Having fun? Meet any cowboys yet?"

"Just one. The one who picked me up at the airport. He's about twelve years old and twelve feet tall, a kid from Mississippi. It's incredible here, by the way, I really love it."

"How's your friend?"

"Fine. And she had a surprise for me. Our other roommate from Berkeley. It's a long story, but she and I haven't spoken in twenty years. She was ready to take the next plane back to New York when she saw me. But I think we made peace last night. I was a real shit to her twenty years ago, I've never forgiven myself for it. And it was really nice to put that behind us."

"Sounds like you've been busy too," he said kindly.

"Yeah, I guess so."

"Well, go back to sleep. I'm sorry I called so early." It was only five-thirty in the morning for him by then, and he was about to go to bed. But he had wanted her to know about Quinn Morrison as soon as it happened. He knew that was what she would have wanted.

"Thanks for calling, Sam. I really appreciate it. I know you did your best for him. Don't feel that you didn't. I wouldn't have been able to do anything different." It was nice of her to say that to him, and he was grateful. She was a good woman.

"Thank you for that, Zoe. Take care. I'll talk to you soon," but as he hung up, he felt sad thinking of her. There was so much there, so much he wanted and admired, and he couldn't get near her. And he sensed her loneliness too. There was an overwhelmingly vulnerable quality about her, and yet she was hiding somewhere, and he was beginning to suspect he would never find her.

At that exact moment, as he went to bed, Zoe was standing in the living room of their cabin in Moose, Wyoming, watching the sun come up over the Grand Tetons. And there were tears rolling slowly down her cheeks at the sheer beauty of it. She thought of Quinn Morrison, and the life he had led. She was sorry he had died, she was sorry for so many of them. There was so much grief in life . . . Ellie . . . and Todd . . . and all the sorrows she'd seen, and yet at the same time there was this overwhelming beauty. And she was suddenly glad she had come. Whatever happened, she had seen the sun come up once in her life over the Grand Tetons. It was impossible not to know there was a God when you saw that. She tiptoed quietly back to her own room, and lay in bed, thinking of Sam, and looking out over the mountains.

CHAPTER 12

On their first morning at the ranch, Zoe went back to sleep for a while after Sam called, but she woke again just as Mary Stuart wandered out of her room. Zoe heard someone stirring, and got out of bed, and the two women met in the kitchen, where Mary Stuart was making coffee. They were both in their nightgowns, and Mary Stuart looked up and smiled at her. Zoe looked more rested than she had before, and surprisingly young that morning.

"Can I make you some coffee? There's tea too, if you want it." But she didn't, and Zoe helped herself to a mug of steaming coffee. "Is Tanya up yet?" Zoe asked, and then they both grinned. "I guess some things don't change."

Mary Stuart looked at her old friend seriously for a moment. They had been estranged for so many years. "No, they don't. I'm glad. I'm glad I came." She looked right into Zoe's eyes.

"So am I, Stu. I wish I hadn't been stupid way back then. I wish we'd talked over the years. I'm just glad we saw each other now. I would have hated to have this stay between us.'' It had gone on for long enough. Ellie had been laid to rest for more than twenty years, and their old battles could be too. Looking back, it seemed so foolish and such a pathetic waste of time. ''I owe Tanya one for asking you here and not telling me.''

''She's a cagey little thing, isn't she?'' Mary Stuart laughed. ''All the way here on the bus she never said a word. I should have suspected something though. She said 'we' a couple of times before I agreed to come, and I think her assistant said something about 'they' and three rooms. I thought she meant the kids. It never dawned on me she'd invited anyone. And it worked out so well for me when Alyssa canceled our trip. I had nothing to do.''

''It's a godsend for me too.'' She thought of the light on the mountains that morning when Sam had called to tell her Quinn Morrison had died. She told Mary Stuart about it, as they sat at the narrow counter in the kitchen alcove, and sipped their coffee.

''It must be depressing work,'' Mary Stuart said quietly. ''I admire you for it, but you just can't win.'' She thought of how awful it had been when Todd had died, she couldn't imagine dealing with that every day. But then again, he had been her son, not her patient.

''You can win for a while. And oddly enough, it's not depressing most of the time. You learn to take the little victories, you get more and more determined to win the fight. And sometimes you lose.'' She lost a lot of the time, it was inevitable. But some of it had to do with the circumstances, and how ready the patient and the family were to let go. Sometimes it was just time, like with Quinn. It was the children she hated to lose most, and the young people, the ones who had so much left to live and to learn and to give. Like herself. But she hadn't absorbed that yet.

''You're lucky you found the right path for yourself so long ago,'' Mary Stuart said, envying her, and enjoying her company. It was easy to remember why they had been such good friends. The rift seemed so unimportant now. In the sunlight of honesty, it had finally vanished. "I do a lot of charity work in New York, a lot of committees and volunteer work, but I've been thinking of getting a job. I just don't know what I'd do. All I've ever really done is be a wife, and mother to our kids."

"That's not bad." Zoe smiled at her, suddenly realizing how much she'd missed her. And in the unexpected twilight of her life, she realized how much she needed her friends now. It was all the more poignant for her because she had always thought she would have so much time, and now she didn't. "Being a wife and mother is a job too."

"Well, in that case," Mary Stuart said, setting down her mug, "I think my job is almost over. Alyssa is grown up. Todd is gone, I'm not even a wife to Bill anymore. We just live at the same address and my name is on his tax forms. Suddenly, I feel useless."

"You're not. Maybe it's just time to move on."

She was right, but the problem was to where. Mary Stuart had been doing a lot of thinking. "I keep looking for the answers, of what to do, where to live, what to tell Bill when he comes back. I don't even want to talk to him right now. But he doesn't want to talk to me either. He hardly ever calls. Maybe he's going through the same thing, and just doesn't want to say it. He must realize that it's all over."

"Maybe you should ask him," Zoe said, and looked at her watch, wondering when Tanya was going to get up, and then she glanced at Mary Stuart. "What time are we supposed to be at breakfast?"

"Eight o'clock, I think." It was seven-thirty by then, and they had to dress, and then Mary Stuart looked at her old friend with a quizzical expression. "Are you leaving today?" Her voice was very gentle.

There was a long pause and then Zoe shook her head. "I'd rather not, unless you want me to. But it's up to you, you've come the greatest distance. If anyone leaves, I should."

Mary Stuart smiled at her gently. "I want you to stay, Zoe,

and I'd like to stay too. Let's put all that stuff behind us. We both loved Ellie, we all did. She would have wanted us all to be together. Of all of us, she was the most loving, the most giving, it would have broken her heart to know that we hadn't spoken for twenty-one years because of her." It was true and they both knew it.

Zoe was frowning, thinking of her. "She deserves to have a broken heart, after what she did to all of us. I think I was so rotten to you at the time because I was so mad at her and there was no one to take it out on."

"I went through the same thing with Todd. I was mad at everyone for the first six months, Alyssa, her friends, myself, the maid, the dog, Bill," she said sadly, "and he still is mad. I think he always will be."

"Maybe he's just stuck," Zoe said kindly. "I was. I was mad for a long time, and when I got over it, you were gone, we had all gone our separate ways. You'd married Bill, I was in medical school, it seemed easier to let it slide, but I was wrong to do that. Maybe Bill is sliding too." It was a fair assessment and Mary Stuart nodded.

"I think he slid right out the door a while back and I didn't notice." She smiled and then looked at her watch again. It was twenty to eight and they had to get ready for breakfast. "What do you say we wake sleeping beauty?" They grinned at each other, and laughing all the way, they tiptoed to her room, and pounced on the huge bed, on either side of her. She was wearing a white satin nightgown and a sleep mask, and she acted as though she were being roused from the dead when they woke her.

"Oh, God . . . stop it . . . I hate you . . . stop that . . ." Zoe was tickling her feet, and Mary Stuart was hitting her with pillows. They were just like two kids, and Tanya was overwhelmed as she tried to hide beneath the covers and found she couldn't. "Will you stop it! Stop that! It's the middle of the night, for God's sake!" She had always hated getting up in the morning, and they always had to drag her out of bed so she wouldn't miss her morning classes.

"Take off your sleep mask," Mary Stuart said. "Breakfast is in fifteen minutes, and the stuff on the desk says we have to be at the corral at eight forty-five to pick out our horses. Get your ass out of bed and get ready." She sounded totally in charge, and Zoe was dragging her out of bed by one arm, as Tanya took off her mask and looked from one to the other.

"Did I hear you say you were going to the corral? Does this mean you're staying?"

"Apparently we have no choice," Zoe said, letting go of her and glancing at Mary Stuart with a spark of mischief in her eye, "if we don't, you'll sleep the week away, and never get out of the room until dinner. We thought we'd stick around and keep you honest. We know how much you hate horses. Without us, you'd probably sit in your room all day, watching television from the Jacuzzi."

"God, what a great idea." Tanya grinned, proud of both of them, they had done it. After all these years, they'd come to their senses and restored their friendship. "Why don't you check back with me at lunchtime, I thought I'd give myself a facial."

"Get your ass out of bed, Miss Thomas," Mary Stuart barked at her. "You have exactly twelve minutes to brush your teeth, comb your hair, and get your clothes on."

"Christ, what is this, the Marines? I knew I shouldn't have asked you two here. I could have brought *nice* people, who treat me *right,* and let me get a little sleep. I'm a very important person."

"The hell you are," Mary Stuart said with a broad grin, "now get out of that bed. You can take a shower later."

"Great. Now I'm going to smell like the horses. Wait till that hits the tabloids."

Both Mary Stuart and Zoe stood with their hands on their hips, as Tanya reluctantly got out of bed, stretching her long exquisite body with a yawn, and then groaned as she headed toward the bathroom.

"I'll get you a cup of coffee," Zoe said as she headed back to the kitchen.

"Make it IV please, Doctor," Tanya said as she turned the bathroom light on and groaned again when she saw her face and hair in the mirror. "Oh, God, I'm two hundred years old and look what I look like. Someone call a plastic surgeon."

"You look great," Mary Stuart laughed as she looked at her. She was so damn beautiful, and the funny thing was she had never really known it. Tanya thought she was plain, and the others always laughed at her for it. Mary Stuart knew she really believed it. "Look what I look like at eight A.M., with no makeup." Mary Stuart frowned at herself in the mirror. Her hair was brushed till it shone, her skin was still beautiful, and she had put on just a hint of pale pink lipstick. She was wearing a blue cotton men's shirt, and a pair of freshly pressed jeans, and a brand-new pair of brown lizard boots from Billy Martin's.

"Christ, look at you," Tanya complained as she brushed her teeth and got toothpaste all over her nightgown. "You look like you just stepped out of *Vogue*."

"She just does that to make us feel bad," Zoe said as she handed Tanya a cup of coffee. They were used to her. Even in college, she had always looked perfect. It was just her style, and in fact they all liked it. She was an inspiration to the others, and always had been. And guys had loved it.

Zoe was wearing jeans with holes in the knees, a pair of cowboy boots she'd had for years, and a comfortable old beige sweater. Her dark red hair was pulled back, and she looked neat and casual and very much at ease in her surroundings. But both of them had to smile when they saw Tanya emerge from the bathroom five minutes later. Even with no makeup on, and having been dragged out of bed, she looked sensational. Tanya was simply a star, without even trying. Her thick blond hair did all the right things, as it cascaded past her shoulders. She hadn't had time to pull it back, and it looked as though she had planned it that way. She had a tight white T-shirt on, and it wasn't indecent in any way, but it was so sexy no man with eyes in his head would have been able to stand it, her jeans looked exactly the way they should, not too tight or too loose, they showed off all the right things, the tight roundness of her seat, the narrow hips, the small waist, the long graceful legs. She was wearing her old yellow boots, and there was a red bandanna tied around her neck, and she had on plain gold hoop earrings. She grabbed a denim jacket she'd brought, her cowboy hat, and a pair of sunglasses, and she looked like an ad for any dude ranch.

"If I didn't love you so much, I'd hate you," Mary Stuart said admiringly, and Zoe grinned. They were all pretty women, but there was no denying, Tanya had something special.

"I've never figured out how you do that," Zoe said, taking it all in, and feeling the same warm glow of affection for her as Mary Stuart. There had never been so much as an ounce of jealousy between them. Even years before, the four of them had been the best of friends, more than sisters. "I always thought if I watched you get dressed, I'd figure it out," Zoe said as they left the room, "but it's like one of those magic tricks, where you can see it done four million times, and there's always that single moment when the rabbit appears, and you just never see it happen. You're the only person I know who can go into a bathroom and come out looking like a movie star three minutes later. I could spend a week in there, and I still come out looking the same, sort of okay, pretty decent, my hair is combed, my face is clean, my makeup is on straight, but it's still me. You come out looking like a fairy princess."

"It's the miracle of plastic surgery." Tanya grinned, enjoying their company, but not believing a word of it. But she thought they were sweet to say it. "If you get enough stuff fixed, you don't need makeup."

"Bullshit," Mary Stuart corrected her. "You looked like

that at nineteen. You used to get up in the morning looking like a caterpillar, and by the time your feet hit the floor, you were a butterfly. I know exactly what Zoe means. You're just too insecure to understand it, and believe what you look like. That's why we all love you."

"Hell, I thought it was my accent." She still had the mildest of Southern drawls. Her fans particularly loved it when she was singing. "I can't believe I let you two get me out of bed at this hour. It can't be good for your health, especially in this altitude. I think it's bad for my heart actually," Tanya complained as she huffed and puffed her way up a short hill to the main building.

"It's great for you," Zoe said matter-of-factly with a grin at Mary Stuart, "and you'll be used to the altitude by tonight. Just don't have any booze to drink."

"Why not?" Tanya looked surprised. She didn't drink much, but she just wondered.

"Because you'll get smashed on the first three sips and make an ass of yourself," Zoe explained, laughing at her, and then reminded her of the time she had passed out after some dance, and they'd taken her home and she threw up all over Zoe's bed and Zoe almost killed her. Zoe and Mary Stuart were both laughing at her, and she managed to look sheepish twenty-plus years later, she was trying to tell them she'd had the flu, and Zoe was saying she'd been just plain drunk, as the three of them exploded into the dining room like a vision of beauty.

There were people at long tables around the room, and helping themselves at the buffet, and everyone looked sleepy and subdued, except for a few guests here and there who looked more animated, and were clearly morning people. There was a rumor that Tanya Thomas was at the hotel, but no one was prepared for what she actually looked like. And laughing with her friends, Tanya looked so relaxed and so young, and so incredibly beautiful that everyone stopped and stared, and Zoe suddenly felt sorry for her. Her two friends closed ranks on her, and they took a table in the far corner. Mary Stuart sat with her, while Zoe went to get them some breakfast, but the whole room was suddenly staring and buzzing, and they both knew it wasn't easy for her.

"What do you think would happen if I suddenly stood up and mooned them?" Tanya whispered, she had her back to the room, and her dark glasses on. She had put her hat on the back of her chair, but even from the back she looked spectacular. She was every inch a star, and the whole world knew it.

"I think you'd make a big impression," Mary Stuart answered her, and they chatted quietly until Zoe arrived with a plate of danish and some bacon, and juggling three yogurts.

"I ordered scrambled eggs and oatmeal for all of us," she said, and Tanya looked horrified.

"I'm going to have to go to the fat farm for six months after this. I can't eat all that crap for breakfast."

"It's good for you," Zoe said matter-of-factly. "You're adjusting to high altitude and you're going to be doing a lot of exercise. Eat a good breakfast. Doctor's orders." She was taking the same advice herself, and Tanya helped herself to a yogurt.

"I am not planning to gain ten pounds while I'm here," Tanya said staunchly, but she was hungrier than she thought, and a few minutes later, she helped herself to a danish. Zoe had gone back to the buffet for more by then, and Tanya glanced at her with a grim look when she returned to the table. She knew without even looking what was happening all around her. "How bad is it?"

"The food? I think it's good." Zoe looked surprised. She had thought the pastry and bacon were delicious, and the eggs had just arrived and they smelled good too. But Tanya didn't mean the food, she meant the people.

"Not the food, dummy. The folks. I can smell it."

"Oh." Zoe understood, and glanced at Mary Stuart as she began to eat her eggs. She hadn't been planning to tell Tanya. "That. Oh, it's probably about par for the course."

"Just tell me so I know what to expect. Are the natives friendly?" She was hoping they'd lose interest eventually, they sometimes did when she stayed somewhere, or sometimes she just had to leave and go somewhere else, but she wasn't planning to do that. She had hoped to remain low-key enough to blend in with the other people, but that was hopeless.

"Well, let's see." Zoe looked at her, amazed at what happened to people whenever they were around her. "Four women want to know if your hair is real, two of their husbands want to know if you've had a boob job, or if they're real. One guy loves your ass. Three women think you've had a face-lift, but five others swear you haven't. There's a bunch of teenage girls dying for your autograph, but their mothers say they'll kill them if they ask, and all of the waiters are already in love with you and think you're gorgeous. I think that pretty much covers it, except for the little Mexican guy who made our eggs and wants to know if the rumor is true that you're originally Hispanic. I told him I didn't think so, and he was real disappointed." As she listened, Tanya was grinning. She knew that Zoe was probably exaggerating a little bit, but it probably wasn't far off the mark. It was always like that. But as long as they stayed in control and kept their distance, she could live with it. If not, they would ruin her vacation.

"Tell the guy who loves my ass it's real, and I'll be happy to send his secretary a Xerox."

"What about the boobs?" Zoe asked her seriously. "Are we prepared to make a statement on those?"

"Tell them to read *People* magazine. It'll be in there next week."

"Oh, that's right, and another woman wants to know your birth sign. She swears you're Pisces just like her sister. She said you could be twins. She wants to show you a picture."

"I can't believe this." Mary Stuart looked at her in amazement. "How do you stand it?"

"I don't. I'm a little crazy," Tanya said with a grin, taking a bite of oatmeal. "They say you get used to it, and maybe I have, and just don't know it." The truth was she was willing to accept a lot of it, it was only when it went over the line or was really cruel that it hurt her. And most of the time it was, which was the problem. This kind of stuff, the birth signs, the questions, the autographs, it was all pretty harmless.

"It would drive me right out of my mind," Zoe said honestly. "I used to cringe for you every time I saw your name in the tabloids."

"I still do," Mary Stuart said. "Sometimes I grab a bunch of them in the supermarket and hide them," she said proudly, and Tanya smiled at her two friends. It was amazing, after two decades in Hollywood and all the people she'd met, these were still the two people she cared about most, and felt closest to. Being with them made her feel safe and protected.

"I don't know how you learn to live with it," Tanya said with a sigh. "It still hurts so much sometimes, the stuff they write, the lies. It makes me want to run away and hide. Sometimes I just think I'll go back to Texas. But my agent says I can't escape it now. It's too big, and it's gone on for too long. He says if I retire it'll just go on forever, so I guess there's not much point in running away. At least this way, I get to sing, and make a little money."

Mary Stuart laughed at that though. "A little money" to Tanya was a king's ransom. She saw the look in her friends' eyes and laughed at herself. "Okay. A lot of money. But what the hell, there have to be some compensations."

"This is one of them." Zoe smiled and looked around her, grateful to be here. "You know, if it weren't for you, I probably wouldn't have taken a vacation for another eleven years. This all just kind of happened spur-of-the-moment."

"What finally made you come?" Tanya asked, she had forgotten to ask her, and Zoe hesitated for only a fraction of a second.

"I got the flu, and I was feeling like hell. And I got a really good relief doctor I know to do a locum tenens for me, that means he's covering for me. That's what he does for a living, it's his specialty, covering for other docs in their practices. He has no practice of his own. Anyway, he said he'd cover for me, and he kind of pushed me. And you had asked me about coming to Wyoming.''

''Good for him,'' Tanya approved. ''Is he married?''

''No. But he's not dating my patients, he's taking care of them,'' Zoe laughed. Sometimes Tanya had a one-track mind. She had always loved arranging blind dates between their friends when they were in college.

''Never mind them. What about you? Is he dating you?'' Tanya's infallible radar had picked up something.

''Nope. I was going out with a breast surgeon for a while, but it was nothing serious and that's over.'' Mary Stuart knew about Adam years before, but she'd never heard about anyone since then. She wondered if there was a serious man in Zoe's life, but she said there wasn't.

''Don't doctors ever go out with anyone else except other physicians?'' Tanya complained. ''Talk about staying within the industry. That's like actors. Talking shop is so boring.''

''No, it's not. Maybe no one else can put up with us, the hours, the pressures. Our interests are pretty narrow.''

''So what about this guy, this 'local tenant' or whatever you said he was? Is he cute?'' Tanya asked her.

''Oh, come on,'' Zoe blushed, and Tanya saw it. ''He's just a doctor.''

''Bullshit! You're blushing!'' Mary Stuart was laughing at both of them and Zoe was squirming in her seat under Tanya's interrogation. ''Aha! He must be cute, and he's not married. What does he look like?''

''A teddy bear. He's big and burly with brown hair and brown eyes. Satisfied? Okay? I've had dinner with him once, and I won't date him and he knows it. Okay?'' Zoe gave it right back to her old buddy, but Tanya was not ready to drop the subject.

''Why not? Is he straight? I mean, in San Francisco, he could be . . .'' She looked apologetic and Zoe groaned.

"You're hopeless. He's straight, he looks okay, he's single, and I'm not interested. End of subject." She was very firm with Tanya, to whom it meant nothing. Tanya had decided that Zoe liked him despite her protestations.

"Why not? Why aren't you interested? Does he have some awful flaw? Bad breath, bad manners, a prison record, something we should know about and hold against him, or are you just being difficult?" Zoe had always been incredibly picky about who she dated.

"I don't have time for anyone. I work all the time, and I have a daughter."

"That's a terrible attitude," Tanya scolded her. " 'This is not a dress rehearsal,' " she quoted her favorite poster. "You can't live alone for the rest of your life, Zoe. It's unhealthy."

"I don't believe this. I'm a middle-aged woman and I can do anything I want. I'm too old to date. Besides, I don't want to."

"Well, thanks for warning me," Tanya said, pushing away her plate. She had eaten everything, even the eggs. "You're a year older than I am, which means I have a year before it's all over. And if you tell anyone I'm that old, by the way, I'll kill you."

"Don't worry," Zoe said, grinning at her, "they'd never believe me."

"They might, but I'll just say you're a compulsive liar. Now, what's this guy's name, he sounds terrific."

"Sam. And you're a nutcase."

"Tell the tabloids. I like him. He sounds great."

"You don't know anything about him," Zoe said firmly, trying to feel calm about it. She wasn't sure why, but Tanya had unnerved her. She had always had the ability to do that.

"I know that you're scared to death of him, which means it must be a serious relationship. If he were a jerk, you wouldn't care. I think you know he'd be perfect for you. How long have you known him?"

"Since medical school. We went to Stanford together."

Zoe couldn't believe she was answering her questions, and Mary Stuart was smiling at both of them, and putting on lipstick. It was just like the old days. They used to have discussions like that over breakfast in Berkeley. Tanya had been so in love with Bobby Joe she thought the whole world should be in love, engaged, or getting married. She hadn't changed much.

"You've known him since medical school? Why haven't you done anything about him till now?" Tanya looked outraged.

"Because we've both been involved with other people, other lives. I lost track of him for a while, now he's doing some work for me. He's a nice guy, but that's it. Now, are we going to ride horses or are we going to talk about Sam all day?"

"I think you should go out with him and give the guy a chance," Tanya grumbled as she got to her feet. She hadn't had this much fun in years, and neither had the others. "I vote for Sam. Let's all discuss this again later."

"I'll be sure to do that," Zoe said, rolling her eyes, and Mary Stuart shepherded them all to the corral. They were the last to get there, and when they arrived, Tanya's appearance once again made a huge sensation. There were whispers, people staring at her, kids shoving each other and pointing fingers. A couple of people snuck photographs, but she turned away from them artfully and quickly. She didn't mind posing for photographs with fans from time to time, but she didn't want the intrusion on her private life, and she was definitely "off duty." The Star Is Out, she whispered to Zoe. But both of her friends were good at blocking people's view of her, and the threesome huddled discreetly in a remote corner, while the woman in charge of the stables called out names, to match people with horses. The night before they had all filled out forms, absolving the ranch of liability, and explaining the extent of their ability and experience with horses. Tanya had written down *Advanced/Hate them/Will ride only intermediate level with friends.* Both Mary Stuart and Zoe were only fair riders. Mary Stuart had more experience, but she hadn't ridden in years, and she had only ridden English. Zoe had ridden several times, but not recently, and none of them were anxious to prove anything. They just wanted to go on easy trail rides. And the ranch had already explained that there were too many guests at the moment to send them out without other guests, but Tanya said she didn't mind that. If it got too difficult because they hounded her or took constant photographs, or she didn't like the people they chose, she could always opt to stop riding. But she was willing to try it for the moment.

As it turned out, their names were among the last to be called, and there were only three other guests left beside them. The head of the corral came over and talked to Tanya personally, as a tall wrangler with dark hair led her horse out.

"We wanted to let the crowd thin a little bit to give you some air," Liz Thompson explained to her. She was a tall, lanky woman with a weathered face and a powerful handshake, somewhere in her mid-fifties. "I didn't think you needed to have fifty people taking photographs while you got your feet in the stirrups," she said sensibly, and Tanya thanked her. "I noticed on your card you're not a horse lover," she smiled, "I think we have a nice old guy for you here." For a minute, Tanya wondered if she meant the horse or the wrangler, but it was obvious from the man adjusting the saddle for her that it was not the cowboy. He looked about forty years old, and he had a powerful build and broad shoulders. But when he looked at her, she saw that he had an interesting, weathered face, and he was eyeing her with interest. If you looked at him for a while, he was almost good-looking. His cheekbones were a little too broad, his chin too prominent, and yet it all fit together right, and he had a drawl similar to her own, and when she asked, he said he was from Texas. But they were from opposite ends of the state, and he didn't seem inclined to pursue the matter further. Most people tried to find some common ground with her. He was only interested in saddling up her horse, adjusting the stirrups for her, tightening the girth for her again, and getting the others mounted. And as soon as she settled on Big Max as her horse was called, he left her. The only way she knew the cowboy's name, since he hadn't introduced himself, was when she heard one of the other wranglers call him. His name was Gordon.

Zoe's horse was a paint mare, and she looked spirited, but Liz had promised she was friendly, and Zoe looked surprisingly comfortable in the saddle. And Mary Stuart was riding a palomino. Big Max was a tall black horse with a long mane and tail, and as he shied a little in the corral, Tanya wondered if he was as sleepy as Liz had promised. She had no intention of battling a wild horse all over these mountains. But Liz explained as she walked by that he'd be fine once he got out, he was corral-shy. The head of the corral was being very attentive to Tanya. Far more so than Gordon, who was busy with the three other guests he'd been assigned, a middle-aged couple from Chicago who introduced themselves as Dr. Smith and Dr. Wyman, but appeared to be married. They even looked alike, which amused Tanya and she said something to Zoe. And then there was a man alone. He looked to be about fifty-five, and Mary Stuart kept staring at him, she could swear she knew him. He was tall and spare and had a mane of gray hair, and sharp blue eyes that examined the entire group with interest. He was a good-looking man and even Tanya couldn't help noticing he had distinguished features. She could see that he had noticed her too, and he smiled when he realized who she was, but he didn't approach her. And he seemed equally interested in the others. And it was only once they were on their way that Mary Stuart sidled up to Tanya on her horse and whispered to her.

"Do you know who that is?" She had finally figured it out. She'd seen him once before, but here he looked different. But Tanya didn't know him. She glanced again and shook her head in answer. "It's Hartley Bowman." It took a minute to register and then Tanya nodded with interest, forcing herself not to glance over her shoulder.

"The writer?" she whispered instead, and Mary Stuart nodded. He currently had two books on the bestseller list, one hard cover and one soft. And he had had a highly respected career. "Is he married?" she asked her friend from New York, and Mary Stuart rolled her eyes at her. She was hopeless.

"Widowed," Mary Stuart supplied, she remembered reading that his wife had died of breast cancer a year or two before. It had been in *Time* magazine or *Newsweek.* And as a writer, he was extremely respected. He looked interesting too, and Mary Stuart would have liked to talk to him, but she didn't want to be like the people who pestered Tanya.

Mary Stuart and Tanya rode on side by side for a while, and Zoe had already begun chatting with the two physicians from Chicago. Tanya was right. Doctors always seemed to hang out together. They were both oncologists, and the wife had heard of Zoe's work and her clinic. And they were chatting animatedly as the horses made their way slowly across the valley. There were fields full of blue and yellow flowers all around them, and the snow-capped mountains were looming high above them.

"It's incredible, isn't it?" Mary Stuart heard a voice next to her and jumped as Tanya rode ahead toward the wrangler. Big Max had tired of moving at a snail's pace, and she had given him his head for a few minutes, which left Mary Stuart alone, but not for long. Hartley Bowman had joined her. "Have you been here before?" he asked casually, as though they were old acquaintances, but the atmosphere at the ranch was very informal.

"No, I haven't," she said quietly, "it's lovely." And she couldn't help glancing at him as he rode along beside her. He was very nice-looking. He had a clean, tweedy look to him. He had lovely hands, she noticed as he held the reins, and a riding style that told her he rode English. She mentioned it to him and he laughed.

"I always feel a little odd in Western saddles. I ride in Connecticut," he volunteered, and she nodded. "Are you from the West Coast?" He was intrigued by her, and the group she was traveling with. He had recognized Tanya immediately and wondered how Mary Stuart fitted into the entourage, but he didn't want to ask her.

"I'm from New York," she said. "I just came out for two weeks."

"So did I," he said, looking very much at ease with her, as he smiled. "I come every year. My wife and I used to love it. This is the first time I've come back since she died." Mary Stuart suspected it was hard for him, but he didn't say it. But she imagined that, having been there with someone before, it had to be lonely for him. "A lot of people come here from the East. It's really worth the trip. I come here for the mountains," he confessed, glancing at them. In truth, they all did, even those who didn't know it. The others thought they came for the horses. "There's something very healing about them. I wasn't going to come again, and I didn't last year, but I found I just couldn't stay away. I needed to be here." He said it pensively, as though surprised at himself for coming. "I normally prefer the ocean, but there's something magical about Wyoming, and these mountains." She understood exactly what he meant. Ever since the day before, she had begun to feel it. It was part of why Jackson Hole had become so popular in recent years. It was like being drawn to Mecca.

"It's funny you should say that," she confessed to him, feeling surprisingly comfortable with him, considering the fact that they were strangers. But he was so open. "I've felt it too. I felt it yesterday when we arrived. It's as though the mountains are waiting for you here . . . as though you can tell your troubles to them, and they're waiting to embrace you." She was afraid it would sound silly to him, but he knew just what she meant as he nodded.

"It must be difficult for your friend," he said gently. "I was watching the people in the dining room, they were transformed the moment she arrived, and without even meaning to, they became completely foolish. She doesn't get a moment without people reacting to her, wanting to be with her, taking her picture, trying to be a part of her aura." It was an interesting analysis, but it was true, and it intrigued Mary Stuart that he saw it so clearly.

"It must be difficult for anyone who's well-known," she said, not wanting to tell him that she had recognized him and read his last six books and loved them. She didn't want to appear starstruck. After being close to Tanya for all these years, she knew just how annoying it could be.

"It has its disadvantages." And then he looked at Mary Stuart with a smile. He had understood perfectly that she knew him. "But I'm not in those leagues. Few are. There are probably only a handful of people in the world who have to put up with what she does. She seems to be very gracious about it."

"She is," Mary Stuart said staunchly.

"Do you work with her?" He didn't want to pry, but he wondered if the two women constantly at her side were her assistants.

"We were college roommates," Mary Stuart explained with a smile.

"And you're still friends? How amazing. Now, there's a story," and then he quickly explained himself before he could alarm her, "for a book, not the tabloids," he specified, and they both laughed.

"Thank you. She gets such a rough break all the time. It's so unfair."

"You stop being human to them the moment you're a star. You no longer matter, you become human garbage," he said sadly, and Mary Stuart nodded.

"She calls it 'life as an object.' She says you become a thing, and anything they do to you then is allowed. She's put up with a lot. I don't know how she does it."

"She must be strong," and then he smiled at Mary Stuart, admiring her impeccable good looks. He loved her style, but he wouldn't have dared tell her. "She's fortunate to have good friends."

"We're lucky to have her." Mary Stuart smiled again. "It

was really serendipity that we came here. It all kind of happened at the last minute."

"How fortunate for the rest of us," he said. "The three of you certainly improve the landscape." He glanced from her to Tanya, looking glorious, as she loped easily along beside the wrangler, but Mary Stuart noticed that they weren't talking, just riding. "She's an incredible-looking woman." He couldn't help but admire her, and Mary Stuart nodded with a smile, completely without envy. "I really enjoy her music. I have all of her CD's," he admitted, looking slightly embarrassed, and Mary Stuart laughed as she smiled at him.

"I have all your books." She blushed as she said it.

"Do you?" He looked pleased and held a hand out to her and introduced himself, though it was obviously not necessary, just good manners. "Hartley Bowman."

"I'm Mary Stuart Walker." They shook hands across their horses' necks, and rode on together comfortably. Tanya and the wrangler were far ahead by then, the trio of doctors bringing up the rear, discussing articles and research, and some new research that had been done recently in oncology at Mass General.

Mary Stuart and Hartley chatted for a while, about books, and New York, the literary scene, other authors, and Europe, when she said her daughter was studying in Paris. They seemed to touch on a wealth of subjects, and they were both surprised when the wrangler turned slowly around and led them back to the corral. It was lunchtime. Hartley and Mary Stuart were still chatting when they dismounted. And she noticed an odd look on Tanya's face when she got off Big Max and handed the reins to the wrangler.

"Are you okay?" she asked as Tanya walked over to join them, and she introduced her to Hartley.

"I'm fine. But our wrangler is really strange. He absolutely would not say one word to me. We just rode out, and then back. He acted like I had bubonic plague or something. He hates me." Mary Stuart laughed at her analysis of the situation. She had never met a man who hated Tanya, certainly not at first meeting.

"Maybe he's shy," Mary Stuart volunteered. He looked pleasant enough. He just wasn't very chatty.

"A lot of them are," Hartley explained. "The first few days they barely say hello, and by the time you leave, you feel like brothers. They're not used to all this big-city stuff, and they're not as chatty as we are," he said, and Tanya looked at him with a smile.

"I thought I'd said something to offend him." Tanya looked slightly worried.

"I suspect Liz told him to behave himself with you, not to say too much. It's got to be pretty impressive for these guys to be around a big star like you," he grinned and looked like a kid then, gray hair and all, "it even makes me tremble a little. I have all your CD's, Miss Thomas, and I love them."

"I've read your books, and I like them too." She smiled at him. It always amazed her when someone important was impressed with her. She never completely understood it. "I like them a lot." They both looked shy with each other, uncomfortable with their own success to a degree. Each of them were stars in their own right. He seemed much more at ease with Mary Stuart than with Tanya, and then Zoe joined them, saying she'd had a great morning. She'd really enjoyed talking to the two doctors. And Mary Stuart introduced her to Hartley.

"What's your specialty?" he asked amiably as they wandered back toward their cabins to wash up before lunch.

"AIDS," she said simply, "and related problems. I run a clinic in San Francisco." He nodded. He'd been thinking about doing a book about it, but he'd been dragging his feet about doing the research. It seemed so depressing. But he was obviously fascinated by what she did, and asked her a great many questions. And he seemed sorry to leave them at their cabin, and said he'd see them at lunchtime. He went off on his own, head down, looking pensive, as he walked toward his cabin, and Tanya watched him.

''What an interesting man,'' Tanya commented as they walked into their home away from home, and she took her scarf off. It had gotten hot since that morning.

''He's crazy about your music,'' Mary Stuart said encouragingly. She would have loved to see Tanya with someone like Hartley, although she had to admit they didn't seem to have a lot in common. Hartley was very smooth and very Eastern, intellectual but worldly somehow, and very polished. Tanya was so much more exuberant and sensual, not wild, but so alive. Mary Stuart thought she needed someone more powerful to tame her, or at least make her happy.

''He may be crazy about my music,'' Tanya said wisely, better versed in the ways of the world than Mary Stuart, ''but he likes you, kiddo. It's written all over him. He couldn't take his eyes off you.''

''That's bullshit. He's intrigued by all three of us. You know, kind of like Charlie's Angels.''

''I'll bet you money he comes on to you before you leave here,'' Tanya said with total certainty, and Zoe rolled her eyes at both of them and washed her hands in the kitchen.

''You two are disgusting. Is that all you think about? Dating?''

''Yeah,'' Tanya said with a mischievous grin. ''Sex. Read the tabloids.'' But they all knew better. Tanya had always been, and still was, very moral. Perhaps even more so than the others, and she'd always been monogamous, even in college. ''I'm telling you what I see. The guy is crazy about Mary Stuart.''

''How crazy can he be? I just met him this morning.''

''Well, his wife died a couple of years ago, right? So he's got to be horny as hell, so watch out for him, Stu. He could be a wild man.'' Mary Stuart and Zoe were both laughing at her, as she pinned her thick blond hair up on her head without looking and instantly looked even sexier than she had at breakfast.

''Why don't you wear a bag over your head or something?'' Mary Stuart said in disgust. ''I don't know why I bother to comb my hair when you look like that without looking in the mirror."

"Yeah, and look how much good it does me. Even the wrangler won't give me the time of day. Christ, I thought the guy's lips had been sewed shut. He never said one word to me. What an asshole."

"Are you trying to pick up the wranglers now?" Zoe shook a finger at her, and Tanya looked insulted.

"I just wanted somebody to talk to. Tolstoy or Charles Dickens or whoever he is was chewing Mary Stuart's ear off, you and the docs from Chicago were talking about disgusting stuff that makes my stomach feel sick, and that left me with Roy Rogers. Well, let me tell you, the guy gets an F in conversation."

"Better than if he got fresh with you," Zoe said matter-of-factly, "or were some crazed fan asking dumb questions."

"Yeah, I guess so," she conceded, "but it sure was boring." They heard the bell ring for lunch then, and were just starting out the door of the cabin when the phone rang. The three of them looked at each other, tempted not to answer, but they knew they had to. Zoe volunteered to do phone duty. It could have been Sam about one of her patients, or Jade. But it was Jean, Tanya's assistant. She had to talk to her about a contract. She was sending the originals for the concert tour, and a red-lined copy by Federal Express, at the request of her lawyer, and he wanted to talk to her as soon as she read it. Just listening to her made Tanya antsy.

"Okay. I'll look at it when it gets here."

"He wants you to send it back right away. No kidding."

"Okay, okay, I'll do it. Anything else major I need to know about?" An employee she'd dismissed had signed a release agreeing not to sue, which was a relief for a change, *Vogue* and *Harper's Bazaar* both wanted to do spreads on her, and one of the movie magazines was poking around to do a really nasty story. "Thanks for the good news," she said, hating to hear all of it. It brought the big bad world right to her doorstep in Wyoming. She couldn't wait to hang up and join the others.

"Everything okay?" Mary Stuart looked at her with concern. Tanya looked upset again, and her friend hated to see it.

"More or less. Someone's not suing for a change, and some lousy magazine is going to run another ugly story. No big deal, I guess." But it was as though they broke off a piece of her soul each time they did it, like an old, stale cookie. And one day, there would be no pieces left at all. She would have no soul left. But to them, it made no difference.

"Don't pay any attention to it," Zoe suggested. "Just don't read it." There had been some critical articles about her when she'd first started the clinic, but that wasn't the same thing and Tanya knew it better than she did. This was so personal, so hurtful, so invasive, and always so ugly.

"Try to forget it," Mary Stuart said, and both women put their arms around Tanya's waist, and the three of them walked up to the dining room, talking like that, with no idea of the powerful impression they made as they walked along. They were three very striking women. And from his deck, unnoticed by them, Hartley Bowman was watching Mary Stuart.

CHAPTER 13

Their ride that afternoon was just as pleasant as the one that morning, and they rode out again in the same groups and configurations. They were assigned the same wrangler and the same horses for the duration of their stay, so Liz, the head of the corral, was anxious to know if everyone was satisfied with their mounts and their cowboys. And no one seemed to have any complaints that she knew of.

Zoe chatted with the doctors again that afternoon, and Tanya tried not to listen as they had moved on to transplants, which was no better than the discussion about severed limbs earlier that morning. And trying to leave Mary Stuart alone with Hartley as they discussed a book they'd both read, she moved ahead again with the wrangler. Once again, they rode for what seemed like miles, in silence. And then finally, Tanya couldn't stand it, and she looked at him from across her horse's neck, but he never even looked at her. It was as though he had no idea who she was beside him. It was entirely up to her to keep up with him, he never once acknowledged her presence.

"Is there something about me that bothers you?" she asked, with an irritated expression. He was really beginning to annoy her. She was not having fun, and she didn't even like him.

"No, ma'am. Nothing at all," he said, without a change of expression. She thought he was going to lapse into silence again and she wanted to hit him with her cowboy boot. He was the most taciturn man she'd ever met, and she couldn't stand it. Usually people at least talked to her, or looked at her, or something. She had never met anyone with reactions like Gordon. But he surprised her after another half mile, while she was debating whether or not it was worth the trouble of trying again, just to see if he would answer. "You're a real good rider." At first, she couldn't believe he'd spoken, and this time he glanced at her sideways, and then looked away just as quickly. It was almost as though her light was too blinding. It was that that was troubling him, but she didn't know that.

"Thank you. I don't like horses." Or cowboys. Or people who don't talk to me. Or anything about you.

"I saw that on your card, ma'am. Any special reason? You taken a bad fall sometime?" She suspected it was the most he'd said all year to anyone, but at least he was trying. He was clearly a man of few words, but she was beginning to wonder if Hartley was right, and he was shy and not used to city people. He should have taken a job doing shoes then, not riding with hotel guests, she thought as she watched him.

"No, I've never fallen. I just think horses are dumb. I rode a lot when I was a kid, but I never liked it."

"I grew up on a horse," he said matter-of-factly, "roping steers. My daddy worked on a ranch, and I worked right along with him." He didn't tell her that his father had died when he was ten, and he had supported his mother and four sisters until they all got married and he still supported his mother, and he had a son he helped out from time to time in Montana.

Despite what Tanya thought of him, Gordon Washbaugh was a good man, and a bright one. "Most of the people who come here say they can ride, think so too, but they're just plain dangerous. They don't have any idea what they're doing. They all wind up in the dust first day out. Not many like you, ma'am." It was a classic understatement and he knew it. He looked at her sheepishly, and she was surprised to see that he was smiling too then. "I never rode with anyone famous. Makes me kinda nervous." He was so honest it impressed her. And she was suddenly embarrassed by her complaints to the others at lunchtime.

"Why would it make you nervous?" His perception of her amused her. It was so rare that she could see herself from that perspective. She never really understood why people were so fascinated, nor why he would be frightened of her.

"Don't want to say the wrong thing, ma'am. Might make you angry."

And then she laughed suddenly, as they rode through a clearing. The light was beautiful on the hills, and in the distance they could see a coyote. "You really made me mad when you wouldn't talk to me this morning," she admitted with a grin, and he glanced at her cautiously. He had no idea whether or not to relax with her, if she was real, and could be trusted. "I thought you hated me or something."

"Why would I hate you? The whole damn ranch wants to know you. Bought your CD's, want autographs. Someone's got a video of you somewhere. They told us not to say anything to you, not to ask questions, not to bother you. I figured it was just better not to talk at all. Didn't want to bug you. The others make such damn fools of themselves. I tried to get them to let someone else be your wrangler. I'm not much of a talker." He was so honest with her that in spite of her earlier assessment of him, she actually liked him. And he was surprisingly clean and well-spoken for a cowboy. "I'm sorry if I hurt your feelings." He brought it down to such real emotions, she started to say he hadn't, but he had, that was the whole point. It hurt her that he wouldn't talk to her. It was something new for Tanya. "I figured it'd be more restful for you if I kept my mouth shut."

"Well, make a little noise from time to time just so I know you're breathing," she said with a lopsided grin, and he guffawed.

"Someone like you, the whole world must chew your ear off. I couldn't believe how crazy they all got before you got here. Must be hard on you," he said matter-of-factly, getting right to the heart of the matter, and she nodded.

"It is," she said softly, able to be honest with him, out in the middle of nowhere, as they loped toward the mountains across a field of wildflowers. It was like seeking truth, or finding nirvana. There was something about the place that touched her deeply. She had come here to amuse her stepchildren originally, and then her friends, but instead she was finding something she had lost from her soul a long time ago, a kind of peace she had long since forgotten. "All those people grabbing at you, taking something from you, taking something away from you, it's as though they suck out your spirit and they don't even know it, but they do . . . sometimes I think that one day it will kill me, or they will." The nightmare of John Lennon being murdered by a fan was vivid for all famous people who had mobs of fans as she did. But there were other nightmares as well, just as lethal in the long run, though less obvious than the gun that had killed him. "It's a crazy life where I come from," she said thoughtfully, "it didn't used to be in the beginning. But it got that way. And I don't think it's ever going to change now."

"You ought to buy a place here," he said, looking straight ahead toward the Tetons, "a lot of people like you come here, to get away, to hide for a while, get their spirit back. They come here, or go to Montana, Colorado, same idea. You could go back to Texas." He smiled at her and she groaned.

"I think I've outgrown that," she confessed, and he

laughed. His laughter was a fresh, easy sound that suited him perfectly and made her smile in answer.

"I think I outgrew Texas a long time ago too. Too hot, too dusty, too empty. That's why I came here. This suits me better," he said as she looked around them and nodded. It was easy to see why. Who wouldn't it have suited?

"Do you live here all year long?" she asked. This was much better than the morning. Even if she never saw him again, at least now they were human beings. He knew something about her, and she knew something about him. She thought maybe she'd write a song about him. The Silent Cowboy.

"Yes, ma'am," he said.

"What's it like?" She was thinking of the song now.

"Cold." He smiled and glanced at her sideways again. She was so beautiful, she scared him. It was easier not to see her. "We get twenty feet of snow sometimes. We send the horses south in October. Can't get around except by snowplow."

"It must be lonely," she said thoughtfully, trying to picture it. It was light-years away from Bel Air, recording studios, movies, concerts. Twenty feet of snow . . . one solitary man . . . and a snowplow.

"I like it," he said. "I keep busy. I get a lot of time to read, and think. I write some," and then he smiled cautiously and glanced at her, "listen to music."

"Don't tell me you listen to me while you're sitting here in twenty feet of snow all winter." The very idea of it was so foreign to her that it amazed her and she loved it.

"Sometimes," he confessed. "I listen to other things too. Country western. I used to like jazz but I don't listen to it much anymore. Beethoven, Mozart." The man was intriguing to her. She had definitely misjudged him. She wanted to ask him if he was married, if he had a family, out of curiosity, not out of any interest in him, but that seemed too personal, and she sensed that he would have been offended. He was careful to set boundaries and stay well behind them. And then, before she could ask him anything else about his life there, they rejoined the others. Hartley and Mary Stuart were chatting easily, and the doctors were still busy dismembering remembered patients, enchanted with their discussions. It was a surprisingly congenial group, and they were all sorry when their trail ride ended. It was four o'clock by then, and they were free to go to the swimming pool, go hiking, or play tennis. But they were all exhausted and Zoe looked it. Tanya had been noticing since the day before that Zoe was paler than she had been in college. Her already fair skin seemed to have gotten even whiter.

The medical couple from Chicago went for a walk to look at wildflowers, and Hartley walked the three women back to their cabin, and they were all startled to see a little boy there. He was just sitting there, and when Mary Stuart saw him, she had a visceral reaction. He was about six years old, and he seemed to be waiting for someone.

"Hi," Tanya said easily. "Did you ride today?"

"Yup," he said, pushing a red cowboy hat back on his head. He was wearing little black cowboy boots with red bulls on them, and little blue jeans and a denim jacket. "My horse's name is Rusty."

"And what's your name?" Zoe asked as she sat down beside him on the deck, grateful to sit down for a moment. The altitude made her breathless.

"Benjamin," he said formally. "My mommy's having a baby, so she can't ride horses." He was more than willing to share the information, and Zoe and Tanya exchanged a smile. Mary Stuart was standing a little distance away, talking to Hartley, but she was frowning and didn't know it. But Tanya had seen it, and she knew why even if Mary Stuart didn't. The boy looked so much like her son Todd at the same age that it made your heart ache. Tanya wondered if Mary Stuart saw it, but she didn't want to say anything to Zoe, for fear Mary Stuart would hear it. And the odd thing was that the child kept staring at Mary Stuart as though he knew her. It was eerie.

"My aunt looks just like you," he offered finally, fascinated by Mary Stuart, although she was the only one of the group who hadn't spoken to him, and didn't want to. She didn't go out of her way to avoid him, but she didn't enter into conversation with him either. She had sensed, more than seen, the resemblance. And Hartley saw something in her eyes that made him wonder.

"Do you have children?" he asked. He had noticed the wedding band on her hand that afternoon, but from things she'd said about deciding where to spend the summer, and the impression he'd gotten that she was alone, he wasn't exactly clear on her marital status. And neither was Mary Stuart.

"Yes, I do . . ." she answered vaguely in answer to his question about whether she had children. "A daughter . . . I . . . and a son, who died," she said awkwardly, and he could see the pain in her eyes and didn't pursue it. She turned away from the boy then, and walked into the cabin with Hartley. She didn't want to see the child a moment longer.

"Was he . . ." he hesitated, wanting to reach out to her, but not sure how to, "was he very young when he died?" he asked cautiously, wondering if he shouldn't mention it at all. But he wanted to know more about her. Perhaps that was why she had come here. Perhaps he had died in an accident with the father . . . or perhaps she was still married. There were questions he wanted to ask her. After riding with her all day, he felt as though they were friends now. They were so isolated from the world they knew, in this remarkable place, thrown together for only moments. If they were to become friends, they had to learn everything about each other very quickly.

"Todd was twenty when he died," she said quietly, trying not to see the little boy beyond the window. He was still chatting with Zoe and Tanya. "It was last year," she said, looking down at her hands for a moment.

"I'm so sorry," Hartley said softly, and dared to touch her hand for an instant. He knew only too well the pain of loss. He and Margaret had been married for twenty-six years when he lost her, and they had never had children. She couldn't. And he had accepted that. In some ways, he had always thought it brought them closer. But now he looked at Mary Stuart and could only glimpse what she had gone through. "It must be terrible to lose a child. I can't imagine it. It was bad enough when Margaret died. I really thought it would kill me. I was surprised when I woke up every morning. I kept waiting to die of grief, and was stunned that I didn't. I've been writing about it in my new book all winter."

"It must help writing about it," she said as they sat down on the couch in the living room. The other two were still outside talking, but she couldn't see the boy now. "I wish I could write about it. But it's better now. I finally put his things away a few weeks ago, before I came here. I couldn't bring myself to do it before that."

"It took me nearly two years with Margaret," he said honestly. And he had only been out with two women so far and hated both of them for not being her. He knew all about the pain of adjusting. At least she didn't have that to deal with, though he still didn't know about her husband. "It must have been very hard on your husband too," he said, fishing for information, but she didn't understand that. He had seen the narrow wedding band, but the way she spoke didn't confirm that she was married.

"Actually," she decided to be honest with him. "It was hard on him. Our marriage didn't survive it."

Hartley nodded. He knew about that too, though not firsthand, but from a cousin who had been through it. It was not surprising. "Where is he now?"

"In London," she said, and he nodded. It was what he had wanted to know. And he assumed that meant Bill lived there. Mary Stuart didn't understand why he had asked her and just thought he was being friendly. It had been a long time since a man had shown an interest in her, and she didn't fully comprehend that that was the case now with this one. For the moment, she just thought they were fellow riders, although she liked him immensely, and was amazed at how easy he was to talk to.

He asked if they would join him for dinner, and she said she'd ask the others, and he left her to do some work, and read his mail. Like many of them, he was managing to maintain contact with his office from a distance, and he was planning to do a little work here. He promised to see her at dinner, and when the others came in, she told them about the invitation. And predictably, they teased her, especially Tanya.

"Quick work, Stu! I like him." She was smiling at Mary Stuart and Mary Stuart threw a small cushion at her in outrage.

"Oh, for Heaven's sake, he invited all of us to dinner, not just me, you dummy. He's lonely. He lost his wife, and he has no one to talk to."

"He seemed to be doing fine with you." Tanya pursued her mercilessly, and Mary Stuart told her she was silly.

"He's very nice, very intelligent, and very lonely."

"And very interested in you. I'm not blind, for Heaven's sake, even if you are. I think you've been married for so long, you don't even see it when guys look at you."

"And what about you and the wrangler?" Mary Stuart teased her right back. They were like freshmen. "He seems to have overcome his speech block. You even had him smiling."

"He's a real character. He lives here alone in the winter, in twenty feet of snow." She didn't tell them that he listened to her music. But there was certainly nothing romantic between them. Just horses.

"I think you're both blind." Zoe addressed both of them. "Hartley Bowman looks like he's crazy about Stu, and unless I've lost my touch entirely, I'd say by the time we leave here, our wrangler is going to be head over heels for Tanya. I predict it for the yearbook." They both laughed at her, and Tanya raised an eyebrow. It was so outlandish, she didn't even bother to comment.

"And what about you, Zoe? Are you going to break up that marriage and run off with the doctor from Chicago?" He was short, round, and bald, and even the thought of it was really funny.

"Unfortunately, his wife is more interesting than he is, which is a real problem. I'd have to run off with her, and that's not my thing, I'm afraid, so I guess that leaves me high and dry here."

"There's always Sam!" Tanya reminded her, and Zoe groaned. That was not a reminder she wanted.

"Mind your own business. Little does he know that he has a champion in Wyoming. Tell you what, Tan, when you come to San Francisco, I'll introduce you, and you can go out with him. You'd like him."

"That's a deal. Now, let's talk about Mary Stuart." She turned her attention to her and Mary Stuart groaned in anticipation. "Tell us about your new friend."

"There's nothing to tell. I told you. He's just lonely."

"So are you, so am I. So is Zoe. So what else is new?" Tanya said, lying down on the couch. Her legs ached. They had done a lot of riding.

"I'm not lonely," Zoe corrected her. "I'm very happy."

"I know, you're a saint. You just don't know you're lonely. Trust me," Tanya said, and they all laughed.

"Forget all these guys, I'm going out with Benjamin," Zoe said with a smile. He was an adorable child, and they had both liked him.

"Great choice," Tanya said, and Mary Stuart said nothing, but asked them what they wanted to do about dinner with Hartley. Should they accept his invitation to sit at his table? "Why not? Maybe we'll get Mary Stuart all fixed up with him."

"Relax," Mary Stuart said soberly, "I'm still married."

"Does he know that?" Zoe asked with interest. Mary Stuart wore a wedding band, but he might have wondered where her husband was and why she had come to the ranch with two women.

"He didn't ask actually," Mary Stuart said, confirming her

belief that he was only interested in friendship. "He asked where my husband was at one point, and I said in London."

"Oh-oh," Tanya said wisely. "You'd better clear that up. I think that's what he was asking, he may have gotten the wrong impression from that." But what was the right one?

"I told him our marriage didn't survive when my son died," she said casually.

"You told him that?" Tanya looked startled. That was a lot to say to a perfect stranger. But they had spent six hours riding side by side. It was more time together than some couples spent in a week's time, and he had been very interested in her.

"Maybe I should tell him I'm still married," though she didn't know for how much longer.. But somehow it seemed presumptuous to just volunteer that information. What if he really didn't care if she was married? "I'll see what seems appropriate. I really don't think he's interested like that," Mary Stuart said demurely, and the other two hooted at her.

"You're both disgusting," she said, and went to take a shower, while Zoe called Sam. She wanted to know what was happening in her office, but he was in a treatment room with a patient. And Annalee told her that everything was going smoothly. She went to lie down after that, and had a short nap before dinner. She was surprised at how well she felt when she got up. Sleep really made a difference.

The three of them dined with Hartley that night. He was intelligent, interesting, and wonderfully worldly. He had traveled everywhere, knew fascinating things, and knew all kinds of intriguing people. And more than that, he was a nice man, and was extremely polite about dividing his attention. He never left anyone out, and all three of them felt as though he enjoyed being with them. But when they walked back to the cabin afterward, and he accompanied them, he walked along beside Mary Stuart. And he spoke to her in a gentle voice that seemed meant for her ears and no others. Tanya and Zoe went inside when they arrived at their cabin, and Mary Stuart stayed outside with Hartley for a while. She wasn't sure how to bring it up, but she thought the others had made a good point that afternoon about telling him that she was married.

"I feel a little foolish saying this to you," she explained, as they sat peacefully beneath a nearly full moon that shone blue on the snow atop the glaciers. "And I have no idea if it means anything to you, but I just didn't want to mislead you. I'm married," she said, and was startled to see a look of disappointment in his eyes. "My husband is working in London for the summer. I realized that what I may have said to you might have given you a different impression. To be honest with you," and she always was with everyone, "I'm planning to leave him at the end of the summer. I needed some time to decide what to do, but our marriage died with our son, and now I think it's time to move on, put us both out of our misery, and end it."

"Will your husband be surprised?" Hartley asked quietly. He was looking at her very intently. He barely knew her, and yet he liked her honesty, her kindness, and her directness. But he was sorry to hear she was still married. Perhaps, in the long run, it didn't make any difference. She sounded pretty definite about it being over with her husband. "Do you think your husband is aware of what you're feeling?"

"I don't see how he couldn't be. He's barely spoken to me for a year. We have no marriage, no life, no friendship. He blames me for our son's death, and I don't think anything will ever change that. I can't live like that anymore. I don't mean to tell you my problems, but I just wanted you to know that I am actually still married for the moment, although I don't think I will be for too much longer."

"Thank you for being honest with me," he smiled. It was incredible even to him how much he liked her. She was the first woman he had really liked since Margaret died, and after only one day, he was crazy about her. But everything here was in triple time. It was very much like being on shipboard.

"I hope you don't think I'm crazy for bringing it up, I just don't want to mislead you. I'm sure it doesn't make any difference to you . . . it's just . . ." She was suddenly mortified to have told him any of it, and she was stumbling over her words. What difference could it possibly make to him that she was married? She was suddenly furious with the other two for influencing her, and she felt really stupid. But as she sat there uncomfortably, he looked at her and he was smiling.

"I have no idea what I'm doing here, Mary Stuart. I wasn't even going to come here this year. I've been feeling sorry for myself for two years, and I haven't looked at another woman. And now suddenly here you are, like a bright ray of sunshine on the mountains, and all I can tell you is that I've never been so bowled over by anyone before. I have no idea what this will be, or what you want, or even what I do, or if you'd even be interested in me, but I just want you to know that I barely know you, but I care very much about you. I hate the fact that you lost your son," he said, as he gently put an arm around her, and he pulled her slowly against his shoulder. "I hated the look in your eyes when you saw that little boy this afternoon, and I wanted to take all that hurt away from you. And actually, although I can't believe I'm saying this, I don't like the fact that you're not divorced, but I'm not even sure that that's important. I have no idea if you'll ever want to see me again after next week, and I'm probably making a terrible fool of myself, and if I am, tell me, and I won't do more than tip my hat at you for the rest of the trip." His eyes were searching hers in the moonlight and hers were full of tears. They were all the things she had wanted Bill to say and he never had. He had completely abandoned her, and suddenly there was this stranger, answering all her prayers. "I just want to be with you, and talk to you, and learn about you . . . and then let's see what happens." What more could one ask? She sat looking at him, unable to believe what she was hearing.

"Am I dreaming this?" she asked, looking at him with eyes full of tears and wishes. Was it possible to find someone like him?

"That's how I felt all afternoon today. Let's not look for any answers quite so soon. Let's just enjoy it," he said, feeling her hair brush his cheek, he closed his eyes, breathing in her perfume. He didn't say another word, he just sat there, holding her for a long time, until he felt her begin to tremble. It was only partly from the chill, the rest was pure emotion. She had only arrived the day before, and seen him for the first time that morning. But she had read everything he'd ever written, and almost felt she knew him, and they had talked for hours and bared their souls, and they shared a powerful attraction.

"You're cold, I'll take you in," he said, wishing he didn't have to leave her. She stopped and looked up at him, and once again he put his arm around her.

"Thank you for everything," she whispered, feeling him close to her, and then he walked her to the door and left her there. She slipped inside, hoping the others had gone to bed, and she was grateful to find they had. But when she went into her own room she found a fax on her bed, from Bill. It was painfully simple.

"Hope all goes well. Work is satisfactory here in London. Best regards to your friend. Bill." That was it. And at the bottom, in her lacy handwriting, Tanya had scrawled across the page, "If I were you, I'd call my lawyer." It was certainly dry, and suddenly life was giving her a brand-new opportunity. A door was closing behind her, but another, just ahead, was beginning to open. And through it, she could finally see sunlight on the mountains.

CHAPTER 14

The next morning, Zoe and Mary Stuart dragged Tanya out of bed together.

"Rise and shine!" Zoe said, as Mary Stuart pulled the covers off and took Tanya's mask off.

"You're both sadists!" Tanya groaned, squinting in the sunlight. "My God, what is that . . . I'm going blind." She rolled over on her stomach and refused to move as the other two pulled her off the bed just as they had in college.

"It's called sunshine, and there's lots of it outside," Mary Stuart said, as Tanya sat slowly upright in pink shorty pajamas. "If I didn't know you better I'd think you were a drunk, the way you wake up in the morning."

"It's just old age. I need a lot of sleep," she said, staggering slowly to the bathroom.

"Well, Big Max is waiting," Zoe added.

"Tell him to go back to sleep, he'll feel a lot better," she said, yawning, but twenty minutes later she was dressed and showered, and she looked as spectacular as she did every morning. She was wearing pale pink jeans and a pale pink T-shirt, her old yellow boots, and a pink bandanna. Her hair was down her back in a long braid, and there were soft tendrils around her face that made her look incredibly sexy.

"That ought to catch your wrangler's attention," Mary Stuart said, when she saw Tanya's outfit. She looked better than ever. "It's a shame you're so ugly." Mary Stuart smiled at her, suddenly anxious to see Hartley. She had thought about him all night, and she felt like a kid waiting to see him that morning. For the moment, they were just friends, but the undercurrent of something more intrigued her.

They were on their way to the dining room, when Benjamin crossed their path again, and Mary Stuart looked as though she'd seen a ghost as he walked beside them. He wanted to stand next to her, and it was almost eerie the way he wanted to be near her.

"Where's your mom, Benjamin?" Zoe asked, sensing Mary Stuart's discomfort. It was easy to see why. Although she had never seen Todd, the child actually looked like Mary Stuart.

"She's sleeping," he said matter-of-factly. "My dad told me to go get breakfast."

"How come she gets to sleep and I don't?" Tanya complained.

"She's eight months pregnant," Zoe explained to her.

"I'm going to look like a hag by the time we leave if you guys don't let me get some sleep. It's not good for your health to wake up this early."

"Who said that?" Zoe grinned.

"I did." Tanya glared at her as they stepped into the main building, and the three of them strode across the dining room a moment later, with Benjamin right behind them. He was sticking to them like glue, and Mary Stuart was determined to ignore him. But when they sat down at the table they'd used the day before, he sat right down with them. Tanya was amused by him, and Zoe liked him too, but neither of them wanted to upset Mary Stuart. They tried to suggest he go sit with his friends, but he absolutely didn't want to.

"It's okay," Mary Stuart said to them finally. "Don't make a big issue of it."

"Are you okay?" Tanya asked her pointedly, and Mary Stuart nodded.

"I'm all right." You couldn't protect yourself to that extent. No matter how much it hurt to see him sitting there, you couldn't create a world without children.

"Nice fax from your husband last night, by the way," Tanya commented as she drank her orange juice. "Very warm and emotional and loving. Nice guy," she said, and Mary Stuart smiled. "Sorry I read it, but I couldn't help it. Are you going to answer?"

"There's not much to say." And then she thought of something. The night before had been almost dreamlike, and she was beginning to wonder if it had ever happened, sitting there with Hartley's arms around her, holding her close, and him telling her he wanted to get to know her. "By the way, I clarified things with Hartley last night, about my husband. You were right, I think he did misunderstand what I said. But now he's clear."

"Did he care?"

She tried to sound cool about it, but the others didn't believe her. "Why would he?"

"Because I don't think he's interested in offering you a secretarial position," Tanya explained as though she were retarded. "The guy likes you."

"We'll see what happens," Mary Stuart said calmly, and couldn't help noticing Benjamin in his red cowboy hat staring at her.

"You look kind of like my mom," he said, looking at her, "and my Aunt Mary."

"My name is Mary too," she said to make conversation, "Mary Stuart. That's kind of weird, isn't it? Stuart was my daddy's name, and he wanted me to be a boy, so that's what they named me."

"Oh," he said, nodding. And then, "Do you have any children?" He was far more interested in her than the others, it was as though he sensed something different about her.

"Yes, I have a daughter, but she's very big now. She's twenty."

"Do you have boys too?" he asked, munching on a danish Zoe gave him.

"No, I don't," Mary Stuart answered, and the child was too young to understand the tears in her eyes as she said it.

"I like boys better," he said matter-of-factly. "I hope my mom doesn't have a girl when the baby comes. I don't like girls. They're stupid."

"Some of them are okay," Mary Stuart explained, and he shrugged, unconvinced in his prejudice about females.

"They cry too much when you push them," he said, by way of an explanation, and Zoe and Tanya exchanged a smile as they listened. Maybe it was good for her to have to talk to him, they wondered silently. Like kind of a vaccination.

"Some girls are pretty brave," Mary Stuart said in defense of her sex, but he lost interest in the subject and ate a piece of bacon, and a little while later he wandered off again when he saw his father. His mother came into the dining room a little while later too, and Mary Stuart noticed that she was hugely pregnant. Her husband had explained to Zoe earlier that the altitude was making her feel wretched.

"I hope you don't wind up delivering a baby," Mary Stuart said in an undertone. "She looks like she's having triplets."

"God, no. There's a hospital here. I don't carry forceps with me. And I haven't delivered a baby since I was an intern. It scared the hell out of me. Delivering babies is a lot scarier than what I do. Too much can go wrong, too many split-second decisions, too many elements you can't control, and I hate dealing with people in that much pain. I'd rather do dermatology than obstetrics," Zoe said with feeling. Mary Stuart said she thought it would be fun, and a really cheerful job, since most of the time it had a happy outcome. Tanya said then that she wondered what it was like having a baby. She had wanted lots of them when she was young, but as her life had unfolded, the opportunity had never happened. And it intrigued Mary Stuart to realize that of all of them, she was the only one who had ever borne children.

"Maybe it was something subliminal they told us at Berkeley," Zoe said, smiling at them. She was happy she had adopted.

"I would have loved to have kids," Tanya said, "I loved having Tony's kids around, they were great children." She wondered if she'd ever see them again, for more than a few minutes. It was all so unkind, losing them, losing him, and when all was said and done, he could just take them and leave her. It made her think that somewhere along the way she should have had her own kids, then no one could have taken them away, and she'd have had them forever, or maybe not, she realized, as she thought of Mary Stuart.

They finished breakfast just in time, and hurried down to the corral. Hartley was already down there, and he looked pleased to see Mary Stuart. Their eyes met and held for a long time, and he stood very close to her as they waited to mount their horses. The doctors from Chicago were back again, and the same groups formed as the day before. Zoe rode with them, and Hartley rode alongside Mary Stuart, which left Tanya and the wrangler to ride ahead again, and this time he tried to make more of an effort.

"You look very nice today," he said, looking straight ahead, and sounding like a robot, and she could see there was a faint flush on his cheekbones as he said it. He was really embarrassed, and she tried to put him at ease as they rode along, but it took a while to do it. After a while, he asked her a few questions about Hollywood, the people she'd met. He asked if she'd ever met Tom Cruise or Kevin Costner or Cher, and he told her he'd seen Harrison Ford in Jackson Hole that summer. She said she'd met them all, and she and Cher had been in a movie together.

"It's funny," he said, looking at her with narrowed eyes, "looking at you, you don't look like that kind of person."

"What does that mean?" He confused her.

"I mean, you're like someone real, not like some movie star or big singer or something. You're just like a regular woman. You ride, you talk a lot, you laugh, you've got a pretty good sense of humor." He glanced over at her with the beginnings of a smile, and this time without blushing. "It's hard to remember after a while that you're the one on the CD's and in the movies."

"If that's a compliment, thank you. If you're telling me I'm a disappointment to you, that's okay too. The bottom line is I'm just a girl from Texas." She was smiling at him, as he admired the pink T-shirt.

"No." He shook his head, glancing at her appraisingly with wise eyes. There was a lot more to Gordon than met the eye on first impression. "There's a lot more to you than that. And you know that. It's just that you're not phony, the way they are."

"The way who is?"

"Other movie stars I've met. They don't even ride when they come here. We've had them all. Politicians, movie stars, even a couple of singers. They just show off a lot, and expect a whole lot of special treatment."

"I asked for a lot of towels, and a coffeepot," she confessed, and he laughed. "Besides, I put on the card that I hate horses."

"I don't believe you," he said, looking more relaxed with her than he had the previous morning. He had hardly dared to speak to her for most of the day before. This was a lot better. While he chatted with her, he was fun to ride with. "You're from Texas," he said approvingly. It said something about her, as far as he was concerned. People from Texas didn't hate horses. "And you're just a regular woman." The funny thing was that she was just that, and he knew it. It was what she had been with Bobby Joe, and Hollywood had screwed it all up, and it was what she had tried to be with Tony. But Tony had wanted a movie star, with none of the problems that went with it. He wanted something that, even with the best of intentions, she just couldn't give him.

"I am a regular woman, but the world I live in doesn't give me much chance to be. I don't have much of a life, to tell you the truth, and I never will now. I hate that, but that's the way it is. The press will never let me have a real life. And even the people who meet me won't. They want you to be what they think you are, and then when they get close to you, they want to hurt you." Even talking about it, it sounded crazy.

"It sounds awful," he said, watching her with interest. He was surprised at how much he liked her. He hadn't wanted to, but she was completely different than he'd expected. He had done everything he could not to be her wrangler, and now he was glad Liz hadn't listened to him. She was actually pleasant to be with.

"It is awful," she said quietly. "Sometimes I think it'll kill me. Maybe it will one day, or a fan will." She said it so sadly that he shook his head as he listened.

"How can you live like that? I don't care what they pay you, it's not worth it," he said, as their horses began loping.

"It's not the money. Not entirely. It's what I do. That's my life. I sing. You can't go backward, you can't hide. If I want to do what I do, then I have to put up with all that."

"It doesn't seem right."

"It's not, but that's reality." She didn't like it, but she knew there was nothing she could do to change it. "Other people hold all the trump cards."

"There's got to be some way to change it, or to live with it, to give yourself a decent life. Other movie stars get away from it, they buy ranches and go places where they can live decent. You ought to do that, Miss Tanya." He really meant it, and she smiled at him, as their horses slowed down again, and Gordon watched her with admiration. She was a great rider.

"Don't call me that," she scolded him when he called her Miss Tanya, "just Tanya is fine." They were almost friends now, enough so to talk about her life. It was like what Mary Stuart had experienced with Hartley. One found oneself talking about the oddest things here. One's hopes and one's dreams, and one's disappointments. It was as though the mountains did something strange and put everything into fast forward.

Hartley was talking seriously to Mary Stuart too, and apologizing if he had overstepped his bounds the night before. When he got back to his cabin, he had been afraid that he might have frightened her by being too forward. They had only just met, and yet he felt so close to her, but she had felt exactly the same thing, and rather than being frightened, she had derived great comfort from it. No one had put their arms around her in a year and she was starving for it. She didn't say exactly that to him, but he understood very clearly as they rode along that she hadn't in any way been offended by his behavior, far from it. And it was a great relief to him, as their horses stopped for a moment and took a drink from a little stream, as he looked at her, and she was smiling. It was magical just being there, and they both felt it.

"All I could think about this morning when I got up was seeing you," he said, with a boyish grin. "I haven't felt that way in years. I don't even feel like working. And for me that's rare, believe me." He wrote daily, no matter where he was or how he felt, or what the conditions of his life were. The only time he hadn't written was when Margaret was dying. He had found then that he just couldn't.

"I know exactly how you feel. It's funny how just when you think your life is over, it all begins again. Life always fools you, doesn't it? When you think you have it all, you lose everything, and when you think all is lost, you find something infinitely precious," Mary Stuart said thoughtfully, looking at the mountains.

"I'm afraid that God has quite a sense of humor," he said

as their horses started walking again, and she smiled at him. "What do you like to do in New York?" he asked, still wanting to know everything about her. First he wanted to know, and then he wanted the chance to do it with her. He was excited to know she was going back to New York after spending a week in L.A. with Tanya. He had business to attend to in Seattle when he left the ranch, and he had to spend a few days in Boston, but then he was going back to New York around the same time she was. "Do you like the theater?" he inquired, and they talked about it for a long time. He had a number of friends who were playwrights, and he wanted to introduce her to them, to all his friends in fact. There was so much that he wanted to tell her and show her and ask her. It was impossible to stand still. The two of them talked constantly, and laughed, and shared ideas, and they were both surprised when they wound up back at the corral at lunch time. They hadn't even been looking where they were walking. Tanya and Gordon were well ahead of them, and the doctors were bringing up the rear very slowly. And Mary Stuart was just dismounting when a horse suddenly came racing past them. There was a small figure clinging to it, and Gordon had spotted it before they did. The horse was shooting right through the corral on the way to the barn, and he instantly broke into a gallop trying to stop it, but before he could reach it a small form flew through the air, and landed with a hard thump on the rocky roadside. At first they couldn't see what it was, it was a bit of something, but Mary Stuart knew less by sight than by instinct. It was as though she felt it almost before she saw it. And then the others saw too. The little red cowboy hat lay beside the small heap that was Benjamin. His horse had run away with him. And without thinking, Mary Stuart jumped to the ground and ran to him, with Hartley just behind her, but when she reached the child, he seemed lifeless. He was unconscious, and when she bent her cheek to his lips, he was barely breathing. And she looked behind her in terror at Hartley.

"Get Zoe!" she shouted at him, and turned to the child

again, afraid to move him for fear his neck or his back might be broken. She was sure he stopped breathing then, but before she could determine it, Zoe was on her knees beside her.

"It's okay, Mary Stuart . . . I've got him." There was very little she could do, and like her friend, she was careful not to move him. She tapped him gently on the chest and he began breathing again, and then she lifted his eyelids. He saw nothing, and there was a large wet spot on the front of his jeans, which meant he was deep in unconsciousness and had lost control of his bodily functions. "Do you have 911 here?" Zoe said loudly to the wrangler, and he nodded. "Call them. Tell them we have an unconscious child, head injury and possible fractures. He's still breathing, but his heartbeat is irregular. He's in shock. Get them here as fast as you can." She looked at him to be sure he understood how pressing it was, and the other two doctors hurried over, having just left their horses. Zoe was still touching him and watching him closely, and Mary Stuart knelt next to the child, holding his hand in her own, although she knew it meant nothing. But she didn't want to let go of him, in case somehow he could feel it. Zoe was continuing to examine him and she looked worried. She was sure his neck wasn't broken, nor his spine, and she was feeling his limbs, when his eyes fluttered open and he started crying.

"Oww!!!" He started to scream, "I want my mommy . . ." He was sobbing and taking in big gulps of air, and Zoe looked happier as she watched him.

"I like that," she said, still checking him all over, and the other two physicians nodded, and as she touched his left arm, he let out a scream. It was broken. But there could have been worse things. And then as he cried, he looked up and saw Mary Stuart, she was still holding his little hand in her own and crying softly.

"Why you cryin'?" he asked, hiccuping on his tears. "Did you fall off the horse too?"

"No, you silly goof," she said, coming closer to him, "you did. How do you feel now?" She was trying to distract him from what Zoe was doing, who was trying to splint the arm with some sticks she asked Gordon to hand her. Hartley was hovering near too, and Tanya was watching, looking shaken. They all were.

"My arm hurts," Benjamin wailed, and Mary Stuart moved a little closer to him, trying not to disturb Zoe. She smoothed down his hair, and if she closed her eyes, it could have been Todd on the ground beside her, she wished it were, it would have been so wonderful to only have to deal with broken limbs or even a head injury. He was alive, he was covered with dust, he was crying . . . but Todd was gone now.

"You're okay, sweetheart," Mary Stuart said softly, as she would have to her own son. "They're going to fix you all up, and I'll bet you get a cast and everyone will sign it and put funny pictures on it."

"Will you?" He clung to Mary Stuart and ignored the others. No one knew why, but maybe it didn't matter. Maybe he had been sent to touch her, to remind her of what Todd had once been, or that there were other children like him. But what good did it do her . . . she had lost her baby . . . and yet somehow, this child had touched her. It was like a visit from her son, or at least his spirit. "Will you go to the hospital with me?" he asked.

"Sure," she said quietly, "but let's see if we can find your mommy. I'll bet she'd like to go with you."

"All she cares about is the baby," he said, in tears again, and now he was pouting as she held his hand and he lay there on the dusty road waiting for the paramedics to come. But now she understood it better. She looked like his mother, so he was drawn to her, and he was angry at his own mother about the baby. Mary Stuart couldn't help wondering if their paths had crossed so she could help him, or perhaps he had come to her to help her. There was obviously a reason for their meeting.

"Benjamin," Mary Stuart said, as she lay on the ground next to him so she could talk to him better, and by then she was as filthy as he was. "I'll bet your mommy loves you better than anyone . . . babies aren't really that exciting. Sure, she'll be happy to have the baby, and so will you. But you're special. You're the first one. I had a little boy just like you, and he was my special, special one . . . always. Because I loved him first. Your mommy is never going to love anyone better than she loves you. I promise."

"Where did your little boy go?" He was intrigued by what she was saying, and he had heard her words very clearly.

She hesitated for only a moment. "He went to Heaven . . . and I miss him a lot . . . he was very special, just like you are."

"Did he die?" She hated to say it to him, but she nodded. "Our dog died," he said, sharing important information with her, and looking deep into her eyes, and then suddenly without warning he threw up all over her. Zoe wasn't surprised, and told Mary Stuart in an undervoice that he had a concussion.

"You're okay, Benjamin. You're okay, sweetheart," Mary Stuart wiped his face with a towel someone handed her, and she stayed with him, as they all did, until the ambulance arrived with the paramedics. He was actually livelier by then, and Zoe was a little less worried about him. He looked a mess, and so did Mary Stuart, but Zoe was almost sure that he had escaped with a concussion and a broken arm, and a few bumps and bruises. He had actually been very lucky. And just as the ambulance arrived, his mother came lumbering down from the cabins as fast as she could. Gordon had sent someone to get her. And she burst into tears the moment she saw him, but Tanya and Hartley and the two doctors were quick to reassure her, and Zoe told her that she thought the damage was fairly minimal considering how fast the horse had been going, and how hard he had fallen, and he hadn't been wearing a helmet.

"Oh, Benjie," she sat down on the ground next to him, and burst into tears as she held him. "I love you so much." She was completely undone as she looked at all of them and thanked them, and Mary Stuart looked down at him, smiling as she cried, wanting to remind him of what she had told him, that his mom would never love anyone better. She had never loved anyone more than she loved Todd. She loved her daughter passionately, and had from the moment she was born, but she had never loved her more or less than her first baby.

She touched his hand as they put him in the ambulance, and then bent down and kissed his cheek, and it tore at her heart again as she remembered the sweet smell of childhood. Even with the vomit and the dirt and the horses, he smelled like a little boy to her, it was just a step beyond the smell of a baby. "I love you, little guy," she whispered to him. It was just like saying it to Todd again and it almost killed her, except that it felt good too. It was as though this child had come to her to open the floodgates of her feelings. "I'll see you soon," she said, and his mother cried and thanked her again, and then they were gone, and Mary Stuart stood there crying and she didn't know what happened but she suddenly felt a powerful pair of arms around her. She knew who it was, and she turned to him and he pulled her close to him and she couldn't stop crying as he held her.

"I'm so sorry . . . I'm so sorry . . ." She didn't even know him, and she was covered with dirt and the little child's vomit, but he didn't care, he just wanted to be there.

"Oh, poor baby . . . I'm so sorry . . . I wish I had been there for you." She looked up at him then and smiled through her tears, wondering how she had suddenly been so lucky. Maybe God thought she had paid enough for once, or maybe it was just blind luck, or maybe she was dreaming.

"He looks so much like my son," she tried to explain it to him, but she didn't have to. The woman with the enormous belly looked so much like Mary Stuart, she could have been her younger sister, it was easy to see the resemblance.

"What a terrible time you've had," he said as the others left them alone, and they sat down on a log for a few minutes so she could regain her composure. But just being with him she felt better. Maybe because he hadn't had an easy time either. His wife had died an agonizing death and he had been with her every moment. But she had made her peace with it finally, and he had been willing to let her go. The doctor said he had to do it, to set her free spiritually so she could die in peace. And she had died in his arms on Christmas morning.

"I'm sorry I'm such a mess. He did something to me . . . he just reached out and touched my heart. I don't know why that happened."

"Some things just happen," he said gently, as he wondered how her son had died, but he didn't want to ask her. And she could sense what he was thinking.

"My son committed suicide," she said as though he had asked her a question, but he hadn't. And she had never said it before to anyone except Zoe. She had never had to. And no one had ever asked her. "He was at Princeton." She told him about it then, and what it had been like, the shock, the agony of it, the funeral, her husband's reaction, all of it. It was a terrible story.

"What a nightmarish experience for all of you. It's a wonder any of you survived it," he said with admiration.

"We didn't. My husband's a zombie, our marriage died a year ago. And I think my daughter would be just as happy if she never had to come home again, and I'm not sure I blame her. I just want to get out of there now, to put it behind me."

"Are you sure?" he asked cautiously, wondering now that he had heard the story. They were all in shock. But what if they came out of it? She and her husband had a long history together.

"I think I'm sure," she said honestly. "I wanted the summer to think about it," and then she smiled, "I never expected anything like this to happen." And she still didn't know what had, or if anything would come of it. Maybe she'd never see him again after two weeks at the ranch. That was a possibility too. She wasn't leaving Bill for him. She was doing it because she had to. "I just need to walk carefully here. I want to do the right thing, for all of us, and I think I know what that is now."

Hartley nodded, and said nothing, he just held her, and a little while later, he walked her back to her cabin. Zoe and Tanya were having a cup of coffee, and Hartley joined them while Mary Stuart went to take a quick shower. They had just heard the lunch bell. And eventually the two women decided to go up to the dining room and get their table. They left Hartley to wait for Mary Stuart. But they were all somewhat sobered by the morning. And Mary Stuart was surprised when she came out of her bedroom, to find that her two friends had gone, and Hartley was still waiting. She thanked him for waiting for her, and he looked at her gently, and she was suddenly worried about him. He had been through a lot too, and he was being very generous with her. She had no right to hurt him by what she was doing.

"I don't want to do anything that will hurt you," she said as she walked slowly toward him. She'd been thinking about it all morning. She was so attracted to him, but she didn't want to be selfish. She hadn't completely resolved the issue of Bill in her head yet, although she thought she was fairly sure of what she wanted to do now. But she still needed a little time before she told him. "You've been so good to me, and I barely know you. You've been kinder than anyone in my life, Hartley, except Tanya."

"Thank you," he said, and sat down on the arm of the couch as he watched her. She was wearing a red T-shirt and jeans, and she made his heart race. "I'm a grown man, Mary Stuart. Don't worry about me. We've both been through a lot, I don't want either one of us to get hurt. But I understand what the risks are. Let me do this. I want to be here with you." She couldn't believe what she was hearing. He wanted to take a chance on her, to see if she left Bill, to wait and see what happened. And then, without saying another word to her, he took two steps toward her and pulled her into his arms and kissed her. She smelled of perfume and soap and toothpaste, everything clean and appealing, and he ran his hands through her hair as he held her. He hadn't kissed a woman in so long he had almost forgotten what it felt like, and neither of them were old enough to give up all they once had. They were like two people who had swum the English Channel and had finally crawled up on shore together, they were cold, they were tired, they were starving, but they were so grateful to have survived, and to be together. He smiled down into her eyes and then kissed her on the lips again, and she had never known a touch as tender. She suspected, without even wanting to, that he would be an incredible lover. She had no idea where this would go, and neither did he, but for the moment, they were here, in Wyoming, together, and it was all they needed.

CHAPTER 15

On their third day in Wyoming, Zoe lay in bed and stretched sleepily. It was not quite seven o'clock and she was going to get up in a few minutes. She could hear someone stirring in the kitchen. Mary Stuart had just gotten up, and she was yawning as she started to go to the kitchen to make a pot of coffee, and she almost jumped a foot when she ran into Tanya.

"What are you doing here?" Mary Stuart said in amazement. She had never gotten up at that hour in her life, not even in college.

"Last time I looked, I live here!" She had made coffee, and muffins, and taken a yogurt out of the fridge, and she looked as though she'd already brushed her teeth and washed her face, and when Zoe came out of her room, she couldn't believe it either.

"Is something wrong?" Zoe looked worried when she saw them. Maybe there was a problem of some kind. There had to be a real emergency to get Tanya out of bed at that hour, and she couldn't believe it when she found out there wasn't.

"Oh, for God's sake, what is it with you two? I just wanted to get an early start." But they weren't buying her explanations.

"I know what it is," Zoe said with a broad grin. It was her turn now. Tanya had pressed Zoe about Sam and Mary Stuart about Hartley. "It's Gordon."

"Don't be stupid," Tanya said, "he's a wrangler."

"What difference does that make?" Zoe said matter-of-factly. "He looks at you like you walk on water."

"Oh, bullshit," Tanya said as she bustled around the tiny kitchen, but there was more truth to it than they knew. The previous afternoon, they had talked of many things while they were riding. Little Benjamin's accident had shaken all of them and turned the mood serious. Gordon had talked about his son. He was grown now and Gordon hadn't seen him in two years, but he was obviously fond of him. Tanya spoke of her failed marriage to Bobby Joe, she considered it her only real one, and still regretted that it hadn't held up to the rigors of her career, although she admitted that by now she would probably have outgrown him, but now and then she still missed him. And now that she was alone again, she wondered what it was all about. What was she going to end up with? A bunch of gold records, a pile of money, a big house? She had no husband, no kids, no one to take care of her when she got old, no one to be with, and share her victories and defeats with. It all seemed so pointless, and the place she had reached in her life seemed so empty. It was what everyone in Hollywood wanted, and the truth was it meant nothing to her. It had been serious stuff to share with him, but he had made a lot of sense, and been very comforting to her. He was smart and practical and down-to-earth, and so was she, and in an odd way they had a lot in common. He would have liked to talk to her some more, but they had to go back to the corral, and the wranglers were only allowed to eat with the guests on Sunday, unless they had a day off, which Gordon did. But Tanya liked talking to him. There were many things she liked about him. And she didn't mind his simplicity or his occasional roughness. He was never unkind, or thoughtless, there was nothing greedy or cruel about him, and he was very intelligent. She even liked the fact that they were fellow Texans, but she didn't feel ready to tell the others.

"Are you keeping secrets from us?" Zoe teased her, and Mary Stuart laughed at her too. But Tanya just ignored them and went to finish dressing. She looked particularly spectacular that day in a pair of bleached jeans, and a peach colored T-shirt. She was even wearing a new pair of boots, a pair of apricot hand-embroidered ones that she had bought a while before in Texas.

And when they went to the dining room for breakfast with the other guests, Hartley was waiting for them. He looked very cheerful, and very comfortable as he put an arm around Mary Stuart, and said a warm hello to the others. He smelled of soap and aftershave, and looked very handsome in a white shirt and blue jeans, and Tanya couldn't help thinking that he and Mary Stuart looked terrific together. They looked as though they were meant to be, and Zoe agreed with her, as she commented on it later, on the way to the stables.

Little Benjamin was waiting for them there, and having everyone sign his cast. Tanya gave him a big kiss and an autograph, and a bunch of young girls asked her for one too, and their mothers let them. People were more relaxed about seeing her around, but no one was taking sneaky pictures of her, which she appreciated. And when Gordon saw her, he waved, he was saddling up a bunch of horses. As always they were among the last to ride, and Mary Stuart sat on a bench with Benjamin on her lap, nuzzling his neck, and talking to him. He was like a gift now.

"You sure scared us yesterday, you wild guy you," she said, remembering the sight of him flying toward the stables on the runaway horse and then sailing into the air, and onto the rocky roadway.

"The doctor said I should have broken my neck, but I didn't."

"Well, that's lucky."

"Yeah, and my mommy cried." He looked at Mary Stuart seriously then. "You were right. She says she's never gonna love the baby like she loves me. I told her you said so."

"Good."

"She said I'd always be special." And then he brought tears to her eyes again with a gesture that hit her like a fist to the solar plexus. "I'm sorry about your little boy," he said as kissed her.

"Me too," she said, as her eyes filled with tears and her lips trembled, and Hartley watched her. "I still love him very, very much," she said, barely able to speak. "He's still very special."

"Can you see him sometimes?" he asked, puzzled by death. They were the kind of questions Todd would have asked her at his age, and she would have tried to answer, but she was honest with him.

"No, I can't. Not anymore. Just in my heart. I see him there all the time. And in pictures."

"What's his name?"

"Todd." Benjie nodded, as though that were sufficient introduction. And then a little while later he got off her lap and went to look at the horses, and then back up to their cabin to his mother. He seemed satisfied with his visit, and then Mary Stuart and Tanya and the others went out with Gordon. Hartley was looking at Mary Stuart, and she smiled. Dealing with Benjamin was still painful. He was so direct with her, but maybe it was healthy for her. It certainly wasn't easy, and Hartley gave her a quick squeeze before she got on her horse and told her she was terrific.

"I don't know what I ever did to get so lucky," she answered.

"Clean living," he teased her. And they had a nice ride

that morning. Zoe was looking tired, so she took it easy, and the doctors had gone for a rafting trip in Yellowstone, so she rode along with Hartley and Mary Stuart. And Gordon and Tanya rode on ahead, and he invited her to the rodeo that night. He was in it.

"Are you kidding? What events do you ride in?"

He looked sheepish for a minute. "Bulls and broncs. I've done it since Texas."

"Are you crazy?" She'd been to those rodeos as a kid. The guys got stomped on and dragged around, half of them were brain damaged before they were thirty, the others had so many broken bones, they walked like old men even though they were in their twenties. "That is a really dumb thing to do," she said, looking angry. "You're a smart guy, why risk your life for a couple of hundred dollars, or a silver buckle?" He had ten of them at home, but so what, if he wound up crippled?

"They're just like your platinum records," he said quietly, not surprised at her reaction. His mother said the same thing, and so did his sisters. Women just didn't get it. "Like what you have to go through to get a gold record, or an Oscar. Look at the torture they put you through, rehearsals, threats, bad managers, tabloids. It's a lot easier riding a bronc for ninety seconds."

"Yeah, but I don't get dragged around on my head in horse shit until I'm brain dead. Gordon, I disapprove of this," she said sternly, and he looked disappointed. Maybe she was a big-city girl after all, and not a Texan.

"Does that mean you won't come tonight?" He looked crushed, and she shook her head, but she was smiling.

"Of course I will. But I still think you're crazy." He grinned at her then and lit a cigarette. "What are you riding tonight?"

"Saddle broncs. That's easy."

"Show-off." She was excited about it. She loved rodeos, and she'd been planning to go anyway. He invited her to come see him at the pens, and she said she would if she could find him. It wasn't always easy for her to get around either. If people recognized her, it would restrict her movements, and she might even have to leave if people really surrounded her. She never went to public events like that without a bodyguard, but she didn't want to this time. She was just going to go in her bus, with Tom, and Zoe and Mary Stuart. And Hartley, if he wanted to join them. But Tanya could hardly wait to see it. And she had just the outfit for it.

She was like a kid going to the fair when they got dressed that night before dinner. She came out of her room wearing soft beige suede jeans with fringe down the side, and a matching beige suede shirt with the same fringe and a suede neck scarf. And she had a cowboy hat exactly the same color. It looked very Western, but she had bought it all in Paris, and the suede was so soft it felt like velvet on her body.

"Wow! You Texans!" Mary Stuart complained. She had worn emerald-green blue jeans and a matching sweater, with black alligator boots from Billy Martin's. And Zoe was wearing stretch jeans with a Ralph Lauren military jacket. As usual, they were the best-looking group in the place, and Hartley had started calling them "Hartley's Angels," which amused them.

It was a lively dinner that night, and Benjamin was running all over the dining room while his mother was threatening to go into labor. She said it had been a traumatic week and she couldn't wait to get home to Kansas City that weekend, and Mary Stuart couldn't blame her. It was not the kind of week you would have wanted to have while eight months pregnant, but Mary Stuart was happy she'd met Benjie. He made her sign his cast for a second time, and right after dinner, they went out to Tanya's bus and left for Jackson Hole with Hartley. He had agreed to join them at the rodeo, and he was enthralled by the bus as they drove there. He loved it.

"I can't believe this," he said, amused by all of it. "And I thought I was hot stuff with a Jaguar."

"I drive a ten-year-old Volkswagen van," Zoe confided to him, and he laughed. But it was for a good cause in her case, every penny she had she put into the clinic to buy medicine and equipment.

"I'm afraid the literary world can't compete with Hollywood," he said apologetically. "You beat us hands down, Tanya."

"Yeah, but look at the shit we have to put up with. You people work like gentlemen. The people I deal with are savages, so I deserve this." She justified it and they all laughed, but no one begrudged it to her, not even Hartley. She worked hard for her money.

And in the comfortable bus, the time passed quickly on the way into Jackson Hole from Moose, and half an hour later they were at the rodeo, and they were nearly half an hour early. The ranch had gotten them great tickets. And it all had a familiar smell and feel to it that reminded Tanya of her childhood. It was just the way Tanya remembered it when she was a little girl. She used to ride her pony over and watch all of it. And when she was a little older she rode in it a few times, but her daddy said it was too expensive, and she wasn't all that crazy about horses. She just loved the excitement. It was like the circus.

They took their seats and bought popcorn and Cokes, just as an official of the rodeo approached her. She wondered if there was something wrong, if they'd had a death threat or a security problem, the man approaching them looked extremely nervous, and Hartley became instantly protective and stood in front of her as the man approached them and asked to speak to Tanya.

"May I ask what this is about?" Hartley asked politely, sensing some kind of danger, or imposition at the very least, as she had.

"I'd like to speak to Miz Thomas," he said with an accent Tanya recognized easily as Texas and not Wyoming. "We have a favor to ask her." He peered over Hartley's shoulder at her and added, "As a fellow Texan."

"What can I do to help you?" She stepped forward. She had decided he was harmless, though annoying.

"We were wondering if . . ." He was sweating uncontrollably, he had been delegated for this task, and he was wishing someone else had done it. And her bodyguard really scared him. He was very well dressed, and a little awesome. It was, of course, Hartley, though she had bought a ticket for Tom too, but she didn't know where he was sitting. "Miz Thomas," the man from Texas went on nervously, "I know you probably don't do this, and we can't pay you anything . . . but we wondered . . . it would be a real honor . . ." she wanted to shake him to help him get the words out, ". . . if you'd sing the anthem for us tonight." She was so startled she didn't answer for a moment. She had done that before, but there was something touching about it. It was a hard song to sing, but in a way it would be fun to do it. Right out in the open, with the mountains all around them. It was such a sweet idea that she smiled at him, and wondered what Gordon would think if she did it. In a funny way, she wanted to do it for him, to wish him luck on his bronco.

"It would be an honor," she said seriously, and meant it. "Where would you like me to do it?"

"Would you come with me?" She hesitated for a moment, always slightly afraid of the crowd, and what could happen to her, and there was no one to protect her. The others looked a little concerned, but no one had recognized her so far, and it was tempting to just go with him and do it.

"Do you want me to go with you?" Hartley asked, he didn't want her to be in any danger, and he was more than happy to go with her to offer his protection.

"I think I'll be all right," she said in an undertone to him. "I'll stay out in the open, and if you see anything strange happen, or a crowd closing in, get the security right away, call the police, just get them out there." But they might not be fast enough and she knew that.

"I don't think you should do this," he said conservatively.

"It's a nice thing to do though. It would mean a lot to them." And it was a gift she could give to Gordon. She wanted to do it for him and the people of Jackson Hole, Wyoming. "Don't worry," she said, patted his arm, glanced at her friends, and followed the perspiring man from the rodeo down a flight of stairs out of the bleachers and around the ring. They were right out in the open and the others could watch her. What they were proposing was that she stand on a box in the middle of the ring with a microphone and sing, or if she preferred, she could do it on horseback. It was a scenario she much preferred. She was a target either way, but she had more mobility on a horse than on foot, and she was a good enough rider to get out of any situation if she had a horse on which to do it. They were more than happy to have her do it on horseback, and they offered her a beautiful palomino which matched her hair and her outfit. It was more theatrical that way anyway. She only hoped she wasn't making herself an easy target for a crazy with a gun. It was an awful way to think, but when she did concerts, she had to. Her agent would have had a nervous breakdown, if he'd known what she was about to do, with no protection, and for free yet. But the little girl from Texas still lived in her. If she had thought when she was a child she would sing the anthem at the rodeo one day, she would never have believed it. It was something she had never done, and used to dream of, as a kid from Texas. And she agreed to do it on horseback. They explained to her that she'd go on in the next ten minutes. And as she looked around, she wondered if she'd see Gordon, but she didn't. No one seemed to be in the least aware of her presence, or what was coming. No one knew she was in the audience, or so she thought, although the people from the rodeo said that the girl at the ranch who'd ordered the tickets for her had said who they were for, which annoyed her a little, but it was hard to control that. Someone always said something. But the crowd at the rodeo was in no way prepared for the announcement that was made as the rodeo began, nor was Gordon.

"Ladies and gentlemen," the grand marshal said into a mike as he sat in the ring on a big, black stallion. "We have a real treat in store for you this evening. The Jackson Hole Rodeo welcomes you tonight, and to thank you for coming here to see our bulls and our broncs and our cowboys, we have a real nice lady who's going to give you quite a treat. She's going to sing our anthem. She's visiting Jackson Hole," and as he said it, Tanya prayed he'd have the brains not to say where she was staying, and the others hoped the same thing as they sat in the bleachers, but mercifully he didn't. "And she's pretty familiar with the rodeo herself. She's a Texas gal . . . ladies and gentlemen," there was a powerful drumroll from the members of the high school band who were about to play the anthem, "I give you . . . *Tanya Thomas!*" And as he said the words, a cowboy opened the gate, and she galloped into the ring on the palomino. She made an incredible sight with her blond hair flying out behind her. She was holding the mike in one hand and the reins in the other, and the horse was livelier than she'd expected, and she was praying she wouldn't fall off before she got to sing the anthem. And according to plan, she galloped once around the ring, and then walked the horse into the middle, smiling at the crowd and waving as they screamed and cheered her. People were on their feet and unable to believe their good fortune. And for a fraction of an instant, she was afraid they would stampede her. She could almost smell it brewing. And she wished she could see Gordon, but she couldn't. He was standing far behind her, straddling the bronc pens, unable to believe what he was seeing, or the crowd's reactions. He was surprised that she hadn't warned him, but he watched as the crowd continued to scream and shout her name, and stamp their feet in rhythm. But she was holding up a hand, and they stopped finally so they could hear her.

"Okay, now . . . I'm excited to see you too, but this isn't a concert. It's a rodeo . . . and we're going to sing our anthem, so let's settle down. It's a real honor for me to be here," she said it with such feeling that they actually quieted down and really listened. "This is a special song for all of us Americans," she said, plucking at their heartstrings. "And I want you to think about what it says, and sing it with me." She bowed her head for a minute and there was an instant of silence and then the band began, and they played it better than any professional orchestra she'd ever heard play it. They were doing it just for her, and she sang her heart out for the people of Jackson Hole, and the tourists, and her friends, and the people of Texas . . . and Gordon. She sang it mostly for him, and hoped that he knew that. She knew what the rodeo meant to him, the same thing it had meant to her as a little girl in Texas. It was the high point of his existence, at least it always had been. But at that moment, the only thing he could think of was her, and what he was hearing and seeing. He had never seen or heard anything more beautiful than Tanya singing the anthem, and he wished he had it on tape, so he could play it forever. It brought tears to his eyes, and to almost everyone who heard her. And they went absolutely insane when she finished. She gave them one last wave and galloped out of the ring, before they could leap over the barricades and mob her. She was out the gate before they could move, and had the mike in the hands of the man from the rodeo who kissed her on the cheek so hard he almost knocked her over, and then she dismounted and literally disappeared into the crowd, and headed toward the bronc pens to see if she could find Gordon. She was shaking with excitement.

No one actually saw where she went, and she moved so quickly that they lost track of her in the crowd. Even Hartley couldn't see her now, and Mary Stuart and Zoe were worried about her, but she knew exactly where she was going. She had hung around rodeos too long not to know how to find the bronc pens, and within two minutes she saw him, still looking dazed, astride pen number five. And as though he sensed her nearby, he looked down and saw her. And he clambered down the rails like a monkey until he stood beside her. He towered over her, and she was beaming.

"Why didn't you tell me you were going to do that?" He looked hurt that she hadn't told him, but he was still moved by her singing.

"I didn't know till I got here. They came and asked me the minute I sat down."

"You were unbelievable," he said proudly. He couldn't believe he knew her. The last few days had been like a dream for him, and now he was standing there talking to her, as though he'd always known her. He was wearing green-and-silver leather chaps, and handmade boots to match them, a bright green shirt, and a gray cowboy hat, and silver spurs that jangled. "I've never heard anyone sing like that," he said in amazement, as people jostled around them, but no one seemed to realize who he was talking to. They hadn't figured it out yet.

"It's a crazy thing to say," she said, feeling shy suddenly, like a kid, and she wasn't sure if he should hear it, "but I did it for you. I thought it might bring you luck . . . I thought you might like it. . . ."

His eyes were a caress as he looked at her, but he felt as shy as she did. "I don't know what to say to you. I just don't know, Tanya . . ." Tanya . . . Tanya Thomas . . . he kept wanting to pinch himself. Was this happening to him? Was she talking to him? Had he been riding with her since Monday? It was crazy. He was dreaming.

"It was kind of my gift to you . . . now you give me one too." He was terrified of what she would ask of him. But at that moment, he would have done just about anything for her. "You stay safe, that's all I want. Take care. Even if it means no score. It's not worth it otherwise, Gordon. Life's too important." She had seen so many people come and go in her life, so many stupid things happen, so many people who risked everything for something that meant nothing. She didn't want him killing himself for seventy-five bucks on a stupid bronco.

In some ways, rodeos were like bullfights. The stakes were just too high sometimes, and you had to know when to cut your losses.

"I promise," he said, sounding hoarse as their eyes met. His knees were turning to water.

"Take care," she said, and touched his arm, and the velvet of her suede suit brushed past his hand and she literally vanished. She had seen people watching them, and before anyone took a picture, or they mobbed her, she wanted to get back to the bleachers. It might be impossible to stay now anyway, now that they knew she was there, but she was dying to see him ride. It took her a full five minutes, but she got back to her seat with no mishap, and her heart was pounding when she got there, but it was because of Gordon, not the crowd or the performance. She had never been as moved by anyone in her life as she was by him, and she knew it could be dangerous for both of them. She didn't need another scandal, and he didn't need his life turned upside down by a singer who was going to get on her bus and leave town two weeks later.

"Where the hell were you?" Zoe was frantic when she got back to where they were sitting, and so was Mary Stuart and even Hartley. They had just been about to call the security when she got there.

"I'm really sorry," she apologized profusely to all of them, "I didn't mean to worry you. It took me a while to get through the crowd, and I ran into Gordon." Everyone accepted it and she sat down and they did too, and half a minute later, Mary Stuart leaned toward her and spoke to her in a whisper.

"You're full of shit, you went to find him." There was mischief in her eyes, and Tanya avoided eye contact with her. She really didn't want to admit it. She was far more smitten with him than she was ready to tell them.

"Of course not." She tried to brush her off and pretended to watch the first event, which was roping, which always bored her.

"I saw you," Mary Stuart said, and their eyes met. Her

friend was smiling. "Be careful," she whispered into Tanya's ear, but as they were talking, half a dozen people approached them and asked Tanya to sign autographs. And since she had made a willing spectacle of herself, she didn't think she could refuse them. It was like that all night, through the team roping, the barrel racing, the bareback broncos, the bulls, and then finally, she saw him. He was riding a fierce, bucking bronco with a saddle. And the thing she hated most about saddle broncs was that the cowboys taped one hand into the horn on the saddle. They had to come off specifically on one side, and be able to get their hand out. And if they didn't, they could be dragged around on their head for ten minutes before the pickup men could catch them. She had seen some horrifying accidents while she was a child in Texas. And she found herself terrified as she watched him come out of the gate on a vicious brown horse that did everything it could to get rid of its rider. His feet were in the air just as they were meant to be, his legs straight forward, his head and torso tilted far back, and he didn't touch the saddle with his free hand. And he seemed to ride forever. He rode until the bell, he had stayed on longer than anyone, and he made a nice clean jump to the ground, while the pickup men went after the bronco and got him. He got an almost perfect score and waved his hat and his taped hand in her direction and then strode across the ring back to the pens, with his chaps and his boots, looking glorious. It had been a real victory for him. And he had done it for Tanya.

They stayed until the last event, a final round of bulls, followed by fourteen-year-old boys on young steers, that made you wonder about the boys' parents. It was certainly not as dangerous as the bulls, but close enough, and Mary Stuart was outraged.

"Those people should be put in jail for letting those boys do that." In fact, one of the youths had been stomped, a boy of twelve, but he was on his feet again within a few minutes. Zoe and the others had been watching closely.

But in spite of some of the barbarism, and the sheer hokiness, Tanya had to admit she loved it, it was everything she had always loved as a child. And as they left, the others couldn't believe the number of people who asked for autographs on the way out, who snapped her picture, and tried to touch her. But the grand marshal had very kindly sent the security and the real police over to her, anticipating that, and she managed to get back to the bus without any real problems. There were still about fifty people standing outside the bus when they left, waving and shouting, and running alongside the bus as it drove away. It was an amazing phenomenon. It was the adoration that always came before the hatred. If she stayed long enough, they would have torn her limb from limb, in order to get a piece of her or maybe some lunatic would really hurt her. It was the kind of atmosphere that always made her very nervous in crowds, or out in public.

"Tanya, you're amazing," Hartley said to her as they pulled away. He was filled with admiration. She was gracious to everyone, while still maintaining her dignity, and trying to give them what they wanted, and yet keep a reasonable distance. But through it all, one sensed constantly how precarious the balance of the crowd was. "I would be terrified of even a little crowd like that," he said sensibly. "I'm an inveterate coward." But she was used to doing concerts in front of as many as seventy-five thousand. Yet even in a crowd like the one tonight, someone could easily have lost control and killed her. And she knew it. "You also have a voice straight from God," he said. "Everyone around us was crying."

"Me too," Mary Stuart said, smiling.

"I always cry when you sing," Zoe said matter-of-factly, and Tanya smiled, touched by all of them. It had been a remarkable evening, and Hartley sat with them for a while when they went back, and then he and Mary Stuart took a walk, and he brought her back around eleven-thirty. They had stood in the moonlight for ages kissing, and Tanya and Zoe thought they were cute and incredibly romantic.

"What do you think will happen?" Tanya asked Zoe as they sat in the living room, talking.

"It would be nice for her if things worked out with him, but it's hard to tell. I have the feeling in a place like this it's a little bit like a shipboard romance. And I'm not sure she's worked it all out in her head with Bill yet." It was astute of Zoe to notice.

"He's been such a bastard to her all year, I hope she leaves him," Tanya said, sounding harder than usual, but she was angry at Bill, and she felt sorry for Mary Stuart.

"But he's been in pain too." Zoe was more familiar with the strain a death in the family put on otherwise decent people. It turned some of them into saints, others into monsters. And Bill Walker had definitely been the latter.

Zoe was going to say something about Tanya's wrangler too, but Mary Stuart came in then, beaming.

"Are we allowed to check for beard burn?" Tanya asked, reminiscent of school, and they all collapsed in laughter.

"God, I'd forgotten what that is," Mary Stuart laughed, and then turned to Tanya. "You were unbelievable tonight, Tan. Better than ever. I've never heard you like that."

"It was fun. That's the good part. I always love the singing."

"Well, you give a lot of people a great deal of pleasure," Mary Stuart said kindly.

They chatted for a little while, and Mary Stuart and Zoe went to bed, and Tanya decided to stay in the living room reading. She was still exhilarated from the rodeo, and her brief performance, and just after midnight, she heard a soft tapping on the window. She thought it was an animal outside at first, and then she looked up and saw a flash of green shirt, and then a face smiling at her like a mischievous boy. It was Gordon. And she grinned when she saw him. She wondered if in some instinctive part of her she had been waiting for him. The thought crossed her mind as she slipped quietly out to see him. It was chilly outside, and she was still wearing her velvety suedes, and she was barefoot.

"Shhh!" He put a finger to his lips, but she hadn't been about to call his name. She had already guessed that he could get in a lot of trouble for being there at that hour, with her. His cottage was down behind the stables.

"What are you doing here?" she whispered, and he beamed at her. He was as excited as she was.

"I don't know. I think I'm crazy. Maybe almost as crazy as you are." It was as though he had known her forever. And he would never forget what she had done for him that night, or the voice with which she sang it.

"You were great," she said, smiling at him. "Congratulations. You won."

"Thank you," he said proudly. It mattered to him. A lot. And just as she had, he said he had done it for her. It was his gift to Tanny, as he called her. It made her seem less like Tanya Thomas.

"I know you did." He was standing next to a tree as she talked to him, and he suddenly leaned against it and pulled her toward him.

"I don't know what I'm doing here. I'm crazy. I could get fired for this."

"I don't want you to get hurt," she said honestly, standing close to him, hoping no one would see them.

"I don't want you to get hurt either." And then he frowned, looking at her. He had never been as afraid as he was that night, not for himself, but for her, when the crowd engulfed her when she left him. "I was terrified . . . I was so afraid someone might hurt you."

"They might one day," she said sorrowfully, it came with the territory for her, and she accepted it. Almost. "It could happen." She tried to sound casual about it, but she wasn't.

"I don't want anything bad to happen to you. Ever." And then he surprised himself with what he said, "I wish I could be there to protect you."

"You can't all the time. Someone could get me coming out of my house any morning, or onstage at a concert. Or at a supermarket." She smiled philosophically, but he looked unhappy.

"You should have guards around you all the time." He would have kept her locked in the house, anything to protect her.

"I don't want to live like that, only when I have to," she whispered. "I'm pretty good in a crowd, as long as they don't go crazy."

"The police said there were more than a hundred people running after you when you left tonight . . . that scared me . . ."

"I'm fine," she smiled at him. "You're in a lot of danger on those crazy broncos. Maybe you ought to think about that instead of my fans," she said, as he pulled her still closer and she didn't resist him. She didn't want to resist him, she wanted to melt into him, to be part of him, and as he looked at her he could think of nothing but her face, her eyes, the woman he had discovered behind the legend.

"Oh God, Tanny," he whispered into her hair. "I don't know what I'm doing . . ." He had been so afraid of her, of being blown away by her, or impressed, but he had never expected this, this avalanche of feelings. And as she put her arms around him, he kissed her as he had kissed no other woman. He was forty-two years old, and in his whole life, he had never felt for a woman what he did for this one. And in less than two weeks now she'd be gone, and he'd wonder if it ever happened. "Tell me I'm not crazy," he said, looking down at her after he kissed her. "Except that I know I am." He looked both miserable and ecstatic all at once, victorious and defeated, but she was just as wildly enamored as he was.

"We both are," she said gently. "I don't know what's happening to me either." It was like a tidal wave that just wouldn't stop and he kissed her again and again, and all she wanted to do was make love with him and they both knew they shouldn't.

"What are we doing?" He looked down and asked her. And then he wanted to know something he hadn't even thought to ask her. "Are you married? Do you have someone . . . a boyfriend?" If she did, he was going to stop now, even if it killed him, but she shook her head and kissed him again.

"I'm getting divorced. It's already filed. And there's no one else." And then she looked at him, it was as though there never had been. And she suspected that if Gordon had been there instead of Bobby Joe, they would still be married.

"That's all I wanted to know. We can figure out the rest later. Maybe there will be no 'rest.' But I didn't want to play games if you were married or something."

"I don't do that," she said softly. "I've never done this before . . . I don't care what they say about singers or movie stars . . . I've never fallen head over heels like this." In fact, she had married the men she'd cared for. She was actually pretty square. But what she felt now for him was almost too much to handle. And then she thought of him and the possible repercussions. "You have to be very careful so no one knows. I don't want you to get in trouble." He nodded, not really caring. He had been at the ranch for three years, and he was the head wrangler at the corral, but he would have gladly given it all up for her, if she'd asked him.

"Tanny," he said, holding her close to him, running his hands through her incredible hair and kissing her again and again. "I love you."

"I love you too," she whispered, feeling more than a little crazy. Neither of them had any idea what they would do about it, if anything, but for the moment, it was more than a little overwhelming. He didn't even want to think about what he was doing.

"Will you come back to the rodeo on Saturday?"

"Sure." She smiled at him, wishing she could sit on the bronc pen with him.

"Don't sing again. I don't want you to get hurt," he whispered.

"I won't," she whispered back, still leaning against the tree with him.

"I mean it." He looked genuinely worried about her. She had marched right into his heart three days before, as though she belonged there.

"Then don't ride the broncs," she teased, but she didn't mean it. She knew he had to, for the moment. Maybe later, he would stop it. If there was a later between them. But how could that happen? They both knew it couldn't.

"I'm going to worry about you now all the time," he said unhappily.

"Don't. Let's trust fate a little bit. It brought us together. It's a complete fluke I'm even here . . . why don't we just see what happens. Life is funny like that."

"You're funny, and I love you." He smiled and kissed her.

They stood there for a long time and kissed and talked. He had a day off on Sunday and wanted to go exploring with her. She offered to take him in the bus, but he just wanted to take her out in his truck, and show her the places he loved, and she agreed to go with him. She had to figure out what to tell the others. She didn't really want to discuss it with them. There was something so magical about what was happening to them, she wanted to keep it private.

"I'll see you tomorrow," he whispered finally, but he couldn't imagine not being able to kiss her the next day, or put his arms around her, but they both knew he couldn't. Maybe he could come back the next night, and go for a walk with her, late like this, but she didn't want him to get in trouble. The ranch management frowned on romances between guests and wranglers, although everyone knew it sometimes happened. But he swore it had never happened to him. He had never done anything like it. And all he could tell himself was that, for a virgin, he had hit the jackpot.

She stood in the doorway and watched him go. He was silent and quick, and he disappeared into the darkness almost the instant he left her. It was after two o'clock by then, and they had been out there for nearly two hours, talking and kissing. And when Tanya went inside, she jumped when she heard a sound. She had thought they were asleep, but it was Zoe putting the kettle on in the kitchen. She looked green and she had a blanket around her. She didn't tell Tanya, but she had raging diarrhea.

"Are you okay?" Tanya asked as soon as she came in, wondering how she would explain what she was doing outside, but she didn't have to. Zoe had guessed, and didn't press her about it. "You look sick."

"I'm all right," she said unconvincingly, and Tanya could see that she was shaking from head to foot, and she was really worried.

"Zoe?" Tanya looked at her with wide, worried eyes, and Zoe just shook her head. She didn't want to talk about it. "Go to bed, I'll make your tea for you." Zoe went back to bed gratefully, and Tanya came in with a cup of mint tea a few minutes later. Zoe was still shaking but she looked a little better. Tanya handed Zoe the mug, and sat down on the edge of the bed. "What's happening?" she asked, looking worried.

"Not much. Just a bug." But somehow, Tanya didn't believe her.

"Do you want me to call a doctor?"

"Of course not. I am a doctor. I've got everything I need here." She had her AZT, a host of other medicines, she even had a shot she could give herself if the diarrhea got out of control again. She nearly hadn't made it to the bathroom. That would have been beyond awful, and it would have taken a lot of explaining.

They sat there for a while, just thinking, both of them, as Zoe sipped her tea and then lay back on the pillows. She looked at her old friend and felt she had to say something. "Tanny . . . be careful . . . what if he's not what you think . . . what if he sells his story to someone . . . or hurts you. You don't really know him." Tanny wondered how Zoe had known, she was one sharp bird, and she smiled as she listened to her. None of it was impossible, but her instincts told her he was genuine, and she usually only got in trouble when she ignored her instincts.

"I think he's all right, Zoe. I know that sounds crazy, because I hardly know him. But he keeps reminding me of Bobby Joe."

Zoe smiled at her wanly. "The funny thing is he reminds me of him too. But the fact is he isn't Bobby Joe. He's his own person. And he could do a lot of things to hurt you." The price the tabloids put on her head was a big one. They would have paid hundreds of thousands of dollars for a story about her. Especially this one. Not to mention pictures.

"I know that," Tanya said cautiously. "And the truth is it's remarkable that I'm still willing to trust anyone, but I am. I may be crazy, but I trust him."

"You may be right," Zoe said fairly. She had always been fair, even when they were young. It was one of the many things Tanya loved about her. "Just don't give your heart away too fast, you only get one, and it's a mess to repair once it gets broken." The two women exchanged a long, slow smile. Zoe would have liked nothing better than to see Tanya find the right guy and be protected.

"What about your heart?" Tanny asked her, as Zoe set her mug down. And she was looking a little better. "Why have you been alone for so long? Is it broken?"

"No," she said honestly, "just full of other people's stories. There's never enough time . . . and now there's my baby. I don't need more than that."

"I don't believe you," Tanya said wisely, "we all do."

"Maybe I'm different," Zoe said, but she looked sad, and sick and lonely, and Tanya wished she could do more for her. She had always loved her like a sister, and Zoe did so much for so many. She was truly a saint of sorts, and Tanya was worried that she looked so ill and was so exhausted. There was no one to take care of her normally, to nurture her, and do for her what she did for others. But she was looking sleepy now, and Tanya turned off the light and kissed her forehead.

"Get some sleep, and if you don't feel better in the morning, I'm calling a doctor."

"I'll be fine," she said, closing her eyes, and she was almost asleep before Tanya left the room. She stood in the doorway for a moment and looked at her. Zoe was already asleep by then, and she was smiling.

And as Tanya walked back to her own room, her thoughts drifted back to Gordon. She knew Zoe was right. He could do terrible things to her and really hurt her. She was the most vulnerable person she knew, and she couldn't afford the same emotional luxuries as other people. He could write an unauthorized biography, or give an interview to the tabloids, he could take photographs of her and blackmail her if she let him, he could do anything from extort money from her to kill her. But how could she live constantly worrying about things like that? And she was always so circumspect and so careful. And now suddenly in three days she had fallen head over heels in love with a cowboy. It was insane, and yet nothing in her life had ever felt more right, or saner. And as she slipped into bed after she brushed her teeth and put her nightgown on, all she could think of was how he looked that night when she told him she'd sung the anthem for him. And all she cared about was to be with him again, in the morning. And as she fell asleep, she could see his face, his eyes, as he rode the bronco . . . his green-and-silver chaps flying . . . his hand held high . . . she was singing for him . . . and he was smiling.

CHAPTER 16

The day after the rodeo, when Mary Stuart woke up, she heard noises just outside her bedroom. She put her dressing gown on and walked into the living room, and she found Tanya there, fully dressed and looking worried.

"Is something wrong?" She didn't even tease her about being up at that hour, and already in boots and blue jeans.

"It's Zoe. I think she's been up all night. She won't tell me what's wrong. She thinks it's a flu of some kind, but Stu, she looks really awful." A thousand horrible possibilities crossed their minds from ulcers to cancer. "I think she should go to the hospital, but she doesn't want to."

"Let me take a look at her," Mary Stuart said quietly, but when she saw her, she was momentarily shocked into silence. Zoe's face was so pale, it was a fluorescent green, and she was dozing. She stood there for a minute, and then they walked out of the room together.

"My God," Mary Stuart said, horrified, "she looks awful. If

she doesn't go to the hospital, we should at least have someone come here to see her,'' she said with complete conviction, and Tanya was relieved to hear her say it.

Tanya called the manager and asked if there was a doctor nearby who could make a house call. They asked what the problem was and she said only that one of her friends was extremely ill, they didn't know what it was, but it could easily have been appendicitis or something that needed immediate treatment.

Charlotte Collins, the owner, called back instantly, and she said she'd have a doctor to them half an hour later.

''You don't suppose it's something serious, do you?'' Tanya asked Mary Stuart as they waited, and Mary Stuart only shook her head, looking worried.

''I just wish I knew. I hope it's not. But she works awfully hard. Hopefully, it'll turn out to be nothing.''

True to her word, Charlotte Collins had Dr. John Kroner there at eight-thirty. He was a young man, with athletic good looks, he looked as though he had played football in college. And it was obvious when he came in that he knew he was coming to see Tanya Thomas. He tried not to look impressed, but he couldn't help it, and she smiled warmly at him, and tried to tell him about Zoe.

''What do you think is wrong with her?'' He sat down, looked at her intently, and listened.

''I don't know. She looks pale to me all the time, and she's tired, but she seemed all right actually until yesterday. She said she had the flu, there was something wrong with her stomach. She was absolutely green, and shaking violently last night. She was up until about two o'clock, and this morning, she looks a lot worse and she has a fever.''

''Any pain as far as you know?''

''She didn't say.'' But she had looked truly miserable. That had to come from something.

''Vomiting? Diarrhea?''

''I think so.'' Tanya felt inordinately stupid, and a moment later, he went in to see Zoe. He closed the door, and they were inside for a long time, and eventually he emerged. It had been an interesting meeting for him. He knew who she was the moment she said her name. He had read everything she'd written. And for him it was even more of an honor to meet her than Tanya.

He had told Zoe he thought she'd feel better in a few days. But she had been honest with him and shared her secret. He suggested she take it extremely easy, stay in bed, drink clear fluids, do everything possible not to get dehydrated, and try to recoup her strength. He was sure she'd be feeling better by Monday. But he felt very strongly that she needed a second week of rest, and he didn't want her going home on Sunday. She looked crestfallen at that, she didn't even know if Sam was free to cover for her for a second week. And she had said darkly that she'd have to call him. She wanted to see her little girl, and go back to work, and she was worried that this was a sign of things to come, but Dr. Kroner told her he hoped it wasn't. She was bound to have isolated incidents like this, but if she was careful to handle them properly, they didn't have to signal a complete collapse of her defenses.

"You know," he said pleasantly, "you know a lot more about all this than I do. I read you in order to help my patients. You've made a real difference to the people I work with. The funny thing is I've always wanted to write you."

"Well, now you won't have to," she said kindly, but she still looked awful. He had offered her an IV of fluids, but she didn't want to upset Mary Stuart and Tanya, and she thought she could accomplish the same thing by drinking.

"If you can't keep it down though, I'm coming back to give you an IV."

"All right, Doctor." He had also suggested that the altitude might have aggravated her situation. She thought that was hopeful. Each time she got sick, she was terrified it would mean a marked degeneration, but so far, she'd been lucky, and she always got better quickly.

Tanya and Mary Stuart were waiting just outside her door when the doctor emerged, and they were deeply concerned by the long visit.

"How is she?"

"She'll be all right," he said calmly. She had warned him that her friends knew nothing of her problem, and she did not intend to tell them. He disagreed with her, but it was her decision obviously, she was the patient, as well as the expert.

"What took so long?" Tanya had been genuinely panicked. It was nine-thirty when he came out. Hartley had come by an hour before, and Mary Stuart had told him they weren't riding that morning. Tanya asked him to tell Gordon. Hartley said he'd ride out with him alone, and if Zoe was better by that afternoon, Mary Stuart and Tanya could join him.

"I'm afraid that was my fault," the young doctor said apologetically, explaining his long visit with Zoe. "I'm a big fan of Dr. Phillips's. I've read every article she's ever written." It was refreshing to have someone be a fan of someone else for a change, and Tanya smiled at him in amusement. "I'm afraid I was picking her brain and telling her about some of my patients." He was really the only practitioner well versed in AIDS in the area, and he had had a million questions.

"I wish you'd come out and told us she was all right," Tanya said snappily, "we were really worried."

"I'm sorry," he said kindly, and then told them he'd be back tomorrow. "Make her stay in bed and drink lots of fluids," he reiterated as he left, but Tanya found when they went in that they didn't need to argue with her. She was already working on a large bottle of mineral water, but she still looked awful.

"How goes it?" Mary Stuart asked her, and she shrugged.

"Not great. He says I'll feel better tomorrow. I've picked up some awful bug here."

"I'm sorry." Tanya felt responsible, and Mary Stuart was instantly maternal, tucking her in, bringing her dry crackers, and a can of ginger ale in case that appealed to her more than water, and a banana to replace the potassium she'd lost with the diarrhea.

"You guys are so wonderful to me," Zoe said with tears in her eyes. She was feeling emotional and she wanted to see her baby. "I really have to get back," she said, and burst into tears, and she was furious with herself when she did. She hadn't meant to. "He thinks I should stay here another week," she said as though it were a death sentence instead of an extended vacation. But she was also coping with everything else he'd said to her about her condition, and they'd had a serious discussion about AZT and her T cells. And somehow, discussing it with him brought the situation home to her again with a vengeance. Unfortunately Zoe knew more about all of it than he did. And she knew what the prognosis was too. She dealt with it daily, and as her two friends looked at her in dismay, she found that she couldn't stop crying. But their being nice to her had made the whole realization harder than ever. She was still adjusting to the realities of her future.

"Zoe, is there anything else bothering you?" Mary Stuart sat down on her bed, looking worried. It wasn't like Zoe to be so high-strung, and it scared her.

"I'm all right," she said, blowing her nose again, and taking a sip of water. But it was all so hard. She was going to die eventually, and she had nowhere to leave her daughter. She had thought of both of them in the past few days, but Tanya had never had kids, and Mary Stuart seemed to feel she was past them. They were all still young enough to have another child naturally, so it wasn't entirely out of the question, but she was afraid to ask them. And it meant telling them that she had AIDS, and despite what the doctor had just said about opening up to her friends and reaching out to them for support, she really didn't want to. But what he had told her was exactly the kind of thing she said to her patients. "I've just been working too hard," she explained.

"Well, then," Tanya said, trying to sound calmer than she felt. She was deeply concerned about Zoe. "Maybe this is an important lesson. Maybe when you go back you need to slow down a little bit, even take in a partner." Zoe had thought of it too, and the only one she'd have been interested in was Sam, but she didn't think he'd want to. He had never had any interest before in sharing a practice, only in doing locum tenens.

"Don't lecture me," she said irritably to Tanya, and surprised both of them. "You work even harder than I do."

"No, I don't. And singing isn't nearly as stressful as taking care of dying patients." But as she said it, Zoe started to cry again, and she felt completely foolish. She was utterly miserable and sorry she had ever come to Wyoming. She didn't want them to see her this way, it was really upsetting. "Come on, Zoe, please," Tanya begged her. "You just feel rotten, so everything seems worse. Why don't you just stay in bed and sleep today. I'll stick around if you want, and by tonight I'll bet you'll feel better."

"No, I won't," she said stubbornly, suddenly angry at her fate, and what it meant for her future.

"I'll stay home," Mary Stuart said firmly. They were fighting to take care of her, and Zoe smiled through her tears as she listened.

"I want you both to go out and play. I'm just feeling sorry for myself. I'll be okay . . . honest." She was starting to calm down, and Tanya looked relieved, as they watched her. "Besides, you both have boyfriends." She teased them and blew her nose again. In crazy ways, their lives were so much more normal, and hers wasn't.

"I wouldn't go that far," Mary Stuart objected with a grin. "I'm sure Hartley would be thrilled to be called my 'boyfriend.' "

"And Gordon would go nuts if he thought anyone knew he said more than two words to me," Tanya added.

"You guys talked for hours outside last night," Zoe said, looking pleased but tired and leaning her head against the pillow. "Just be careful," she warned her again, and Mary Stuart nodded. They both knew that Tanya was sensible usually, but sometimes she led with her heart, instead of her radar.

"Why don't you get some sleep," Mary Stuart said gently and Zoe nodded, but in a funny way she didn't want them to leave her. She just wanted to be there with them, and stay close to them. It was almost as though they had become her parents.

"I have to call Sam," she said sleepily. "I'm not even sure he can stay another week for me. If he can't, I'll have to go home no matter what and at least see some of my patients."

"That would be really stupid," Tanya told her. "In fact," she looked at Mary Stuart pointedly, "we won't let you. We're holding you hostage." Zoe laughed at them, and then tears filled her eyes again and Mary Stuart leaned over and kissed her.

Zoe was still completely overwrought, and as Mary Stuart looked at her eyes, it was as though there were someone frightened and sad trapped inside her. And somehow, she had to try one more time. She didn't want to intrude, but she wanted to help her. As she leaned over her, she asked her one last question. "Are you leveling with us? Is there anything you want to tell us?" She didn't know what made her ask, but she just sensed that Zoe was sitting on the edge and wanted to tell them something, but was afraid to. She didn't answer at first, and Tanya had been standing in the doorway and she turned and watched them, and then added her voice to Mary Stuart's.

"Zoe, is there?" They both sensed that she was keeping something from them, and they weren't sure what, but they knew it was important. "Is something wrong with you?" All of a sudden she had the overwhelming feeling that Zoe had cancer, but as she looked at them her eyes filled with tears again, and her voice was very small when she answered.

"I have AIDS, guys." There was a deafening silence in the room, and without saying a word, Mary Stuart leaned forward and hugged her. By then, she was crying too. At least cancer might have been cured, but AIDS couldn't.

"Oh, my God," Tanya said and walked back into the room,

and sat down on the bed next to Zoe. "Oh, my God . . . why didn't you tell us?"

"I just found out recently. I didn't want to tell anyone. How can I take care of my patients if they think I'm sick? I have to be strong for them, and for so many people. But I've been thinking about it so much, about what it means to my life, my career . . . my baby. I don't even know what to do with her when I die, or if I get really sick." She looked from one to the other then, in terror. "Will you take her?" They were the best friends she had, and she would have loved to know that Jade was with them.

"I will." Tanya spoke up instantly, without hesitation. "I'd love to have your baby."

"And if for some reason, Tanya can't, I will." Mary Stuart said it strongly and firmly, but Zoe was still worried, though grateful.

"What if you're with Bill, and he doesn't want her?"

"I'm going to leave him anyway," she said in a clear, sure voice, and Zoe believed her. "And if for some reason I didn't, I would then for sure, if he wouldn't let me take her." And she meant it.

"And I don't have anybody telling me what to do," Tanya said with a warm smile, holding her friend's hand. It was small and frail and icy. "But you have to take care of yourself. You could live for a long time. You owe her that, and us, and your patients. What about this doctor covering for you? Have you told him? You're going to need his help so you don't overdo it." It was exactly what Dr. Kroner had told her that morning. But she didn't want to tell Sam either. It was enough that Tanya and Mary Stuart knew. Now they would nag her, and worry about her, and tell her what not to do. But on the other hand they would also support her and love her. It was the same dilemma she saw with all her patients. On balance, with Tanya and Mary Stuart, she was actually glad she had told them. Now she knew that Jade could go to Tanya, and she could draw up the papers. Hopefully, it wouldn't happen for a long time, but you never knew.

"I really don't want to tell him," Zoe said, referring to Sam. "Word would spread like wildfire, and I just don't want that. It diminishes my impact on my patients."

"On the contrary," Mary Stuart said seriously, "I think it increases it. They'll know then that you really know whereof you're speaking." And then she wondered something, though she was almost embarrassed to ask her. "How did you get it, by the way?"

"A needle stick from a little girl with AIDS. She squirmed and so did I, it was just bad luck really. I wondered at the time, but I decided to be philosophical about it. I almost forgot, and then I started getting sick. I denied it for a while, and then I finally got tested. I just found out before I called you," she said to Tanya, and Tanya sat on her bed, holding her other hand and crying.

"I just can't believe this," Tanya said, feeling badly shaken.

"I'll be okay. I'll feel better when my gut settles down again," Zoe said, looking a little stronger. They were so supportive of her that she felt terrible to have upset them. They looked worse than she did.

"I want both of you to go out and play. I don't want you sitting here all day," she said firmly. It was nearly lunchtime.

"We will if you promise to get some rest," Tanya said, and Zoe nodded.

"I'm going to sleep all day, and by tonight, hopefully, I'll feel human."

"You have to be okay by tomorrow night," Mary Stuart said practically, "so we can all learn the two-step. Let's get priorities straight here." They all smiled through their tears, and the three of them held hands for a long moment. And Zoe thanked her lucky stars that she had come to Wyoming. Being with them had been the most important thing that had happened to her in ages, and it had settled her daughter's future. She had made her peace with Mary Stuart, and she was even coming to terms with the fact that she had AIDS. She hated the thought of it, but she knew somehow that if she did the right things, perhaps she could prolong her life and improve the quality of it. It was the best she could do now. And then the three of them made a pact and Zoe made the others promise her not to tell anyone that she had AIDS. If anyone wanted to know, she wanted them to say she had an ulcer, or even stomach cancer. They could say anything except that she had the AIDS virus, and was dying. She didn't want to deal with their terror or their pity. And her friends agreed to support her in her deception.

She sent them out finally, and when Mary Stuart and Tanya walked out, they both started crying, but they didn't say anything until they were out of earshot.

"Oh, God, what an awful day," Mary Stuart finally said when they were halfway to the stables. They didn't even know where they were going, they were just walking and crying, with their arms around each other. "I can't believe it."

"You know, it's funny. I kept thinking she was very pale. She always had that translucent kind of skin that goes with her red hair, but she's been paler than ever since she got here," Tanya said, thinking back over it, "and she gets tired very easily."

"Well, this explains it." Mary Stuart looked devastated, and was grateful that they had made peace now. "Thank God she told us. What a terrible burden to take on alone. I hope we can do something to help her."

"She needs to tell the guy who's covering for her, Sam. He really has to help her, or she has to find someone else who will," Tanya said practically, thinking of the future.

"I guess that explains why she won't date," Mary Stuart added.

"I don't see why she can't, if she's careful," Tanya said thoughtfully. "I'm sure other people do. She can't completely isolate herself, it's not healthy. Oh, God, I can't believe this," Tanya muttered, and they both blew their noses in unison, just as Hartley and Gordon walked toward them, leading their horses. They almost walked right into them, and both men saw immediately that they'd been crying, and wondered what had happened.

"What happened?" Hartley asked. He had been very worried when Mary Stuart had told him they couldn't ride that morning. And Gordon was terrified that Tanya had come to her senses and was now afraid to face him. But it was obvious now that something much worse had happened to them. And at first neither woman answered.

"Are you all right?" Gordon asked Tanya cautiously. She looked as though someone close to her had died. It wasn't that bad, but it would be, someday. This was just the introduction.

"I'm okay," Tanya whispered, brushing his hand with her fingers, and he felt an electric current run through him. "How's your friend?" Tanya didn't answer, and she saw that Mary Stuart was talking to Hartley and crying again. She knew Mary Stuart was too discreet to break her promise to Zoe and tell him Zoe had AIDS, but Tanya suspected she might say she had cancer, which was what the three of them had agreed to tell Hartley and Gordon. And Tanya chose to do the same thing with Gordon. He felt terrible when he heard, and he could see easily how close they were. "I've known her since I was eighteen. That's twenty-six years," she said miserably, and he wished he could put an arm around her shoulders, but he didn't dare. He was working.

"It sure doesn't look it," he said, and she smiled at him.

"Thanks. I'm probably ten years older than you are," she said. "Officially, I'm thirty-six, in case it matters. But I'm really forty-four."

He laughed at the complications. "Well, I'm really forty-two, and I'm really a wrangler, and I'm really from Texas, and I was starting to panic. I figured you'd woken up and come to your senses and never wanted to see me again or something." He had been in a total state all morning, and could hardly pay attention to Hartley. Fortunately, no one else had ridden with them.

"I was up at six o'clock to get ready to see you. I couldn't sleep I was so excited. It's like being fourteen years old and falling in love for the first time." It was like when she had fallen in love with Bobby Joe in eighth grade, only more so. "It was all I could think of all night . . . and then, this morning, everything went crazy. She was so sick, and I called the doctor. And he sat with her for hours, and then she told us."

"Is she going to be all right? For now, I mean. Should she be in a hospital?"

"He doesn't think so," Tanya explained, "unless she gets worse here. But she wants to go home and go right back to her practice."

"She's an amazing woman." And then he looked down at her, suffering for her friend, even before she lost her. The thought of it almost killed her, and it reminded her of Ellie. That had been so heartbreaking for all of them. And Zoe would be even worse when it happened.

"You're an amazing woman too," he said gently. "I've never known anyone like you. I never expected you to be so real. I thought you were going to be the fanciest woman I ever met, instead you're the most human, the most down-to-earth, the plainest." It wasn't an insult, but a compliment, and she knew that. "Do you think you can still get away on Sunday?"

"I'll try. I want to see how she is first," but she also knew that it would be their only chance to be together. He worked every other day of the week, and the following Sunday, when he'd be off again, they were leaving.

"Is this real, Tanny?" he asked her suddenly, as they stood there, under the oak trees. He wanted it to be, he wanted to believe it was everything he thought it was, but he was desperately afraid that she was just some fabulous movie star who had come up from Hollywood, was going to play a little bit and forget him. But that didn't seem like her. He didn't even dare say it.

"It's real," she whispered softly. "I don't know how it happened, or when," she smiled then, "you annoyed the hell out of me when you wouldn't talk to me on Monday. Maybe that's when it happened. But whenever it did, I've never known anything like this. It's real, Gordon, believe me," she said softly, and she looked as bowled over as he did.

"I didn't talk to you because I was afraid to, and then you didn't turn out to be the way I thought, and I just couldn't help it. I just wanted to ride around those hills with you forever."

"What are we going to do now?" She wanted to see him and talk to him and spend time with him, and see what they had here, but she didn't want to cost him his job and get him into trouble.

"Can I come back and talk to you tonight?" he asked softly so no one would hear them, and she nodded, and raised her eyes to his with a small smile.

"We'll ride tomorrow. I think this afternoon we'll stay with Zoe, unless she's sleeping or something. I want to check on her again after lunch. What about tomorrow night? Will you come and teach me the two-step? The brochure says the wranglers will teach us, and I'd like to hold you to it." In spite of their horrendous morning, she was teasing him, and he loved it. His eyes were as full of love and excitement as hers were. It was just a shame they couldn't really indulge it. But this had its high points too, it was tender and secret. "Will you teach me, Mr. Washbaugh?"

"Yes, ma'am. I'll be there." It was one event he was expected to attend, and he intended to take full advantage of it. "And on Saturday, I'm in the rodeo again."

"I'll be there," she whispered.

"Are you going to sing again?"

"Maybe." She smiled. "It was fun." But it had also scared them both a little. "I'll see what the crowd looks like."

"You looked great on that palomino." She would have

loved to ride off on it with him. "And Sunday is ours, and we'll see how next week goes."

"That sounds pretty good." She smiled at him, this was very new for both of them, and more than a little scary. They wandered back to Hartley and Mary Stuart then, and as he left them, Gordon brushed his hand against hers, and it tied her stomach in a knot being so close to him, and not being able to do anything about it. She was dying to kiss him.

"How was your ride?" she asked Hartley, and he looked sympathetic.

"A lot nicer than your morning. Mary Stuart was just telling me about Zoe. Pancreatic cancer is an awful thing. I had a cousin who died of it in Boston." Tanya nodded, grateful to know her friend's story. "I'm so sorry."

"Me too," Tanya said, and exchanged a glance with Mary Stuart. "She could go on for quite a while apparently, but eventually there might be complications." It was complicated lying, but he was nodding agreement.

"That's exactly what happened to my cousin. All you can do is make her as comfortable as possible, let her do what she wants, and be there if she needs you." His saying that reminded Tanya that she had forgotten to tell Gordon she was taking Zoe's baby eventually. She wanted him to know, for a variety of reasons. And she wanted to see his reaction. She couldn't believe that she was actually testing the waters for a future with him after three days, but if it was even a remote possibility for some later date, she wanted to know how he would react to a number of things, and one of them was Zoe's baby.

Hartley walked them up to lunch, and the three of them talked endlessly about Zoe, her health, her career, her clinic, her child, her future, her brilliant mind, her enormous devotion to mankind. They went on endlessly about her, and the subject of their admiration and sympathy was sitting in her bedroom, thinking. She knew she had to call Sam, but she was stalling about it. She needed to ask him if he'd cover for her for a few more days, but she was afraid he'd hear something more in her voice, and she wanted to keep it from him. But while she sat mulling over what to do, and whether she should just leave a message for him, the phone rang, and it was providence, because Sam was calling her to ask her advice about a patient. She needed a major change in medication, and Sam wanted to be sure he was doing what Zoe wanted. He was actually surprised to find her in her room, he was planning to leave a message, but thought he'd check first, just in case she was there for a minute.

"I'm glad I caught you," he said, sounding pleased and then asked her the question, and she gave him the answer. She was happy that he'd asked, so many other people didn't give the primary physician that courtesy to make the decision.

"I really appreciate your asking me," she told him. It was why she liked having him cover for her instead of other people. Other relief doctors had screwed up many of her patients while she was gone, and never even bothered to tell her.

"Thanks for saying that," he said. He sounded busy and happy, and he said he was taking a rare lunch break. "You don't get fat around here, I'll say that much. I haven't run this hard since med school." In the past he had covered for her at night, or an afternoon, so she could go to dinner, or the theater, or have a glass of wine without worrying about it at a social event. This was the first time he'd done a whole week for her, and he loved it. "You run a great show here," he said admiringly, "and all your patients love you. It's mighty hard to live up to."

"They're probably not even asking for me by now." She smiled. "They're all going to come in asking for Dr. Warner."

"I should be so lucky." And as he listened to her, he thought she sounded a little strange, like she was tired or in bed or had just woken up, or been crying, and it suddenly struck him as odd, and he asked her about it. It was just an instinct, and she was so startled to be asked if she was really all right or upset about something that it silenced her for a moment, and then she started crying again, and couldn't answer. And he heard that too, and suddenly in his head, there were alarm bells.

"Did something happen to one of your friends?" he asked her gently. "Or to you?" He was an extraordinarily intuitive person and that scared her.

"No, no, they're fine," she said, and then realized she had to ask him about the following week while she had him on the phone, and she decided to try it. "Actually, I was going to call you anyway. We're having such a good time that I was wondering if . . ." She faltered and pressed onward all in the same breath, hoping he wouldn't notice. ". . . if you could maybe do another week for me, possibly less. But at worst, I'd come home a week from Sunday. I wasn't sure if you were free, or how you felt about it, and I wanted to ask you."

"I'd love it," he said quietly, but he had listened to every intonation in her voice and he was convinced she was crying. "But something's wrong, and I want to know what it is so I can help you."

"Really nothing," she continued to lie to him. "But can you do another week at the clinic?"

"I told you I would. No problem. But that's not the issue. Zoe, what's wrong? There's always a piece of the puzzle you don't show me. Why are you hiding? What's wrong, baby . . . I can hear you crying . . . please don't shut me out . . . I want to help you." He was almost crying too, and at her end she was sobbing.

"I can't, Sam . . . please don't ask me . . ."

"Why? What is it that's so terrible that you have to hide and carry all your burdens alone?" And then as he asked her, he knew. It was the same thing she saw every day, and he was seeing now. The ultimate scourge, the greatest shame, the final sorrow. She had AIDS. She didn't tell him, but he knew it. "Zoe?" She could hear in his voice that something had happened. And at her end of the phone, she was very quiet. It explained a lot of things, why she wanted no relationship with anyone, why she had looked so ill that day. It happened to a lot of doctors who treated patients with AIDS. You tried to be so careful, but it happened. You made a mistake, someone moved wrong, you stuck a child and pricked yourself, you were tired, you got sloppy, whatever the reason, the result was final. "Zoe?" he said again, and his voice was very gentle. He was only sorry not to be in the same room with her so he could put his arms around her. "Did you stick yourself? I want to know . . . please . . ." There was a long, long silence, and then a sigh. It was so hard fighting him. Her secret was out now.

"Yeah . . . last year . . . she was a little kid and very wiggly."

"Oh, God . . . I knew it. Why didn't you tell me? I've been so stupid, and so have you. What are you doing? Why are you hiding from me? Are you sick now?" He sounded panicked. She had AIDS, and he'd done nothing to help her except cover her practice. His mind and heart were racing. "Are you sick?" he asked her again, sounding still more forceful.

"Kind of. It's not serious, but the doctor here wants me to take it easy for a few days. I think I'll be all right by Monday. He says give it a full week to avoid secondary infection."

"Listen to the doctor. What is it?" He sounded suddenly clinical and she smiled. "Respiratory?" She didn't sound like it though. Aside from the tears, her voice was normal.

"No, the usual horror that comes with this disease. Raging diarrhea. I really thought I was going to die last night. I'm amazed I didn't."

"You're not going to die for a long time," he said matter-of-factly, "I won't let you."

"I've been through this myself, Sam," Zoe said sadly. "Don't do this to yourself. Remember, that's how I started in this business. The man I lived with got a bad transfusion. I started the clinic because of him. But it was the hardest thing I ever did, watching him die, and I had a lot of good years with him before that. I won't do that to anyone, and I sure won't start that way. That's starting at the ending. I won't do it."

"Do you regret you did it? Are you sorry? Do you wish you hadn't been with him?"

"No," she said clearly. She had loved Adam till the end. But she didn't want Sam to go through what she had gone through.

"What if he had said he wouldn't let you? What if he tried to send you away?"

"He did more than once," she smiled. "I just didn't listen. I didn't go. I wouldn't have left him," and as she said it, she thought about what she was saying, and then faltered, "but that was different." And then she wondered. "I would have felt cheated if I hadn't been there," she said pensively, thinking of Sam. But in some ways she hardly knew him, in other ways she'd known him forever.

"Why are you trying to cheat me?" he said bluntly, no longer willing to be put off, or pretend, or hide his feelings. "I'm in love with you. I think I have been for years. Maybe even since Stanford. I think in those days I was just too stupid to know it. And once I figured it out, you never gave me the opportunity to say it. But I'm not going to let you stop me now. I want to be there for you . . . I don't care what this miserable disease does to you . . . I don't care if you get diarrhea, or sores on your face, or pneumonia. I want to help you stay alive, I want to do your work with you, Zoe . . . I care about you and Jade . . . please let me love you . . . there's too little love in the world, if we've found some, let's share it. Don't throw it away. Your having AIDS doesn't change anything, it doesn't make me not love you, it just means that what we have is more precious. I won't let you throw it away. It means too much to me . . ." He was crying now, and she was so moved, she couldn't speak through her own tears. "Zoe . . . I love you . . . if I weren't covering for you here, I'd get on the next plane and tell you in person, but you'd probably kill me if I did that, and left no one minding the store." He laughed through his tears then and so did she.

"Yes, I would, so don't you dare leave the clinic."

"I won't, but otherwise I'd be there tonight. Besides, I miss you. You've already been gone too long," he complained.

"Sam, how can you be so crazy? How can you do this to yourself?"

"Because you don't get choices about things like this in life. You fall in love with the people you fall in love with. Sorry if it's inconvenient, sorry if you're sick. I could fall in love with some awful woman tomorrow and have her fall under a train. At least you and I know the score here. We have some time, maybe a lot, maybe a little. I'm willing to take what we can get. What about you? Are you going to waste this?"

"You'd have to be so careful." She was still trying to discourage him, but he wouldn't listen. He was absolutely sure of what he wanted from her.

"Being careful is a small price to pay, isn't it? It's worth it. God, I miss you so much, Zoe. I just want to hold you, and make you happy."

"Will you work with me? Full-time, I mean, or even part-time?" That was almost as important to her, maybe more so. She had a responsibility to a lot of people, even more than to herself as far as she was concerned. And she needed Sam to help her. But he was more than willing.

"I'll work with you night and day if you want," he said, and then thought better of it. "Actually, I'll do the night and day stuff, you do a little less, please. And let's take some time for us. I don't want you wearing yourself out anymore. Let's take good care of you. All right? Just like we tell the patients. And you'd better listen to me. In your case, I'm the doctor."

"Yes, sir," she smiled, and wiped her eyes again. It had been an emotional morning. She had told her two best friends and Sam, and none of them had let her down, on the contrary, they were three extraordinary human beings. And then Sam startled her yet again.

"Let's get married," he said, and she couldn't believe what she was hearing. He was truly insane, but she loved him for it. She was smiling broadly when she answered.

"You're certifiable. I won't let you do that." She was horrified but deeply touched that he would offer.

"I would have wanted to marry you whether you had AIDS or not." And he meant it.

"But I do, and you don't need to do that to yourself," she said sadly.

"What if this were one of your patients? I know you. You'd tell them to do whatever made them happy and seemed right to them."

"How do you know this is right?" she asked gently.

"Because I love you," he said, praying she'd hear him.

"I love you too," she said cautiously, "but let's not rush into this, let's take it slowly." He liked what she was saying, because it meant she thought she had some time to make decisions, and that meant she was optimistic, which was important. But he really did want to marry her. But he knew he might convince her more easily in person.

"I'm awfully glad I called you today," he said happily. "I got advice about a patient, a job, full-time preferably, and possibly a wife. This was a very fruitful conversation," he said, and she laughed.

"I can't believe I left a lunatic like you in charge of my clinic."

"Neither can I. But your patients love me. Think how happy they'll be when we're Dr. and Dr. Warner."

"I have to take your name too?" She was laughing. She really did love him. She had been so fond of him for so long, but she had never allowed her feelings for him to move forward. She had been too busy taking care of her patients to let herself be anything more than a doctor, and mother.

"You can call yourself anything you like if you marry me," Sam told her magnanimously. "I'm very open-minded."

"You're crazy," and then she grew serious for a moment, although they were both in good spirits. "Thank you, Sam . . . I think you're wonderful," she said honestly, "and I really do love you," she said softly. "It scared me before how much I liked you, but I was determined not to get you into a mess like this. And you walked yourself right into it. You can still change your mind if you want."

"I'm here forever," he said calmly.

"I wish I were," she said sadly.

"You might be. If I have anything to do with it, you will."

"At least my work will be . . . and the clinic . . . and Jade . . . and you . . . and my friends . . ."

"If you ask me, it sounds like a lot to stick around for."

"I'll do everything I can, Sam. I promise."

"Good. Then get a lot of rest while you're there and come back healthy, and check yourself into the hospital if the diarrhea doesn't stop."

"It has," she said, and that reassured him.

"Drink a lot of fluids."

"I know. I'm a doctor. Don't worry. I'll be good. I swear."

"I love you." It was odd. It was so totally unexpected. He was so happy suddenly. She loved him. She had AIDS, it was terrible news, and yet in some crazy way he was happy, and so was Zoe. She was still smiling when Mary Stuart and Tanya came in later after lunch to check her.

"What happened to you?" Tanya asked suspiciously. "You look like the cat that swallowed the canary."

"I talked to Sam. He's going to come to work at the clinic full-time."

"Wow, that's terrific," Mary Stuart said enthusiastically, she knew what a relief that was for Zoe.

"No, no, wait . . . she's lying," Tanya said, narrowing her eyes and looking at their old buddy. "There's more, and she's not telling."

"No, there's not." But she was laughing as she said it. It was a far cry from the intensity and sorrow of the morning.

"What else did he say?" Zoe was grinning from ear to ear as she tried to avoid Tanya's question.

"Nothing. I told him," she hesitated, looking more serious suddenly, "that I was positive." She hated to say the words, and then she looked at her friends with wide eyes filled with disbelief, still unable to believe what he had said to her at lunchtime.

"What did he say to you?" Mary Stuart asked gently, and Zoe turned to her with a broad smile of amazement.

"He asked me to marry him. Can you believe that?" The other women's jaws dropped, and they looked at her in delighted disbelief, but it was Tanya who spoke first.

"Let's get you healthy so you can go home to this guy, before someone else grabs him. He sounds terrific."

"He really is." Zoe had no idea what she was going to do yet. But she was going to be with him, and work with him, and let herself experience everything that life offered her, and if he really wanted to marry her, then maybe she would. But whether or not she married him, she knew she loved him, and that was the most important.

"Well, I'll be damned," Mary Stuart said, enormously impressed by Dr. Sam Warner.

The three of them talked about it for a little while, and then Mary Stuart and Tanya went out for the afternoon, since Zoe seemed to be doing so much better. Hartley and Mary Stuart went for a hike that afternoon, and talked about a number of things, especially Zoe and a man who was brave enough to marry a woman he loved and knew was dying. They both thought it was an extraordinary gesture, and they loved him for it.

And Tanya went out riding with Gordon. They were lucky that day. No one else in her party wanted to ride, Hartley was on the hike with Mary Stuart, and the doctors from Chicago had gone fishing that afternoon, so they were actually alone, without even planning it. Gordon took her to a waterfall in the mountains on horseback, and they dismounted for a while, and lay in the tall grass among the wildflowers while he held her and they kissed, and it took a superhuman effort not to let it go any further, but they wanted to move as slowly as they could, despite the limited time they had. They already felt as though they were on an express train. But it was the most beautiful afternoon of her life, as she lay looking up at him, and then he lay next to her, and they looked at the mountains. They walked for a while, hand in hand, leading their horses, talking about their childhoods, and they talked about Zoe too, and Sam's remarkable love for her. They were brave people in a hard world. And in her own way, Tanya was too. She had come a long way in her life, and now suddenly, there was someone solid and warm and kind beside her. It frightened her a little bit to think of what the press would make of it, and she tried to warn him of the damage they could do, the hurt they could inflict, but he didn't seem to care, and he told Tanya to look around them.

"As long as we have this, how can you care about all that? It is so unimportant. We're all that matters, and what we are to each other."

"And if we don't have this anymore?" she asked, looking around her, and thinking of going back to California.

"We will," he said quietly, "we have to. As long as we have something here, a place we can come to, to get sane again, maybe the rest of that insanity won't matter." It was an interesting idea, and she liked it. Maybe he was right, and she should buy a place in Wyoming. She could certainly afford it. She could even sell the house in Malibu. It was huge, and she almost never went there.

"I feel as though I'm standing on the edge of a whole new life," she said, as they stood on a bluff, looking out over the valley. They could see buffalo, and elk, and cattle, and horses. It was an amazing sight, and she could see easily why he loved it.

"You are standing on the edge of a new life," he said calmly, and then he turned her toward him again, put his arms around her, and kissed her.

CHAPTER 17

On Friday morning, Zoe was still asleep when Tanya tiptoed in to look at her, but she seemed peaceful, she'd eaten well the night before, and Mary Stuart agreed when she came in that Zoe's color was better.

They were just going out to ride, when she got up, and wandered into the living room in her nightgown, and they were pleased to see that they'd been right. She looked a great deal better.

"How do you feel?" Mary Stuart asked solicitously. They were both so worried about her.

"Like a new woman," Zoe said, almost sorry she told them. She wondered if she shouldn't have said she had AIDS, but the cat was out of the bag now, and it meant a lot to her to have them support her. "I'm sorry I was so much trouble yesterday." Tanya wanted to tell her how sorry she was that Zoe had pricked her finger the year before, and contracted AIDS, but she didn't.

"Don't be silly." Their eyes met and held and they each

knew what the other was thinking. There was real love there, and compassion and caring. They were the kind of friends that came along once in a lifetime. "We want you to take care of yourself. Stay in bed today, get lots of rest. I'll come back at lunchtime to see if you need anything," Tanya said as she put an arm around her. She was surprised to realize that under the flannel nightgown, Zoe was incredibly frail, even more so than she looked. There was barely any meat on her.

"Do you want us to stay with you?" Mary Stuart asked generously, and Zoe told her that she didn't.

"I just want you two to have a good time. You both deserve it." They'd all been through rough times in different ways, death, divorce, all the trauma of which life was made and that challenged one's very survival.

"We all deserve a good time," Mary Stuart said, "so do you."

"I just want to get back to work," she said, she was beginning to feel really guilty for being so lazy, and a second week away seemed absolutely sinful. But she knew she needed to recover from the little episode she'd just been through.

"Be a good girl and be lazy." Tanya wagged a finger at her, and a few minutes later she and Mary Stuart left for breakfast.

Hartley inquired about their friend, and they sat and talked quietly about her over breakfast. They thought she was very brave, and Tanya was grateful that Sam was being so supportive.

"He must be quite a man," Hartley said admiringly when Mary Stuart told him of Sam's reaction when Zoe told him. They still hadn't said she had AIDS and they didn't plan to. He thought she had cancer.

"She might recover," he said hopefully, but it was obvious that he thought it was unlikely and so did they. "I knew another couple who did something like that, got married in the face of a terminal prognosis. They were the most remarkable people I ever met, and probably the happiest, and I think she lived a lot longer because of it. He just refused to let her go, she fought valiantly, and I think their love added years to her life. I've never forgotten them. I don't think he ever remarried when she died, he wrote a book about it, about her, and it was the most touching thing I've ever read, I cried from beginning to end, but I can't tell you how I admired him. He loved her more than any man could love a woman." There were tears in Mary Stuart's eyes as she listened, and she wished that more than anything for Zoe.

Sam called Zoe that afternoon, and they talked for a long time. He wanted her to promise him, seriously, that they'd get married, and she was still accusing him of being crazy.

"You can't propose to me," she said, touched and flattered and moved to tears by what he was saying, "you don't even know me."

"I've known you for over twenty-two years, I've worked with you off and on for five. I've probably been in love with you for the last twenty, and if we both were too dumb to see it then that's not my problem. You're so busy taking care of everyone else all the time, Zoe, you don't even see what's happening right next to you. I want to be there for you," he said, and his voice was warm and gruff and sexy when he said it.

"You already are there for me, Sam," she said softly. He was amazing.

"I'll be here for you as long as you want me. Besides, we haven't even had our first date yet."

"I know. You haven't even tasted my lasagne." There were so many things for them to do, so many things to discover about each other.

"I'm a great cook. What's your favorite kind of food?" He didn't know things like that about her, and he wanted to know them all now. He wanted to spoil her, and be there for her, and take care of her. He wanted to make history, and have her recover. But if she didn't, he'd be there for her too, until the bitter end. He knew now, to his very soul, that it was his destiny, and nothing she could have said to him would dissuade him or change that.

"My favorite kind of food?" She was smiling at his question. She almost didn't remember that she was sick. She felt better today, and she was so happy. It was all about now, about just being there at this very moment, and not worrying about tomorrow. "Actually . . . I think, takeout. You know, fast food, you stick it in the lab closet and eat three mouthfuls between patients."

"You're disgusting. No more of that. Nothing but gourmet meals for you. Maybe I should do catering instead of locum tenens." But he was going to be full-time now, and they both loved the idea. The idea of working with her daily really pleased him. Besides, he could keep an eye on her and make sure she didn't overdo it. "Speaking of which," he had reminded her, "we need to find a new relief, you can't take calls for me if we're going to be together." She was already assuming, as he was, that they would be together most of the time. The idea certainly appealed to her, now that he knew her situation, and she had a feeling that the relationship was going to be even better than either of them expected. And for a moment she smiled and thought of Dick Franklin. She could never have done anything like this with him, he would never have been there for her. She was just damn lucky she had known Sam Warner, and she knew it.

"We can cover for each other some of the time," Sam said practically, "and I'll ask around if anyone knows someone good who could cover for us. There's a guy I did some work for whom I like, and a woman who's done a lot of AIDS work at General. She's young, but she's good. I think you'd like her."

"Is she pretty?" Zoe asked with concern, and he laughed.

"You've got nothing to worry about, Dr. Phillips." But he sounded pleased. "I didn't know you were jealous." This was all so crazy and so wonderful. It was as though it had all come together like magic.

"I'm not, just smart and careful."

"Fine, I'll put the word out, we're only looking for guys or ugly women to relieve us . . . Zoe, I love you." There was something so tender in his voice that it brought tears to her eyes as she listened to him.

"I love you too, Sam," she said, and he promised to call her later that afternoon, when he was finished working.

"Your patients are stacking up outside, I'd better get back to work before I close your clinic. Get some rest, and I'll call you later."

"I think I might go to dinner tonight," she said, looking up at the ceiling as they chatted. She really was feeling a lot better.

"Don't push too hard. Just take it easy, remember. I want to take you out when you get back, so rest up. There's a new restaurant on Clement I want to try." It all sounded so alive and so real, and so hopeful.

And she said as much to Dr. Kroner that afternoon when he came by. But she didn't have to, he could see it. She was still a little dehydrated, and he wanted her to push fluids more, but she looked like a new woman. He knew that she was aware that she would have times like that, terrible moments, and episodes of illness or despair, and then she would rally. Eventually the bad times would outnumber the good ones, but not necessarily for a long time. She could go on like this for a long time before it got worse, or it could get worse very quickly. No one could predict it, and she knew that better than he did.

"Can your locum tenens guy stay on for a while?" he asked after he had checked her, and sat down to chat in her cabin.

"Actually, yes, he can," she laughed, thinking of all the things Sam had said since the day before. "He can stay for quite a while. He's agreed to come in full-time." She was smiling as she said it.

"That's terrific," he said, looking pleased for her, and a little surprised that she looked so happy. The episode of the day before seemed to have left her almost ecstatic. It was an unusual reaction for someone who was potentially as sick as she was. "But how much of the work do you think you'll be willing to let him take on? You have to agree to give some of it up, Dr. Phillips," he said, and she nodded, but she couldn't stop smiling.

"Actually, I think he'll be taking on quite a lot." She paused as she looked at him. "He wants to get married," she said, feeling like a kid again, and not even a sick one. She wasn't even sure if they would, but the fact that he wanted to touched her deeply. Knowing that he wanted to be there for her meant everything, with or without a wedding. The wedding was only frosting on the cake, the important thing was that he'd be there for her, in sickness and in health, for better or worse. That was all that mattered.

Dr. Kroner congratulated her, and he looked pleased for her. Things certainly seemed to be working out well for her, and that was important. She said that she had told her friends about her illness too, and it had been very emotional for all of them, but she felt great support from all the people who really mattered to her.

"You know how much that means," he reminded her. It was important not to make oneself vulnerable by telling the wrong people about the disease, those who couldn't handle it, and would shrink from patients in horror. But most people had a small core group who could make a difference, and now she had one.

They talked about her plans for a while, and her work, and her clinic, and Sam, and Jade, and the things she wanted to do when she got home. He reminded her not to overdo it, and she promised she wouldn't, but he said he didn't believe her.

"You're probably right," she laughed. She couldn't wait to get back and see her patients, but she was having fun in Wyoming too, and she thought it was doing her good. Like the others, she had felt the same pull here. There was something almost mystical about the mountains.

And then he asked her something that surprised her. He said he wanted a favor from her, and she couldn't imagine what it was. But she was deeply touched when he asked if she would visit some of his patients. She was so knowledgeable and she had so much experience, it would be invaluable to him if she would see them. He only had about half a dozen, but he read everything he could, and had a huge library on AIDS-related research. He had copies of all her articles, he said. But having her actually consult with him would be the greatest help he could think of.

"Not until you're feeling stronger of course . . . maybe in a few days . . ." He looked up at her with hopeful eyes, and she told him she'd be happy to do it. In fact, she was honored.

"What kind of visiting services do you have?" she asked with interest.

"Not bad," he said modestly, grateful for her interest. "We have a wonderful hospice group, and some terrific nurses. I see everyone I can. I go out to them, I try to rally their friends and families to help them. We're trying to organize some kind of a small central kitchen run by some friends, a little bit like Project Open Hand in San Francisco, on a smaller scale. I hope we never need to service that many people. For the moment, fortunately, we don't have that many cases. But with the influx of people from urban areas, people in the entertainment business, writers, people who just want to escape, I think that, conceivably, we could wind up with a lot more people coming here who have AIDS, possibly even in late stages, and in need of treatment. I'd appreciate all the input from you I can get," he said, and she nodded soberly. She promised to send him some additional books too, volumes that had been useful to her, and even some of the articles Sam had recommended to her. They started discussing alternative medications then, and by the end of the afternoon they discovered they'd been talking shop for nearly two hours. She was tired by then, and he suggested she take a nap before she tackled dinner. She wanted to go to the dining room, to watch the two-step lesson they were having afterward. It sounded like fun and she knew the others were going. And she wanted to go with them.

"I'll come and see you at the hospital in a few days, or maybe you want me to do house calls with you. See what works best for you," Zoe said helpfully, "I'm open to anything, just leave me a message." They were doctor and student now, more than doctor and patient, but he knew that she was well aware, better even than he, of what she needed. She thanked him again for his help the day before, and when he left, she lay down again and fell asleep. She was sleeping soundly when the others came back from riding. It had been a pleasant afternoon for them. They had paired off as they often did now, Hartley rode with Mary Stuart, and Tanya rode on ahead with Gordon. And she was happy to hear he was coming to the dancing lesson in the main living room that night. It was one of the rare occasions when the wranglers were not only allowed to mingle, but asked to. And Gordon was particularly popular because everyone said he was such a good dancer.

Zoe woke up in time to get dressed, and chatted with her friends. With Zoe feeling so much better again, in spite of what they now knew of her disease, they were all in surprisingly high spirits. But their romances had them all laughing and talking and giggling. And once again it reminded all of them of the old days in Berkeley.

"God, it's like being kids again, isn't it?" Tanya said, still amazed at what was happening to each of them. "Do you suppose it's the water here?" She hadn't had as much to say to anyone in years as she seemed to with Gordon, and Mary Stuart and Hartley looked as though they had always been together. They were amazingly comfortable and completely at ease, and they seemed to have identical, or at least compatible, views on almost every subject.

"I've never known anyone like him," she said. It made her think of living with Bill, even before Todd died. There had always been a considerable divergence of opinion between them, but she'd thought it was interesting, and even at the best of times, there had been a fair amount of amicable conflict. She used to think it gave texture to things, and it shed new light on a variety of situations. But in Hartley's case, everything was so much smoother. Now she saw what it was like being with someone who had the same ideas about things, shared the same views, it was like dancing with Astaire and being Ginger Rogers. She and Bill were no longer even in the same ballroom.

She was halfway out the door that night, in bright red jeans, a matching sweater, and lipstick exactly the same color and her dark hair pulled back, when the phone rang. The others had just gone on ahead, and she had stayed to look for the bright red cowboy boots she'd bought at Billy Martin's. She had just pulled them on and run out the door when the phone rang. And she was tempted not to answer. But it didn't seem fair to the others, it could have been a call from Zoe's child or one of her patients, or something warning Tanya of danger, or a potential problem. She hurried back into the room, carrying her red cashmere shawl, and picked up the phone, sounding breathless.

"Hello?"

"Is Mrs. Walker there?" She didn't recognize the voice at first. It was a man and she couldn't imagine who was calling.

"This is she. Who is this?" she said formally, and then was startled by the answer.

"Mary Stuart? It didn't sound like you." It was Bill, and it only underlined how remote they had become. Neither of them had recognized the other. But she hadn't spoken to him in days. Most of the time now, they exchanged brief and extremely uninteresting faxes.

"It didn't sound like you either. I was just running out to dinner."

"Sorry if this is a bad time," he said drily. It was three o'clock in the morning for him. And she couldn't imagine why he was calling.

"Is Alyssa all right?" Her heart skipped a beat as she asked him. It was the only reason she could think of now for him calling.

"She's fine," he said calmly. "I spoke to her yesterday, they're having a ball in Vienna. They had just arrived from Salzburg. They're all over the place, but it's fun for them. I don't suppose we'll see her now all summer." Mary Stuart smiled at the description of what she was doing. It sounded just like her.

"If you talk to her again, tell her I love her. She hasn't called me. I think the time difference probably makes it too difficult. But I figured she was okay, or she'd have called you. It's late for you. What are you doing up at this hour?" They were like business associates exchanging news, there was nothing personal between them.

"I was working late, and I was stupid enough to drink coffee this afternoon, so here I am, awake at this ungodly hour, so I figured I'd call you. The time difference never really works for me either." Neither does our marriage, she wanted to add, but she didn't.

"It's nice of you to call," she said, but sounded unconvincing. She didn't even want to try anymore. She didn't want to warm up to him. She had made her decision. She wanted out now. And it had nothing to do with Hartley Bowman. It had everything to do with William Walker.

"What are you doing there? You haven't told me a thing in your faxes. In fact, I don't think I've heard from you in several days, have I?" He didn't even remember. But it didn't matter to Mary Stuart.

"You don't tell me much either," she said pointedly.

"There's nothing to tell, I'm working. I'm not going to Annabel's or Harry's Bar. I'm sitting on my duff day after day, night after night, getting ready for this case. It's not much fun, but I think we're going to win it. We're very well prepared."

"That's nice," she said, looking down at her red leather boots, and thinking of her husband. But as she listened to him, she found all she could think of now was Hartley. And

Bill suffered from the comparison. She couldn't imagine having this conversation with Hartley Bowman, or having the year she had just shared with him. She couldn't imagine any of it, or wanting to live through it again, or even continue any longer.

"What about you?" He was pressing her, and she didn't seem to want to talk. He noticed it too, and wondered about it.

"We're riding every day. It's incredibly beautiful here. I've never seen anything like it. The Tetons are spectacular, better than Europe."

"How are your friends?" Why was he so interested suddenly? She couldn't understand it.

"They're fine." She didn't say a word about Zoe. "In fact, they're waiting for me for dinner." She didn't tell him about the two-step lesson afterward, or about Zoe's illness. There was nothing she wanted to share with him. It was over.

"I won't hold you then. Give them my best." She was about to thank him and say good-bye and there was an awkward pause at his end. It was late for him, and she hadn't seen him in weeks now.

"Stu . . . I miss you." There was an endless silence after he said it. She didn't want to mislead him now, and she didn't know why he was doing this. After a year of silence and pain, why would he? Maybe he just felt guilty, or was sorry about what they no longer had, just as she was. But she wasn't going to play games with him, and she wasn't going to let him hurt her again. He had hurt her too much already. The doors were closed now. She wondered, from the hour and his tone, if he had been drinking. It wasn't like him, but it was late and he was alone, it was possible. Whatever the reason, she wasn't buying.

"Don't work too hard," was all she said. A month before, six months before . . . a year before . . . she'd have felt like a monster for what she wasn't saying. But now she felt nothing at all as she said good-bye and hung up the phone, and hurried out the door to meet the others for dinner.

The two-step lesson that night was even more fun than anticipated. All the guests came, and Zoe sat wrapped in a blue cashmere shawl, she was wearing a soft chamois dress and beautiful turquoise earrings, and she looked lovely as she sat there. Some of the other guests had worn skirts that swirled as they danced. Tanya looked spectacular as usual in a white lace antique Victorian dress that managed to make her look both innocent and sexy. And Gordon looked totally overwhelmed by her when he saw her. He was wearing jeans and a clean cowboy shirt, a black Stetson and black boots. Tanya told him when they met that he looked like a cowboy in a movie. And Charlotte Collins asked that Gordon do the demonstration. He had apparently won several prizes for his two-step.

"Not just for riding bulls and saddle broncs, although he won't tell you that," she teased. She was a wise and canny old woman. And she was keeping a motherly eye on Zoe, who was content to sit on the couch. She was not yet feeling up to dancing, but she was having a good time chatting with John Kroner, who had come for dinner and the evening. Charlotte invited him frequently, and he had come tonight just for the pleasure of seeing Zoe and to get a chance to talk to his hero.

"Has anyone here ever done the two-step before?" Charlotte asked, as Gordon came forward and several return guests raised their hands awkwardly, and Tanya couldn't help laughing.

"Not since I was about fourteen, Miss Charlotte."

"That's right," Charlotte smiled warmly at her, "we have a girl from Texas. Will you give it a whirl?" she asked, as though Tanya would be doing her a favor, and the guests instantly applauded. If they couldn't hear her sing, at least they could watch her do the two-step.

"I'm afraid I'll disgrace myself," she laughed, "and you," she said to Gordon as he approached her. But the temptation to dance with him was too great, the lure of him too strong, and she slipped her hand gently in his and headed for the middle of the floor as they turned on the music, and Charlotte explained to everyone how you did it. Gordon went through the motions with her slowly first, and then with the next song, he spun her around, walked her forward and back and twirled her, and everyone clapped, they looked fantastic together. It looked like a professional demonstration, and Gordon looked as though he were going to die of joy as Tanya twirled lithely around him and he took her in his arms as the song concluded.

"You Texas turkey," he whispered to her with a broad smile, "you're better than I am. Don't tell me you haven't done that in a while."

"I haven't," she whispered back, but she'd had a great time. And they danced again, as the other couples joined them, and everyone tried and most of them stumbled. She and Gordon danced four more times, and then he changed partners and showed several others how to do it. But at the very end, he came back to her, and they did it one last time. Everyone had had a great time, and people were admiring her, but they left her alone now. They hardly even whispered when they saw her. She was a familiar sight here, and she was very comfortable on the ranch, and even more so with Gordon.

When the music was over, he stood around, and several other wranglers were talking to the guests as well. After five days together, they were all good friends, and a relationship had developed among them, though none quite as intense as Tanya and Gordon's. But much to their relief, absolutely no one seemed to suspect what had happened.

"I had a great time," he smiled down at her, and she looked up at him with eyes full of excitement and laughter.

"Me too. You're a good dancer, Mr. Washbaugh."

"Thank you, ma'am." He stretched out his drawl and bowed to her and they laughed as Charlotte Collins joined them.

"You two should enter the contest at the state fair," she said with a broad smile. "It sure is pretty when it's done right."

"I'm afraid I'm pretty rusty," Tanya said modestly. But she and Bobby Joe had entered all those contests and won them.

"Is everything all right?" Charlotte asked. She had been very concerned about Zoe. John Kroner hadn't told her what it was, but he said her condition was serious, and it concerned her. "Dr. Phillips is looking a little brighter." But she was still pale, and in spite of her animated look, she seemed very fragile.

"She's feeling a lot better tonight," Tanya said, looking relieved but still somewhat worried. When she took a little distance from her, she noticed again how pale and thin Zoe was. It was hard not to, but when you were talking to her, she was so alive and so intense that you forgot it.

"I see you're going back to the rodeo tomorrow," Charlotte said with a smile. Tanya and the others had just ordered tickets before they went to dinner.

"Are you going to sing again tomorrow night? You were the talk of the town after Wednesday."

"I'd like to," Tanya smiled generously, tossing her long blond hair over her shoulder, and she saw out of the corner of her eye that Gordon was frowning. "We'll see if they ask me, and how the crowd looks." If she saw a lot of drunks, or it looked rowdier than it had on Wednesday night, then she wouldn't.

"Oh, they'll ask you. It was the high point of the year in Jackson Hole. Maybe the decade. You were nice to do it." She smiled and then moved on to the other guests, and Gordon was still frowning.

"I don't want you to do that," he whispered. "I don't like the way people get when you're close like that. If you're up on a stage, with security, they can't hurt you."

"Yes, they can," she said honestly, and she knew they might someday. She had worn a bullet-proof vest at a concert in the Philippines once and swore she'd never do that again. She had been shaking from head to foot and ready to throw up through the entire concert. "That's why I rode the horse the other night," she said matter-of-factly. "I knew I could get the hell out of Dodge if I had to."

"I don't like you taking chances," he said, not wanting to be overbearing with her, but genuinely worried.

"I don't like you riding bulls and broncos." She looked him straight in the eye while she said it. She knew this cowboy life. She came from it. And she knew the price you paid, and its dangers. But she knew her own world too, better than he did.

"Tell you what," he said honestly, "we ever make a go of it, and I'll give up the bulls and broncs."

"I'll hold you to it," she said softly, and then she wanted to be honest with him too, "but I can't give up concerts, Gordon. That's how I make my living."

"I know that. I wouldn't expect you to. I just don't want you to do some two-bit thing to be nice to them, and get hurt. It's just not worth it. They don't deserve it."

"I know," she sighed, looking up at him. It was hard to believe they were having this conversation, negotiating their future, what they would each give up and what they wouldn't. But there was no harm done, if it ever happened. "I just like to sing for the hell of it sometimes, without the promoters and the contracts and the hype and all the bullshit. It's fun to just do it."

"Then sing for me," he smiled.

"I'd love that." There was an old Texas song she would have loved to sing for him. She had sung it as a kid at high school dances, and it had gotten popular since, but she had always thought of it as her song. "I will one day."

"I'll hold you to that too." There were a lot of promises floating between them.

They all stood around and talked for a while, and then Mary Stuart and Tanya took Zoe back to the cabin. Gordon had promised to show up later, if he could. He said he would just tap on her bedroom window. She told him which one it was, and then they left, and Hartley walked them back, and then sat outside with Mary Stuart. Tanya and Zoe were inside the cabin chatting.

Mary Stuart told him about the call from Bill before dinner, and he looked at her thoughtfully while she told him.

"He's probably realizing what he's missed, and what he's given up for all these months," he said, thinking about it, and looking at her. "What are you going to do if he wants to fix it?"

"I can't imagine it," she said honestly, "but I realized something when I talked to him tonight. I don't want to do that. I can't go back again. We can't undo the last year, or what happened to Todd. I don't think I'll ever forgive him for how he's behaved. That's a nasty thing to say, and it's mean-spirited of me, but to be honest with you, I think he killed it."

"And if he didn't? If he comes back and tells you how much he loves you and how wrong he was, what then?" He wanted her to think about that before they made a mistake. They were both extremely attracted to each other, but they were being very cautious, and that was just what he wanted. He didn't want to get decimated either.

"I don't know, Hartley. I'm not sure. I think I know. I believe it's all over for me. I suppose there are no guarantees until I see him. I think I'll be sure then."

"Why are you waiting until September for that?" It was a question she had been asking herself lately too. Originally, she had thought she needed time, and she was glad she'd have the summer in which to think. But ever since she'd been here, she realized that she was ready to tackle it now. It had even occurred to her that she might fly to London to talk to Bill, and she said as much to Hartley.

"I think that's a good idea," he said gently, "if you feel ready for it. I don't want to push you." They had known each other for five days, and it had been an extraordinary experience for both of them, but it was possible that it was all a dream, an illusion, or maybe it was real and something very special. Only time would tell. But first, she had to deal with her husband. Neither of them wanted to do anything confusing before she did that. And as tempting as it was to just fall into bed with each other, she knew they wouldn't.

"I'm going to Los Angeles with Tanya when I leave here. I was going to stay a week, but she's busy anyway." She was thinking out loud and sharing it with him. "I think I'll stay for a few days, and then fly to London. I came here to think, and to decide what I wanted. And I knew the moment I came here. I think I knew before that." She had known when she left her apartment in New York that she would never live there the same way again. She had been saying good-bye to her old life when she left it, and she knew that, and she said as much to Hartley.

"There's something about these mountains that gives you the answers to many things. I missed coming here after Meg died." He smiled at Mary Stuart then and took her hand in his. "It would be amazing if I found my new life here, if I came here to find you," and then he looked at her sadly, "but even if nothing comes of this, if you go back to him, I want you to know how happy you've made me. You've shown me that I'm not as alone as I think I am, that there is someone out there who can make me fall in love again. You're a beautiful gift I never expected, you're a vision of what life can be when two people love each other and are happy." He was exactly the same for her. He was living proof that there was someone in the world who cared about her, that she could talk to easily, and who could love her. And she didn't want to give that up now. He wasn't asking her to, but he wanted her to be sure of what she wanted to do about her husband before moving toward him. Mary Stuart felt certain she had made her mind up.

"I don't think seeing him is going to change anything," she said gently, holding Hartley's hand in her own and kissing it. He was so dear to her, she had grown so fond of him in such a short time, and they felt incredibly protective about each other. But they also knew that she needed to prove to herself what she still felt for Bill and what she didn't. And Hartley didn't want to rush her, but she insisted he wasn't.

"It was so strange when he called me tonight. It was like talking to a total stranger. I didn't even recognize him at first, nor him me, and I couldn't figure out why he was calling. It's sad to feel so far away from someone you once loved. I never thought it would happen to us."

"You weathered one of life's cruelest blows," he said sympathetically. "Most marriages don't survive it. The statistics are staggering. I think it's something like ninety-seven percent of people who lose children get divorced. You have to be awfully strong to withstand that," he said kindly.

"And I guess we weren't."

"I love being with you, Mary Stuart," he said, smiling at her, and changing the subject. He wanted to move ahead with her, to be in New York with her, to go to Europe with her, to share his friends and his life and his career. There was so much he wanted to do with her, and he was anxious to get started. He had been alone for two years, but he knew he had to wait a little longer. She had to go to London to see her husband. But once she'd gone, if she was sure, the possibilities were limitless, and he knew that. There was nothing else left to hold them back from each other, although he was still a little bit concerned about her daughter. He had never had children of his own, and he wondered if Alyssa would resist him, if she would blame him for the divorce, and choose to hate him out of loyalty to her father. In fact, the divorce wouldn't have been because of him, but it might be hard for her to accept that. He had spoken to Mary Stuart about it that afternoon, and she admitted that she and Alyssa would have to do some very serious talking. But on the other hand, she wasn't willing to stay with her father just for her. Alyssa had to make her own life. And as Mary Stuart saw it, her own life was better than half over, this was her last chance possibly to make a life with a person she could really care about and who loved her. She wasn't going to let the chance pass her by out of loyalty to something she no longer had with a man who could no longer love her. She wanted to be with Hartley.

They sat together for a long time, talking about the past, the present, and the future. And it was all agreed. She would go to London the week after they all left Wyoming. She didn't think she'd stay in London for more than a few days, possibly less if Bill didn't want to discuss it further. And she might try and meet up with Alyssa somewhere for a day. She wasn't sure if she would tell her yet, unless Bill thought they should, otherwise she thought telling Alyssa her parents were getting divorced could wait until September. But she just wanted to see her, if Mary Stuart could even find her on her trek around Europe. And then she would go home again, and get her life organized. She had no idea what Bill would want to do with the apartment. If he would want to keep it, or sell it, if he wanted to live in it, or thought she should. But she had already made her mind up about that too. She didn't want to live there. It was all too painful, and a constant reminder of tragedy every time she passed Todd's room. Whether or not his things were there made no difference. She knew he had once lived there, knew exactly where the Princeton banner had been, and the trophies, and the teddy bear on his bed when he was little. His things were put away now, and it was time for them to put their things away too. It was time for a whole new life for all of them, and hopefully, if she was very lucky, and the Fates were kind to her, hers would be with Hartley.

"Would you like to come to Fisher's Island with me when you get back?" he asked cautiously. "I have a funny old house there. I haven't been there much since Margaret died, but I thought I'd spend some time there in August." She looked at him gratefully then, and nodded. He had his ghosts too, his old haunts, his routines. They both did.

"I'd love that. I didn't really know what to do with myself this year, with Bill away for so long. I was going to go out and see friends in East Hampton."

"Come and stay with me then," he said, nuzzling her neck.

He wanted nothing more than to wake up next to her, to listen to the ocean and make love to her all afternoon and all night and all morning, and talk into the wee hours, and share his favorite books with her. He had already discovered that she was a passionate reader and they loved almost all the same authors. He had some wonderful first editions he wanted to share with her. He wanted to walk down the beach holding her hand, and tell her all his secrets. But they had already shared most of them, riding through the wildflowers across the foothills and thc valleys of Wyoming. It was already wonderful, and it could only get better.

It was late when he finally pulled himself away from her, and they were both satisfied with their plan, that she should go to London after the following week, and then come and spend time with him on Fisher's Island. It was the trip to London that was so important. And as he said good night to her, he asked her one last painful question.

"And if he wins you back?"

"He won't," she said, kissing him.

"He would be a fool not to," Hartley whispered, and then kissed her. And if he did, Hartley knew he would have to find the way back without her. "Maybe we should figure out a signal," he said, "so I'll know if my life is over or just beginning."

"Stop worrying," she said, and they kissed again, but he couldn't help it. He wanted her so badly. "I love you," she said, and meant it to the depths of her soul. She barely knew him, and yet she knew she could spend the rest of her life with him, and never regret it for a moment. He was completely different from Bill, and yet she knew that she could have lived a lifetime with either of them and been perfectly happy. But her time with Bill had come and gone. And her time with Hartley was just beginning.

CHAPTER 18

On the way to the rodeo, they were all in high spirits again. Zoe had decided not to come, she said she felt up to it, and she looked fine, but she wanted to marshal her strength, and she thought the rodeo would be too taxing. She had stayed home with Hartley's latest book, which he'd given her, and she wanted to call Sam, and talk to the baby.

Tanya and Mary Stuart were going to the rodeo, and Hartley had come with them. He was wearing a new cowboy hat he'd bought in town that afternoon, and he had bought one for Mary Stuart. Tanya said they looked like fancy Texas ranchers. The hats had been steamed and shaped for them, the crown had been raised on hers, the brims trimmed on both of them. They were the real thing, and they made a handsome couple. Funnily enough, they had both worn navy blue, it was something Hartley said couples sometimes did unconsciously when they were particularly in tune with each other. But it warmed Tanya's heart to see them.

"You two are so cute," she said, sitting on the couch on her bus, swinging one leg over the other. She was anxious to see Gordon. Hartley was aware of that situation too, but he was extremely discreet, and Tanya knew he would keep their secret. But like Gordon, he was worried about her safety.

"Shouldn't you have security with you?" he asked sensibly, and Mary Stuart nodded. She thought the rodeo was dangerous for her too. But Tanya insisted that it wasn't.

"I would in L.A. normally, at something like this, but the people are so decent here. They're not going to hurt me. The worst they're going to do is ask me to sign a bunch of autographs and that's not so bad. It seems so showy to take a bunch of security guys with me to a small town rodeo. It looks so Hollywood, I'd be embarrassed to do it."

"But maybe it's smarter," he persisted. "At least be careful," he warned, and she smiled at him. She loved the fact that he was so good to Mary Stuart. She had never really liked Bill Walker. She always thought he was too hard on Mary Stuart, and expected so much from her. In Tanya's opinion, he had completely taken her for granted. He had the perfect house, the perfect wife, the perfect children, and he expected it that way. She wondered how much he'd ever really appreciated it, how often he'd thanked her, if ever. But she was sure that he was going to be stunned now when Mary Stuart told him it was over. Even his faxes to her made Tanya mad. They were so cold and so aloof, and so unfriendly. Hartley was entirely opposite from Bill, he was warm and kind and solicitous, and concerned about everyone around him. She really thought he was perfect for Mary Stuart, and they looked fabulous together. They even looked a little bit alike, except that his hair was gray and he was ten years older. And he made Tanya promise that she'd be careful that night, and ask for help from the police if she had the smallest problem.

"Just stay close to us, and don't go wandering off," Mary Stuart warned, sounding as though she were talking to Alyssa.

"Yes, Mom," Tanya teased, but she was so excited she

could hardly sit down when they got there. The bus pulled into the parking lot, bumping over ruts, and narrowly avoiding kids on horses.

But as soon as Tanya got off the bus, they were waiting for her, not just fans, but the same man and the officials who had approached her on Wednesday. They wanted her to sing the anthem just one more time, just the way she had, just the way God meant it to be sung, they said. They were so hokey that somehow they touched her. She signed half a dozen autographs while talking to them, and Hartley and Mary Stuart were looking concerned, but they both knew that this was what her life was. And she hated to let her fans down. In the end, she agreed to sing again. They had the same palomino for her, and this time she asked if she could sing another song either before or after. They suggested she do it right after the anthem, and she wanted to sing "God Bless America." It was what the rodeo always made her think of.

"What about one of your own songs, Miss Thomas?" the grand marshal asked hopefully, but she said she wouldn't. She didn't want to sing her stuff with a high school band, without a rehearsal, and besides, this wasn't the place for it. It was "God Bless America" or nothing, and they took it.

She went to find her seat with Mary Stuart and Hartley, and she looked at the livestock pens, but she didn't see Gordon. And a few minutes later they came for her again. People were looking at her, and she knew they had recognized her, but other than a few kids, no one had dared approach her. And she went off to do her bit for them, wearing blue jeans and a red shirt, and Mary Stuart had lent her her new red cowboy boots that looked terrific. They still wore the same shoe size. She was wearing her hair loose again, and a red bandanna around her neck, and a number of heads turned as she walked by them. Just watching her you knew she was someone special.

"She's an amazing girl," Hartley said admiringly, as she strode away, and he watched her make her way through the crowd, looking poised and gracious. She had a wonderful way about her that was both good manners and kindness. There was nothing of the prima donna about her. "I worry about her safety though. There's something about the mentality of music fans that always unnerves me. All I ever have to do is sign a book or two, but people in her shoes bring out all the crazies."

"I always worry about her too," Mary Stuart admitted, keeping her eyes glued on her. She knew she was on the far side of the ring now, and several riders were exercising their horses.

And then he asked her an odd question. "You don't think it's serious, do you, between her and the wrangler?" He glanced around to make sure no one had heard them. But there was no one in the seats near them whom they knew, and no one from the ranch sitting behind them.

"I don't know. Why?" Mary Stuart was worried that he knew something she didn't.

"It just seems like an odd combination. She's so sophisticated, and he's from another world. Her life must be very complicated. I think it would take someone pretty unusual to withstand that."

"That's true," she agreed, but he reminded her so much of Bobby Joe, an older, wiser version. And she was sure that, even if only unconsciously, Tanya sensed that. "But he's a lot like her first husband. And she's not as sophisticated as she looks. In some ways, Tanya is part of all this. The rest of her life just kind of happened. In her heart of hearts, she's just a kid from Texas. Who knows? It might work." Who knew about anything? It was all blind luck. And maybe nothing would ever come of it, but she really hoped for Tanya's sake that it worked out with Gordon. And just as Mary Stuart thought of him, she saw him. He had climbed up on the railing above the bullpens, and was watching Tanya get on her horse and say something to the grand marshal.

And as he sat there watching her, he couldn't believe his good fortune. This couldn't be happening to him, he told himself, it didn't work like this. People like Tanya Thomas just didn't get on a horse and ride off into the sunset with you. He kept trying to remind himself that it was probably just a game for her, a fun part of her vacation, and yet he knew from talking to her that she was genuine and sincere, and he believed everything she told him. They had kissed and talked and pawed each other outside her cabin until three o'clock that morning. And now he sat looking at her prancing around the ring on the palomino they'd loaned her, and the crowd fell instantly quiet. There were a few screams, and he could hear some of the fans shout her name, but as she looked at them, and moved around the ring, they fell silent. She had an amazing power and charisma.

And then she sang for them, the anthem as she'd promised them, and then slowly she began to sing "God Bless America," until people literally cried as they heard her. She had a powerful voice that floated up to the skies and enveloped all of them, and even Gordon wiped his eyes when she was finished. She smiled broadly at them all then, and waved at them as she made the horse dance, and then she galloped out of the ring with a good Texas yell and the crowd went crazy. If they could have followed her, they would have all run out of the ring and grabbed her. But she was careful this time. She was off the horse and gone before they knew it. She kissed the grand marshal on the cheek, and thanked him for letting her sing both songs, and then she literally disappeared into the crowd as he started after her. She quickly took off the red shirt and tied it around her waist. Under it, she'd been wearing a white T-shirt. It transformed her instantly, and just as quickly she pulled her hair back, and braided it, and slipped a rubber band on the end, and by the time she got to the bronc pens, she looked completely different, and Gordon was surprised to see her.

"Well, that was a quick change," he said, admiring her, standing as close to her as he dared, and aching to kiss her.

"That's the whole idea." She took his cowboy hat off and put it on her head, and it disguised her even further.

"Good move," he said, and he was glad she was being careful. "That was a knockout," he said, referring to her singing.

"I've always thought that should be our anthem, instead of the 'Star Spangled Banner.' I really like it."

"I like anything you sing," he said, still looking a little awestruck. "You could sing 'Smoky the Bear' and you'd make me cry, Tanny."

"That's good to hear," she said, her eyes caressing him. Then he bought her a beer and they shared it. She stood with one foot up on the pen, drinking his beer, with his rodeo hat on, looking like a real cowgirl.

"Tanny, you knock my socks off," he whispered, and she laughed at him.

"You do a pretty good job on mine too," she teased, and they watched the rodeo together for a little while, and then she went back to the others so they wouldn't worry. "Ride safe. Tell the horse that if he hurts you, I'll come back and shoot him."

"Yes, ma'am," he said, as she put his hat back on him, it would have been the perfect moment to kiss her, but he was afraid to. If there were a photographer around, they'd be all over the papers. He also didn't know if Charlotte Collins was there that night. And the cowboys would have talked for sure. They both knew they were better off keeping their secret.

"I'll try and come back later. Otherwise, come visit," she whispered before she left. He had promised that afternoon to come to her cabin again, they loved to sit and talk and neck in the moonlight. She had a date with him the next morning. She was going to take her bus into Moose, and he'd pick her up there in his truck, and they'd spend the day together. There were a million places he wanted to show her.

She wished him luck again, and went back to her seat, where Mary Stuart and Hartley had been waiting. They hadn't spotted her in the crowd from the moment she'd left the ring, but when she came back to them, they could see why. She had taken her shirt off and pulled her hair back.

"That was smart," Mary Stuart praised her and asked where she'd been, although she had a pretty good idea before Tanya told them.

"At the bronc pens," she said, sounding pure Texas, and Mary Stuart laughed at her.

"I remember when you sounded like that all the time. I used to love it."

"I been in the big city too long," she said, pulling out her drawl, and in spite of the change of costume, people around her were starting to point and whisper. Mary Stuart gave her her new dark blue hat to put on, and Tanya hid quietly beneath it, keeping her eyes down.

She watched most of the events with interest, and then Gordon came on. He was riding bareback tonight, which was even harder and more dangerous. Tanya hated all of it, and most of all the breathless feeling of watching him in midair being bounced around by a wild beast that could easily have killed him. Everything was going well until suddenly the horse literally flew into the air, and did a jackknife leap at the gate of the bullpen. He was willing to do almost anything to get rid of his rider, and did, he pounded Gordon against it, and when he eventually fell off, the horse dragged him fifty feet by one hand, but at last the pickup men got him. He was doubled over when he left the ring, and holding his arm. But at the last moment, he turned and waved, and she knew he had done it just for her, so she wouldn't worry. She wanted to run and find him and find out if he was all right, but she didn't want to draw too much attention to herself, so she waited a little while, and watched him from where she was sitting. He had climbed back on the bullpen again, but he seemed to be nursing the arm, and the announcer congratulated him on a real nice ride. He got the second highest score of the evening, but at what price glory.

"You think he's all right?" Tanya leaned over and asked Hartley.

"I think he is, probably. They'd have taken him away or called for the paramedics if he wasn't." But it shocked all of them to see how many of the cowboys left the ring obviously injured. They limped out, they held their backs, dragged their legs, cradled their arms, their heads were banged, their guts were hurt, and they came back to do it again three days later. The announcer even congratulated one of them for coming back after he'd gotten a "real bad concussion ridin' the bulls on Wednesday." As far as Tanya was concerned, it wasn't brave, it was just plain stupid. But this was the world they lived in. Even the five year olds were out in the ring during the intermission chasing raffle tickets and tickets for free days at the county fair tied to the tails of calves and young steers, and Mary Stuart kept complaining to Hartley that they were going to get trampled. But this was how they lived in Wyoming. It was like the running of the bulls in Spain, it made sense to them. But even to Tanya, who had lived in Texas, it all looked dangerous and more than a little crazy.

"This macho shit is going to kill me," she said to Hartley as they watched one young bull rider nearly get killed when the bull dropped him unexpectedly and then stomped on what must have been his kidneys. They called an ambulance for him, but he still crawled out of the ring, nearly on hands and knees, with some assistance. And the audience cheered him. "This is a lot worse than what I do," Tanya said, and Hartley and Mary Stuart laughed. And a little while later, she went back to the bronc pens to check on Gordon.

"Are you okay?" she asked with worried eyes when she got there. She had given Mary Stuart back her hat, because she didn't want to get it dirty, or lose it if someone grabbed it from her. That happened to her sometimes. People snatched articles of clothing from her and ran off with them as souvenirs. It was really annoying, and always scared her a little. "How's your arm?" she asked him quickly, and he smiled at her concern.

She could see that his hand was swollen, but he had put ice on it and claimed he didn't feel it.

"You're lying, you big fool. If I shook your hand right now, or held it, you'd probably hit me."

"No, but I might cry a little bit," he teased, and she laughed at him in spite of herself.

"You people are nuts," she scolded him. "How's the guy who got stomped by the bull?"

"He's okay. He didn't want to go to the hospital. He's pretty tough. He'll be peeing blood for a week, but he's used to it."

"If you keep doing this, I'm going to kill you," she said fiercely. "It's bad for my nerves."

"You're good for my nerves," he said, moving closer to her, and she could smell his aftershave mixed with the smell of horses. He noticed a couple of people watching her then, and turned so he would block her from their line of vision. It was Saturday, and there were more people here tonight, and a lot of them were drinking. "I want you to be careful when you leave, Tan. You hear?"

"Yes, sir," she said, and saluted. She wasn't worried. She liked to think she was invisible, or that she wouldn't be recognized if she didn't want to be and wouldn't make eye contact with them, but he knew better.

"People know you're here, Tan. Tell Hartley to get the cops to help you out. It's Saturday, and a lot of people are drunk out there."

"I'll be fine," she reassured him. "I'll see you later." She touched his cheek then and disappeared, and he watched her for the rest of the rodeo, sitting in the bleachers. He didn't see her leave, because he was talking to some of the other men. They were talking about a cowboy who'd been disqualified from the saddle broncs, and offered a reride but refused it. The politics of cowboys.

Mary Stuart and Hartley made their way out with Tanya between them, and they could see the security nearby, keeping an eye on them, and several of the local police. And there were the usual cluster of fans, waving pens and begging for autographs, and a number of them took pictures of her, but it was all harmless, and Tanya didn't feel threatened. And they were twenty feet from the bus, when two men shoved their way in front of her and there was a flash of cameras, and she noticed a TV videocam just behind them. They were the local newsmen and they wanted to know what had made her sing the anthem, and if she'd been paid, had she ever been to a rodeo before, and was she going to move to Jackson Hole now. She tried to be pleasant with them and still make her way in a forward direction, but they provided a roadblock and she couldn't get to the bus and she couldn't move them, and the security people were so busy pushing back fans that they were helpless to assist them. Hartley tried moving the reporters on, but they provided a wall in front of them, snapping photographs, taking videos and shooting questions at her, and suddenly it was as though they had sent up flares. All the fans in the area realized where she was and what had happened, and she couldn't get past the cameras to safety. Tom had the bus door open for her, but he was instantly shoved aside, and a dozen fans poured into the bus past him, looking for her, grabbing things, trying to see what they could, taking pictures. And the police were suddenly shoving everyone, as Tanya was pulled and her shirt was torn, someone yanked her hair, and a drunk standing next to her tried to kiss her. It was terrifying, but through it all she kept trying to shove her way past the newsmen but they wouldn't let her, and Hartley and Mary Stuart had been separated from her by a seething mass of fans who wanted to tear her limb from limb. They didn't know what they were doing. They just wanted to have her. The police had their bullhorns out by then, and they were warning the crowd to stand back, and shouting at the cameramen who had started it, and by then there were fifty people on the bus and they were tearing down the curtains. And as it was happening, Tanya realized she was really in trouble. She couldn't get away from them, and they were pushing her, grabbing her, clawing her. There was no getting away from them, and in the midst of it all she felt a powerful arm around her waist, and felt herself lifted off the ground as she saw a hand punch someone, but she didn't know who it belonged to. She was being dragged along the ground, and then lifted into the air, and half carried, half dragged toward a truck. She thought she was being successfully kidnapped, and then she saw that it was Gordon. He had lost his hat, and his shirt was torn too, but he had a look in his eyes that said he was going to kill someone if they touched her. He was the only thing standing between her and real destruction. The police were far behind them.

"Come on, Tan, run!" He shouted at her, pulling her along, as the others tried to follow. He had parked his truck as close as he could to the crowd when he saw what was happening, and left the engine running, and her feet pounded as hard as they could on the rough ground, as four marshals on horseback galloped past them. But they had reached Gordon's truck by then, and he pushed her inside, leaped into the driver's seat, and took off, nearly running over half a dozen people and several horses. But he didn't stop for anything. There was literally a riot behind them. He kept his foot on the accelerator until they were a mile away, and then he pulled over and stopped to look at her. They were both shaking.

"Thank you," she said in a trembling voice. She was shaking from head to foot. It had been awful. It had been one of the most dangerous situations she'd been in recently, because the crowd was uncontrolled and she didn't have adequate security to help her. If he hadn't been there, she might have gotten killed, or badly hurt, and they both knew it. "I think you saved my life," she said, trying not to cry as he took a deep breath and looked at her, wanting desperately to protect her.

"Don't tell me saddle broncs are more dangerous than that. Give me some mean son of a bitch horse any day compared to that stuff. What happens to people? Those are perfectly normal folks out for a Saturday night at the rodeo. They take one look at you and they go nuts. What is that?"

"Crowd craze. I don't know. They want to own you, even if they have to tear you apart to do it, even if they come back with just a piece of you, a shirt, a piece of hair, an ear, a finger." Her head hurt, so many people had pulled her hair trying to get a piece of it to save. It was truly an insane business. She was smiling, but neither of them thought it was funny. She had hated leaving Mary Stuart and Hartley to fend for themselves, but she couldn't help them and she knew the police would.

"It was those goddamn photographers," Gordon said, putting an arm around her and pulling her close to him. She had just told him about the pulled hair and he couldn't believe it. "If they'd let you through, you could have gotten on the bus and you'd have been okay. But those assholes put up a roadblock so they could get a story."

"Well, they got one. A lot better one than just asking me if I got paid to do the anthem."

"Shit," he said, shaking his head. He could just see the headline. TANYA THOMAS CAUSES RIOT IN WYOMING. He could see now how her life got out of hand so easily. He wondered how she stood it. "Is this worth it to you, Tan?" he asked, looking at her, he honestly wondered why she did it.

"I don't know," she shrugged, "sometimes. It's what I do. I used to say I was going to retire, but I don't want to let them win. Why let them stop me from what I want to do just because they make my life miserable?"

"Yeah, that's true. But maybe you need to rethink this. You got to protect yourself somehow."

"I do. At home I've got security and barbed wire, electric gates, cameras, dogs, all that stuff," she said as though it were normal.

"Sounds like Texas State Prison. I mean something else, some way that people aren't going to rip your hair out of your head every time you go buy yourself an ice cream." He was deeply impressed by what he'd just seen and more sympathetic than she knew. As far as he was concerned, it was inhuman.

"Can you get me to a phone?" she asked then, looking worried. She wanted to call Tom on the bus, and let him know she was all right and hadn't been abducted by a stranger. She'd been kidnapped by a friend, she smiled at him, and told him what she thought when she first felt his arm around her. He had been so powerful she knew she had no hope of resisting.

"Poor kid. All I wanted to do was get you out of there as fast as I could."

"And you did," she said gratefully as he stopped at a 7-Eleven. He watched carefully as she used the phone, to make sure no one had recognized her, and Tom answered on the first ring. Hartley, Mary Stuart, and the police were waiting with him. They knew that if she was okay, she'd call the bus, and Hartley had suspected that it was Gordon who had taken her, but he hadn't wanted to say it. They had said only that she had friends at the rodeo, and they were hoping she had gone with them. Mary Stuart was immensely relieved to hear her.

"Are you all right?" she asked, still shaking herself. It had been a horrible experience even for them, and it reminded all of them of how difficult Tanya's life was.

"I'm fine. I look a mess, but nothing's broken. It just scared me. I'm really sorry, Stu. Is Hartley mad?" It was a miserable experience to go through. When she was single, before she and Tony were married, there were guys who wouldn't go out with her, because they said trying to take her to a movie was like college wrestling.

"Of course not," Mary Stuart said, incensed, "not at you. He's furious at the press for what they did. He said he's going to call the owner of the paper and the local news station tomorrow."

"Tell him not to bother. I'm not even sure they were local. Someone may have tipped off the wire services, or cable TV. I didn't see where they were from. It doesn't make any difference. They won't do anything about it anyway. How bad does the bus look?" Mary Stuart looked around, still upset by what they'd done. The fans had grabbed ashtrays, cushions, broken some plates, torn the curtains down, but none of it couldn't be repaired. The driver said something to her and she repeated it to Tanya.

"Tom said it's as bad as Santa Fe, but not nearly as bad as Denver or Las Vegas. Does this happen to you regularly?" Mary Stuart looked even more aghast at the list of comparisons. Poor Tanya, what a nightmare.

"It happens," Tanya said quietly. "I'll see you later," but Gordon touched her arm then.

"Don't make any promises," he said softly, blushing faintly. He would have suggested going to a roadhouse just for a drink so they could relax, but he didn't dare. He really wanted to take her to his place to unwind, so they could talk and sit by a fire. He didn't want to sit outside with her tonight. She'd been through too much, he wanted to take her home and put his arms around her. And who knew what might happen. Tanya read volumes in his eyes and nodded with a smile.

"Don't worry about me. I might be home late. I'm in good hands."

Mary Stuart knew Tanya was with Gordon. "See you tomorrow then?" she teased, and Tanya laughed.

"You never know. Give Zoe my love and tell her she picked a good night to stay home. And tell Hartley again how sorry I am."

"Stop apologizing. We're sorry for you. And thank our friend for me. He did a good job."

"He's a good man." Tanya smiled at him as she stood in the phone booth.

"I think so," Mary Stuart said softly. "Take care of yourself, Tan. We love you."

"I love you too, Stu. Good night," she said, and hung up, and then turned to him and he put his arms around her. He just stood there holding her, and then he put her in his truck, and drove her home to the little cabin behind the corral. He drove in as quietly as he could and turned the lights off, and they sat there for a moment. It had been quite a night for both of them, and Tanya was still feeling shaken. His bronco ride had been nothing compared to what came later.

"Are you okay, Tanny?" he asked gently.

"Yeah. I think so." They were about a quarter mile from her cabin, but she had no desire to go there. "Stuff like that always shakes me up for a while."

"Do you want to come in?" he asked. He would have understood if she didn't, if she wanted to go home and go to bed. But he wanted to be with her, and even though this wasn't allowed, it was better than being seen coming out of her cabin. He would have lost his job in either case if someone saw them together, but Gordon had decided days before that he thought she was worth it. "You don't have to do anything you don't want to, Tanny," he said kindly. "I'll take you back up to the cabin if you like."

"I'd like to come in," she said quietly. She wanted to see where he lived, what he had, what he liked, she just wanted to be with him.

"I think everyone's out, but we need to be kind of quiet about it." She knew how much trouble he'd be in if someone saw them, and she worried about it. The other cabins were nearby, although his was less accessible than most. But she didn't want anyone to see them.

"Is this all right for you?" she asked with worried eyes, and he smiled the smile that tore her heart out.

"About as all right as it gets," he said, and then got out of the truck, and strode quickly into his cabin. She followed him in and he locked the door, pulled down the shades and turned on the lights, and she was surprised at how orderly it was, and how pleasant. She had expected it to look a lot rougher and a lot more disheveled. The cabin itself, as it had been provided to him, was nicely decorated, with a denim couch and Western decor, and all around the room he had put photographs of his son, his parents, a horse he'd loved. There were books and magazines in neat piles, some tools in a neat box, and an entire bookcase filled with music. She was surprised by how many albums of hers he had, but she also liked his other choices.

There was a living room, a large kitchen with a dining area, and that was neat too, though the refrigerator was all but empty. He had what she called bachelor food. Peanut butter, an avocado, two lemons and a tomato, some soda water, a lot of beer, and a lifetime supply of Oreo cookies.

"You must not do a lot of cooking." She laughed.

"I eat in the staff dining room," he said, pointing out, as he pulled out a refrigerator bin, that he also had eggs, bacon, jam, butter, and English muffins.

"I'm impressed," she laughed, and he put a pot on for some coffee. He had whiskey and wine and offered her both, but she said she wasn't a drinker, although after the fracas at the rodeo he thought a shot of whiskey might have done her good, but she said she didn't want it. And as she walked out of the kitchen again, with a mug of coffee in her hand, she glimpsed his bedroom. It looked small and spare. There was a bed, a dresser, and a large comfortable chair. He pointed out that he didn't spend a lot of time there. But it was nice being in his world, seeing where he lived, and she felt surprisingly at home there. It was nicer than a lot of homes she had seen in her lifetime.

"It's almost as big as the house I grew up in when I was a kid," he said, smiling. "There were two bedrooms, my parents had one of them, and there were six of us kids in the other."

"Sounds like where I grew up," she smiled. "I'd probably still be there, if I hadn't gotten a music scholarship to Berkeley. That changed my life," she said, thinking back, and to the women she had met there.

"You changed mine," he said softly, as they sat down on the couch, and he put an arm around her. And a few minutes later, he put on some music. It was so peaceful there, she couldn't imagine any harm ever coming to her with him. She felt completely safe and totally protected. They started to kiss again after a while, and all the terror and the relief and the sheer horror of what had happened that night seemed to flow away from her as he held her. They kissed for a long time, and then he looked at her. He didn't want to do anything she didn't want, or would regret later. At any time, he would have taken her back to her cabin if that was what she wanted.

"Tanny?" His voice was gentle in the dark. He had turned off the lights and lit a fire, and the music lulled them as they held each other and kissed and slowly discovered each other's bodies. "Are you all right with this, Tanny? I don't want to do anything you don't want," he whispered.

"I'm fine," she said softly, and kissed him again, giving him her whole heart, her whole soul, and he lay on the couch next to her, and slowly peeled off her torn T-shirt. And as he took off her clothes, he was overwhelmed by the beauty of her body. She was like a young girl in his hands, she was tanned and honed, and had limbs that never seemed to end, and they both lay there naked side by side as he smiled at her. He had never been happier in his life, or loved a woman more, as she wrapped her arms around his neck, and gave in to what he had wanted almost since the day he met her.

They went into his bedroom after that, and she slept in his arms, and when he awoke at dawn and looked down at her, he wondered if he was dreaming, if this was all a fantasy and it would end by morning. She would go back to Hollywood and forget she'd ever met him. But as he thought about it, she opened her eyes and looked up at him and told him how much she loved him.

"I'm scared," he said in the soft light of dawn. He had never admitted that to anyone before, but he said it to her, just as she told him all her secrets. "What if this never happened? . . . What if it all goes away again, what if . . ."

"Stop it . . . I love you . . ." she said. "I'm not going anywhere. I'm just a girl from Texas," she smiled, "don't you forget that." He laughed in the soft morning light, and they made love again, and it was ten o'clock when they woke up again, and she strolled into his living room stark naked.

"Oh, my God," he said, staring at her. "How did this happen to me?" He sat on the edge of the bed with a look of amazement, and she laughed happily.

"I think we both figured it was a good idea, some time around midnight. Or were you drunk?" she teased, but he still looked awestruck.

"I don't mean that . . . I mean look at you. Lawd, lawd . . . look at that woman. It's Tanya Thomas walkin' buck naked around my living room holding a cup of coffee from my kitchen." She laughed at the way he said it, and he laughed too. It was a crazy thought, all of it. Him, her, the place her life had gotten to, the fact that people wanted to tear her clothes off and rip her hair out.

"You look pretty good to me too," she grinned, and she proved it to him in his living room on the floor and on his couch, and then back in his bed. He was torn between spending the day making love to her and showing her all the things he wanted to share with her. It was a tough decision, but he told her that the best time for them to leave would be when everyone went to lunch. So at noon, they made a quiet getaway, and much to their delight no one saw them. She was wearing her jeans, an old hat, and she tied an old workshirt of his just beneath her breasts. She looked spectacular, and he shook his head in mock amazement at his fate, as she put on the radio and turned up the music.

She had left a message for the others at the ranch that she'd be back sometime that night. She wanted to spend the whole day with him, and she did.

They'd gone to a waterfall that day, and he had driven her high into the mountains. The view had been incredible, and they had gone for a long, long walk, while he talked about his childhood, his family, his dreams. She had never felt as comfortable with anyone in her life. And on their way back to town, he stopped at an old ranch. He said it had been one of the finest in town once, but the owner had died, and it wasn't showy enough for the kind of people coming to Jackson Hole now. A couple of movie stars had looked at it, and some German guy. Gordon knew the realtors. It was being offered at a fair price, and it needed some work, but most people thought it was too far out of town and too rustic. It was about forty minutes from Jackson Hole, and it looked like something in an old cowboy movie to Tanya. They walked around and peeked inside. It had a good-size ranch house, and three or four decent cabins for employees. It had stables that were in disrepair, and a big handsome barn, it needed some fixing up, but the meat was there, and it was obvious to Tanya that Gordon loved it.

"I'd like to buy a place like this myself one day," he said, squinting out at the mountains. You could look right down into the valley from where they were standing. There were some beautiful rides, and it was good land for horses.

"What would you do with it?"

"Fix it up. Breed horses probably. There's good money in that. But you've got to have start-up money to do it." It seemed a shame to him that no one had ever bought the place. He thought they were all missing the point. And Tanya agreed with him. She liked the ruggedness of it, and she could just imagine hiding away in a place like that all winter. You could do great things with the ranch house.

"Could you get in and out of here in the snow?" she asked, and he nodded.

"Sure. The road is good. You could get out easily with a snowplow. You'd have to send some of the horses south, but you could probably keep some here, with a heated barn." And then he laughed at himself for making plans with a ranch he didn't own. But Tanya was glad he'd shared it with her.

They drove around for a while after that, and then he took her to dinner at an old ramshackle restaurant half an hour out of town, where a lot of old cowboys hung out. There were fancier places he would have taken her to, but he was afraid that anywhere they went, people would recognize her, and they'd start another riot. But she liked the funny old place they went to, and after that they went back to his place. She'd had a great time, and knew she should go back, but she didn't want to. She sat in his living room with him, listening to music. And then, for the fun of it, he put on his favorite CD of her singing, and she sang it for him, and he couldn't believe what he was hearing. He felt sure that he was dreaming, he said, and she laughed at him.

"No, you're not," she laughed, and started to take his clothes off.

"Yes, I am," he said, laughing too, "this is a fantasy, just look at what I'm dreaming . . . I'm listening to Tanya and she's taking my clothes off . . ."

"No, she's not," she denied what was happening, as he took hers off too, "and you're not taking hers off either . . ." They were laughing, and playing with each other and kissing, and he couldn't believe how much he loved her or how she excited him. And a minute later, they wound up back in his bedroom. And they didn't look at the clock again until long after midnight.

"Maybe I should just move my things in here," she said sleepily, with a deep, sexy voice that drove him wild, and he smiled, thinking of what she had done to him and how much he liked it.

"I'm sure Mrs. Collins would be glad to help us. I'll just tell her I'm offering you my cabin for the rest of the week." They both laughed.

"Or you could move in with us."

"That would be nice," he approved, and she started making love to him again, as he moaned and writhed beneath her tongue and fingers. "Oh, God . . . that is nice, Tanny . . ." They lay together until the dawn, and then she knew she had to get up before someone saw her. But she hated to leave him.

"I don't want you to," he said sadly, watching her dress

after he showered with her in his tiny bathroom. And that had almost started everything again, but this time he knew they couldn't. "What am I going to do when you go?" he asked, looking like a lost child, and she smiled at him. She wanted so badly to be with him. And she knew he was referring to Sunday when she had to leave for L.A., to continue fighting her battles.

"Why don't you come with me?" she asked, knowing it was a wild idea, but she didn't want to leave him either. But he was far wiser than she was.

"And how long would that last? What would I do? Answer the phone? Carry in flowers for you? Answer fan mail? Be your bodyguard? You'd hate me after a little bit, and so would I. No, Tanny," he said sadly, "I don't belong there."

"Neither do I," she said unhappily, not sure how to resolve the problem.

"But it's your life, not mine. You'd hate me after a while." He was smart. That was exactly what had happened to Bobby Joe. He had truly detested her by the time he went back to Texas. "I don't want to do that."

"So what happens to us?" she asked, looking panicked.

"I don't know. You tell me. I could come to visit once in a while, for as long as you could stand it, or I could. You could come back here. You could get yourself a place here, it might do you good. A place to come to and get sane again after the kind of lunacy we saw the other night. If you lived here, it'd be different. You could live here part of the year, Tan . . . and I'd be here waiting for you. If I had a life with you here, going to L.A. with you would make some kind of sense. I'll do anything you want, stay, let go, disappear, wait for you, I just don't want to go L.A., give up my whole life, and watch you come to hate me."

"I could never do that," she said honestly. She hadn't hated Bobby Joe either.

"I'd hate myself and you'd know that. Come back here," he said, winding his arms around her, and bringing her so close to him that she couldn't breathe as he kissed her. "I'll be here, waiting for you. Forever, if you want."

"Will you come to L.A. sometimes, really?" She was worried about him now. What if she never saw him again? If he forgot her the moment she was gone, if he moved on to another ranch, another town, another singer? She was every bit as frightened as he was.

"Sure I will," he reassured her about coming to L.A. "As long as it's just for a visit. What about your living here, at least part-time?"

"I've never thought about anything like that," she said honestly, giving it some thought. "I kind of like it."

"I think you'd love it."

"If I bought a ranch, would you run it for me?"

"Yeah," he said, thinking about it, as they sat on his bed, talking. "But I don't want to be your employee."

"What does that mean?" she asked, looking puzzled.

"It means I don't want you to pay me," he said quietly, and she could see in his eyes he meant it.

"How are you going to live then?" She was worried about him, and she wanted to work it out with him. There had to be a way they could do it.

"I've got some money saved up. I haven't worked all these years for nothing. I could buy some horses, do some breeding, do some extra work here on the ranch. I could work for room and board at your place. We could work it out," he said, pulling her close to him again. "I'm not worried about it." He was feeling better again, he loved her so much, he knew he could do anything with her, as long as they were on equal terms, just so he didn't wind up feeling like one of her employees. But she liked his ideas, and she was thinking about it while he kissed her.

"I don't want to leave you," she said again. He knew she meant that week and not that morning.

"Then don't," he said hoarsely, wanting to make love to her again. He had never had another relationship like this one. It challenged him to his very soul, and physically she drove him crazy. "Don't go."

"I have to. I've got a bunch of engagements for the next few weeks, and I have to cut a record." And then she thought of the concert tour she'd agreed to. She told him about it while she got dressed, and he listened. "Gordon, would you come with me?" It would mean exposing him to the press, but sooner or later they both knew that would happen, just so long as they were ready for it.

"I'd come if you want me to," he said, thinking. In a funny way, it appealed to him, in another way, it didn't. He wanted to be with her, and to protect her from all the garbage she went through. But the idea of being part of all that really scared him. But he knew that if he was going to be with her, he had to at least share in her world some of the time. He couldn't expect her to spend all her time hiding with him in Wyoming. "I'd do it," he said, and she kissed him. "I don't know what we're going to do, Tan. Your life is pretty complicated, but we'll work it out if we have to." And then he asked her an odd question.

"What about kids? How come you never had one?" He had been wondering about that since he met her. She was such a warm, caring person that it seemed strange to him she'd never had children.

"The time was never right. I was always married to the wrong person at the wrong time, being pushed around by managers and agents. They probably would have killed me if I'd gotten pregnant." He nodded, it made sense to him, but he was sorry for her. He thought she would have been a good mother.

"Would you still want one?" he asked, looking at her thoughtfully, and she was startled by his question.

"I don't know," she said honestly, "I did a few years ago." She had tried to talk Tony into it, but he hadn't wanted more kids, and he said it was too much trouble. "My doctor thought it might take some real effort at my age." But just his asking about it made her think about it again, and she was surprised to realize, the idea was appealing. And then she laughed, he was certainly turning her life around. He was trying to talk her into moving to Wyoming, living on a ranch, and having a baby. She said as much to him and he laughed. "Talk about a change of lifestyle. I feel like Heidi." And then she looked at him honestly. "I might want a kid, would it matter if I didn't?"

"Whatever you want," he said, leaning over to kiss her again and starting to take her clothes off, but they both knew she had to leave before the ranch came alive and everyone started working. "I just think it would be great to have a child with you," he said. He hadn't felt that way in years. He hadn't felt any of this, and then she told him about Zoe's baby, and asked how he'd feel about it if Zoe left Jade to her. She had meant to ask earlier but never had the chance. But he didn't see any problem with it. As far as he was concerned, that was up to Tanya.

It took all the strength she had to tear herself away from him, and finally she was dressed, and he was in his jeans and barefoot, standing in his living room. He was holding her in his arms, and he never wanted to let her go, not for a single minute. It was six o'clock, and in three hours, they'd be riding together again, but she didn't want to leave him.

"I can't leave you for three hours," she said with huge eyes looking into his. "How am I going to leave you on Sunday?"

"I don't know the answer to that either." He closed his eyes and held her for a long moment. "You'd better go though." He glanced at his watch, and he knew that any minute the wranglers would leave their cabins for the corral, and most of the employees would leave for breakfast. "Will you come back tonight?" He looked at her with worried eyes, and she smiled.

"What do you think?" She kissed him good-bye, and with a wave she was gone, hurrying up the road in the early morning sunlight, as the first fingers of sunshine streaked across the top of the mountains. She looked up as she walked along, thinking of him, and the time she had spent with him. He was everything she had ever wanted, and never expected to find. And now, suddenly here he was in Moose, Wyoming. There was a lot to think about now, to figure out, to plan, to decide. All she knew for sure was that, in a single week, a cowboy from Texas had changed her life forever.

CHAPTER 19

On Monday morning, when Tanya got back, Zoe was already up and making herself a cup of coffee. She was feeling fine again, not even as tired as she had been before she had come to Wyoming. And she looked up when she saw Tanya come in, and wagged her finger at her.

"And what have you been up to? Let me guess . . . a religious retreat!" It was a lie Zoe had once told for her, to cover for her with her parents, when she had gone away for the weekend with a boyfriend.

"How did you guess?" Tanya laughed, beaming from ear to ear, not just because of the fantasies she and Gordon had shared for the past thirty-six hours, but the feelings she'd discovered for him.

"Does this mean you're giving up Hollywood, and moving to Wyoming?"

"Not yet," Tanya said, helping herself to a cup of coffee.

"Is this just a passing affair, or should I be hearing wedding bells?" After only a week it was more than a little premature, but the ranch seemed to have a remarkable effect on the people who met there.

"I think that's a little soon," Tanya said sensibly, "and he's smarter than Bobby Joe. But then again, he's a lot older. He says he won't come to L.A., except to visit."

"Good for him," Zoe approved. "It would eat him up in about five minutes. I'm glad he's smart enough to know that. It's not that I don't think he's up to it. I just don't think he'd like it."

"Neither does he. He got a taste of it the other night, and I think it turned him off forever."

Zoe nodded seriously. "Mary Stuart told me. Tom called last night, he said the bus is okay again. He was able to replace or fix everything but the curtains."

"Do you believe that?" Tanya asked in disgust, just as Mary Stuart joined them, looking sleepy.

"Believe what? Hi, Tan, how's your sex life?"

"Be sure not to beat around the bush, will you?" Tanya laughed. She loved the relationship they shared, and it was so wonderful being back together.

"So how is he?" Mary Stuart asked with interest.

"Will you stop!" Tanya hit her with a pillow, and Mary Stuart laughed mischievously. She wanted all the details.

"Look, I haven't slept with my husband in a year. Now I'm involved with a guy who doesn't think we should do it till I figure out if I'm getting divorced or not, what else is there for me to do except live vicariously through my friends?" She turned her glance then to Zoe. "That goes for you too. Any action with Sam when you get back, I want to know it."

"Hopefully, by then, you'll be getting yours too." Zoe gave it right back to her and they all laughed.

"God, we're all a mess, aren't we?" Mary Stuart shook her head as she assessed them, but the truth was, they knew they weren't. They had all had good lives, but hard ones, enormous advantages and tremendous pains, they had paid high prices for all the blessings they had had, and now was no different.

Each one of them had to leap through a hoop of fire in some way, to get what they wanted.

"Actually, I think we're pretty great," Tanya said, looking at her two best friends with pride. "And I love you both, just in case you want to hear it."

"Ahhh . . . the postcoital haze of love for mankind . . ." Mary Stuart said, and Tanya hit her with the pillow again.

"You're disgusting," Tanya said, still laughing, and then she looked at her friends again, wanting to share at least something with them. She could hardly stand it. "I'm in love with him," she said, glancing from one to the other and they both laughed, but Zoe answered.

"No kidding," she said. "We figured that out."

"I don't mean, I'm just lusting for him, I mean I love him." They were both quiet then, as they watched her, and Mary Stuart spoke to her gently.

"Your life is awfully complicated, Tan. Make sure he can make it better for you instead of worse. Make sure he can handle it before you leap off the cliff hand in hand."

"I will," Tanya said, but it was Gordon who was being truly careful. "He's scared to death of all that. He's smart that way."

"I'm glad," Mary Stuart said, and then told them the plan she'd made with Hartley. "I'm going to London."

"Back to Bill?" Tanya looked startled, wondering what had happened in her absence.

"No, just to talk to him," Mary Stuart explained. "I was going to wait until the end of the summer, but I don't want to. I guess I knew what I wanted to do when I left New York. There's really no point waiting."

"Are you sure?" Tanya asked her quietly. They were all making such enormous decisions.

"Very much so."

"Does he know you're coming?"

Mary Stuart shook her head in answer. "I thought I'd call him in a few days."

"What if he tells you not to come?"

"I'm not giving him the option," she said simply. "Those days are over."

"Amen," Zoe said, always the independent spirit among them.

"How's Sam?" Tanya asked as she went to get dressed.

"Still crazy," Zoe said with a broad smile, and then she told them she was going into town that afternoon to see some of John Kroner's patients.

"I thought you were supposed to be on vacation," Mary Stuart scolded.

"It's no big deal. I'd really like to do it."

"When are you going in?" Tanya asked with interest.

"I thought I'd ride this morning, have lunch with all of you, and then go into town. Charlotte Collins said someone could give me a ride."

"I'll take you on the bus, I want to go into town myself this afternoon to do some errands." She asked Mary Stuart if she wanted to go into town too, but she said she wanted to stay with Hartley. And with that, they all went to get ready. It was almost like getting dressed for classes every morning, and they reached the stable looking bright and fresh-faced a little over an hour later, after breakfast. Gordon was disappointed to hear that Tanya had other plans that afternoon. She said she had to go into town with Zoe.

"Will you come back to the cabin tonight?" he asked, looking like a kid, as they rode ahead of the others.

"If you'll have me," she said, and they exchanged a look that would have been worth millions to the tabloids.

"I love you," he whispered, and she answered him, and then they loped across the field side by side in total harmony. It was as though in the past day and a half their souls had been welded together. She felt bonded to him, and he would have followed her to the ends of the earth, anywhere except L.A., she teased him, as they headed back to the others.

"I told you, I'll come for a visit."

"When?" she asked, pinning him down, knowing how busy

she'd be for the next month. But he explained that he couldn't leave the ranch now for more than one day a week till the end of August.

"When can you come back here?" he asked, more to the point, but she didn't have much spare time either. She ran through her commitments in her head, and figured out that she had a free week at the beginning of August.

"I could be back in three weeks," she said, and he nodded as Hartley joined them. The doctors from Chicago had left that weekend, as had Benjamin and his parents.

"That seems like forever," Gordon whispered to her before Hartley could hear them. But it did to her too. But there was nothing she could do for the moment. She had free time again in September, and he could come back to L.A. with her. It was going to be interesting. Commuting to Moose, Wyoming.

"It's beautiful today, isn't it?" Hartley said, looking up at a Wedgwood sky as Gordon and Tanya grinned at each other and nodded.

They had a good ride till noon, and then went in to lunch, but Gordon didn't join them. His horse had thrown a shoe, and he had paperwork to take care of. New guests had come in the day before, and although he didn't have to ride with them, since he was already assigned to Tanya's group, he still had to make sure that the other wranglers were doing their jobs and there were no problems with the horses. In the end, it was just as well that Tanya was busy that afternoon, since two women from New York fell off their horses during a loping lesson in the corral, and he had to take a mare to the vet that had sprained her ankle.

Tanya dropped Zoe off at the hospital that afternoon, and John Kroner was waiting for her, and then she went off to do her errand. She had made an appointment that morning. And it worked out perfectly. Everything was taken care of in time for her to get some shopping done too. She bought a pair of turquoise cowboy boots, and picked Zoe up in plenty of time to get back to the ranch for dinner. They were waiting for her outside when Tom pulled up in the bus, and John Kroner waved when they left. Zoe looked tired, but pleased, as she lay down on the couch across from Tanya.

"How was it?" Tanya asked with a warm smile.

"Interesting. He has some very nice patients," Zoe said, and they had been so grateful to meet her. It was almost embarrassing, and the staff had made a huge fuss over her. But she had really gotten to like John Kroner. She had invited him to join them for dinner one night with his friend. He was a radiologist and had moved to Jackson Hole the previous year from Denver. They were nice young guys, and had both been extremely kind to Zoe. "I really like him."

"Is this competition for Sam?" Tanya raised an eyebrow at her, "or is he too young for us?" she teased her old friend, and Zoe laughed at her assumption.

"Neither, you dolt, he's gay, or hadn't you noticed?"

"Actually," Tanya looked at her thoughtfully, "I hadn't. Oh, well. You've got Sam. What more do you want?" She was in great spirits, and Zoe laughed at her as they rode back to the ranch.

"You're hopeless. What did you do today?"

"Just some errands and stuff." The shops were great and they had all bought suedes and leathers and cowboy hats on their previous excursions. "I got some great turquoise cowboy boots."

"I'm sure they'll look great at Spago. You've been here too long. I did that once in Aspen. Knee-high pink cowboy boots that I somehow convinced myself would look great at the hospital. I still have them, brand-new, never worn, in the back of my closet." The two of them chatted and laughed all the way back to the ranch, and when they arrived, Hartley and Mary Stuart were having a quiet conversation in the cabin. They never seemed to run out of things to talk about, and it was obvious when the other two came in, that the couple had been kissing. It was like interrupting teenagers making out on the couch, and Mary Stuart blushed at a raised eyebrow from Tanya.

"Stop that!" she said under her breath to Tanya as she went to get Hartley a Coca-Cola.

"What did I do?" Tanya said, feigning innocence, but they were all like kids again, and it felt terrific. It was a much-needed counterpoint to the far too serious traumas of their lives, from suicide to divorce to AIDS to tabloids. And a little teasing and fun and romance between them was not only harmless but therapeutic.

"What are we doing tonight?" Zoe asked as she sat down, tired after an afternoon of seeing patients, but exhilarated by her conversation with John Kroner. "Tango lessons? Snake dance? Anything exciting going on?" The ranch provided a fair amount of entertainment, although Tanya and her friends didn't always join in, mostly so Tanya could keep her distance.

"I think it's just regular dinner," Mary Stuart explained, and then glanced at Tanya. It was her turn to raise an eyebrow. "Will you be joining us tonight, Ms. Thomas?"

"Of course," Tanya said innocently. "Why wouldn't I?"

"Would you like me to answer that?" Mary Stuart grinned wickedly and Tanya looked prim.

"No, thank you." She was leaving them after dinner to join Gordon, but they didn't know that.

They had a pleasant dinner, the four of them, and Zoe went to bed early after her busy afternoon. Hartley and Mary Stuart decided to go into town for a movie, and by eight o'clock, Tanya was walking down the road to the corral in her old yellow cowboy boots, and her blue jeans and a big white sweater. She thought she could smell smoke in the air, and wondered if someone was having a cookout.

She had thought to put a cowboy hat on so no one would see her face quite so easily, and when she got to his door, she knocked once and slipped inside. She didn't want to hang around outside the cabin. And he was sitting on the couch, watching TV, and waiting for her.

"What took you so long?" he asked expectantly, looking like a kid waiting for Santa Claus, and she laughed softly as she locked the door behind her. He had already drawn the shades and pulled the curtains to keep their secret.

"What took me so long? Dinner was at seven, and it's five after eight. I thought that was pretty good. I almost ran here."

"Next time eat faster," he said with a broad boyish grin as he stood up to kiss her, and a moment later she was locked in his arms, and they both had their clothes off. They never even made it to the bedroom, but lay on the couch, making love, in front of the TV, oblivious to what the announcer was saying, and it was only afterward, as they lay there for a while, talking quietly, that he realized they were saying there was a fire on Shadow Mountain, and he sat up to listen.

"Is that close by?" she asked, noticing the worry on his face.

"Right above us." He was listening intently to what they were saying, and suddenly she remembered smelling smoke in the air when she'd been walking down to the cabin to see Gordon.

The announcer said that the fire was confined to a small area, but the winds had just picked up, and the parks department people were worried. He made reference to a fire in Yellowstone several years before, and showed old footage of utter devastation. And then they went back to the normal program.

"They may call us out tonight," he said quietly, looking at her. He was concerned for the ranch, and thinking about the horses.

"Would you rather I didn't stay here tonight?" she asked. She would have understood if he said she should go back to her own cabin.

"I don't see why not," he smiled. "No one has to know you're here. They're not going to evacuate the ranch unless it turns into a real big one." He went outside for a minute to look up at the sky. He could see some smoke, but there was no glow from the fire, and he wasn't worried. And when he came back inside, he was more interested in Tanya than Shadow Mountain.

He played some of his favorite music for her, and played with an old guitar, and she sang softly for him, so no one would hear them. She loved it when they sang together, and he laughed, as he touched her face with a gentle hand.

"It's just like singing to records." They sang together again, and they shared a sandwich around midnight. He had gone to buy some groceries that afternoon after his ride with Mary Stuart and Hartley, and he told Tanya how much he liked them. "They've got something going, don't they?", he smiled. He had spotted it from the first morning. "Is she divorced?"

"She will be. She's leaving her husband. I think she's going to London next week to tell him."

"Is he English?" She shook her head, he was interested in her friends and her life, and the things she cared about. He was interested in everything about her.

"He's working there for the summer," Tanya explained.

"Why's she leaving him?" They were sitting at his kitchen table, when he asked her.

And Tanya sighed as she thought about it. "Her son killed himself last year. I don't know all the details, but I think her husband blames her for it. She didn't do anything to provoke him to it, I just think Bill doesn't know who else to blame. Their marriage pretty much fell apart after it happened."

"Maybe it wasn't all that solid before that."

"Maybe," she said softly, but she didn't agree with him. "I think it was. I just think it was too much of a blow for them. And now she's too hurt by what her husband's done. I think it's pretty well finished."

"You think she and Mr. Bowman will wind up together?"

"I hope so," Tanya smiled, with a gentle hand on Gordon's arm. "What about us? You think we will?"

"We'd better," he said, leaning closer to her, and looking

into her eyes. "If you try to get away from me now, I'm going to come riding down Hollywood Boulevard on one of those saddle broncs, and come and get you." The image was wonderful and she laughed at him.

"I thought you were giving them up."

"Not till I come and get you." They were both laughing, and she stood in his kitchen naked, with her long legs, wearing his shirt open as she washed his dishes. It was a photograph he would have loved to have, but he knew he'd remember it forever. She was so down-to-earth he couldn't get over it. She was just what she claimed, a plain old girl from Texas, but she sure as hell didn't look it, and no one else in the world would have believed it for a minute. "You blow me away," he said, standing behind her, as he put his arms around her waist, and leaned his chin on her shoulder. "Next week, I'm going to think I was hallucinating all this time." It made her sad to think about a time when she wouldn't be there.

"Will you call me?"

"I'll try," he said, and she put the dishes down and turned around and they were belly to belly.

"What do you mean, you'll 'try'? Will you call me or won't you?" She looked worried.

"I'll call you. I just don't like phones all that much. But I'll call." He didn't have a phone in his cabin, and he didn't want to use the ranch phone, and give them a record of it. Most of the time they just paid for their calls at the end of the month. He'd have to go to the 7-Eleven. And it worried her even more that she couldn't call him. It wasn't a great situation. "You'll just have to come back quick, that's all."

"I promise. Three weeks, if I can. I've got to move some things around." She had already called Jean, and asked her to do it, and now she had more reason to than ever. "And you better come to L.A. after the summer," she warned in a sexy undertone, but he was grinding against her, and distracting her from what they were saying.

"I will, I swear. I'll tell Charlotte I need time off at the end of August." She had already started to figure out gaps in her schedule when she could come to Wyoming. She could fly straight into Jackson Hole if she changed planes in Salt Lake City or Denver. It was certainly an interesting prospect, and she loved it.

They went to bed shortly after that, and were lying in each other's arms, having just made love again, when they heard a pounding on the door, and Tanya jumped about a foot. Gordon grabbed his jeans and ran to the door as he climbed into them. He pulled open the door as soon as he had them on and saw one of the ranch hands.

"The park service just called. We have to evacuate."

"Now?" Gordon looked stunned, but when he looked up at the sky, he could see that over Shadow Mountain it was bright orange. "Why didn't they warn us?"

"They put us on standby around midnight, but Charlotte thought they'd have it in control by now. The wind just changed," he explained. There was a brisk breeze, and he saw lights coming on in all the other houses. "Charlotte's rounding up the guests. We have to get the horses and run them down the valley." There was another ranch nearby, and they'd done it before, but it was dangerous to move that many animals with so much speed. Either the people or the horses could get injured.

"I'll be out in five minutes," he told the boy, and went back inside to talk to Tanya. He locked his door again, so no one could burst in, and he told her as quickly as he could what had happened. "They'll move you to another ranch," he explained. "If you call your driver, he can come out and get you. I've got to get the horses. We've got two hundred head to get out as fast as we can," he said, moving quickly, and then he stopped for an instant and kissed her. "I love you, Texas girl, don't worry about us, we're going to make this thing work, even if I have to go to Hollywood to do it." He knew she was worried, and he was concerned too, but he was determined to do it. But now he had to turn his mind to other things. "Get dressed," he told her before he left. "Just stay off the road, go alongside it in the tall grass and no one will see you. They're too busy to worry about you right now. Go back to your cabin. I'll see you later."

"Can we do anything to help?" She felt stupid just getting on her bus and moving to another ranch, when there were people and animals in danger.

"That's my job," he smiled, jamming his hat on his head, and grabbing an old denim jacket. "See ya," he said, and was gone with a last look over his shoulder. She felt like the little woman as she stood there. And she quickly put on her clothes and did as he told her. And as he drove his truck down the road, he smiled when he saw a rustle in the tall grass moving toward the cabins. He knew exactly what it was, and he mentally put his arms around her and kissed her.

But as soon as he got to the corral, his work was cut out for him. They had to get all the horses out of their stalls, into the main corral, and they were going to herd them across the valley. The trick was seeing that none of them got hurt or lost, or stampeded. He rounded up ten good men and four women to do it. They needed all the help they could get, and they had already called ahead to the next ranch. They were emptying their pens and making room for them. And if the fire traveled that far, they would all be in terrible trouble. But for the moment, the winds had shifted in the opposite direction.

Gordon was shouting directions at all of them, and riding an old paint mare that he knew would be good for the job, just as Tanya walked into the cabin.

"My God, where were you?" Mary Stuart was looking unnerved, and Zoe was putting her clothes on. They had just been called, and they knew exactly where Tanya was, but they didn't know how to find her. "They called to say we have to evacuate, and I didn't want to tell them you were in the wranglers' cabins," Mary Stuart said, still looking nervous.

"Thanks for that," Tanya smiled, and dialed Tom. She asked him to come to the ranch, and told him what had happened. She was going to offer the bus to transport as many people as they wanted. There were nearly a hundred guests at the ranch at the moment.

"Do you think the ranch will burn down?" Mary Stuart asked anxiously, just as Zoe walked into the room in a heavy sweater and jeans, carrying her doctor's bag. It was chilly, and there was a stiff wind out.

"No, I don't think the ranch will burn down. Gordon says this happens from time to time, and they always control it. What are you doing?" she asked, as she turned to Zoe.

"I'm going to offer them a hand. They've got firefighters going up there."

"Are they asking for volunteers?" Tanya looked surprised. Gordon hadn't given her the impression that the guests would be helping, and at that exact moment Hartley arrived, and said they were wanted in the main building as fast as they could get there. Everyone looked slightly tousled and very concerned, in an assortment of rough clothes and peculiar outfits, as they hurried up the hill to the main hall. Mary Stuart chatted with Hartley, and seemed calmer when she got there. She was holding his hand, and he was carrying a briefcase, he'd been working on a manuscript off and on since he got there. The other guests were carrying an odd assortment of things they didn't want to lose, from briefcases, to fishing equipment, to handbags.

Charlotte Collins was waiting for all of them, and she explained calmly and succinctly that she was sure there was no real danger to the ranch, but it seemed wisest to move the guests to another location, should the winds change. They didn't want to be caught in a situation that presented any danger to anyone, or where they had to move too quickly. They were all being taken to a neighboring ranch, and they would be made as comfortable as possible in the spare rooms they had, and their living rooms would be made available for their exclusive use for the duration. There weren't enough rooms for everyone of course, but they were hoping that people would be good sports about it, and they were sure that they could come back in a matter of hours. Charlotte hoped that, in the spirit of the ranch, they would look upon it as an adventure. She was very bright and very cool, and very cheerful.

Sandwiches were being made, she said, and thermoses of coffee being prepared, and she indicated that transportation would not be a problem. She said their biggest concern was getting the horses out, and that was being handled at this very moment. Tanya thought of Gordon as she said it.

She said that everyone would be moved out in the next half hour, and they would, of course, keep them posted. And with that, the meeting ended, and there was a huge hubbub of voices as people milled around, discussing what was happening with each other and Charlotte. Tanya made her way to her and let her know that her bus would be available at any moment. And they were welcome to use it for transporting people to other locations.

Charlotte said she was very kind, and they'd be grateful to use it. She explained too that there were busloads of volunteers going up to fight the fire on Shadow Mountain, at which point Zoe stepped in, and asked if she could go up with them. She had a medical kit with her, and Charlotte knew she was a physician. She hesitated for an instant, knowing she wasn't well, and then agreed to let her do it. They always needed medical assistance, and she knew Zoe was well enough to provide it. Whatever her long-term medical problems were, and John Kroner had hinted to her that they were severe, she was certainly fine at this point.

"We'd appreciate that, Dr. Phillips," she said as two other guests came forward, also carrying their bags. Zoe didn't know them, one was a gynecologist from the South, and the other was a heart surgeon from St. Louis, but they were certainly all capable of doing what was needed. "I've got a truck going up in a few minutes," Charlotte told the three physicians, and the three of them conferred, and showed each other their supplies. None of them were well prepared for burns, but Charlotte said she had a kit just for that purpose, and someone brought it to them. It was enormous and very helpful.

People started getting in vans provided for them then, and twenty minutes later, Tanya's bus arrived, and Charlotte started funneling people into it. They had almost everyone loaded up in half an hour. Hartley and Mary Stuart had been among the first to get on, and Tanya had stayed behind to talk to Charlotte. "Could I go up the mountain with you, Mrs. Collins?" she asked her quietly, and the older woman reminded her to call her Charlotte. "I'd like to help if I can. I know you've got volunteers up there. Maybe I could lend a hand, or assist Zoe." Charlotte Collins hesitated for only an instant, and then nodded. They needed all the help they could get, but she didn't want the other guests to know that. It was frightening enough just to see the night sky blazing above them. It was bright red now.

Tanya ran to tell Mary Stuart. She shouted onto the bus that she was staying. Mary Stuart seemed to hesitate and then nodded. Hartley was right beside her. And a moment later, Tom took off with the other vans, and Charlotte directed the handful that had stayed into trucks. There were half a dozen men, the three doctors, and Tanya, and they headed up the mountain in Jeeps, trucks, and vans, along with dozens of wranglers and ranch hands. They were a small, efficient army. And all the while, Tanya kept wondering how Gordon had fared with the horses.

They traveled up the mountain for nearly half an hour and then they reached the barricades where they had to leave the trucks. They were directed to go the rest of the way on foot, and join the others on the line. They were passing buckets of water, while planes overhead were dropping chemicals on it. The fire was blazing hot, and there was a constant roaring sound, like a huge waterfall, and they had to shout to be heard above it. Tanya took her sweater off, and tied it around her waist, she was wearing one of Gordon's T-shirts, and she had never been so hot in her life. She could feel her face getting blistered, and sparks were flying around them. It was terrifying as they fought the blaze, and they weren't even in the front lines. She couldn't even imagine what it must be like for the others. She was sorry she didn't have gloves as she burned her hands, and she could feel the ground hot beneath her boots, as trees fell and the wind raged on, and small animals rushed past them, heading down the mountain, but there had already been endless carnage. And she saw Zoe from time to time. They had formed a medical station with some doctors and nurses from town. People were starting to arrive in droves to help and it seemed like hours later when she saw Gordon. He walked right past her, and then he turned around with a look of amazement, and he came back for a minute to see her. He wondered if anyone knew who she was, and he doubted it. She was just standing there, working like all the others. She took a break for a minute then, she'd been working for hours, and her arms were so sore she could hardly lift them.

"What are you doing here?" He looked tired and filthy dirty, but the run to the other ranch had gone well. All the horses were safe there, and he had come up to fight the fire with the others.

"Zoe and I volunteered. I figured they could use some help."

"You sure look for enough ways to get into trouble, don't you?" He shook his head at her, he didn't like the idea of her fighting the fire. If the wind changed, some of them could get trapped. It was easy to get killed fighting a fire like this one. "I'm going to the front, be sure you stay back here, I'll come back and look for you later." She wanted to tell him not to go, but she knew it was his job, he had to defend the ranch from the fire with the others.

The planes continued to drop chemicals on the fire all night, and at noon they were all still there. Most of them were ready to drop they were so tired. And mattresses were brought up and laid on the backs of trucks, so people could sleep and form shifts. There were as many as ten people sleeping in the back of each truck. They were so tired they would have lain down anywhere and passed out. It was early in the afternoon when Tanya finally saw Zoe. She hadn't seen Gordon since that morning.

"Are you all right?" Tanya asked with a look of concern, but Zoe looked surprisingly well and very calm.

"I'm fine," she smiled. "We've done pretty well, nothing but small casualties so far. They say that if the wind doesn't change, they'll have it out by nightfall. I saw Gordon a while ago. He said to say hi if I saw you."

"Is he okay?" Tanya looked worried, and Zoe smiled as she nodded.

"He's fine, scorched his arm a little bit, nothing much. I think he's sleeping in the trucks right now." The two women stood together drinking coffee for a little while, and then went back to their stations. It was something of an adventure for them, and they both liked the fact that they were useful. And they were planning to tease Mary Stuart for not coming. They both knew she hated being anywhere near road accidents, and fires, and anything frightening or out of control or potentially dangerous. Tanya was actually glad she had evacuated with Hartley, there was no real reason to be here. It was just nice to be able to lend a hand, and Tanya was happy to be there near Gordon, even if she never saw him. And this way, she could keep an eye on Zoe.

They were there till four o'clock that afternoon when the forestry service told them that the fire was officially in control. They thought they'd have it out completely before nightfall. A cheer went up all around, and half an hour later a band of filthy but happy people went back down the mountain. They went in trucks and vans and cars, they went on foot, and they talked and joked, and shared stories of what had gone on at the top, or off to the side, or on the trucks, or in the air. Everyone had a story. Tanya was walking when Zoe and the other doctors rode by. They looked tired but as though they were having a good time, and Tanya saw John Kroner among them. She waved at them and they drove on, and she walked slowly down the hills toward the valley. She was tired, but she didn't mind the walk, as she looked across the valley at the mountains. They were always there, her friends. She knew she would always love them.

"Need a ride?" a voice behind her said, and she turned to see who it was. It was Gordon, driving his truck with a black face and a hard hat. His eyes had been covered with goggles, and she could see where he had burned his arm. It was covered with a bandage.

"Hi there, you okay?" she asked, and he nodded. He was exhausted. They were offering food in the dining room, and he didn't even think he'd have the strength to eat it. She hopped in with him, and instinctively she leaned over and he kissed her, and then they both looked shocked at what they'd done. It seemed so natural to them now, and they reminded each other that, particularly in this crowd, they had to be careful. "I'm sorry, Gordon, I wasn't thinking."

"Neither was I," he said with a broad smile. All he wanted was to go back to bed with her, and sleep for about twelve hours, and wake up next to her in the morning.

"What do you do about the horses now?" she asked, taking a swig of water from his thermos. It smelled of smoke, but she was desperately thirsty.

"We'll bring them back tonight. I'll come get you when I'm done," he looked at her with a smile, "if that's all right with you."

"Sounds good to me." She lay her head back against the seat, looked out the window, and started singing. It was just an old Texas song, one of her favorite ones. He knew it too, and he started singing with her, and the people they passed smiled. As she sang, they began to realize who she was, and they were amazed to realize that she had come with them. It impressed a lot of them, and it had made a big impression on Charlotte Collins. Tanya had worked like a dog all night. She had been on the mountain for seventeen hours with all the others, and worked harder than most whenever Charlotte saw her. And Zoe had done the same. She'd actually had a great time with the other doctors.

When they got back to the ranch, before they brought the guests back, the dining room was opened to all the workers, and a huge meal was served of fried eggs, omelettes, sausages, bacon, steaks, fried tomatoes, there were cakes and ice cream, and fried potatoes.

"The only thing they don't have is grits," Tanya complained with a grin as she took a seat next to Gordon.

"Damn right, they don't know how to eat here," he laughed with her. They chatted easily and Zoe came and sat next to them, along with John Kroner and his lover. They talked about the fire for an hour, and then slowly everyone went back to where they came from. But Gordon still had to round up his crew to go and get the horses.

"You're going to be dead tonight," Tanya whispered to him as they walked out of the dining room, "are you sure you want me to come by?"

"What do you think?" His eyes, as he looked at her, told the whole story.

"I think you're one tough hombre, Mr. Bronco Man," she said, and nearly kissed him.

"Watch that, or I'll be out on the highway with my thumb out, looking for a job on another ranch."

"I doubt that." She had seen that night how hard he worked and what a great job he did. Charlotte Collins would have been crazy to can him. "But I'll be careful, I promise." They were just too comfortable, it was as though they were meant to be together.

"Maybe you should hang on to this one," Zoe said of Gordon with a smile, just as the bus returned, and they spotted Mary Stuart.

The bus and the vans came back at seven o'clock, and there was an informal buffet dinner waiting for everyone, in the same hall where she and Zoe had eaten with the volunteers, and they really weren't hungry.

But they sat with Hartley and Mary Stuart anyway, talking about their adventures. They hadn't even had time to get back to the cabin yet. Zoe had been putting away supplies after the fire, and Tanya stuck around to help her after Gordon left to get the horses. But a noticeable camaraderie had sprung up among all those who'd fought the fire, and Zoe commented on how perfect for each other Gordon and Tanya seemed to her whenever she saw them together.

By the time they got back to the cabin that night, the fire on the mountain was completely out. It was on the news, and word spread all over the ranch quickly. Tanya got in the shower, and then soaked in the Jacuzzi for an hour, and as she got out of the tub and wrapped herself in a large towel, she heard a tapping on her window. She pulled back the curtain and saw a filthy black face there, with his goggle marks, and she wanted to reach out and put her arms around him. Mary Stuart and Zoe were already in bed. None of them slept the night before, and both of them said they were exhausted. Tanya was tired too, but she was waiting for Gordon, and it had taken hours to soak the smell of smoke out of her skin and her hair. She was all pink and clean now and smelled of perfume. He was beckoning her to come with him. He was too tired to wait, he was dead on his feet, but she signaled to him to hold on for a second, and she ran to the door of her cabin. She had had an idea as she lay in the Jacuzzi.

She turned the light out outside and in the living room, so no one would see them there, and she stood talking to him from the doorway.

"Come on," he said urgently, he was anxious to get going.

"I want you to come inside. No one's going to know. The others are asleep, and after last night, if anyone sees anything, you can tell them you were talking to me about the fire." It had been an unusual day and night and he hesitated only for a minute, and then slipped into the living room and closed the door behind him. All the curtains were closed, and she beckoned him straight into her bedroom.

"What's up?" he asked nervously. "I don't think we should spend the night here."

"I want you to have a Jacuzzi," she insisted. "You're exhausted. Come on. If you want to go after that, I'll go with you." He knew he'd never want to go anywhere ever again once he took his clothes off, but he didn't argue with her. He didn't have the strength. They'd had a hell of a time getting the horses back, and he was beyond exhausted.

She turned on the tub for him, and helped him peel his clothes off. He was like a little kid only too happy for the assistance, and a moment later he got into the huge sunken tub, and she turned on the jets, and he lay there with his eyes closed, feeling as though he had died and gone to Heaven. He opened his eyes once as he started to drift off to sleep and looked at her. "Tanny, I can't believe this." She didn't tell him that her life at home was even more luxurious. That wasn't the point between them. She just let him soak in the tub, and she washed his hair for him, while he lay there luxuriating. It was the best gift she could have given him, and she was glad she had insisted he come in with her.

He lay in the tub for nearly an hour, and then he glanced up at her. He hadn't been to sleep yet, but he looked a hell of a lot better. "Want to come in?" he asked, and she laughed. She was still wrapped in a towel from her own bath, and she couldn't believe that he could even think of such things, as tired as they both were. But the moment she got in the tub with him, it was obvious that he had other things on his mind than sleeping.

"I can't believe you. I thought you were dying an hour ago."

"I've been resurrected. Select parts of me anyway." She laughed at him, he was certainly in good form, and they made love in her Jacuzzi. It was midnight when they got out again, and they'd been in the water for so long that she said she felt like a little shriveled-up raisin. "You shore don't look like one," he drawled, caressing her bottom, and then she turned and looked at him.

"Do you want to go back to your place or stay here?"

He thought about it for a moment, and knew he was a fool, but he just couldn't resist it. Just this once, he decided to take a chance. "I may regret this, especially if you don't kick me out around five-thirty. That's real important."

"I will," she promised him.

"Then let's stay here . . . I don't think I'll make it to my cabin." Even more than that, he didn't really want to. They slipped into her enormous bed, and he thought he'd never felt anything as comfortable. The sheets were clean, her flesh was smooth, she smelled of perfume and soap, even her hair was clean. He had never felt better in his life, and he was asleep even before she could turn the light out.

He held her close to him all night, and she woke him up gently, as promised, at five-twenty. She had set her alarm clock.

"I hate to do this to you, baby," she whispered into his neck, and he rolled over and put an arm around her. Even in his sleep he was affectionate with her, and she loved it. "You've got to get up."

"No, I don't," he said in the dark, with his eyes closed. "I died and went to Heaven."

"Me too . . . come on, get up, sleepyhead . . ." He opened his eyes finally, and with a groan he got out of bed, and slowly put his clothes on. They were still filthy from the fire, and he was clean, but he only had to wear them as far as his cabin, and then he would shower again, and dress for work. But he hated to leave her.

"Thank you," he said, as he stood looking at her, "that was the nicest gift anyone could give me," he meant the Jacuzzi as much as her loving, and she smiled at him.

"I thought that would do you good." And as they stood there, she remembered it was Wednesday. "You're not riding in the rodeo tonight, are you?" she asked, and he hesitated and then shook his head.

"I think I'd either fall asleep or fall off before I got out of the pen. I think I'll pass tonight."

"Me too," she said, after the fiasco on Saturday night, she hadn't planned on going either.

"Why don't we spend a quiet night listening to music? Do you mind coming to the cabin again?"

"No, sir." She smiled and kissed him, and told him she would see him later. And then he slipped out on silent feet and was gone before anyone could see him. And when she saw him at the corral at nine o'clock, he looked clean and organized and official in a white shirt, a cowboy hat, and a pair of jeans. The horses were all sorted out and saddled, everyone looked rested again. Other than a faint smell of smoke in the air, you would never have known that anything had happened. But it was all anyone could talk about all day. The fire on Shadow Mountain.

It was a peaceful day for all of them, and that afternoon, after lunch, Mary Stuart called Bill in London. He was working in his room, and he sounded a little surprised to hear from her. She usually sent him faxes now and rarely called him. But he seldom called her either.

"Is something wrong?" he asked, startled to hear her voice. It was ten o'clock at night in London.

"No, I'm fine," she said matter-of-factly, and asked him how work was, he said it was fine, and then there was an awkward silence. She told him about the forest fire then, and that Zoe and Tanya had volunteered, but she had been evacuated to another ranch. She didn't say that she had gone with Hartley. And then she totally stunned her husband. "I thought I'd come to London next week," she said quietly.

"I told you," he said, sounding irritated. "I'm busy."

"I'm well aware of that. But I think we need to talk. Otherwise I'm not going to see you till September." Apparently that didn't bother him. But it bothered her a lot. That was part of the problem.

"I might be back at the end of August."

"I'm not going to wait another six weeks to see you," she said simply.

"I miss you too," he said, still annoyed, "but I'm working day and night. I told you that. Otherwise, I'd have had you come with me."

"Would you rather I just send you a fax?" she snapped at him. It was ridiculous, he wouldn't even take the time for her to tell him it was over.

"Don't be disagreeable. I don't have time to see you."

"That's the entire point of my visit. You don't have time to speak to me either, or make love to me, or be my husband. I don't actually think it has as much to do with time, Bill, as interest."

"What exactly are you saying?" he said with a little chill running up his spine. He was suddenly beginning to understand what she was saying, the faxes, the silences, the fact that she didn't call. He was getting it. But very, very slowly. "Why are you coming over here?" he asked her bluntly. He had always hated surprises.

"To see you. I won't take a lot of your time. I won't even stay in the same hotel if you don't want me to. I just think that after twenty-one years, we ought to say a word or two to each other before we throw the whole mess in the trash can."

"Is that how you feel about us?" He sounded both appalled and startled, but she couldn't deny it.

"Yes, it is, and I'm sure you feel that way too. I just think we ought to talk about it."

"I don't feel that way at all," he said, sounding crushed. "How could you say that?"

"The fact that you can even ask me that is the saddest thing I can think of."

"We've both been through a great deal . . . And I have this very important case in London . . . you know that . . ."

"I know, Bill." She sounded tired listening to him. He was so totally without insight that she wondered if it was even worth her while going over to see him. Just talking to him depressed her. "We'll talk next week."

"Are we talking or signing papers?" he said, sounding angry.

"That's up to you." But it wasn't. It was up to her. And she knew it. He'd probably go on like that forever, married to a woman he never touched, looked at, or spoke to. As far as she was concerned it was not too appealing. And having just spent ten days talking to Hartley constantly, the idea of going back to a silent, loveless marriage made her suicidal. She just wasn't going to do it. It was over.

"It sounds as if you've already made up your mind," Bill said unhappily, and she almost said that was the case, but if she had there would have been no point going to London. And somehow she felt that she had to give him a chance to defend himself, to at least explain why he had treated her so badly for the last year, before she told him. But it was a bit of a kangaroo court, and she knew it. "Are you flying from New York?" he asked, as though that made a difference, but of course it didn't.

"I'm coming from L.A., as soon as I leave Tanya."

"Is this her idea?" he asked, as though she couldn't have thought of it herself. "Or your other friend, the doctor?"

"Her name is Zoe. And no, it's not their idea. Bill, it's mine. I thought all this out before I left New York, and I see no point waiting two more months to tell you."

"Tell me what?" He was really pressing her. He heard what she was saying and the way she sounded, and he was beginning to sound panicked. It was pathetic. Instead of panicking now, he should have noticed the situation six months earlier, or even two. That might have made a difference. Now it wouldn't.

"I'm telling you I'm miserable with you, or hadn't you noticed? And you're just as miserable with me. And don't be dishonest about it."

"It's been a hard time, but I'm sure it'll be fine," he said, denying all the agony of the last year, the bitterness, the silence, the hatred.

"Why would it be fine? What is possibly going to change it?" She had asked him to see a therapist months before and he had refused. He was not dealing with it, and he was hiding. How could it possibly get any better? But he sounded as though he was fighting for his life now.

"I don't know what's going on here." He sounded completely confused, and totally unprepared for her accusations, as though he had never expected her to notice, as though he could just park her somewhere and beat on her occasionally, and come back one day if he felt better. Well, it was too late. And suddenly he knew it. "I don't understand why you're coming over." He was still trying to deny it.

"We'll talk about it next week," she said, unwilling to pursue it any further.

"Maybe I can come to New York for a weekend," he said, as though having her come to London was too threatening. But she wasn't going to wait a moment longer than she had to.

"You don't need to do that. You're busy. I won't take up too much time. I promise. I'm going to try and meet up with Alyssa."

"Does she know you're coming?" Did everyone? He sounded utterly panicked.

"Not yet," Mary Stuart said coolly. She had loved him for too long, given too much to him, and waited too long for it to get better. And now she had nothing left to give him. She wasn't even sorry. "I'll try and track her down before I come."

"Maybe we can all spend a weekend together," he said, sounding hopeful.

"I don't want to do that. That's not why I'm coming. I'll come to London to see you for a day or two, and then I'll fly to wherever she is." She was not going to let him hide behind their daughter, or have him play little family at her expense.

This was between her and her husband and no one else, and she didn't want Alyssa with them.

"You can stay longer if you want. As long as you're coming over . . ." His voice trailed off but he was beginning to sense that it was pointless. He was not a complete fool, and he had never heard her so heartless or so angry. It never even occurred to him that there might be someone else. She didn't sound that way, and she was not that kind of woman. He felt certain that she had always been faithful to him, and he was right. But he had never, ever heard her so angry. It was more than anger, it was disdain. He knew now that it had gone too far. And he knew exactly what he was going to hear when she came to London. He respected her for coming to tell him herself and not writing to him, but that didn't make it any better.

He was crushed when they hung up. She could have saved herself the trip. He knew precisely what she was going to tell him. All he could think of to do was send her a fax. And when she got it an hour later, she looked at it and threw it in the garbage. It fell on the floor instead, and Zoe picked it up that afternoon and shook her head when she read it. The poor guy really didn't have a clue. He was hopeless.

"Looking forward to seeing you next week. Warm regards to you and your friends, Bill." For a drowning man who was fighting for his life, he might as well have been clinging to a toothpick. And it seemed obvious to Zoe, or anyone who knew Mary Stuart, that he was not going to make it.

CHAPTER 20

By Thursday, they were each clinging to the last of their days, like worry beads they were each hanging on to for different reasons. Of the three of them Zoe was the most excited to go home, she'd been talking to Sam every day, she was feeling well, and she was anxious to see her baby. But she still loved being at the ranch, and felt that each day there was an opportunity to get stronger. It was like going to Lourdes, she said jokingly, she could look up at the mountains and pray and she knew she would go home a whole person. And John Kroner even said there was something to that.

But for the others, each day less was an agony of sorts, a priceless gift they had lost, something they knew they would never again recapture. In the face of their departure, Hartley was beginning to fear that they had been too cautious, that they should have had an affair, that they should have done more than kiss and hold each other, and learn all about each other. He saw what Tanya and Gordon had, and he suddenly envied them. But when he talked to Mary Stuart about it on Thursday afternoon, she told him he was being foolish. They had done the right thing for them, and he knew that. She reminded him of how much they had both been through, how much loss, how much pain, and how much wiser for them to proceed with caution. She didn't want to begin their relationship by feeling she had cheated on Bill, or left him for Hartley. She didn't want guilt trailing them for the rest of their lives, and Hartley smiled at her, relieved by what she was saying. For a short time, he had panicked.

"As long as there is a 'rest of our lives,' then I'm not worried." Neither of them were completely sure of it, and there was still her trip to London to live through, but it certainly looked as though they were going to wind up together. And anyone watching them for any length of time would have put money on it, particularly Tanya and Zoe.

"I think I'm going to go crazy when I know you're in London," Hartley said sheepishly. He was such a nice man, and he was so attractive. He had invited Mary Stuart to go to Seattle with him. He was talking to a library there that wanted to build a wing in his honor, and from there he was flying to Boston, to discuss a lecture he was going to give at Harvard. It was going to be an interesting life for her, if she joined him. He was anxious to have her read his work too, and he had given her pieces of the manuscript he was working on. It had been a great honor for her, and suddenly the prospect of finding a job no longer seemed as important. Hartley was going to keep her very busy.

But she declined his offer to travel with him when they left Wyoming. She wanted to go back to Los Angeles with Tanya, spend a day or two with her, and then fly on to London. She needed to get it over with, to clear her head. And she would meet him back in New York as soon as it was over. It would be better for both of them, she'd be free then. And she was more than willing to spend the rest of the summer with him at Fisher's Island. He wanted to give a dinner party for her, to introduce her to his friends, and let them know the good times had come again after nearly two years of solitude and silence. He was ready to come out of hiding.

"I'll call you the minute I've talked to him." Mary Stuart smiled gently as they walked along. They had ridden that morning, but decided not to ride that afternoon. They wanted to be alone and do some hiking.

"Maybe we should arrange some kind of a signal."

"Like what?" She tried to imagine what she would feel like in his shoes, and she sympathized although she thought he was unduly nervous about it. Her trip to London was nothing more than a courtesy, as far as she was concerned, especially after her last conversation with her husband. "What kind of signal do you have in mind?" she smiled gently.

"One if by land, two if by sea," he laughed, and then frowned as he thought about it. And then finally he looked at her with worried eyes. "Just send me a fax with some kind of a message. And let me know when you're coming. I'll pick you up at the airport."

"Stop worrying," she said, and kissed him, as they walked slowly back toward the ranch, holding hands, just as Gordon and Tanya galloped back from Shadow Mountain. They had been surveying the damage after the fire, and it was fairly extensive. They were talking about it on the way down, when Tanya noticed a man on foot coming out of a clearing. He looked like sort of a wild mountain man, he was wearing torn clothes and had long hair, and in spite of the rubble and the charred wood everywhere, he was barefoot. He stood watching them for a little while, and then he disappeared into the tree line.

"Who was that?" Tanya asked as they rode on. He had looked strange, and he'd been carrying a rifle.

"There are guys like that who live up in the mountains from time to time. They travel around the national parks. The fire probably drove him out and he's looking for a new campsite. They're harmless." Gordon looked unconcerned as they rode on, and Tanya smiled as she thought of something. She had asked him about a ride she wanted to take tomorrow. He said it was possible, but they would have to start early.

They were back at the corral on time at the end of the afternoon. She left him there, and they both knew she would be at the cabin later that night. She was spending all of her evenings there, after she had dinner with the others, and she was back before they got up in the morning. It was the happiest time she'd had in years and none of them begrudged it to her.

She had dinner with them all that night, and all of them were in good spirits. Hartley and Mary Stuart looked relaxed, and Zoe had spent the afternoon at the hospital visiting John Kroner. She enjoyed his company and he was grateful for her input with his patients. They were all laughing and telling jokes, and it was later than usual when she left them in the cabin. Even Hartley suspected where she went although he didn't know how long she stayed there. But Gordon was a nice guy and they seemed surprisingly well matched. It actually didn't shock him.

She walked down the path, as she always did, and the sky was filled with stars. It was such a pretty night, she almost hated to go in, and she could hear the horses neighing softly when she went by them. He was waiting for her, as he always did. He had music on, and he'd made coffee for her. They sat and talked for a while, and inevitably they made love, and as she lay with him, she wished she could turn the clock back. Time was moving much too quickly. They were lying in the dark and talking late that night when she thought she heard a crashing sound, a dog barked, and then the horses suddenly were neighing loudly. Gordon turned his head in the dark, and listened to the sounds, and then the dog barked again, and it sounded as though the horses were going crazy.

"Is something wrong?" she asked quietly.

"I don't know. Sometimes something spooks them, a coyote sneaks down to the corral, or someone walks by. It's probably nothing.'' But ten minutes later, it hadn't stopped, if anything it was worse, and she could hear banging sounds, as though some of the horses were rearing in their stalls, and Gordon decided to put his clothes on and check them. ''I'm sure they're fine,'' but he was responsible for looking in on them in case anything happened. And she knew she couldn't go with him.

''I'll wait here,'' she said, watching him move around in the dark. He had put on jeans and boots, and pulled a sweater over his bare chest. He looked so handsome as he stood there in the moonlight that she almost wanted to stop him. She kissed him long and hard and felt him aroused and he laughed softly in the darkness.

''Hold that thought, I'll be right back.'' He headed for the corral at a run, and then she saw him slow as he rounded the corner. She was peeking from his kitchen window. And she couldn't see anything. Other than the noise the horses had made, and were still making now, everything seemed to be peaceful. But he didn't come back for a long time and after an hour, she got worried. She didn't know if one of the horses was sick, and he had to stay with it, or if something had happened. And she couldn't call anyone for help, or ask someone to check. She decided to put her own clothes on and look for him. At worst if she met someone, she could say she hadn't been able to sleep and had gone for a walk. They wouldn't know where she'd come from.

She walked slowly toward the corral, and it seemed quieter suddenly, but as she turned the corner she saw them. It was the mountain man, he was pointing a gun at Gordon, who stood very still talking to him, and then she saw that several of the horses were smeared with blood, and one was lying on the ground, and she noticed a huge hunting knife he was brandishing at Gordon. It took her a moment to realize what was happening, and then slowly she backed away and began to run, and just as she turned the corner he saw her, and as he did, a shot rang out. She had no idea where he'd shot or who, or if he was shooting at her, she just kept running. She knew she had to get help and fast, and she prayed that he wasn't shooting at Gordon. She couldn't even think of that now. There were no more shots, as Tanya's feet pounded onto the porch of the nearest wrangler's house and she hammered on the door. It was one of the men she knew, a young boy from Colorado, and he came to the door with a blanket wrapped around his middle. He thought it was probably another forest fire. Sometimes when a fire was put out, an ember smoldered for a while and then set it off again, but he saw from her face that something much worse than that had happened. He knew instantly who she was, and she grabbed his arm and tried to pull him with her.

"There's a man with a knife and a gun in the corral, some of the horses are hurt and he's got Gordon. Come quickly!"

He had no idea how she knew and he didn't ask her. He dropped the blanket and put on his pants, as she turned away while he finished dressing. He was still zipping up his pants as he came out on the porch, and pounded on the door of the cabin one door over. The lights went on, the man came out, the young man Tanya was with told him to call the sheriff and round up the others, and then he and Tanya headed for the corral at a dead run in time to see the man jump on one of the horses and gallop off toward the mountains. He was still brandishing his gun and shouting obscenities at them, but he didn't shoot at anyone. Two horses lay dead, one stabbed, the other shot, and Gordon was lying on the ground bleeding profusely. There was blood everywhere, and it was spurting from his arm. Tanya understood instantly what had happened. An artery had been cut and he was going to bleed to death in a matter of moments. She grabbed his arm and applied pressure to it, and shouted at the other wrangler to run to her cabin and get Zoe, and as she looked at him she could see Gordon fading away on her. But for a second at least the blood had slowed. She was already covered with it, and it was all over the ground, and the horses were going crazy all around her.

"Come on, baby . . . come on . . . Gordon, talk to me . . ." She was trying to keep him conscious while putting pressure on the artery, but she could see that he was going. "No!" she shouted at him, but she didn't have a free hand to slap his face or do anything but slow the blood down. "Gordon! Wake up!" She was shouting and crying all at once, as the others began to arrive. They were stunned, and it took a minute for them to understand what had happened. No one had heard anything and as she tried to explain and hold Gordon's arm she saw Zoe flying down the hillside in her nightgown. She was carrying her doctor's bag, and as she reached them, Tanya saw that she was wearing rubber gloves, to protect Gordon from her illness.

"Make room for me," she said to the men, "that's it . . . thanks." She knelt beside him and looked at Tanya.

"Someone slashed him with a hunting knife." Zoe could see he had all but taken his arm off. "I think he hit an artery, it was gushing like a pulse." She had taken first-aid years before and this much she remembered.

"Don't let go," Zoe instructed her, and tried to check it out, but even just moving the arm a tiny bit, a geyser of blood hit them both and the ground around them. Tanya shifted the pressure again, and Zoe made a tourniquet as best she could just above her, but he was in bad shape, and in shock, and she wasn't at all sure that he'd make it. Tanya could see that too and she kept shouting his name as the other men watched in horror. Charlotte Collins had been called by then, and two of the wranglers were grieving over their lost horses. The man had been insane. The wrangler she had woken up was telling all of them what he had seen, and what seemed to have happened.

"How soon do you think the ambulance will come?" Zoe asked one of the men.

"Ten, fifteen minutes," they answered, and she looked pained. Gordon wasn't looking good, and there wasn't much she could do here. He needed blood, oxygen, and an operating room as fast as he could get there. But just as she began to give up hope, a siren screamed through the night, and the wranglers directed it right down to where Gordon lay. He had just lost consciousness and his pulse was thready. He had lost a lot of blood, and Tanya was sobbing as she kept pressure on the wound while Zoe kept trying to reassure her. Other than the tourniquet, there was nothing she could do now, except keep track of his vital signs, and pray he made it.

She told the paramedics as much as she knew immediately and they had him on a stretcher in seconds. Zoe got in with them and someone handed her a long slicker to cover her nightgown with. It was all they had, and Tanya asked if she could go with them. The paramedics were holding his wound now, and Gordon was as white as paper.

"How about if I drive you?" a voice asked, and Tanya saw that it was Charlotte Collins. There was no disapproval in her face, only gratitude, and Tanya nodded. She let the ambulance go ahead, there hadn't been room for her anyway, and Zoe didn't want her there if he died, which she thought was likely. It was easier for Tanya to ride right behind with Charlotte Collins. Tanya told her about seeing the man earlier that day, carrying a rifle, and Gordon thinking he was harmless.

"Most of them are, some are disturbed. There was a terrible story a few years ago, some guy recently out of prison in another state murdered a whole family in their sleeping bags, but that kind of thing doesn't happen here often. Most of us don't even lock our doors at night," she said, glancing at Tanya's obvious terror for Gordon. She wished she were in the ambulance. She couldn't believe what had happened to him. It was incredible, and it had all happened so quickly.

It felt like a thousand years getting to the hospital, and neither of them spoke again on the way. Tanya was clearly too jangled to make conversation. And Charlotte was deeply sympathetic. She knew more than Tanya thought. There was very little that happened on the ranch that escaped her notice. It wasn't what she recommended to her staff, on the contrary there were severe penalties for fraternizing with the guests, but now and then odd things happened. Life was life, and rules were something else sometimes. She just hoped that he didn't die now. The rest could be sorted out later.

When they reached the hospital, a code blue had been sent out, and they were met by a dozen staff, a gurney from the operating room, and two surgeons were already scrubbing. They asked Zoe if she wanted to come in, and she said she didn't think that she was needed. She thought she'd be more useful in the waiting room with Tanya. She had kept him alive for the ride, that was about all she could do for him. The rest was up to the emergency room staff and the surgeons.

"How is he?" Tanya asked hoarsely.

"Alive" was all Zoe could say for him at that point, but she knew she had to be honest with her. "But barely." Charlotte shook her head in dismay at her answer, and they both held Tanya's hands as she cried and they waited. Tanya wasn't even embarrassed to have Charlotte see her cry. She didn't care what she knew now. All Tanya knew was that she loved him.

The police came after a while and questioned her. She told them what she knew and where she'd been, and Zoe worried about her. When that got out, she'd be in the tabloids again, and it wouldn't be pretty. Tanya Thomas "screwing around" at a dude ranch with the wranglers. Charlotte thought of it too and went to have a word with the officers. They nodded and left. There wasn't much they could do to suppress evidence or testimony and no one wanted them to, but nobody needed to call the papers. They were very sympathetic, and they knew Charlotte. They also promised to send the sheriff into the mountains to look for Gordon's attacker, and recover the horse he'd stolen.

John Kroner even turned up after a while. Someone had called him at home, since he was the physician for the ranch, and he sat and talked softly with Zoe. He went up to the O.R. to see what he could find out, but Gordon was still hanging in the balance. The artery had been sewn, but there had apparently been a lot of damage and blood loss. Tanya just sat there with her eyes closed after a while, and Zoe and John took a little walk down the hall together.

"She doesn't look great," John said to Zoe once they'd walked away. "Did the guy go after her too? What was she doing at the corral at midnight?" Zoe looked at him and smiled, he was naive, but he was young, and she had come to trust him since she'd been there.

"She's in love with him." That explained all of it, and John nodded.

It was another hour before the head surgeon came to them, and he looked so grim Tanya almost fainted when she saw him. Zoe was holding tightly to her hand, and Tanya was already crying before he said a word. He looked right at her, as though he understood the situation perfectly. He had no idea who she was and he didn't care. He could see what was happening to her and who he needed to speak to. "He's going to be all right," he said in a single breath, and Tanya burst into sobs and clung to Zoe.

"It's okay, Tan . . . it's okay . . . he's going to make it . . . shhh . . . baby."

"Oh, God, I thought he was dead," she said as the others turned away discreetly and let her vent her terror. The surgeon explained to Charlotte that there had been ligaments and nerves involved, but he thought Gordon would be fine. He didn't even think he'd need additional surgery, just therapy, and a week or two of convalescence. He had lost a lot of blood, but Tanya and Zoe had both acted quickly and saved him. The doctor had decided not to give him a transfusion, and he thought that if he did well, and wasn't in too much pain, and didn't run a fever, he might even go back to the ranch the next morning. Charlotte nodded, and thanked him, and then the surgeon turned back to Tanya.

"Would you like to see him?" He smiled at her. "You and the doctor here did a fine job hanging on to him for us. Without you holding that artery, he'd never have made it. He'd have been gone in minutes.'' Tanya nodded, unable to speak for a minute.

"Is he awake?'' she asked, as she followed him down the hall. The others had decided to wait in the waiting room, and were talking animatedly about what had happened.

"More or less,'' the doctor smiled at her, thinking what a pretty woman she was. He figured her for about thirty, and had no idea that she was Tanya Thomas. "He's a little groggy and a little drunk, but he asked for you as soon as he woke up. You're Tanny, right?'' She nodded.

She followed the doctor into the recovery room and put on a gown, there were half a dozen nurses standing around, and twice as many machines from what Tanya could see, but he lifted his head and smiled at her when he saw her.

"Hi, baby,'' he said, and she leaned down and kissed him.

"You scared me to death,'' she said.

"Sorry . . . I was trying to keep him away from the horses, and he got me.''

"You're lucky he didn't kill you,'' she said, still shaken by the entire evening.

"The doctor says you saved me.'' A long look passed between them that no one could mistake and she kissed him again.

"I love you,'' she whispered.

"I love you too,'' he said, and then turned his head toward her and closed his eyes for a minute. She asked the doctor if she could stay, and he said she could, if she wanted. And she went out and told Zoe.

"Are you sure?'' Charlotte Collins asked. "I can bring you back tomorrow.''

"I'd like to stay,'' Tanya said quietly, and then she looked at Gordon's employer apologetically. "I'm sorry about what's been happening . . . about him . . . I don't mean to create trouble for him.'' But there was no way to hide it now, and Charlotte nodded, smiling.

"I know. Don't worry about it. Everything's all right. Just

be careful.'' Like Zoe, she was concerned about Tanya. Zoe said something to her before she left, about being mobbed by the press. And Tanya told her not to worry. No one had the least idea who she was at the hospital.

The two women left, and John Kroner went home, and she went back to Gordon. He was sleeping. And they set up a small cot in the recovery room for her, and at six in the morning, they moved him to his own room and she went with him. He was awake by then, and claimed that he was fine, but he looked pretty rocky.

''I feel fine, let's go home,'' he said, but he was too dizzy from the loss of blood to sit up, and Tanya shook a finger at him.

''Yeah, you look great. Lie down and be quiet.'' She scolded him and he laughed. This was a golden opportunity to push him around, and he loved it.

''Just because you saved my life doesn't mean you get to tell me what to do for the rest of my life,'' he said, looking peevish, but he couldn't help looking at her and grinning. ''You look tired, Tan,'' he said then, looking worried.

''You scared the hell out of me.'' But she had one more thing to do on the way home before she could sleep. And she was disappointed, she had wanted to go on a ride with him. She had Tom coming for him, and he could lie down in the back and take it easy.

The doctor said he could leave at noon, because he had developed no complications and had no fever, and Tom came for them, as Tanya had asked. Gordon whistled from the wheelchair as he saw the bus arrive.

''Subtle, aren't we?'' He grinned. ''How am I going to explain this to Charlotte? Or are we totally blown out of the water?''

''I'd say she got a small clue last night, while I was clutching her arm in the waiting room, waiting to hear from the doctor. Actually,'' Tanya said seriously, ''she was very decent about it. I think she understood completely.''

"I hope so. Getting slashed in the middle of the night with you around wasn't exactly in my plans," he said, still looking a little unnerved by it. But he seemed reasonably healthy, although she could tell the arm hurt. He wouldn't admit it, but he winced when he moved it. They had given him painkillers to take home, but he claimed that all he needed was a shot of whiskey.

She settled him in the back of the bus in one of the beds, and propped his arm up comfortably on pillows, and he grinned at her as she handed him a Coke, and they took off for the ranch, but after a while he glanced out the window and looked puzzled.

"I hate to tell you this, Tan, but your driver is going by way of China."

"I thought you'd like a little scenic tour on the way back." He didn't want to tell her he wanted a scenic tour of his bed, he was afraid to hurt her feelings, so he nodded, and kissed her.

"I just want you to know, I'm not going to let this affect our sex life," he said, and she laughed.

"Let me tell you, about midnight last night, your sex life was the least of your problems." Neither of them could believe what had happened.

She noticed just then that they had almost reached their destination. She glanced out the window and saw it. They had come around a bend, and were looking out over a bluff, just beneath the mountains. It was a place she had gone to with him the week before, and he recognized it as he looked out the window.

"What did you want to come back here for?" He looked amused and sat up, as he looked outside. "I love this place," he said. He wondered if she was just being sentimental, and he leaned over and kissed her, but she was laughing.

"I hope so," she said.

"Why?"

"Because I own it."

"You what?" He looked completely confused by what she was saying. "You do not. This is the old Parker Ranch. I've known it for years. I brought you here last Sunday."

"I know." She looked extremely pleased with herself as she kissed him. "I bought it on Monday."

"You're crazy." He looked completely overwhelmed and for a minute she was afraid he'd be angry. "Why did you do that?" He wanted to believe all this, but he just couldn't. He had brought her to see a ranch on Sunday, and the next day, she bought it. It defied the imagination.

"You told me I should buy a ranch here."

"So you did?" He stared at her. "Just like that?"

"The realtor said it was a great investment, and the price was fairly okay, so I figured I'd try it. I thought we'd do what you said. You can breed horses here, I can commute. You can do some stuff for Charlotte Collins. You help me run my little ranch. But we fix it up first. And we'll see. If we hate it, if you run off with some other rock star, if you decide to move to L.A. and give up broncos, I can always sell it. I figured we'd try it."

"Oh, baby," he said, and grabbed her close to him with his good arm. He knew it was for real now. No kidding. "You are amazing."

"Will you help me do it?"

"Of course I will," he said breathlessly, after what she'd done for him, there was nothing he wouldn't do now. She had proven herself in every way, and he knew he'd never forget it.

"I wanted to ride over here with you today, and show you."

"I can't believe this." He was still beaming as they pulled away and he looked at her again in amazement. "You really want to do this with me?" It was such a leap of faith for her, such a gift for both of them, it defied the imagination. He really did feel as though he'd died the night before and gone to Heaven. "How can you be so decent and so trusting?" he asked.

"Just stupid, I guess." She smiled and took a sip of his

Coke, and settled him back on his pillows. "Is there any reason that I shouldn't?"

"No, ma'am," he said proudly, "you're going to have the best little ranch in Wyoming. When can we start fixing it up?"

"As soon as you can fly again," she pointed to his broken wing, "it's ours next week." It was hers of course, but she was going to share it with him. She figured she'd give it to him as a wedding present if they got married, but that was for later. She still had to get her divorce from Tony, and it wouldn't be final till Christmas. But after that . . . the possibilities were endless. The sky was the limit.

When they got to the ranch, and people saw the bus arrive, the whole staff was waiting outside his cabin, and they cheered as Tom helped him down the steps and into his cabin. Tanya was walking behind them. She was too afraid to hurt him if she moved his arm wrong. Everyone wanted to talk to him, tell him how glad they were that he was okay. They had brought him books and candy and food, and tapes. He had everything he needed. And now he had a woman who loved him, and the ranch he had always dreamed of. It brought tears to his eyes when he was finally alone with her again in his cabin.

"I still can't believe you. Nothing in my life has ever been like this."

"Me too," she said. "I love it here, and I want to be with you."

"I'll come to L.A. too, whenever I can," he reassured her.

"You don't have to if you don't want to." She had learned that lesson now. She lived in a difficult world, and if he didn't want to be part of it, she wouldn't force him.

"I want to. You've seen my world, you're part of it now. I want to see your world too. We can have both, as long as we understand each other."

"My world can be brutal," she said sadly, "it'll hurt you terribly, even if you're careful. Nothing's sacred. I don't want them to hurt you." But as it turned out, she couldn't stop them. The whole story was in the paper the next day, fed to the wire services, and it was on the front page of the tabloids, about how Tanya Thomas had gone to a ranch two weeks before, had an affair with a cowboy, and bought him a ranch a week later. It said how much she had supposedly paid for it, and added roughly a million dollars. And then it told the story of each of her husbands. Most of that was wrong, and all of it was ugly. The headline in the tabloids was A QUICKIE, OR HUBBY NO. 4? WHICH IS IT, TANYA? It approximated how much money he made a year, and how much she did, and it ridiculed her in every way. It cheapened him, it made her sound like a whore. It even made her look like a fool for singing the anthem at the rodeo, and they had the pictures they'd taken outside the bus there. It even told the story of how he'd been stabbed allegedly by another wrangler fighting over her in the corral. It made the knifing sound like a fight between two men vying for Tanya, and the article claimed she'd nearly been killed trying to stop them. She sat in her room at the ranch, feeling sick as she read it. The trouble was, there was always just enough truth in those stories to make people wonder. And she was worried about Gordon. What would he think of her when he read it?

"Don't read that shit," Zoe said, furious at what they'd done to her. And then she couldn't help asking. "Did you really buy him a ranch? It's probably bullshit, but I wondered."

"No, I bought me one. But he's going to help me. I think I've gotten smart enough not to try and drag him into my life. He's happy here. I don't want to spoil that, so I want to spend some time here."

"That's fair," Zoe said. "I just wondered. And Tan, I'm sorry."

"Me too," Tanya said miserably. "I used to wonder who talks, but I guess they all do. The cops, the press, the nurses, the ambulance drivers, the hairdressers of the world, and the tourists, the realtors, even friends sometimes. It's hopeless. Everyone supplies a tiny little piece of information and then they weave it into a knife and stab you with it, right through the heart.'' She wondered how Gordon was feeling. Rotten probably. How could he not? They managed to make everything good look sleazy. She had stayed with him the night before, and cooked dinner for him, and she hadn't even left him till daylight. It wasn't much of a secret now that she was with him. And when she'd gone back to her own cabin, she'd seen the papers. The others were thinking about hiding them, but they knew there was no point. She'd find out eventually, and it was better to face it.

''I can't believe those bastards,'' Mary Stuart said in fury to Hartley. He'd experienced it too, though never to that extent. And his success was different from Tanya's. Writers weren't usually devoured by tabloids, except for a few select ones. But Tanya was fair game, as far as they were concerned. And they loved to hate her.

She took the paper with her when she walked back to Gordon's cabin later that morning. The others had gone out for a last ride, and John Kroner had come over to go with them. He was riding with Zoe. Tanya was sorry not to go, but she wanted to be with Gordon. And now she wanted to talk to him about the papers. But the moment she walked in, she knew he'd seen it. There was something pained in his eyes, a kind of embarrassment, and she wondered if it was over between them. She looked at him long and hard. He was sitting on the couch, watching TV and drinking coffee. It had been on the news too, with a picture of him, and the slasher story, but she didn't know that. He couldn't believe how they could distort the truth that way. And as he looked at her, he wondered what she was feeling.

''How's the arm?'' she asked, and he moved it a little bit to show her he could. But it wasn't the arm she was worried about now. It was how he felt about her after the story in the paper.

''You paid too much for the ranch,'' he said matter-of-factly, and she looked at him as she sat down. He had read the story.

"How do you like making headlines?" she asked, watching his eyes. He hadn't reached out his arm to her yet, or told her he loved her. He was digesting what had happened.

"I can think of better ways to do it, like shooting a reporter. I'd like to."

"Get used to it," she said, with a hard edge to her voice. They had done this to her before, but never quite as viciously, or as cruelly. They had demeaned him, they had made her look ridiculous and cheap and like a slut. It was typical of what they did. Life as an object at its finest. "This is what they do all the time, Gordon. They do it constantly. They take everything you do and turn it to shit. They make you look cheap and stupid and they misconstrue everything and misquote you. There is nothing sacred. Can you live with that?"

"No," he said simply, looking her right in the eye, and her heart stopped. "And I don't want you to either. If that's how they treat you, then I want you to stay here."

"But they do it here too. Who do you think gave them the story? Everyone. The realtor, the nurses last night, the paramedics, the cops, the grand marshal at the Rodeo. Everyone wants to feel important, and in order to do that they sell my ass out."

"They can't. I own it," he said with a glimmer in his eye, and she looked at him ruefully.

"As a matter of fact you do," she said, wishing it hadn't happened, that they hadn't been dragged through the papers, "but I want you to face the fact that everything we do or I touch is going to end up like this. If I have a baby, they're going to claim it's someone else's because I'm too old to have one, or they'll say I screwed the mailman, if we hire a cleaning woman they're going to say you're fucking her because I'm in L.A., if I buy you a present sometime, they're going to say how much it costs before I even give it to you, and then make you look like a gigolo because you accepted it in the first place.

They're going to beat on us every day, in every way they can, and if we have kids, they're going to torture them too. It doesn't matter if I live here, or there, or in Venezuela, that's what my life is, and I want you to see that now, or you're going to hate me later. And even if you look at it and think it won't bother you, understand that after it has happened and happened and every dentist you go to, or dry cleaner, or hooker, God forbid, because I'd kill you," she added, and he grinned, "but every single person you do business with, with only one or two exceptions, will sell you out and make you look like garbage. And maybe the ninety-third time it happens to you, you'll start to hate me. It's happened to me before. I know what happens. I know how it feels. It erodes your life like cancer. I've lost two husbands to it, and the third one was so corrupt he sold my ass out to the tabloids more than anyone else did." It was her second husband, the manager, who had done that.

"Sounds like you've had a great life," he said, she had never told him that much about it, but he suspected it was painful.

"What are you expecting, Tanny?" he asked her sadly, but he could see it in her eyes now. "Are you expecting me to leave now? If you are, you'll be disappointed. I don't scare that easy. And I know what your life is like. I see the tabloids. I know the kind of crap they write. And you're right, it feels different when they write about you. I opened the paper this morning and I wanted to kill someone. But you're not the one who did it. You're the victim, not the asshole."

"People forget that," she said unhappily, "and they can't take it out on them. There's nothing you can do to them. It's not even worth suing them, no matter how much they lie, you just sell their papers for them. So in the end, you'll end up hating me because they hurt you."

"I love you," he said clearly, as he stood up and looked at her. "I love you. I don't want this to happen to you. And yeah, I'm going to hate it when they say this stuff about me, and there's plenty to say. I'm just a dumb cowboy from Texas, they'll all think I'm after your money. They're going to say you picked me up here. So what? You're real. I'm real. It just means I can't sit on my ass in Wyoming all the time, like I thought. I'll have to spend more time in L.A. protecting you, because I'm sure as hell not going to let you take this crap without me. Maybe we'll both have to commute for a while, until you get tired of it and decide to breed horses with me."

"I'm not giving up my career," she said, looking worried. "Even with all this shit, I like what I do." And she loved the singing.

"So do I. I would never ask you to give it up. And maybe it won't work living here part of the time. But I'd like you to try it. Let's see what happens. I want to be with you, here, there, wherever. I love you, Tanny. I don't give a damn about what they say about us."

"Do you really mean that? Even after all this?" She waved the paper at him.

"Of course I mean it." He grinned at her, and then he came over to where she sat and kissed her. "They said you lured me to bed with promises of buying me a ranch. When did I miss that part?"

"You were sleeping," she grinned, "I whispered it to you."

"You're an amazing woman, and I don't know how you put up with all this garbage."

"Neither do I," she said, leaning her head against him, as he sat down beside her and put an arm around her. "I hate them."

"Don't waste your energy. But I'll tell you one thing. You need to be a lot more careful. No more singing at rodeos, no more floating around hospitals thinking no one knows who you are, no more just marching in and buying ranches. Let's get a little sneaky about this, okay? You can hide behind me if you want to. I don't care what they say. In my case, it's probably all true anyway. Let me take the heat for you."

"Gordon, I love you. I thought you'd never want to see me

after today." She had been so worried as soon as she saw the paper.

"Not likely," he grinned. "I was sitting here trying to figure out if I could talk Charlotte into a weekend off next week, so I could come to L.A. and surprise you. Maybe with the broken wing now, she'll let me go for a few days since I'll be pretty useless."

"Would you do that if you can? I'd love it."

"I'll try. She and I are going to have to sit down and have a serious talk next week anyway. I'd like to start working here part-time after the summer."

"Don't forget Europe and Asia next winter. It'll be a nightmare."

"You make it sound terrific," he smiled. "I can hardly wait."

"Neither can I." She looked at him, thinking of how different her life was going to be now, with Gordon to take care of her and protect her. She wanted to be there for him too, but no one had ever treated her as he did.

"Where are we going to be at Christmas, by the way?"

"I forget . . . Germany . . . London . . . Paris . . . maybe Munich." She couldn't remember.

"How about getting married in Munich?" he said softly as he kissed her.

"I think I want to get married in Wyoming," she said, "looking up at the mountains where I found you."

"We can work that out later," he said, pulling her to her feet and into his arms, holding her with his good arm, "we have something else to work out before that," he said, pulling her toward his bedroom. "It's time for my nap." But she suspected he wanted to see if everything was still working. It was painful to realize this was their last day together. They spent the whole afternoon in bed, while everyone else was riding. He fell asleep in her arms, and she held him for a long time, unable to believe her good fortune. And she had almost lost him two days before. It didn't bear thinking.

* * *

Hartley was very quiet that afternoon as they rode alone, he was trying to cope with the idea of losing her, if she didn't come back to him after London.

"Don't do that to yourself," Mary Stuart said gently when he told her what he was thinking.

"I have to. What if you don't come back? What will I do then? I just found you, and I can't imagine losing you so quickly." He didn't say it to her, but he knew he'd write about it. It wouldn't change anything, but at least it would allow him to work out the feelings. "You can't promise me you'll be back, Mary Stuart. You don't know that."

"That's true. But we have so many losses in life. Why taste them before they happen?"

"Because the taste is too bitter when you don't. I'll miss you so much if I lose you," he said nostalgically, and she leaned over and kissed him.

"I'll do my best to return very quickly." And she meant to, but he surprised her with what he said next.

"Don't even come back if you can save your marriage," he said wistfully. "Margaret and I almost divorced once. I had an affair when we'd been married for about ten years. It was very stupid of me, and I never did it any other time. I don't know what happened, we'd been having problems, we were dealing with the fact that she couldn't have children then and it was very difficult for her. She kind of went crazy for a while, and she put a lot of distance between us. I think she blamed me, as much as herself, because she couldn't get pregnant. Whatever the reason, I did it, and she found out. We were separated for six months because of it, and I continued the affair, which was even more stupid. By then I thought I was in love with her, and it was even more complicated. She was French, and I was in Paris with her. I went to New York to tell Margaret I was going to divorce her. But when I got there, I found that everything I had always loved about her was still there, and so were all the things I didn't like as well, and all the reasons why I had cheated on her in the first place. She had all the inadequacies, the neuroses, the irrationalities that made her difficult, and all the things I adored about her as well, her honesty, her loyalty, her creativity, her wonderful sense of humor, her bright mind, her discretion, her sense of fairness. There were a million things I loved about her." He had tears in his eyes when he said it, and so did Mary Stuart. "When I went back to New York to say good-bye to Margaret, I fell in love with her all over again." He took a breath and looked out over the mountains. "I never went back to the woman in Paris. She knew when I left that it would happen that way. She'd said so. We had worked out a code. She said she couldn't bear long explanations, and she didn't want them. Two words would do. If I'd worked it out with Margaret to leave her, all I had to do was write, '*Bonjour,* Arielle' in a telegram. That was a long time ago," he smiled, "before faxes. And if Margaret and I got back together, 'Adieu, Arielle' would do it. She was extremely down-to-earth, and very much no-nonsense. I left for New York promising her she had nothing to worry about, and met my Delilah, she chopped off my hair, won my heart, and I never left her side again . . . the telegram read 'Adieu, Arielle.' And I never saw her again. That was what she wanted. But I never forgot her." It was a sad story and it touched Mary Stuart. "If that happens with us, Mary Stuart," he looked into her eyes and meant every word of it, "I want you to know that I won't regret this for a moment, and I will love you forever. I will move on, and I will recover. Arielle married a very important minister, and she became a very successful writer, but I'm sure she never forgot me. I never forgot her." He smiled wickedly then. "Margaret never forgot her either. I never quite lived that down, but I think she forgave me. It was an awful mess for a while when it first happened. But I just want you to know I won't regret this, it's been the happiest two weeks of my life here with you." And she had finally helped him get over losing Margaret. He was feeling much better.

"It's been the happiest two weeks of my life too," she said.

"And I won't forget you either. But I don't think I'll stay with Bill, Hartley, I really don't." And she truly meant it.

"You never know what will happen between two people. See what happens when you talk to him. If I had left Margaret then, I would have missed sixteen more years with her, and they were great ones. Be open to whatever happens. That's the fairest thing I can tell you."

"I shall always love you," she said softly.

"And I you. That's what you can send me in the fax then." He had found the code they'd been seeking. " 'Adieu, Arielle,' or "*Bonjour,* Arielle,' to let me know what happens."

"It'll be '*Bonjour,* Arielle,' " she said, looking certain as they rode back to the stables with the wrangler standing in for Gordon.

And as they rode, Zoe was having coffee with John Kroner. They had become fast friends in the two weeks she'd been there. She'd gone to the hospital to see him several times, and he loved coming to the ranch to see her. He had promised to visit her in San Francisco.

"There's a patient I'll want to consult you about soon," he was saying. "I just started him and his lover on AZT. He's HIV positive, they both are, but so far they're both asymptomatic."

"You're doing the right thing then. You don't need me," she smiled comfortably at him. She was sure Sam would like him too, and she was anxious to introduce them. Sam had been calling her daily, more to talk about them than her practice. And she found she liked it. "You're doing a great job with your patients," she encouraged John again, and thanked him for his help when she wasn't feeling well. "You know," she said philosophically, "I have so much empathy for them now," she was referring to her patients. "I used to think I understood what it was like for them, hearing that death sentence and then waiting for it to strike them. I felt it so much for them. But I still didn't really understand it." She looked right at him so intensely. "I never knew until it happened to me," she touched his hand then, "you don't know what it's like, John. You can't imagine."

"Yes, I can," he said quietly. "I'm HIV positive too. I'm the patient I just mentioned. We both are. And when we start getting sick, I want to come to you for a consultation," he said matter-of-factly, and she looked stunned. She didn't know why she was, but she hadn't expected it. He had AIDS, and so did his lover.

"I'm so sorry."

"It's all right," he said philosophically, "we're all in this together." There were tears in Zoe's eyes when she hugged him.

They all had a quiet night that night. Hartley and Mary Stuart spent hours talking, Zoe was on the phone with Sam in her room, and Tanya was at the cabin with Gordon. They were all talking about their plans, their dreams, the things that had happened at the ranch, and how much they wanted to come back here. It had been magical for all of them. And Tanya and Gordon were talking about their plans for the ranch she had just bought. They had all but forgotten the tabloids. He had talked to Charlotte that afternoon, and he was coming to see Tanya in L.A. the following weekend. This was the beginning. And they were both excited about all of it. There was so much Tanya wanted to share with him. He wanted to walk down Sunset Boulevard, see the Pacific, meet her friends, see the studio where she rehearsed and recorded, she wanted to spend the weekend with him in Malibu, walk down the beach with him, and take him to Spago. They were going to do all of it if they could, and two weeks later, she would be flying back to Wyoming to see him.

"I wish I could go with you tomorrow," he said sadly. "I hate to think of what you have to face alone there."

"I wish I could stay here," she said, and meant it. She hated to leave him, this place, and the mountains.

"You'll be back," he said, pulling her close to him, and she closed her eyes, trying to engrave it on her memory for when she left it. She knew it would never be quite like this again. They would not be in this cabin, sealed off from the world. It would never be this simple again. They would be in their own house, and they would be part of the world after this. It would own a piece of them, and grab whatever it could take from them. Right now, they were safe here, and she loved it. And she hoped that they could re-create some of that at the ranch she had just bought in the foothills.

"I want it just like this," she said to him, and he laughed.

"Could we have it just a tad bigger, Tanny? I stub my toe every time I get out of bed here." He was a big man and it was a small house, but he knew what she meant, and he had lots of ideas about it. He had been gathering thoughts for years about a ranch of his own and he knew just what to do now.

They talked late into the night, and made love at dawn, just as the sun came up, and then he wrapped her in a blanket and they went outside and watched the light on the mountains. It was exquisite.

"It's going to be a beautiful day," he said, "I wish you'd be here with me." She could hardly bear the thought of leaving.

None of them could. They were all crying as they said good-bye at the bus. Hartley held Mary Stuart in his arms for ages. John Kroner and his friend had come to say good-bye, and they both hugged Zoe and all the others. And everyone applauded when Gordon kissed Tanya right out in the open.

And they all thanked Charlotte Collins when they left. And all three women were crying as they boarded the bus. Mary Stuart stood there forever looking at Hartley. And Tanya hung out the window and warned Gordon to stay away from broncos. He waved his hat at her for as long as he could with his good arm, and Zoe wondered if she'd ever see the place again, while Mary Stuart silently prayed that she'd see Hartley in New York after her trip to London. A thousand questions had been born at the ranch in those two weeks, but they did not yet have all the answers.

And as Tom drove the bus away, they all sat quietly, lost in their own thoughts, thinking of the people and the dreams they'd left there. They didn't talk for a long time, and they kept to themselves. Tom planned to have them in San Francisco at midnight.

CHAPTER 21

When the bus pulled up to Zoe's house, they were all asleep. They had stayed up for hours, laughing and talking about the men in their lives. They made something to eat and shared it with Tom, and eventually they fell asleep. It had been a big day for them. And Tanya had to wake Zoe up when they got there. She was in a deep sleep and smiled when they woke her. She had made them promise to come in a minute and see her baby, even though she'd be sleeping, and they'd both agreed to it.

Tanya woke Mary Stuart too, and the threesome walked up the steps to Zoe's house, and waited while she found her key in her handbag. She opened the door as quietly as she could, and they tiptoed into the living room, on their way upstairs to see the baby. And as Zoe walked in, she saw that there were toys everywhere, a plate of food, and a bottle, and then she saw them. Sam was sound asleep on the couch, with Jade in his arms. They had waited for them for hours. Inge had gone upstairs to bed long since, and Sam had kept Jade up so she could see her mommy. And the three women looked at them with warm approval.

Zoe took a few steps toward them, and bent to kiss the sleeping child, and then Sam opened his eyes and saw her. He barely moved, and smiled as she looked at him, and then she kissed him too, gently on the cheek at first, and then on the lips as her two friends watched her.

"I missed you," he whispered, and then he stood up to meet the others. He was still carrying Jade and she was sound asleep and didn't stir. They had become good friends in the past two weeks and she really loved him. She had been perfectly happy to fall asleep in his arms, waiting for her mommy. "She was dying to see you," he explained, and Zoe smiled. "Me too," he said, putting an arm around her. "Are you okay?" He looked concerned and she nodded.

Mary Stuart and Tanya were anxious to get going. Tom wanted to drink a lot of coffee and keep driving, and get to L.A. by morning. They had another six hours of travel ahead of them, and it was time to go now, though they would have liked to spend more time with Sam and Zoe, but they knew they couldn't. And it was time for Zoe to be with Sam now.

He still had an arm around her shoulders when they left, after a tearful good-bye, and Sam and Zoe waved from the stairs as the bus pulled away, and then he took Zoe inside, and set Jade down on the couch, and gently took her mother into his arms and kissed her.

The bus reached L.A., on schedule, at six o'clock the next morning. It had been almost twenty-four hours since they left Wyoming. And when they got to the house, Mary Stuart found a fax from her husband. He was inquiring about exactly when she was arriving. She had her reservations made, but she had not yet told him. And there was a long list of messages for Tanya, from her lawyers, her secretary, and her agents. But looking at it now, after being in Wyoming for the past two weeks, it all seemed less important. And as the sun came up over L.A., Mary Stuart and Tanya sat at her kitchen table. It was an enormous room, and it felt good to be home in a way, but they both missed Wyoming. They had left a great deal there. And they sat in the kitchen, talking about Gordon and Hartley. It had been an extraordinary trip for all of them, it was hard to believe now it had happened.

"When are you going to London?" Tanya asked. She didn't know either.

"I thought I'd stick around today and tomorrow, and go Wednesday," she said, "unless you want me to go sooner."

"Are you kidding?" Tanya said easily. "I wish you'd stay forever. And I hope you come back soon." They had both made Zoe promise to stay in touch, and they were talking about spending a weekend with her somewhere, maybe in Carmel, if she felt up to it, or Malibu at Tanya's, or even in San Francisco. They all thought it sounded terrific. They were not going to let time or distance or, worse yet, tragedy get between them.

Tanya spent the entire day working with her secretary, and trying to make decisions after two weeks away, and late that afternoon, Gordon called her. He was fine, working in the corral, missing her like crazy, and he'd gone up to see the house, and had a contractor drawing up plans for her. He said they'd be ready to move in, in no time. And she told him about all the horrors of coming back to work in the real world. He told her to just hang in until he got there.

"I can't wait," she said, her eyes filling with excitement.

"Neither can I," he said, closing his eyes, and imagining her just the way she looked in his cabin in the morning. He couldn't wait to set up their ranch now.

They talked for a long time, he had gone to a pay phone to call her. He kept putting quarters in, and he refused to let her call the number, or call her collect in future. He was stubborn. And he promised to call her again the next day, and asked her to say hello to Mary Stuart. She had heard nothing from Hartley but she didn't expect to. They had agreed not to call each other until she settled matters in London. And she didn't even know where to reach him in Boston or Seattle. She knew he'd be home on Thursday. And she knew what the code was. "Adieu, Arielle," or "*Bonjour,* Arielle," depending on what happened with her marriage.

Tanya took her to Spago that night, and introduced her to Wolfgang Puck, the owner, and she explained who everyone was. Victoria Principal was having dinner with a big group. George Hamilton was there. Harry Hamlin . . . Jaclyn Smith . . . Warren Beatty . . . And George Christy of the *Hollywoood Reporter* was at a corner table. And everyone knew Tanya, but it was one of the few places in Hollywood where, no matter how big the star was, they never disturbed her.

She and Mary Stuart talked for a long time about everything, and Mary Stuart seemed to have made her mind up. She went shopping the next day when Tanya went to rehearsal. And they went to bed early that night. Gordon had called again, and there was a fax from Bill, confirming her arrival. He had said absolutely nothing personal at all, and Mary Stuart shook her head when she saw it.

And the next morning when she left, she and Tanya clung to each other and cried. She didn't want to leave at all, and they both wanted to turn the clock back and leave for Wyoming.

"It'll be okay," Tanya encouraged her. "It'll be fine. Just think of Hartley." It was all Mary Stuart could think of, as she left, and all the way to London. She even wrote him a letter. It would be their first, she smiled to herself, the first she'd written to him. Maybe he'd even keep it. He was wonderfully sentimental. She told him how much he meant to her, and how wonderful Wyoming had been, how empty her life had been before she met him. She was going to mail it when she got to the hotel in London.

The hotel had sent a car for her. She was staying at Claridge's after all. It seemed easier than going to another hotel when he was staying there. But she had reserved her own room. She had no idea if Bill knew that. But actually, the hotel had told him.

She went through customs easily, and reached the hotel shortly after. It was all very civilized, and when she reached Claridge's they ushered her upstairs like a visiting dignitary from another country. And they informed her that Mr. Walker was in the suite he was renting as his offices, with his secretary, he was working. But she did not call him as soon as she reached her room. She wanted time to regain her composure. She washed her face and combed her hair and as usual she looked impeccable in a black linen suit that had traveled perfectly from L.A. to London. It was typical of Mary Stuart.

And when she had ordered a cup of tea, and finished it, she called him. By then, it was ten o'clock in the morning. But she had no idea that Bill was going crazy. He knew her plane had gotten in at seven. He assumed she had gone through customs by eight, and gotten to the hotel at nine. And he had called the desk to confirm it. He knew she was in her own room, and hadn't called him. He had been agonizing ever since then. But Mary Stuart was in no hurry. It was Thursday by then. She had allowed a day for this, and as she had been unable to reach Alyssa, she was flying to New York on Friday. It was certainly a circuitous route from Wyoming.

He answered on the first ring when she called him. It was awkward even speaking to him now, and she gave him her room number, and he said he'd come right down to see her. He left his secretary and told her not to disturb him. He was going to an important meeting.

Mary Stuart opened the door and looked at him, and it was painful to see how familiar he looked, how much like the man she had loved for so long until the year before. But she knew this man was different. They both were.

"Hello, Bill," she said quietly as he came in, and he was about to put his arms around her, but when he saw her eyes, he decided not to. "How are you?"

"Not so great actually," he said, and surprised her.

"Is something wrong?" It was odd for her, of all people, to ask him.

"I'm afraid so," he said, sitting in a chair, and stretching his long legs out before him.

"What happened?" She assumed the case wasn't going well, and she was sorry to hear it. He had certainly put enough time and effort into it to win it.

"Actually," he said, looking at her mournfully, and seeming very young to her. He looked vulnerable and kind of pathetic. "I've fucked my life up pretty badly and yours." She was startled by the way he looked, and even more so by the way he said it. She wondered if he was going to make some terrible confession, like an affair since he'd been in London. But in some ways, that might make it easy. This was not as easy for her as she'd hoped, just telling him their marriage was over. Suddenly he was a real person, with wrinkles and flaws, and things she had once loved about him.

"What do you mean?" she asked, looking puzzled. What did he mean, he'd fucked his life up?

"I think you know exactly what I mean. That's why you're here, isn't it? I figured that much out, stupid as I am. And as men go, I've been pretty dumb. I've spent the last year with my head buried in my desk somewhere, thinking that if I ignored you long enough you'd go away, or my misery and my guilt would, or Todd would come back, or the stupid things I said to you would be forgotten. But none of that seemed to happen. It just kept getting worse. I felt more awful every day, and you've come to hate me. That was actually pretty predictable, given the way I behaved. The only one who didn't predict it though was me, which is pretty awkward." He said it all looking like a kid, she had to smile at what he was saying. Sometimes he was very endearing. "Anyway, I don't suppose any of this surprises you. I think I'm the only one around here who's amazed not only by my stupidity, but my behavior. So now you've come to let me know very politely, and in person, which is very kind of you, my dear, that you're going to divorce me." He was the criminal helping the executioner set up the guillotine, and agreeing all the while that he deserved it. It actually made it harder to kill him.

"Where have you been all year?" she asked. It was the one thing she had wanted to ask him. "How could you have completely hidden from me, frozen me out? You never even spoke to me, or answered questions." It had been like living with a robot. Or a dead man, and he had been.

"I was unhappy," he said. He was the master of understatement, and she kept silently reminding herself to think of Hartley. "So what do we do now? Did you bring the divorce papers with you?" He figured she had them ready when he talked to her in Wyoming. It had all suddenly come clear to him, and he knew exactly why she was coming.

"Was I supposed to? Do you want them?"

"Do you have them with you?" He looked ready to sign them, and it annoyed her even more to see how willing he was to give up on what they'd had for twenty-two years. He really didn't care at all, from what she could see. And it infuriated her even further.

"No, I do not have our divorce papers with me," she said angrily. "Hire yourself a lawyer or draw them up yourself. I can't do everything, for God's sake. I came over to talk to you, not have you sign papers."

"Oh." He looked startled. He had also gotten the message when the concierge told him she had her own room. He had been about to tell the housekeeper to prepare for another guest in his room, and it crushed him when he realized she wasn't going to stay with him. That certainly delivered the message. "You're very angry at me, Stu," he said sadly, looking at her, wishing he could take it all back, or change it. "I don't blame you. I've been a complete bastard to you. I can't even give you an excuse, although you deserve one. All I can give you is an apology. I've been confused ever since Todd died. I felt so guilty, I didn't know who to blame. I blamed myself, but

I couldn't stand it, so I pretended to blame you. But I never really did. I was always convinced it was my fault."

"How could it be your fault?" She was stunned by what he was saying. "It wasn't anyone's fault. It was horrible for all of us, even Alyssa. None of us deserved it. I got really angry at him when I cleaned out his room, and the funny thing is I felt better after I did that."

"You cleaned out his room? Why?" Once again, she had surprised him.

"Because it was time. I put everything away, and packed up his things. I gave away his clothes to people who could use them. I think I thought that if I left his room there long enough, he'd come back to it. I finally figured out that wasn't going to happen."

"I think I figured that out here in London."

Then she shocked him again. "I want to sell the apartment. Or you can do what you want," she corrected herself, "but I don't want to live there. It's too depressing. None of us are ever going to recover as long as we live there." Everyone had said not to make hasty decisions, and they hadn't. It had been a year now. "You can live there if you want, but I won't." When she went back to New York, she was going to look for an apartment, unless she decided to live with Hartley. She still hadn't decided. And she knew he would do whatever she wanted.

"Never mind the apartment," Bill finally said bluntly. "Do you want to live with me? I think that's the issue." He almost fell out of his chair when she answered, although he had expected it, he still didn't want to hear it.

"No, I don't," she said calmly. "Not the way it's been for the past year. I would, the way it used to be. But that's all over."

"What if we could go back again? If it could be like that, the way it was before, then what?"

"That doesn't happen," she said sadly, and when she looked up she saw tears in his eyes and she was sorry for him.

She had cried so much for the past year, she couldn't cry anymore. For her, it was all over. "I'm really sorry."

"So am I," he said, looking vulnerable and human. It was sad, the body snatchers had brought him back too late, but it probably didn't matter anyway, it was only for a visit. If she had agreed to go back to him, he probably would have been rotten to her again, and stopped talking to her, she thought as she looked at him. She didn't want to chance it. "I'm sorry I was such a damn fool," he said, his lip trembling, his eyes filled with tears. "I just didn't know how to handle what happened."

"Neither did I," she said, her eyes filling with tears in spite of herself, "but I needed you. I had no one." She sobbed as she said it.

"Neither did I. I didn't even have me, that's what was so awful. It was like I died along with Todd, and I killed our marriage."

"You did," she accused him openly. This was why she had come to London. She at least wanted him to know why she was leaving. He had a right to know that. But he just sat there, crying. And he looked so miserable while he did, she just wanted to put her arms around him, but she forced herself not to do that.

"I wish I could take it all back and do it differently, Stu, but I can't. I can't do anything but tell you how sorry I am. You deserve a lot better than this. You always did. I was a total shit and a complete moron."

"What am I supposed to do with that?" she said, pacing around the room suddenly. For the first time, she looked angry and flustered. "Why are you telling me now what a bastard you were? Why didn't you do something about it?"

"I didn't know how to stop. But I figured it out once I got here. I realized what a mistake this was as soon as I got to London. I was so lonely I couldn't think straight. I wanted you here. I wanted to ask you to come, but I was too embarrassed to do it, and you were having a good time at some goddamn dude ranch. You probably fell in love with a cowboy, for all I know,'' he said, looking miserable, and she stared at him and wanted to shake him.

''You are a complete jerk,'' she said, with total conviction. She should have said it months ago, and was sorry now that she hadn't.

''I'm sorry. I didn't mean that to be insulting, I just meant I deserved it.''

'You deserve a good swift kick in the behind, and you have all year, William Walker. What do you mean you were lonely when you got here? How could you be stupid enough to set yourself up here for two or three months and just dump me in New York? Why should I even be married to you anymore?''

''You're right. You shouldn't,'' he said humbly.

''Good. I'm glad we agree on that. Let's get divorced.'' She had finally said it. It was over, but he was staring at her and shaking his head at her, which confused her further.

''I don't want to,'' he said, looking like a kid refusing to go to the dentist. ''I don't want to divorce you,'' he said firmly.

''Why not?'' She looked exasperated.

''I love you.'' He looked straight into her eyes as he said it, and she looked away from him and out the window.

''It's a little late for that, I'm afraid,'' she said sadly. She would never believe again that he loved her. He had proved otherwise for an entire year now. He had ignored her, abandoned her, shunned her, frozen her out, gone to London for two months, and he had never offered her a moment of comfort when their son died. He had cheated her of everything he owed her as a husband.

''It's never too late,'' he said, still looking at her, but she shook her head. She knew different. ''Are you saying you could never forgive me? That's not like you. You've always been so forgiving.''

''Probably too much so,'' she said wisely. ''I don't know why, but I do know it's too late for me. I'm really sorry,'' she said, standing up, and turning her back to him, as she looked out at the rooftops of London. She wanted to end their discussion. She had told him she wanted a divorce. This was what she had come for. And she had a fax to send . . . "*Bonjour,* Arielle" . . . She wanted Hartley to find it the moment he walked into his apartment on Friday.

But she hadn't realized that Bill had come up behind her, and she jumped a foot when he put his arms around her. "Don't do that, please," she said, without turning around to see him.

"I want to," he said, sounding desperately unhappy, "just one last time, please . . . let me hold you . . ."

"I can't," she said miserably, and turned around to face him. He had his arms around her and his face was inches from hers, and he wasn't letting go. She wanted to tell him she didn't love him anymore, but she didn't have the guts to say it. And it wasn't true yet. But it would be one day. It would just take time. She had loved him for too long for it to disappear overnight. But he had hurt her too much for her to want to love him. The only trouble was, she still did though.

"I love you," he said, looking right at her, and she closed her eyes. He was still holding her and he wouldn't let go, and she didn't want to see him.

"I don't want to hear it." But she didn't move away either.

"It's true. It always was. I love you . . . oh, God, even if you leave me now, please believe that. I will always love you . . . just like I loved Todd. . . ." He was crying again, and without meaning to, she bowed her head, and put it on his shoulder. She could suddenly remember how painful it was, when it had happened to them, and Bill hadn't been there for her. He had been so dead and hurt and frozen that he couldn't help her. And now he was crying for their son, and so was she, as she clung to her husband. "I love you so much," Bill said again, and then he kissed her, and she tried to back away, and pull away from him, but she couldn't. Instead she found herself kissing him, and hating herself for it. How could she be so weak? How could she give in to him? And the worst thing was that she wanted to kiss him.

"Don't," she said, when he stopped, and they were both breathless. But she found that kissing him had soothed the hurt even if it didn't end the pain. And then he kissed her again, and she kissed him, and it felt like she never wanted him to stop, for forever. "This is not appropriate," she said breathlessly. "I came here to divorce you."

"I know," he said, kissing her, and then suddenly it had gone much further. He was touching her and holding her and she was kissing him, and neither of them could understand their attraction for each other. It hadn't happened to them for a year, and now suddenly they were both overwhelmed with desire, and before either of them knew what had occurred, they were in bed, and she had never wanted him as much or been more aroused by him, and he was seized with passion for her as he had never known it. The room was strewn with their clothes, and they were both exhausted when they finally stopped. It had been a year for both of them, and as she lay and looked at him, she grinned, and then suddenly she laughed, it was all so absurd, and he was smiling.

"This is disgusting," she said, still grinning at him. "I came here to divorce you."

"I know," he said, but he was still smiling. "I can't believe this. I don't know what happened . . . let's do it again . . ." And an hour later, they did. They talked and they made love, and he lay in her arms and cried for their son, and what he had done to her, and they made love again. He never saw his secretary again that day and she had no idea what had happened to him except that he had said he was going to an important meeting, and that was what she told everyone who called him.

They were still naked and in bed at six o'clock, and they were spent. He asked her if she wanted room service, but all she wanted was to be with him, and she slept in his arms. And when she woke the next morning, he was looking at her, praying it hadn't been a dream. The one thing he knew in his life, with all the uncertainties he'd found, was that he didn't want to lose her. And he told her that over breakfast. He had ordered a huge breakfast for both of them, they were starving, for food and each other. And as they sat and talked, he asked her what she wanted to do that day. He made it sound as though they were on vacation.

"Don't you have to work?" she asked, finishing her omelette, and taking a sip of coffee.

"I'm taking the day off. If you're going back to New York, I want to be with you before you go," and then with a sad look, he added, "I'll take you to the airport." But after breakfast, they made love again, and had almost missed her plane by then. She could have made it if she'd leapt out of bed and dressed in a hurry, but she didn't want to. She wanted to stay. For a day, a week, the duration of his stay. Whatever it took. Maybe forever. And she said as much to him as they sat together in the bathtub.

"Will you stay?" he asked ever so gently, and when she nodded, he kissed her.

"All I have with me are cowboy boots and jeans, and about two proper city dresses." She smiled at him and he looked happier than she'd ever seen him.

"You'll be all the rage in London. Do we have to have separate rooms?"

"No," she said seriously, "but I still want to sell the apartment." He thought it was a good idea too. It was time for them to move on, to heal, to find each other again, and with any luck at all, start over. He had every intention of making that happen, and he was grateful to her for letting him do it. He swore the nightmare of the past year would never happen again, and after all the talking they'd done, she believed him.

He said he wanted to take her out that afternoon, just for a walk, so he could be with her and talk to her, and remember how sweet it was to walk beside her. But he had to stop at his office first. He had promised his secretary when he called that he'd sign some papers. And Mary Stuart had said she would meet him in the lobby.

She dressed quietly, thinking of him, and the time they had shared, and she jotted the note with shaking hands once she was dressed. She was wearing a brown linen dress, which was the only other respectable dress she had brought to London, and her hair wasn't as neat as usual. She looked younger and just a little bit disheveled. She had already told Bill that if she stayed, she had to go shopping. But she wasn't thinking of that now, she was thinking of him, the man who had ridden through the wildflowers with her in Wyoming.

She went downstairs and spoke to the concierge, and he said it was no problem to send it for her, although he reminded her that her husband had a private fax already set up in his office. But she preferred to do it with the concierge, she explained, and she gave him the fax number. She had written out two words, and her eyes filled with tears as she handed him the paper.

"It will go out immediately, madam," he said, and she trembled at the pain it would cause, for both of them. But he had been wiser than she was. He had realized better than she had what might happen.

The paper said "Adieu, Arielle." Nothing more. Just that. And she never mailed him her letter. There was no point now. That had been her promise to him. Just two words and no explanations.

"Ready for some air?" Bill asked when he came downstairs. He thought she seemed quiet again, and he was worried, and he saw when he looked at her that she'd been crying. They'd been in her room for nearly two days, but they had settled a lot of things, and he put his arms around her again right there in the lobby.

"It's okay, Stu . . . I swear it'll be all right . . . I love you." But she hadn't been thinking of him. She'd been saying good-bye to a friend. And then, she took her husband's hand,

and they walked out into the sunshine. The doorman watched them as they walked away, hand in hand, and he smiled. It was nice, and so rare, when you saw happy couples. Life seemed so easy for them. Or maybe they were just lucky.